CONTENTS

Almost Human	1
Prologue	2
Chapter 1	7
Chapter 2	17
Chapter 3	30
Chapter 4	44
Chapter 5	64
Chapter 6	79
Chapter 7	92
Chapter 8	107
Chapter 9	121
Chapter 10	135
Chapter 11	148
Chapter 12	165
Chapter 13	184
Chapter 14	191
Chapter 15	209
Chapter 16	223
Chapter 17	231
Chapter 18	245
Chapter 19	256

Chapter 20	262
Chapter 21	273
Chapter 22	281
Chapter 23	297
Chapter 24	303
Chapter 25	307
Chapter 26	312
Chapter 27	319
Chapter 28	330
Chapter 29	340
Acknowledgement	347
About The Author	349
Books By This Author	351

Almost Human: Discovery is written in UK English. Some spellings differ from US English spellings.

ALMOST HUMAN

Discovery

To ▮▮▮▮

Thanks for reading,

Ashleigh Revero
x

PROLOGUE

Friday 10th April 2082

Poly-Gen Site, Fairtock

Nicole was brought back to the present with a start as Hobson's harsh and abrupt voice rang in her ears, "Do you need assistance with this task, Ms Wilks?"

He stood with his arms folded across his chest, peering at her through square shaped glasses that seemed to make his unusually far-apart eyes bulge. His stern face never faulted and his expression seemed to be silently screaming for somebody's blood.

Nicole shook her head. She could feel tears attempting to push their way out of her eyes, but she remained steadfast and stoic. Hobson gave a curt nod but offered no more words as he blustered out of the room. Somebody was going to pay dearly for this.

Jenson offered her a sympathetic half-smile. "It won't be long Nicole, and all this will be behind us. Just a few more hours for you, and only a couple more months for me. We will get through this," he whispered. He pressed his thin lips together and cleared his throat, then as he pushed open the door, his face returned to his standard stern expression before he barked, "Don't be too long about it. This isn't a job that should take all day," as he left the room.

Once alone, Nicole shook with the weight of the task she had been asked to perform. She held her breath, her hands clamped over her mouth, trying not to allow the sounds of her anguish to escape with her tears.

A few short breaths later and she had shoved the pain and the self-hatred far enough away that it wouldn't hinder her work. She opened her eyes, ready to begin. The incubation pods were lined up on the large, pristine, white work surfaces, each one connected to an array of high-tech equipment that hummed and beeped as it monitored the subjects inside.

Nicole looked at the readouts of the first pod, trying to understand why these infants needed to be terminated. It would make it a little easier to know for sure that they were not developing properly, or that they were sick and wouldn't survive anyway. She studied the information, but there was nothing to indicate any problems. All the vital organs were developed perfectly. Brain function was normal, each of their senses were working exactly as they should, the nervous system, endocrine system, digestive system... everything fine and within normal limits.

These experiments were made in batches of fifteen. Each infant in a single batch were genetically related – they came from the same human donors. They were technically siblings. It wasn't uncommon for a 'faulty' batch to have one or two perfectly healthy babies, but they would incinerate the entire batch regardless. The HGMR were interested in the batch as a whole, and only the strongest would go on to be mass produced.

Nicole moved to the next incubation pod and assessed the information. Another perfectly healthy infant as far as she could see. The next, and the next, and the next. None of these infants deserved to die.

It was as she was desperately assessing the eighth pod, that she realised the reason. The blood group. These infants were the wrong blood type.

Her body felt numb as she fully understood the situation. Fifteen perfectly healthy babies. She was about to murder fifteen PERFECTLY HEALTHY BABIES!

She took a moment to compose herself, trying to detach herself from this place and this situation. Her mind worked hard trying to block out the guilt. She didn't allow the thoughts to enter, as she scrubbed her hands and donned her PPE. What a terrible task for a final day in hell. The hopeful thoughts crept in: this would be her last day. Everything was in place and tomorrow she would start her new life, in a new city, with a new name. She would be free of the horrors of PolyGen. It felt sickening to feel any sliver of happiness right now. To think she was about to end fifteen lives of fifteen perfectly healthy babies and then she was going to simply leave, shrug her shoulders and forget all about it.

She tried to remind herself that these were experiments, not real human babies. It wasn't the same as killing human babies. These infants were simply faulty government stock. She clenched her jaw as she willed herself to believe it.

Nicole let out a shaky breath as she opened up the first pod, thankful that the sleeping infant did not stir. This phase of testing was the worst, because the babies resembled human newborns. They had a gestational age of approximately 40 weeks. If they were being grown inside women, they would be ready to be born about now.

Nicole drained the fluid from the pod and the perfectly formed, brown skinned infant looked even more perfect in the air. She detached the brain scanner that was attached to the infant's head, but the baby did not stir. She had the poison ready, just a quick injection in the back of the neck, and the child would die quickly and painlessly. She turned her head away and screwed her eyes shut as she plunged the needle into the child's body and pumped the chemical inside. It usually took between fifteen and forty-five seconds before the infant stopped breathing. She methodically removed the artificial placenta that provided food and waste disposal, then lastly, the breathing apparatus was removed from the baby's face.

In less than a minute, the baby had gone limp. She tried not to look at its face or pay attention to its gender. The more detached she was, the easier it would be. She placed the infant in a grey zip-lock bio-hazard bag, and then into a much larger bright yellow bio-hazard bag that said, 'For Incineration Only' in large red letters.

Nicole took a minute to catch her breath. One down. Only fourteen more to go. She worked methodically, moving along to the next incubation pod and repeating the sequence as though she were merely performing a mundane cleaning task. Time passed in a blur, and she paid as little attention as possible to what she was doing, trying her hardest to block the feelings, the emotions, the memories.

When she reached the final pod, she allowed herself a second to feel relief. It was almost over.

She drained the fluid and the baby's legs jerked. Its eyes sprung open and she closed her own eyes tight, willing herself not to look. Sometimes, they woke up. It was always harder when they were awake.

Making a special effort to turn her head away from the infant, and not look at its face, she readied the syringe. She mentally counted herself in. 3...2...1... her hand came closer, needle poised and ready to shoot the poison into this tiny body, when the purest cry she had ever heard left its lungs.

"Shhhh," she found herself soothing the baby. Almost as though her body was working without permission from her brain, she removed the breathing mask from its face and found herself holding the baby in her arms. This was forbidden. They were never to handle the merchandise.

Why? Why? Nicole, how stupid are you? She silently berated herself. Whatever had possessed her to pick up and hold this child? It gurgled and cooed and settled in her arms and her heart constricted. How could she kill this child now?

She looked down at the infant. A boy, she realised. He was perfectly formed. His small and delicate features were perfectly proportioned, and he had a smattering of black fuzzy hair on his head. He looked just like Thomas; her own child who had been so cruelly taken from her at the tender age of three.

Without warning, without any knowledge of what she was doing, she lifted the child higher to her face, and buried her nose in him, taking in his scent. He smelled new and pure and perfect.

She swallowed as tears leaked from her eyes and sobs racked her chest. Why did she lift this child up in her arms?

The fleeting idea passed through her mind, and she shook it away venomously. She could not save this boy.

But… what if I could? The voice persisted. *What if there was a way to smuggle out this child without getting caught?*

CHAPTER 1

Wednesday 22nd February 2102

Gromdon Slums, Harpton Main

Jay winced as he opened his eyes, the blinding pain in his head was a force to be reckoned with. He blinked a few times and tried to focus, trying to work out where the hell he was. It was daylight, but it was cold, and he could hear heavy rain hitting the tin roof of the building he had slept in.

Bringing his hands to his face, he roughly rubbed his eyes and tried again to focus on where he might be. He remembered very little from last night, but the feel of the rough stubble on his cheeks confirmed it had been a few days since he'd last shaved. He wondered how he looked. *Probably not good*, he thought.

Jay gingerly pushed himself up to a sitting position and took in his surroundings a little more. He appeared to have slept in an empty, disused warehouse. It was filthy with grime and litter, the high up windows so thick with dirt you could barely see out of them. He saw the empty vodka bottle next to him, and the headache, extreme thirst and dry throat suddenly made a lot more sense.

The familiar feeling of shame and disgust filled him as he remembered what he'd done the night before and how he came to be here. He knew he needed to sort himself out and get his life together.

He reached for the empty bottle, just to see if it was in fact empty. He hated himself a little more for being disappointed. As he slumped back against the wall, an unnerving thought shot through him. *The money. Where is the money?*

His hands patted down his jacket pocket and relief swelled in him as he felt the small square lump concealed inside. The relief was short-lived when he opened the wallet to find it almost empty. *All the cash, what happened to all the cash?*

His eyes travelled to the vodka bottle on the floor and his spirits sank further. He couldn't quite believe he had spent his whole temporary cash allowance on alcohol. The ban on his digital account was still in place for another three days, and he had no access to his money. His heart pounded in his chest as the reality set in. How was he going to get by with no money?

At least he still had his ID. He could still prove he was a legitimate citizen, and not a real casher.

This was his own doing. He had been arrested two weeks ago for being drunk and causing trouble. *It was all a misunderstanding, really; he wasn't intentionally causing trouble... the other guy had started it...* he thought bitterly. But when the authorities scanned his ID, and saw he'd been in trouble for substance abuse and had some previous arrests on his record for being violent in his younger years, they came down hard and doled out an instant ban. The general view from the government was, if you can't behave like a legitimate citizen, then you can live like a casher until you learn.

In truth, Jay wasn't a violent man, at least not anymore. He'd had his fair share of trouble in his younger years, but age had mellowed him, and he was usually a calm and placid individual these days. But the anniversary of Tanya's death had snuck up on him. He hadn't expected the grief to hit him quite this hard, and when things got tough, he turned to the only thing he knew would help. The vodka.

The memory of his dead girlfriend invaded his mind and all

the ways he missed her swam to the surface. She was such a good person. He shook his head in disgust. If she could see him now, what would she say to him? He would be such a disappointment to her.

He opened his wallet again and fully assessed the damage. There was still some change in the coin section, and he was thankful he could get a coffee at least. Pushing himself off the floor with a groan, he tried to work some feeling back into his stiff, aching legs and sore back. He made his way towards the exit at the back. The door was closed, but there was a smashed in window at ground level which had a large, corrugated metal sheet pulled across to keep it covered. He vaguely remembered dragging it across the gaping hole last night to keep the draft and the rain out. He realised now that he wasn't alone in this building. There were others dotted about on the floor. He was lucky to have kept his shoes, never mind his wallet and phone.

The corrugated metal makeshift door made a loud screeching as he pulled it open, and he heard one of the men asleep on the floor mumble in complaint. His eyes stung as the fresh morning light hit him, even though it was a dull and dreary day. It was still raining, but since his clothing was still damp from the night before, he supposed it didn't really matter too much. He stepped out into the alley where the fake door let out and tried to work out his location.

Judging by the look of the place, he decided he must be in Gromdon. Gromdon was the poorest part of Harpton Main, and he'd somehow ended up in the centre of the slum town. At least he could spend his remaining cash here, that is, if he could keep hold of it long enough. He looked up and down the alley, but he didn't know which way to go.

Once outside, the air began to clear his head and lift the fuzz from his brain. He set off walking, trying to ignore the smell of rotting meat. It was most likely rotting dead person, and he didn't think his delicate stomach could handle that so early in the morning.

At the end of the alley, he turned left and saw the shanty

town. Rows upon rows of makeshift houses, some made from tents, some from precariously placed large pieces of metal or wood. None of it looked clean, safe, or sanitary. He could hear babies crying and dogs barking.

He turned around and took the right turning instead. It led him onto another side street, where he had a view of Harpton Main city centre in the distance. From here, the skyscrapers looked magnificent. It was a beautiful city, and the people who lived there were happy to turn a blind eye to the poor and the desperate immigrants who lived down here.

Now he'd found his bearings, he had a better idea of which way to go. He walked along the streets; they sounded eerily quiet to his ears. He was used to the noise of traffic and the sound of phones ringing and people laughing and chatting. Here though, in Gromdon, it was not legal for cashers to drive cars or own mobile phones. Those things were restricted to legitimate citizens only.

The rain had eased as he walked out of the poorest part of town. He could tell he was still in a casher part of town, but at least the buildings were more solid than the makeshift slums back the other way. He could see the river, it looked a filthy brown colour, and was full of trash. There were women further down who appeared to be washing their clothes in the murky water.

It hit him hard how little he had done for the cashers since Tanya died. She worked hard for a charity who helped the refugees; she volunteered a lot of her time, energy, and money. She would work in the free kitchens, donate to the food bank, and made a point of shopping at the cash market, where their home-made knick-knacks and clothing, and home-grown food were sold for cash or bartered for other goods. Sometimes, she went into the slums with other volunteers, and brought them medicine and bottled water, or soap and cleaning supplies. She even sponsored a young girl named Gabriella to go to school and live in the children's home in Helstain.

Jay had at least kept up that promise to Tanya after she died.

He took over the fees from the school and children's home, so that Gabriella could have a chance in life. She was still in a very disadvantaged position. No form of identification meant they would always treat her like lowlife scum, a drain on society. She would always be looked down upon and seen as a second-class citizen. Even with an education, she will probably struggle to find well-paid work. The cash rate is poor. Cashers are desperate, and will work for a pittance, and the wealthy can get away with paying it.

The familiar feeling of shame nudged at him again. *What would Tanya think of me now?* He was a better man with her in his life. It's not that he didn't care anymore about the casher situation, but it was so much harder to do anything to help without Tanya there to push him on.

He made a silent vow to come back to Gromdon, and help somebody in some way, no matter how small. Any gesture, no matter how insignificant it might be, would make a difference to some of these poor peoples' lives.

He smiled a little, knowing that it would be a much better way to honour his girlfriend, rather than getting drunk and fighting.

He continued down the riverbank and over the bridge. From here, he could hear the distant hum of traffic and he knew he was getting closer to proper civilisation. There were real solid buildings and roads, some electric lighting, and billboards spouting the usual government propaganda. There was a small building on the corner with a flashing sign that said CASH ACCEPTED HERE. He made his way over and pushed open the door to the little cafe. It was grim inside, rust seemed to be the only thing holding the grubby tables and chairs together, and the wooden counter had deep scratches along the top, filled with years' worth of grime. Still, it was warm at least.

There were no other customers, and Jay wondered how hard it was to run a business in an area like this, between the cash world and the legitimate society. Most cashers don't have the luxury to spend their pennies on frivolous things like coffee, and he couldn't imagine why any legitimates would meet here, unless they had shady business to attend to away from the watchful eye of the government security cameras that were placed on every street corner in the legitimate society.

"How much for coffee?" he asked the scruffy-looking man behind the counter.

The man eyed him suspiciously and Jay tried to make himself more presentable, running his hand through his untidy hair, trying to pat it down at the back. His hair was short, brown, and wavy, but often unruly when he hadn't styled it.

"Cash price? Or Legit?"

"Um… Cash." The price for cash purchases was usually higher. It was seen as an unsavoury way to pay, and it was time-consuming to bank it all up at the end of trade, not to mention unsafe. It was very difficult for thieves to steal from your digital bank account, the law enforcers could always trace it. But cash, cash was untraceable.

The man told him the price, and Jay counted his coins. He was thankful he had enough; he hadn't realised how cold he had become. Now he was inside, his body was shivering. He gripped the cup in two hands, allowing the heat to penetrate his fingers, and the steam to hit his face. It might not look like the best place, but the coffee smelled good.

Jay was coming round now; the coffee bringing him back to his senses, and his fuzzy head was easing. It was only as he looked at his watch that he realised he was meant to be at work. He was meant to be at work yesterday and the day before that too, but he hadn't shown up. He was too drunk. He was trying to piece together the last few days. Had he really been drinking for three solid days? There was no wonder all his cash had disappeared.

He wondered if he would even have a job to go back to. Reaching into his jacket pocket, he pulled out his phone and checked his messages. There was a string of texts from Maarku asking him where he was, and if he was okay, and several missed calls from the office, and one from Mr Johnson's personal number. That didn't look good, Frank Johnson was one of the top bosses. He never made social calls.

He opened his emails up and saw a lot from work, some from his direct line manager getting increasingly angry as the messages went along. Lots of "Where the fuck are you, Jay?" and threats of him losing his position. He couldn't afford for them to fire him. 40 was the wrong age to be looking for new work. Getting in contact immediately would be his best option, but he simply didn't have it in him. He didn't know what he should say to them. Telling them he missed three days of work because he was drunk didn't seem like a viable excuse.

Another man entered the cafe, and Jay instinctively concealed his phone back inside his jacket pocket. He didn't need anyone to know he was a legitimate citizen. They would take everything he had if they wanted to.

He finished his coffee and made a swift exit. *Great,* he thought, as the rain started to pour again. He set off walking in the general direction of home. It was a fair distance, and he had considered catching the train, but he couldn't purchase a travel token with a ban on his cards.

He'd been walking for over half an hour now and he was still in the cash town. He'd forgotten how big the area was, and how many immigrants there were in Harpton Main. Well, not just in Harpton Main, but across the country. It wasn't surprising really, considering that after the war, people flocked to New America from all over the world.

New America had closed its borders long before the war. It was a fully controlled country, broken away, sealed off and separated from its counterpart – The American Republic. But the war had displaced most of the world, with entire countries left decimated and uninhabitable by nuclear warheads and chemical and biological weapons. Many immigrants had fled the devastation in other parts of the world and settled here illegally. The population had increased by a third, and still the immigrants kept coming. The government had turned its back on these desperate people, claiming that New America's limited resources were for New American citizens only. They refused to give the immigrants any form of identification, and without identification, options were restricted.

Solid buildings came into view, and Jay recognised the area. He had been here with Tanya and the other volunteers before. The people were still poor, but most of them had jobs and homes, although it was technically illegal to rent or buy property for cash, rich legitimate's will always find loopholes in the law. A lot of the rich bought cheap property on the outskirts of town and rented illegally for cash, except, they would never declare that cash was being paid. It was only illegal to charge rent. It wasn't illegal to allow a 'friend' to live in your spare house for free. It was quite the money-making scheme since there were no minimum standards to upkeep for the properties, and cashers couldn't complain to anyone about diabolical living conditions, because they shouldn't be there in the first place. The things the legitimates took for granted, like electricity and running water, were not legally available to be paid for with cash. Any casher living in a real house, connected to the grid, was exceptionally lucky. He'd never really given much thought to how hard life must be for these people.

He turned into a side street that he was sure would bring him out onto a main road. The street was dirty; there was an old filthy mattress with rusty springs poking out of it, and papers and cardboard littered the ground. There was a large dumpster overflowing with rubbish, a foul smell emanating from it.

Jay looked ahead of him and laid eyes on a young, frightened looking woman crouched by a doorway. He heard them then, the two men taunting her.

"Come on, princess. Don't be shy," one jeered at her.

The other was shouting at her to take off her top. "Show me your tits. I want to see how much you're worth."

They sounded drunk and threatening, and Jay knew he couldn't just leave her there. She looked so small and fragile, and terribly afraid. He had to help her, especially knowing what these two men's intentions were.

Without thinking, he shouted from where he stood, "She's with me. Leave her alone." Nerves caused his heart to flutter rapidly in his chest as he walked towards them and stood, squaring up to them with false confidence.

The two men rounded on Jay. They were drunk, or maybe drugged. Maybe both. The first man spoke up in his jeering voice, "How much you charging for the girl?"

Jay felt sick. "She's not for sale," he said in his most authoritative voice. He chanced a glance at the girl and saw how she stood motionless, looking at the floor in front of her. Her face was passive, almost expressionless. He had expected her to have made a run for it by now, but it occurred to him that she was probably too afraid.

Her clothing was wet through and a little too big, the black hoody was pulled up over her head, obscuring the top half of her face from view and he noticed she wasn't wearing any shoes.

The second one jeered at him, "I'll give you double what she's worth. I like the small ones. They squeal louder." He was laughing at his own disgusting remark.

"You'd better shut the fuck up!" Jay wasn't in any fit state to be fighting. His hangover was still very present, and his head was pounding again with the stress of this new situation, but there was no time to worry about that. The first punch came hard and took Jay by surprise. The well-set and stocky men were heavier than Jay, but older and out of shape. It surprised him that the larger of the two could move so swiftly.

There was a sharp jolt of pain as the punch connected with his face and he staggered backwards. His hands came up to his nose where the blood was streaming, and he felt a little dazed.

There was no time to recover before the other man was on him, forcing him to the ground. The first one hit him hard in the head as he fell to the floor, the other was kicking him in the ribs and the groin. He was still so drunk that he couldn't put up much of a fight. The only thing he could do to protect his body was to curl into the foetal position and hope for the best.

When he spotted the shorter man pulling out his pocket-knife, the small amount of fight he had in him disappeared. His final thoughts as he lost consciousness were of Tanya. At least he had died doing something that would have made her proud. He'd given his life to save a casher from being a victim of rape. He wouldn't be a complete disappointment to her after all.

CHAPTER 2

Wednesday 22nd February 2102

Gromdon, Harpton Main

Jay felt confused and groggy when he awoke. His body ached from top to toe and his head throbbed from the hangover.

Slowly, he opened his eyes and groaned as he tried to make sense of his surroundings. He was inside another disused, empty building, similar to the last, but much smaller. He couldn't think how he had ended up here; this was becoming a weird habit.

The realisation hit him he wasn't alone. A girl was here – the one he'd tried to save. He turned to see her crouched beside him, and found her hands were cradling his head, lifting it slightly from the floor.

"Drink," she said, holding a bottle to his lips. Jay obeyed and took a deep drink, grateful for the water. She set his head back on the hard floor with care and moved back towards the door.

It took a few minutes for Jay to come round to his senses. He took his time rolling onto his side and pushed himself into a sitting position. He groaned as the sharp pain in his side bit at him, and the girl reached into her bag and pulled out some pain relief medication.

"Take them," she said, as she placed the pills next to the water bottle.

Jay looked at the girl, then at the pills. "Thanks," he said, pouring two pink tablets into his hand. It renewed his focus as he took another long drink from the water bottle. He looked at the girl and asked, "What happened?"

She didn't answer him; she only stared at him.

"Did they hurt you?" She still didn't offer him an answer, so he asked again, "Those men. Did they hurt you?"

"No."

"They just left?" He couldn't believe they hadn't tried to hurt her. She didn't answer him, and he let it go.

He inspected the neat stitching on his stomach, "Did you do this?" he asked her, impressed with her skills.

"Yes."

"Wow, thanks! Will I need to see a doctor, do you think? I can't tell how deep it is. It hurts like hell! Did it look deep to you?"

"No. It is a surface wound. Not deep enough to cause any damage. Keep it clean and covered. It will heal."

Jay pushed himself to his feet, and the girl seemed to tense with nerves. She stared at him with distrusting eyes, and he realised he must seem terrifying to her. It was hard to say how long he had been out cold, but moments before they met, she was being threatened by two men. She would no doubt feel very vulnerable enclosing herself in an empty room with a man she didn't know, no matter how injured he may be.

Jay held out his hand to her and said, "My name's Jay. What's yours?"

She made no move to shake his hand, and it hung, useless, in the air between them.

"Edel," she said, after a long, strained silence.

Jay couldn't help noticing how cold and abrupt her speech was. She was straight to the point and there was no friendliness to her at all. He let his arm drop from the space between them.

Relief and surprise filled him as he found his wallet, his identification, and his phone all still present. Even his watch was still attached to his wrist. This girl had helped him, maybe even saved his life, and she hadn't stolen from him. Yet there was no doubt in his mind that she was a casher.

"Thank you for helping me," he said.

There was no answer. It made him question what terrible trauma she'd been through to leave her so withdrawn and despondent. He'd seen it before, many times with the girls that Tanya had helped. Some of them never made full recoveries. He was so grateful to her for one; saving his life, and two; not stealing his possessions, and he felt so sorry for her. She looked cold and her clothes were damp, and she was barefoot, he noticed with sympathy.

He cleared his throat and offered her a gentle smile, then said, "Look um, I've got no cash, but I do have a home. Why don't you come with me, and I'll get you warmed up, I'll dry your clothes and get you a hot meal?"

She didn't move, and she continued to stare at him. He assumed she didn't trust him. "I'm a legitimate. I'm not lying. Here," he reached into his pocket and produced his identification. It had his full name, Jaydon Powell, printed in bold, and his address underneath. "See, I live in Helstain," he said, pointing to the address on his ID card. "I don't want to hurt you. I only want to help."

The girl seemed to consider his offer. She didn't speak, but after a few seconds, she looked up at Jay and gave a slow nod of her head.

Jay made deliberately slow movements as he approached the girl. She seemed unsure of him, and he didn't want to make her more uneasy than she already was.

His body ached from the attack, and his side was sore from where the knife went in, but the painkillers she had given him had been effective in taking the edge off. Whatever those pills were, they were impressive.

He opened the door and peered outside. There was no sign

of the two men, everything looked okay. "This way. Come on." He was attempting to sound confident, but in truth, he was trying to remember where he was, and which direction was home. Once he'd found his bearings, he set off at a good pace. It surprised him how the pain had worn off to nothing more than a dull ache, and his hangover had eased too. Again, he wondered what was in those pills.

Edel kept pace with him, but always walked a little behind, never at his side, and never in front. Jay assumed she was still wary of him. It shocked him, how she had agreed so readily to go with him. She must be desperate.

She still made no effort to communicate with him, and he wondered if she was regretting her choice now and was looking for a way to get out of this situation. He'd never fully appreciated how hard it must be to be a casher. And worse still, to be a female one. A large proportion of them had been abused in one way or another. The government didn't care about them, and the cash areas were lawless. The police were only required to help legitimate citizens, these poor girls had nobody to look out for them. Thinking back to the blank and expressionless look on her face when those two men were leering at her, it was obvious why she did not move or run away. These poor girls' upbringing makes them believe it is an unavoidable part of life, and it is all they are worth. There isn't a lot of point in fighting it. He hoped that wasn't the reason she had agreed to go with him. Perhaps she wondered if he would want something from her in return for his kindness.

He made a few feeble attempts at conversation, but she didn't respond. He asked her if she lived in Gromdon, and he asked her about her family – if she had one, and where they were, but she kept her eyes down and only continued to walk as if she hadn't heard him speak. After that, and one more feeble attempt to reassure her he would not hurt her, he gave up. It was obvious this was going to be more difficult than he first thought, but he couldn't turn her away now. He kept thinking how afraid she must be, and how she needed his help.

They were leaving the cash area now and entering a legitimate citizen's area. Most still considered it to be a poor area, but not 'cash poor'. All the buildings were solid, and they all had running water and electricity. They all had internet access and many of the people had cars. Jay noticed how jumpy the girl seemed. Every noise had her twitching. Her head lurched in sharp, jerking movements towards each sound, as if she was hearing the noises for the first time and it made her look so odd. He wondered if maybe this was the first time she had ventured out of Gromdon. Perhaps she'd never seen or heard traffic before.

When she walked, she appeared almost robotic. There was no natural sway to her arms, and she held her shoulders back, keeping her upright in a perfect but abnormal looking posture. He thought about how fear and anxiety do strange things to people. He hoped she would relax a little soon.

As they headed across the streets, Jay came to an abrupt stop. Edel stopped just behind him, and her eyes narrowed as he turned to look at her.

"You have no shoes!" he said.

She didn't seem to understand what he was getting at.

"We're about to cross the boundary line into the nicer part of town. The law enforcers will be there, to keep the cashers out. You need something on your feet."

She looked at him but did not answer. He began to take off his shoes and socks and handed her his socks. "Look, I know they're not exactly clean, or dry for that matter, but socks will draw less attention than bare feet."

She took them without question or hesitation and slid them over her bare and dirty feet. If she found wearing a strangers' damp and sweaty socks in any way unpleasant, she certainly didn't show it to Jay. He had expected a small amount of resistance. He wouldn't have wanted to wear them if it was the other way around.

In truth, they would grant her admission to a legitimate area, if she had a legitimate citizen to vouch for her. There were a multitude of reasons why a legitimate citizen may want to bring a casher in, from cheap labour, to adult entertainment, and as long as the legitimates were happy to take responsibility for them, that was fine. However, any trouble at all, and the legitimate citizen who vouched for them would be in a great deal of trouble with the law. But she was wet, scruffy and had nothing on her feet, and he didn't want people to know she was a casher in case they thought he had bought her. It wasn't unusual for legitimates to buy casher girls and pass them around amongst some of moral-less men, as though they were nothing more than cheap entertainment. She looked so afraid that he worried that would be what people would assume.

They walked through the town. It was a lot nicer here; the streets were large and roomy, and well-maintained trees lined the walkways. Most of the housing was tall apartment blocks, but they all looked to be a decent standard, clean and well maintained. There was a park across the street, large and green open fields with beautiful trees dotted about, and a large pond, with ducks floating on the water.

Jay saw the girl looking at the park and wondered what she made of it. There wasn't a lot of green in Gromdon. A lot of the area was industrial. The docks were there, and the factories and the steelworks. A lot of the cashers found work in these places.

He tried again to make conversation with Edel. "Beautiful, isn't it?" he asked, gesturing to the park. Her body visibly jumped when he spoke, as though he'd caught her doing something she shouldn't have been. She averted her eyes from the park with one rapid movement and remained silent as she looked down at the ground in front of her. Jay let out a sigh and again in a quiet murmur, he told her, "It's okay, I'm not going to hurt you."

She didn't look up; her eyes stayed firmly fixed on the ground ahead of them, her posture still in the same unnatural and rigid position.

He considered telling her she didn't have to come with him

if she didn't want to, telling her she still had the option to change her mind. But then he remembered how cold and wet they both were and how hungry she might be. She probably assumed the offer of help came with strings attached, but was so desperate, she chose to come with him anyway. The thought made him sick. He was only trying to help the poor girl, but instead of feeling safe, she was anticipating being forced into having sex in exchange for food. No amount of telling her he wouldn't hurt her would make any difference. She would always be expecting it.

Jay crossed the street and entered the park. Edel following him, still walking a couple of paces behind. She was almost silent when she walked, her feet barely making a sound. Even her breathing was silent, unlike Jay, who was a little out of shape these days and finding the long walk back home a bit of a challenge. She was so quiet; he found himself looking back at her at regular intervals, just to make sure she was still there.

"It's not much further now. Helstain is just at the other side of the park," he said, trying to keep his tone cheerful and friendly, hoping it would put her at ease a little.

The rain had stopped again, and the sun was attempting to show itself. It was still bitterly cold, though. Jay was looking forward to getting home, just to get out of his wet clothes and get warmed up. His feet were freezing with no socks, but he reminded himself that at least he was wearing shoes.

They hadn't entered far into the park when Jay spotted the man in the grey uniform. He noticed them straight away, and it looked to Jay as though he was speaking on his radio. The girl seemed to tense a little at the sight of him as well.

"It's okay. I have my ID. If he asks, just tell him you're with me and nothing will happen."

Her eyes shifted from the man in grey to Jay and back again. She didn't make a sound, and Jay was beginning to wonder if she had some sort of mental health problem.

The man was walking over to them now, with a strong and authoritative stride. He gave the air of importance, and seemed like someone who wouldn't take any nonsense, though he was polite when he spoke to them and asked to see their identification.

Jay handed the officer his card, and he scanned it with his small hand-held device. He asked for his thumb print and then asked him the personal security questions tied to his digital ID tag.

Once he was satisfied that Jay was a legitimate citizen, with every right to be in this area, the officer turned his attention to Edel. "ID please, Miss," he said, polite and calm.

Jay spoke up on her behalf, and said, "She's with me."

The officer looked the girl up and down and took in her scruffy appearance and lack of shoes. He looked back at Jay, then back to Edel.

"Miss; Are you here of your own free will?" he asked her, a gentle sort of kindness to his voice. Jay felt mortified. What did this guy think? That he had kidnapped her or something!?

Her eyes locked onto the man's face as she spoke a single solitary, "Yes."

"She's my guest, right Edel?" Jay said, with a friendly smile on his face. He felt that if the officer knew he knew her name, then they would be more easily believed. He couldn't believe how dirty it made him feel, knowing what this man was thinking of him.

The officer didn't look convinced, but he had performed his duty. He had to take her answer at face value. The legitimate man was doing nothing wrong. Most boundary officers didn't even bother to ask, they turned a blind eye to situations like this.

The officer stepped aside and gestured with one arm that told them they were free to go. Jay couldn't help but notice the uneasy look the man had on his face as they left. He wondered how responsible the officer felt for what might happen to the girls he let through here with wealthy, legitimate men.

Jay hadn't considered how wet the grass would be after all the rain that had fallen. As they continued through the park, trudging over the sodden ground, it dawned on him how soaked this poor girl's socks would be, and how her feet would be icy cold. But she showed no discomfort. She still hadn't spoken to him since the brief conversation at the abandoned building, and he was tired of trying to get a response out of her, so he kept his thoughts to himself.

At the other end of the park, they emerged onto another street. There was housing across the road. Large, detached properties set back from the street, with spacious and spotless gardens in the front. It was a pleasant area, but Jay didn't live here. Helstain was an upmarket part of town and if you could afford one, the houses were fabulous, but Jay's budget would not stretch that far. He lived a little more central, in a more urban part of the area.

He walked through the streets, Edel still following him. She still seemed to startle at every noise. He had hoped she would have relaxed a little by now, but she was tense, like a coiled spring. Jay was hoping he didn't bump into anyone he knew. He'd been AWOL from work for three days, and now he was bringing a dirty-looking casher to his house, early in the morning, and he was filthy, sweaty, and reeked of vodka. It wouldn't exactly paint a wonderful picture.

As they walked past the children's home, he prayed Gabriella wouldn't be around to see him. He couldn't help but look for her as they passed by the school, but she wasn't there. There were some teenage children hanging around by the front gates, all dressed in their green blazers and grey skirts and trousers. They all wore the emblem of a sword pointing down through three coloured rings, and the tall flags positioned at either side of the main entrance to the school were the same. Jay saw the girl's eyes sweep across the building and the flags, and he wondered if maybe she felt a stab of envy for the ones who were lucky enough to attend school and had the safety of a charity backed home. Most cashers didn't receive an education, only the lucky ones who were sponsored or taken in by charity programs. The government only want to invest in their legitimate citizens' futures.

It was still around another twenty minutes before they reached Jay's street. Most of the buildings here were tall apartment blocks, but there was a small convenience store on the corner, and a coffee shop next door to it. Further down, there were bars and restaurants, and in the opposite direction, a bank.

Jay looked at the girl. Her agitation seemed to grow, her head jerked, and eyes darted in every direction, and she looked quite mad. It made him question if it was a good idea to invite her into his home after all.

He walked up the steps to his building and held open the door for Edel. She entered in silence, offering him only a strange and distrusting look as she passed him. It made him feel uncomfortable, as though he were doing something wrong.

It was warm inside, and he was pleased to be out of the chill of the cold outside air. He didn't wait for the elevator, but opted for the stairs instead, deciding that being in a small and confined space with him wouldn't do anything to help this girl relax.

They reached his apartment, and he held open the door again for Edel. She stepped inside and her eyes swept across the room. Jay's ears flamed with red hot embarrassment, and he began to apologise for the state of his home. He had forgotten what a mess he had left it in. Empty beer bottles and cans littered most of the surfaces in the kitchen and covered the table. There was a half-eaten pizza still in its box on the floor by the sofa, and coffee cups and dirty dishes filled the sink.

In normal circumstances, he wasn't such a slob, and if he'd known he was going to have company, he certainly wouldn't have allowed his house to get into this state. But, as the anniversary of Tanya's death had approached, the grief hit like a tidal wave, knocking him back into the same pit of depression he had found himself in when she died so suddenly a year ago. He felt disgusted as he looked around. This girl probably kept a cleaner house, and there was a high chance she lived in the slums.

"Um... here, why don't you get warmed up? You can use the shower. It will help. If you leave your clothes by the door, I will get them dry, and you can borrow something of mine in the meantime." He pointed to the door towards the back of the apartment.

She looked at him, and her eyes followed his hand.

"Would you like me to show you how to switch the water on?" He didn't wait for a reply. He casually strode across the room and opened the bathroom door, letting out a silent hope he had left it in a half decent state.

She followed him into the small room, and he showed her how to adjust the temperature. "I'll just be outside. Shout if you need anything," he said. Then, as an afterthought, he said, "You don't need to worry. I won't try anything."

He closed the door behind him as he left and hoped that she believed he wouldn't hurt her.

He crossed the room, turned on the TV out of habit more than anything else, and began clearing up the mess of all the empty bottles and cans. He was halfway through washing the dishes when the news report caught his attention.

BREAKING NEWS

There was a number flashing across the screen, and they were showing images of an explosion somewhere. At first Jay thought it was a terrorist attack, or a 'people's uprising' again, but the news reporter was talking about something far more sinister.

The words 'SECRET GOVERNMENT ORGANISATION' and 'GENETICALLY MODIFIED HUMAN' were being thrown around. Apparently, a building had been blown up. It was called Poly-Gen, a government testing facility in Fairtock, where they carried out genetic experiments.

At first, Jay thought it was a joke. It sounded so ludicrous. It was true that the government were very secretive, and they had complete control over all their legitimate citizens, and the country was more of a dictatorship than a democracy, but the authorities had always maintained that everything they did, and the control they exercised over the population, was for the good and the safety of the people. Jay wondered how human genetic experimentation would be of any good to the people of New America.

He turned his attention back to the news report. "These individuals are identifiable by the code etched onto their skin, above the left wrist, and on the back of the neck. It will resemble a bar code and looks like a tattoo. It is their only easily distinguishable feature. They have no specific race, they appear to be approximately 20 years of age, average height, with a small to medium build. If you spot one of these individuals, DO NOT APPROACH."

The number flashed up on the screen again. "We have specially trained government operatives who are equipped to deal with this particular threat. Once again, DO NOT APPROACH."

Jay was dumbfounded. This was a sure-fire way to cause widespread panic. Why would they keep something like this top secret and then make it public once something has gone wrong? The government owned the media. They told them what to report and what to keep buried, so there was no way this story got out by accident.

Jay wondered if there would be another revolt of the people, but it seemed a little pointless when disagreeing with the government was not tolerated. Even making a harmless comment or joke online would have the authorities breathing down their necks and have them investigated for not being patriotic. And since there was no anonymity anymore because a person's online presence was tied directly to their identity, they would always know if a person was making waves or causing trouble. People weren't allowed to express opinions, publicly disagree online, or report their own stories. The government only let out what they wanted people to know. They weren't a free nation, just sheep being herded into blind obedience. The government even put sanctions on technology in a bid to keep control over the population. There had been no technological advancements in the last hundred years or so, except of course for the spyware the authorities used to keep control of the people. They didn't want people to be able to think for themselves.

Jay flicked through the channels on the TV. This story was on every single channel. The same information, the same number to call. It was as though they had every intention of trying to cause a panic.

He didn't have time to worry about it right now, though. He was on a mission to help a poor casher and prove to himself that he could be someone his deceased girlfriend would be proud of.

CHAPTER 3

Wednesday 22nd February 2102

Branley, Harpton Main

Gemma disembarked the train in Branley, as though she was going to work. She had her casher's work permit in her purse; it was a small card with her photo and her work address printed on it. It wasn't the same as a digital ID the government issued to legitimate citizens. It only gave her permission to be in the area for work purposes.

She was dressed in her uniform, minus the apron and name badge. The white shirt and black trousers were the only set of smart clothing she owned, and she hoped it would draw less attention to her as she entered the city.

It was still quite a distance to the city centre from Branley, but without identification, or a work permit specifying Harpton Main city centre, she was unable to buy a travel token to get her there. Branley was still much closer than walking from Gromdon.

She felt self-conscious as she wandered through the streets, wondering if people knew she was committing a crime simply by being there. She passed by her workplace; the restaurant was still closed. It didn't open until eleven. She couldn't help but worry if border patrol stopped her, they would want to know why she was in the area so early. Maybe she could say it was delivery day or something.

She held her head steady and tried not to look as she walked past a boundary patrol officer. There was a man on his knees, begging them to grant him access to his workplace, but he wasn't carrying his work permit, and he had no form of identification. He was desperate, almost crying, saying he would lose his job if they didn't let him in.

The guard didn't care. He hit the man across the face with his baton and Gemma heard his yelp of pain before the guard's cold and uncaring voice boomed out, "You know the rules. No ID, no access."

Gemma continued to walk on, knowing that if they stopped her in the city, she could expect the same treatment. As she drew closer, she could see the beautiful shiny skyscrapers across the river. She loved the city, but she had never been here alone.

She crossed the footbridge over the river and paused to look at the beauty of it. The river didn't look like this in Gromdon. It was a filthy brown colour and full of rubbish, and the occasional dead body. The river was wide here, and there were pristine white boats sailing along at a leisurely pace. There were men across the way, sat up on the riverbank fishing. Gemma wondered why they spent their days fishing in the river, if they weren't planning to eat the fish, especially on such a cold, wet and dismal day. Danny had told her they do it for sport, but she couldn't get her head around it. When a casher catches a fish, they wouldn't dream of letting it go. Not when their families were starving.

She walked along the footbridge; the wind whipping up and catching her umbrella, blowing her long dark hair around, and sticking it to her face. She hoped the umbrella wouldn't break, she'd only bought it a few weeks ago, and she couldn't afford a replacement. As she approached the other end of the bridge, she took a few deep breaths to steady her nerves. This was the city centre. She was breaking the law.

She walked further into the city, through the major streets and roads. She was thankful that she'd been here so many times before with Danny, or she would have no hope of finding her way around. The roads were busy with traffic and noise, and she knew if she hadn't had so much experience of how to use the pedestrian crossings, she would be stuck not knowing how to get across the roads. Nobody seemed to notice her as she walked along. She was doing a good job of blending in.

She passed the billboards. They were always the same. The government was always trying to influence the legitimate citizens and vilify the refugees. One was reminding citizens to check stranger's identifications and report the presence of illegitimates and refugees in high-class areas. Another was advertising the new digi-pay systems, and the huge discounts people could get for shopping online. It wasn't fair; it seemed to Gemma that very few legitimate citizens needed discounts, yet, online shopping and digital payment systems were only available for legitimate citizens. The government controlled everything, and you needed a digital ID to get online.

She finally arrived at "The Grid", which was what they called the area with all the skyscrapers. Gemma had never seen them this close before. A funny feeling hit her stomach as she stood and looked up, straining to see the tops of the buildings. She felt almost dizzy, and so impossibly small as she stared up at them. They looked beautiful from across the river where Danny lived, but here, so close to them, their sheer size felt unnerving, and being surrounded by them gave her a sense of claustrophobia.

She tried to get her bearings. The building she needed was easy to spot from far away, but now she was in the middle of it all, she was lost. She considered asking for directions, but then they might ask to see proof of her eligibility and she didn't dare chance it.

She meandered through the built-up city and tried not to draw attention to herself. The rain had stopped, and she packed her umbrella away in her plain black shoulder bag. She stopped in a quiet space and redid her hair, trying to undo the damage of the wind and rain, and pulling it into what she hoped was a tidy-looking ponytail, praying she still looked smart enough to pass for a legitimate citizen. There were plenty of restaurants and bars here though, perhaps nobody would bother her if they thought she worked at one of those.

She finally found the building she needed. It was beautiful, all glass fronted and immaculately clean. It was a large building, with several entrances, and it took her a few minutes to work out which door she should use.

She took a few moments to collect herself; she didn't particularly enjoy confrontation, and Frank made her incredibly nervous. He always made her feel so worthless, and he was so condescending. He patronised her as though he thought she was stupid.

Gemma walked as confidently as she could towards the door, and pushed it, but it didn't open. She tried it again, but it still didn't budge.

There was a lady behind the reception desk looking at her, staring at her with an unfriendly expression. The woman made no move to acknowledge Gemma or open the door for her. Gemma looked from side to side and spotted the intercom system to the left of the door. She pressed the buzzer, and the bored sounding voice of the receptionist came through the speaker.

"Yes?"

Gemma tried hard to sound confident as she spoke, but she was sure her voice was as shaky as her legs, as she said, "Hello. I've got an appointment to see Frank Johnson."

The receptionist eyed her through the glass. "Name?"

"It's Gemma. Gemma Fletcher."

Gemma watched as the woman behind the desk tapped on her computer and then picked up the phone. The conversation was short, and a moment later, the door buzzed, and Gemma pushed it open.

It was warm inside, and there was the pleasant smell of

coffee and baked goods wafting through the air. She couldn't help but notice how beautiful it was inside the large and airy room. The main desk was curved into a crescent shape, giving a modern feel to it, and the floors were polished and shiny. Gemma's shoes made a click-clack sound as she walked across it. Everything about it screamed money and status. There was even abstract art displayed on the walls and the lighting was artistic too, large glass balls hanging down from the ceiling in a spiral shape over the desk, and two more further back lighting up the rest of the room. Gemma had never been inside Frank's workplace before, and she didn't know where she should go. She approached the desk to see if the unhelpful woman could direct her.

The receptionist flicked her long, straight, blonde hair and gave Gemma a cool and unfriendly look. "I don't appreciate being lied to. You don't have an appointment to see anyone," she said with a curt tone.

The heat rose in Gemma's cheeks. She hadn't expected to be called out like that. The receptionist held out her hand with an expectant stare, and Gemma stared back at her in confusion.

"ID," the woman barked at her and shot her an impatient scowl.

Gemma made a show of looking in her purse, but the receptionist wasn't buying it. She pressed a button under the desk. A portly, middle-aged security guard appeared and spoke to the woman. They were both discreet, but Gemma could still hear them.

"I think we have a casher here. Get rid of it, will you?"

The guard turned to Gemma. He was wearing a grey and black uniform and had a photo ID pinned to the top pocket of his shirt. "Come with me, Miss," he said, and grabbed her by the arm with his pudgy fingers. It was a tight grip, firm enough to stop Gemma from getting free of him, but he wasn't unnecessarily rough with her, and there was a sort of gentleness to his voice when he spoke.

He steered her past the reception desk and towards a plain

side door. Gemma realised it would reflect badly on the business if people saw them removing immigrants from the premises. Her insides shrivelled as the humiliation gripped her. She felt like she was something dirty and shameful.

The receptionist smirked at Gemma as the guard led her away, but the smirk was soon wiped clean when Frank's booming voice pierced the quiet. "What is going on here?"

The receptionist didn't miss a beat. She answered in a calm and almost bored voice, "She has no ID. I was only following procedures, Sir."

The security guard had eased his grip on Gemma as soon as Frank appeared. Gemma turned to face her boyfriend's father and saw him pin the receptionist with an icy stare. "I said I would see her," he said. His voice was both quiet and angry, and it made Gemma shiver with nerves.

He turned his attention to the security guard and said in a more placid tone, "I'll take it from here. Thank you, Malcolm."

The guard gave an apologetic nod and a half smile to Gemma and turned to Frank to make his apology. "Sorry, Sir. I thought I was doing the right thing."

Frank pursed his lips as though he had something to say, but the guard's radio buzzed and he hurried away, no doubt thankful for the interruption.

Gemma noted the scowl on Frank's face as he looked her up and down. He held his hand out in front of him and gestured for Gemma to follow. She knew Frank was an important man, but she didn't have a full understanding of what his work entailed, only that he was very wealthy, and owned a lot of companies. They took the elevator in silence, and Gemma couldn't help but wonder if it was some sort of mind game, to make her feel insecure, or if he just didn't want to speak to her.

Once they reached the correct floor, Frank showed her to his office. It was not what Gemma had expected. It was a large room, with double doors, and inside there was a small, curved glass desk with a middle-aged woman sitting behind it, and plush purple chairs along the back wall, facing a fish tank full of different tropical fish. Frank walked past the lady at the desk and said, "I don't want to be interrupted. Any problems, have Bilson handle it, or take a message." It was only as he continued to walk that Gemma realised that this was where he had people wait to see him. He must be *very* important.

She hadn't spotted the double doors at the back of the room. This time, the doors opened into an enormous room, with extravagant floor-to-ceiling windows overlooking the city. She would have been impressed by the breath-taking view if she wasn't so nervous. Frank's desk was enormous and immaculate. She noticed the framed picture of Danny, and next to it, one of the whole family– himself with his wife Michelle, Danny, and Lyssi, Michelle's daughter.

The sight of Danny's picture gave her some comfort. This wouldn't be an easy conversation.

Frank closed the door and walked around to his chair behind the desk. He motioned for Gemma to sit in the chair opposite. She obediently took her seat, not knowing what else to do.

There was a strong tension between them, the silence was almost painful on her ears. Frank was studying her with a careful interest, considering the best way to begin. Eventually, he cleared his throat and said in a business-like manner, "I take it you're here about my offer. What did we agree? $10,000 was it?"

Gemma's face flushed crimson. How could this man think so low of her? She held her head high and met his eye, as she slowly said, "We didn't agree on *anything*."

Frank held her stare and sat back in his chair. "Huh. $10,000 is a very generous offer, Gemma. I wasn't expecting greed. But, what else should I expect from someone like you? Go on then – name your price."

"I don't want your money," she spat. "I love Danny! And he loves me."

Frank let out a mean and derisive laugh. "Don't be a fool, Gemma! How long do you really think this relationship can last? I know what you're up to. What do you think? That you can marry into my family and take half of Danny's fortune? Gain your citizenship and live comfortably for the rest of your days? It will not happen. I'm going to make sure it doesn't happen. You won't use him like that."

"We love each other," she spoke with a quiet sorrow. She wanted to shout and scream at him, but she simply wasn't able. He made her feel so insignificant; she knew her feelings didn't matter to him.

Frank shook his head. "You don't even know him. Not properly."

She spoke with slow and concise words this time, as if Frank was an idiot. She needed him to hear this. "I know EVERYTHING about him."

Frank's eyes snapped up and met Gemma's. He looked visibly shaken but was quick to recover himself. He held her gaze for a minute and then, with a forced calm, he asked, "What do you know?"

She could tell he knew what she meant. "He told me *everything*," she said again, with emphasis on the last word.

This was the first time she had ever seen Frank speechless. He stared at her with his mouth gaping open and Gemma took her opportunity to continue. "He loves me enough to share his biggest secret with me. He *trusts* me enough to share his secret. And here you are, trying to pay me off, like I'm nothing. Like I mean nothing to him. And why now? We've been seeing each other for years. Why are you suddenly trying to get rid of me?"

Frank didn't answer her question. Instead, he asked her, "What do you want, Gemma? Why did you come here? Look, I'll double my offer: Ten to leave, and ten to keep quiet about whatever it is he's told you."

"You're not listening, Frank. I'm not interested in your money. I love Danny. I came here to tell you to stick your money. I don't want it."

His expression was one of pure disbelief. "Then what do you want?"

"All I want is for you to give me a chance. You don't even know me. You just assume I'm with Danny because he's rich. It's not like that." Emotion was causing tears to form in her eyes and her voice was unsteady. She was angry with herself for it and roughly brushed the tears away as they fell onto her cheeks. She continued on, "We've been seeing each other for almost three years, and I've never asked him for anything. Not once! I've never asked YOU for anything. But you don't like me. You won't even give me a chance. You're an elitist. You don't like me because I'm poor, or because I'm not a legitimate citizen. You treat me like I'm a criminal or something, but I'm a good person. I'm a better person than you."

Frank didn't have an answer to that. He opened the top drawer of his desk in silence, pulled out a box of tissues, and handed her one. She took it and gently dabbed her eyes and wiped her nose.

Once she had recovered herself a little, she said in a much calmer voice, "How do you think Danny would feel if he knew you had tried to buy me? If he knew you were interfering in his private life?"

Gemma shook her head with deep sorrow and stood to leave. Frank seemed to panic, almost jumping to his feet, and shouted, "Wait! Wait, Gemma! Are you going to tell him?" He sounded desperate.

She turned back to look at him and gave him a sad smile as she shook her head. "Why do you think so badly of me, Frank? Why would I ever tell him about this? What makes you think I would ever want to hurt him like that? He thinks the world of you. He would feel so betrayed if I told him what you had tried to do today."

Frank looked down in defeat, a guilty look on his face. Gemma hoped he felt as bad as she thought he should.

"Look, where are you going now? Back home?" His tone was gentler now, kind even. "Let me get you a car. You're not allowed in the city without a legitimate to vouch for you. I don't want you getting arrested. Besides, its freezing outside."

Not wanting to be petulant, she accepted his offer and thanked him. He pressed a button on his desk and a woman's voice spoke up "Yes, Mr Johnson?"

"Felicity. I'd like you to organise a car, please. ASAP. Put it on my personal account."

"Yes, Sir."

The line clicked off, Gemma realised the person he was speaking to was the middle-aged woman at the glass desk in the other room. She must be his personal assistant. She wondered what he was like to work for.

"Can I get you something while you wait? Coffee? Tea?"

He'd caught her off guard. She couldn't understand his sudden change or why he was being nice to her.

"No, thank you. I'm fine." She tried to sound polite as she declined his offer and hoped she hadn't offended him.

"Gemma," he paused after he spoke her name, as though he wasn't sure how to phrase his next sentence. "I'm sorry. It seems I have misjudged you."

She was so taken aback; she didn't know what to say. Though her face must have said it for her because Frank cleared his throat and looked uncomfortable as he averted his eyes from hers. He didn't strike her as someone who was used to admitting when he was wrong.

"I hope you realise; all I was ever doing was trying to protect my son. I love him. More than anyone will ever know."

She met his eye as she lifted her chin a fraction, her face set in steely determination, as she answered, "Me too."

Frank nodded. It looked as though he was about to say something else when the phone on his desk buzzed, and the receptionist's voice came through. "Mr Johnson?"

"I expect this will be your car," he said to Gemma, as he pressed the button. "Yes?"

"There is a phone call for you, sir. He said it was urgent."

"Get Bilson to handle it. Or take a message. I told you I didn't want interrupting," he snapped at her.

She didn't seem phased by his tone at all, perhaps she was

just used to dealing with him. "It's a Mr Marcus Jenson. He said it was of a personal matter, and that you would most definitely want to take this call. Should I take a message?"

"NO!" he almost shouted at her. "No. please, put him through. Thank you, Felicity."

Frank picked up the call as soon as the phone rang. Gemma wandered over to the large windows overlooking the city and tried to look like she wasn't listening. It was hard not to hear though.

"Jenson. Is everything okay?" she heard him ask.

She couldn't hear the other side of the conversation, but Frank sounded worried.

"No. I've been in the office all morning. I've not seen the news."

Gemma looked at the people down below. They looked so small from up here, and so carefree, just casually going about their day. Then she remembered she was in the city centre. Those people *were* carefree, or at least, they didn't have the same set of problems as the immigrants.

"Jenson. Now isn't the best time to talk. Can we meet? Tell me when and where. I'll make it work."

Gemma was still staring out of the window. Whatever that phone call was about, Frank certainly didn't want her overhearing it. She saw him scribbling on a piece of paper and watched him fold it up and put it in his jacket pocket. He flashed her an uneasy smile, then pressed the button again and said, "Felicity. Cancel all my appointments. Something unavoidable has come up. I will be out of office for the rest of the day."

"Yes Sir." she said, in a business-like manner. It sounded to Gemma like she had to deal with this type of thing often.

A moment later, it buzzed yet again, and Felicity's voice came through the speaker.

"What now?" he snapped at her.

"The car you ordered has arrived Sir." Gemma thought she was very professional. She didn't sound as though Frank's attitude bothered her in the slightest.

"Ah yes. Sorry. Thank you, Felicity," he said, hurriedly.

He shot Gemma an expectant look as he stood from his chair. She allowed him to escort her to the front door and out to the car. He held open the door for her and she clambered in. He told the driver, "Take her wherever she needs to go."

Gemma thanked him as he closed the door and watched him out of the window as the car drove away. She had never been in a chauffeured car alone before, and she wasn't sure what she should do. She didn't know if she was supposed to make conversation with the driver or sit in silence. Fortunately, the driver, who was used to ferrying people to and from Frank's offices, was pleasant and chatty.

"Where to Miss?" he asked, catching her eye, and offering her a cheerful smile through the rear-view mirror.

"Um... Gromdon please."

There was a slight pause before the driver recovered himself and said, "Gromdon? Cash town?"

That familiar feeling of embarrassment and inferiority swept over her. "Yes," she mumbled.

"Do you have an address or–" He trailed off, and she knew he didn't want to ask if she lived in the slums. She gave him the address of her house, thankful that she had an address to give. She knew she was lucky; she lived in a house with running water and electricity. It was more than most people in her situation had. If her landlord was caught illegally subletting to cashers and paying for amenities on their behalf, he would be in some serious trouble.

The driver was chatty and didn't seem to mind one bit that he was driving a casher to Gromdon. He talked about the weather, about working for Frank, about the city, and about the government, and the state of the country, and how sorry he felt for all the immigrants. Gemma couldn't decide if he was being genuine or simply trying to sound like he cared. It was unusual for legitimates to be on their side.

"Hey, did you see the news?" he asked, changing the subject.

"No. What's happened?" She thought back to when Frank was on the phone. Hadn't he spoken about not seeing the news yet?

"It's everywhere. Literally everywhere. You can't miss it!" He sounded excited now, as though he had some juicy piece of gossip he just had to share with someone.

"The government has been doing experiments on humans. And now they've all escaped and blown up the science lab! And now they're telling the entire country to watch out because they're supposed to be really dangerous or something! I mean... What kind of world do we live in, really? They put sanctions and limits on our technology, keep us in the dark and say it's for our own good, yet they have advanced scientific breakthroughs enough to make some sort of superhuman?"

"What are you talking about?" Gemma couldn't quite believe what she was hearing.

The driver continued on in the same excited tone, as though this was the most thrilling conversation he had ever had with anyone. "Apparently, they've been at it for years. They made them – some sort of superhuman in case we had another war. And now they're out and they don't know where they are."

The driver pressed a button, and the radio came on. "I've been listening to it all morning. It's all they're playing, over and over. It must be bad if they want everybody to know about it. They're saying these things are dangerous, and that we're not supposed to approach them, but you wouldn't know if you met one unless you got close to it. They say that they look just like us, and the only thing that is different about them is that they have a bar code tattooed on them or something."

Gemma listened to the voice on the radio. It was on repeat, cycling through the same information. How there had been an explosion at the Poly-Gen facility in the early hours of this morning, how a small number of "experimental human soldiers" had escaped and what to look for, and how to identify them. The driver was still chuntering away about how there had been no technological advancements in the last century, and how come the government didn't want the people to know what was available in other countries. "This just proves my theory though! It isn't that we haven't made advancements in science. It's that they government don't want us to have the technology. They can't control us so easily if we have access to the things the rest of the world probably have. I mean, communication tech hasn't moved on in over a hundred years," he said, pointing to his phone, "and we are still driving cars with combustion engines, yet they can make genetically modified humans?"

Gemma was only half listening to him and trying to concentrate on the news report. "I don't understand," she said. "The Poly-Gen facility is in Fairtock. There's nothing there but desert and scrubland, for miles and miles. Why are they trying to cause a nationwide panic? They couldn't have got very far if it happened less than 12 hours ago."

The driver caught her eye in the rear-view mirror. "How do you know what's in Fairtock?"

She changed the subject hastily. "Frank said you would take me anywhere," she paused, not wanting to be cheeky. "Would it be too much trouble to take me to Helston instead, please?"

"Helston! That's a no cash zone! Why would you possibly want to go to Helston?"

"Because my boyfriend lives there. He's a legitimate."

"In Helston? *Your* boyfriend lives in Helston?" his attitude irritated Gemma. She gave him Danny's address, and the driver looked at her in disbelief. "That's one of the most elite areas in the whole of Harpton Main. I can't take you there. Not without someone to vouch for you."

"Frank said to take me anywhere I wanted to go. I'd like to visit my boyfriend. In Helston."

The driver looked uneasy. "What's your boyfriend's name?" He asked. It was obvious he was expecting her to falter.

She felt a deep sense of satisfaction as she said with a smile, "Danny. Danny Johnson. Frank Johnson's son."

CHAPTER 4

Wednesday 22nd February 2102

JoBi Corp Offices, Harpton
Main City Centre

Frank saw Gemma off and turned back to his office building. He marched in with a serious business air about him, taking the elevator up to his floor, and hurried back to his office. There were still a few loose ends to tie up before he set off to meet Marcus Jenson.

He called Bilson, his right-hand man, or 'second in command' as they liked to joke, to explain he would be out of office for the rest of the day, due to unavoidable, unforeseen circumstances, and would need him to handle anything that cropped up, while denying him a real explanation about what was keeping him from his work.

Felicity had already cancelled his appointments for the day, but he had made a promise to call into one of the warehouses for a meeting with one of the under-managers. Jay was one of the best, but he had some sort of struggle with alcohol. Frank knew all about that. His first wife, Janet, was an alcoholic before he lost her to suicide.

He found Jay's number in the online personnel files and tried to call to apologise for being unable to make the meeting today, but the call went through to voicemail. There was no way he'd be able to commit to another day without checking his schedule, and he didn't want to appear callous, so he decided not to leave a message. He could always try again later. Whatever this meeting with Jenson was about, it was more pressing.

He switched on his automatic out of office email response, grabbed his keys and left without speaking to Felicity, who was busy on the phone. Instead, he offered her a simple nod as he made his way to the elevator and down to the underground parking facility.

Frank waited until he was inside the car before he called Danny. He couldn't risk anyone listening to his conversations at work. Danny picked up on the second ring "Dad! Have you seen the news?!"

"Yes. No. Sort of, Jenson called. Are you safe?"

"Yeah, of course I'm safe. Why did Jenson call?"

Frank couldn't quite believe how dumb his son was sometimes. "To tell me about the breakout. He wants to meet; he has all the inside knowledge. I'll be gone most of the day, we're meeting in Hawley."

"Hawley? Are you gonna be okay?" Danny sounded concerned and Frank couldn't blame him. Hawley had a reputation for being unsafe.

"Yes. I'll call you when I'm home."

Danny's voice changed to one of surprise when he said, "Gemma's here! In one of your cars!"

"Um, Danny, I've got to go. I'll call you later. Bye," he snapped, and ended the call, seething. He had assumed Gemma was going back to Gromdon. He inputted the address into his navigation system and set off driving, praying she would keep her mouth shut about their earlier conversation.

The drive was long and tedious. He listened to the news, but there was nothing new. Huge explosion. Genetically modified super humans. How to identify them. Not to go near them. Very dangerous... It seemed so odd. If anything, this seemed

45

like something the government would want to keep secret. Why panic an entire nation?

He finally approached the turnoff for Hawley, and it wasn't much longer before he was in the city centre. The place they were meeting was not a high-class establishment. It was a place in a questionable neighbourhood, neither rich nor poor, with a good mix of cashers and legitimates. It was an old-style diner, with stools by the counter, that served coffee and fruit pies. There was a large flashing neon sign outside that said "CASH ACCEPTED" in bright lights.

Frank knew he would have to leave his car and walk to the diner. It wasn't safe to park his car in this neighbourhood, not without leaving himself open for being mugged. If people suspected he had any money, they would target him for sure. If only he had thought to change his clothing before he set off. Being well dressed made him stand out like a beacon. He was thankful his skin was dark. There was a general expectation that black people would be cashers, so maybe he would go unnoticed as he made his way through this poor town.

Once he had located some underground parking, he removed his watch then took his phone out of his jacket and concealed it in the glove box, along with his wallet and his ID. He didn't want to risk anyone knowing who he was.

As he arrived at the diner, he spotted Jenson sitting at a booth at the back, perusing the menu; his untidy, greying hair was poking out from behind the printed sheet that was obscuring his face from view. As he lowered the menu, Frank noticed how this man had aged. He was no longer a young man; he was in his late fifties, but he looked it these days. His jawline was hard and jagged, his thin lips almost colourless.

"Frank!" Jenson greeted him with warm enthusiasm, and they shook hands.

Frank eased himself into the seat opposite, and they talked for a minute, as though they were nothing but old friends catching up.

"It's been a while! You look well," Jenson said.

ALMOST HUMAN

"I'm doing okay. How are things with you?"

He smiled. "Still enjoying my retirement." He nodded as he spoke. "How's the family? Is Danny okay?"

Frank nodded. "Everyone is fine, thank you. Michelle and I are well, Lyssi is studying hard at school, and Danny has moved into a house with his friend, Tony."

Jenson's eyebrows raised up. "He's living with a friend? Does this guy know?"

Frank nodded. "They've been friends a long time. He knows." His tone was clipped as he spoke, making it obvious that he was not impressed that Tony knew the truth.

"Does it worry you?"

Frank shook his head, but his face betrayed his lie, as he said, "No, it's been a long time since Danny's last episode. I'm sure he's just fine."

Jenson nodded as the server approached to take their order, and he quickly changed the subject to fishing. The ease at which this man could jump into a topic and act as though that's all they had been discussing since their arrival was impressive. But no doubt, Jenson would be well practised at this sort of thing.

They placed their order of coffee and as the server left, they got down to business.

"How bad is it?" Frank asked. He wasn't sure he wanted to know the answer.

"I've been in touch with the HGMR. They wouldn't say much, as I don't work for them anymore, but they wanted my input on what I think their next moves will be. They say there are eight escaped XJ5s and two XFs and an M. The M is who is thought to have instigated the breakout."

Frank was a little unsure what the codes meant. He understood HGMR stood for Human Genetic and Mutations Research. They were a secret branch of the government that the common man knew nothing about until now. XJ was the project his wife had worked on, and he had heard of the XFs but he wasn't sure what they were. "What is XF and M?" he asked.

"XF was originally a social experiment conducted by Multa-Gen, almost 50 years back, when the HGMR were playing around with their eugenics program. Multa-Gen were tasked with breeding a race of people with superior intellect, but who were totally compliant. They wanted to see if it was possible to create a group of people who primarily used the analytical part of their brain but weren't free thinkers. The XFs are incredibly intelligent, but they don't have any understanding of lies or manipulation. They are as naïve and gullible as children in that respect. The experiment was deemed a success, but there was no use for the XFs. They were due to be terminated, but someone at the top saw potential to utilise them at Poly-Gen. Every laboratory should have a small number of 'employees' who follow orders to the letter, never answer back or complain, and have no empathy for the subjects they are testing. And the fact they have superior intellect and photographic memory meant they were the ideal candidates to compile the data from the XJ experiments. They worked on the XJ4 project, and so knew everything there was to know when we perfected the formula and moved on to XJ5."

"And M?"

"They are a separate project, created around 30 years ago. They are/were ordinary humans, born to ordinary families, not developed in a laboratory like the XJs and XFs. Most were military, some spies. The scientists were working on enhancing their strength and intelligence. They were most impressive during their heyday, although the XJ project blew project M out of the water when it came along."

"So, how did they escape?"

"My money is on the M. You've got to understand how things work over there. I've been saying it for years... The XFs handle all the security, and much of the data compilation. Their main design specification was superior intelligence and when the HGMR decided to utilise them at Poly-Gen, they were only supposed to help compile the data from the experiments. But their capacity for memory, coupled with their analytical brains, made them perfect for the running of the security systems. Now they have a lot of responsibilities that they weren't originally designed for, but they are good at it. One of their newer responsibilities included monitoring the M's. M's are traced and tracked, heavily monitored and tested, but they are human. They have complaints and free will and objections, like anybody else, yet they are sort of stuck. They are under the thumb of the government, owned if you like, it's not as if they can walk whenever they feel like it, they are seen more of as tools than as people. The HGMR matched each M with an XF, as a monitor. The XF was to record everything about the M, every scrap of information. I've been saying for years that we shouldn't allow them to form personal connections like that. What would stop a friendship forming between the two, when they are meeting with one another at such regular intervals? The XF's have too many responsibilities. They have all the access codes, all the security codes, and they program all the systems themselves. They maintain all the tracking devices and the compliance chips. It would be easy to break out if you could coerce one into helping."

Frank paid close attention, trying to take it all in. He hadn't realised there were other projects out there or other research facilities doing similar work with genetics.

"Whenever I brought this up with the HGMR, they dismissed my concerns. They were confident that the way they designed, raised, and controlled the XFs would be sufficient to never have them question the order at Poly-Gen. The HGMR didn't believe they would ever question the rules or what they were taught. And they wanted to keep the test results as accurate as possible. They said there would be more margin for erroneous results if they didn't keep the XF monitors consistent. They basically advised me to concentrate on my own work with the XJs and mind my own business."

The server reappeared with their drinks, and the subject turned back to fishing. "I told him he was using the wrong sort of bait. You need those fat meaty worms in those waters. He sat there all day without even a nibble..." Jenson let out a natural sounding laugh, then continued, "It was the longest and most boring trip of my life."

It astounded Frank how natural Jenson sounded. As the server left again, Frank picked back up where they had left off.

"So, you think this M person convinced the XFs to turn off the security systems? And then what? They all just walked out?"

Jenson nodded. "Yes. That's precisely what I think!"

"Wait... but I thought there was an explosion. Didn't they blow up half of the facility? The news said there were over 250 deaths."

Jenson slowly shook his head. "The HGMR were responsible for the explosion."

"They blew up their own site? Why?"

"The escape happened five days ago, Frank. Not last night."

Frank stared at Jenson, unable to comprehend what he was saying. "I don't follow..." he said.

Jenson sighed. "Human Genetics and Mutations Research is a branch of the government that the government doesn't want to admit to having anything to do with. They tried to drop any affiliation with them fifty/sixty years ago, when they were working on their eugenics program and the country went mad over it. There is going to be a huge investigation, everyone will want answers. The government must be seen to be looking for answers as to why there are people doing genetic experiments on humans. As soon as the escape happened, they moved their research to another site. Now they can say the explosion destroyed all their research and experiments."

Frank stared at him in disbelief. "They blew up their own people to cover up what they were doing?"

Jenson looked sombre. "Yes. I knew a lot of the workers who died. The government will do anything to protect their research."

"So that's why they've made it public then? Five days is a long time. They could be anywhere by now, couldn't they?"

Jenson nodded. "They could. They're worth a lot of money. Especially the XJs. And they're dangerous. The HGMR wants to recover them as fast as possible. Making everyone aware of the threat is one way to get people on the lookout. If everyone knows what they are looking for, the missing XJs should find it difficult to hide. I doubt they will fit into society, anyway. They are too different to humans."

"Danny's not!" Frank said. He couldn't help sounding defensive.

"The ones raised at Poly-Gen are. They have been heavily abused, controlled, and conditioned. It's not like they are able to function in the real world. They have never even been outside."

The two men sat in silence for a moment, drinking their coffee. Frank was thinking about what he had just learned. If Janet still worked there, she would have been one of the expendable workforces who was killed in the explosion. If Jenson had still been working there, would he still be alive today? The obvious answer was yes. He would have known about it. Maybe he would have even been responsible for it.

"Does Danny know about the escape?" Jenson asked.

"Yes. It's all over the news. Do we need to worry?"

Jenson shook his head. "Nobody there knows about him. Only me, and I intend to keep my promise to you and Nicole."

"Janet," Frank corrected him.

"Yes, of course. Sorry. I still remember her as Nicole."

"Me too." A sad smile graced his lips. "We were happy when she was Nicole, and I was George, before she'd ever become mixed up in that whole mess."

"I am sorry for what happened. I truly thought after she got away from that place, she would be okay. That she would forget about it and go on and live her life with her new identity. She had so much to live for."

Frank nodded. His wife was never the same after she entered that place. Nicole and George were a happy couple with a comfortable life. They both had careers they enjoyed, and then they were blessed with a child. He would give almost anything to go back to those days, but then, he wouldn't have married Michelle, or be a father to Danny and Lyssi. He wasn't sorry for how his life had turned out.

"So, Danny has moved out? How do you really feel about that?" Jenson asked, changing the subject from Frank's dead wife.

"He's a big boy. He's sensible. I'm sure he knows what he's doing."

"How has he been? Any unusual behaviour?"

Jenson always made Frank feel uneasy when he started asking questions like this. He trusted Jenson to a certain degree, after all, he was the one who had helped Janet get out from under HGMR's control, and he had never revealed to anyone how she had smuggled out one of their infants. But Frank couldn't help wondering if this man's interest in his son was more scientific than friendly. Danny was the only one of his kind to be raised away from the Poly-Gen research facility, and the XJ project had been Jenson's life's work. It would be only natural for him to want to make comparisons.

"Danny is fine. Just like any other 20-year-old *man*," Frank glared at Jenson with a pointed look. Danny wasn't a child anymore, and he wasn't one of Jenson's experiments either. He was a grownup, with a house, a job, and a girlfriend.

Jenson cast a thoughtful glance at Frank. "It's been a while since I last saw or spoke to him, that's all. I'm the only person who can help Danny understand who or what he is. You might not care to hear it, but Danny isn't just like any other 20-year-old man. He is vastly different. Possibly dangerous, and burying your head in the sand about it will change nothing."

"He's fine."

"He's been seeing his girlfriend a while now, hasn't he?" Jenson asked. The question sounded so casual, but Frank heard the obvious weight behind it. The XJs weren't made to form close connections with others.

"You know he has. I know he has discussed it with you in

your meetings," he said tightly. "Look, I appreciate your help, and your insight, Marcus. I really do. But you need to back off. He's fine. I'm fine. His girlfriend is fine."

Frank had hoped that would be the end, but Jenson continued. "I take it the control techniques I taught him are working then? He hasn't lost control of himself for some time?"

Frank shook his head. "Not for a long time. He's doing very well," he lied. Admitting that Danny was no longer living at home because he had gone into full meltdown and tried to kill Lyssi was the last thing he wanted to do. Michelle said she wasn't prepared to have him in the house anymore, and Danny felt so guilty, and he was so worried it might happen again, he didn't even argue.

They finished their coffees in silence, both lost in thought about what they had been discussing.

"There is one thing Danny should be aware of," Jenson said, as they were getting ready to leave. "I'm not saying that they will go down this route, but if they do, Danny will need to take care and look out for himself."

"What are you talking about?"

"One of the sure-fire ways to track the missing XJs would be to use the others to locate them. They have extra senses to us, Frank. They can sense each other."

Frank's mouth fell open. "What do you mean? Sense each other? How?"

Jenson shook his head. They were back to talking in whispered tones again.

"Frank, they were specially designed to work in teams. A single XJ is dangerous. A group of them working together are unstoppable. They can sense each other, locate each other if they are close by, and they react to each other in ways that are difficult to explain. It's almost like a hive mind situation, except they're not reading each other's minds, more like feeling each other's feelings." He paused for a minute, then said, "What I'm saying is, if the HGMR decide to use their controlled XJs to search for the missing ones, they might accidentally find

Danny..."

Frank's heart beat a little quicker in his chest. He had no idea of this special talent that his son possessed. "Does Danny know about this? That he can do this, I mean? Did you ever tell him?"

Jenson shook his head. "No. I couldn't imagine a time where he would ever need to be privy to that information. I didn't think he would ever meet another XJ – and he still probably won't. But one of his greatest struggles is the fact he is so different to us. I didn't want to tell him he's more different than he imagines. I didn't see how that would help him."

"Do you think I should tell him? Is it something he should be told about?"

"I think the HGMR will use the controlled XJs as a last resort. They wouldn't want anything to interfere with the research on the prototypes. The current XJ5s are only for experimentation. The plan was never to use them commercially. But, if they have trouble finding the missing ones, they might decide to go down that route."

Frank rubbed his face. This was a lot to take in.

"I might not work for them anymore, but I am a respected scientist in the field. The XJ5 project was my baby, and I expect they will contact me to ask my advice and opinions on how to proceed with the capture of the missing subjects. Of course, I will pass on everything I find out. If they decide to go forward and use the XJs to locate the missing ones, then I would advise Danny to apply to temporarily leave the country."

"Leave the country? Why?" There weren't that many safe places outside of New America, and the country was very selective about who they let in or out.

"Danny, as far as anyone knows, is your biological son. Your man Tyler did an excellent job with his fake birth registry and digital ID. He appears to be a legitimate citizen from a wealthy family. Nobody would think twice about stopping him from leaving the country for business purposes. The missing XJs cannot leave the country unnoticed. I doubt the HGMR will search for them outside of New America."

"I understand. Thank you, Marcus."

"Frank, do you understand what would happen to Danny if they ever discovered that he existed?"

Frank swallowed. He had spent the last 20 years trying not to think about it.

"He would never leave that facility! And his life would not be worth living." There was a hardness to his voice when he said, "I'm not proud to admit that I have spent a good portion of my life torturing children and adolescents in the name of science. But there it is. If Danny was among them, I would have tortured him too. The others continuing the research would be VERY interested in Danny."

It was the first time Frank had ever witnessed Jenson reference the things he used to do at Poly-Gen. He wondered how he could sit there and so brazenly admit to torturing children. How could he live with himself? The things he had done were by choice and were far worse than the work they forced Janet to carry out, yet she was so tortured with guilt that she drank her sorrows away until the weight of her conscience became too much, and she killed herself. Jenson didn't even seem sorry. It was all so matter-of-fact to him.

Frank had listened to enough. He got to his feet and offered Jenson his outstretched hand.

"I'll be in touch if I find out any more news on how they plan to proceed with the search."

"Thank you, Marcus." He reached into his jacket pocket and pulled out some cash. He didn't want anyone being able to trace him to Hawley or being able to pin him down as being in contact with an ex Poly-Gen scientist. It wouldn't take too much digging to find out his real name was George Wilks, and he was the husband of Nicole Wilks, the Poly-Gen genetics researcher who disappeared 20 years ago. And from there, it wouldn't be a big jump for anyone to work out how Danny fit into the equation.

He left, feeling worse for seeing Jenson. The idea that any person with a heart could live with themselves after the things he'd done was beyond Frank's comprehension. He would never understand how he could have had an escape plan in place, then simply turn his back on it and give it all up for a promotion. Jenson *chose* to be there in the end. He *chose* to hurt those children.

Frank saw how his wife wrestled with the weight of her conscience until it took her life. It didn't sit well with him that Jenson saw the XJ project as nothing more than a science experiment. He didn't consider them to be in any way human or have feelings. To his mind, they were nothing more than tools, or items of stock, to be controlled and used for a purpose. They weren't meant to have feelings or independent thoughts.

It made him question Jenson's motives in wanting to keep a relationship with Danny. If he hadn't been so desperate for help and answers, he might have taken Danny and ran a million miles away when Jenson showed back up in their lives. But Danny was out of control, and there was a time when Frank thought he was beyond help. He would get consumed by fits of rage and he was so strong, there was nothing anybody could do to stop him or calm him. In truth, Danny had frightened Frank when he got into those states, but thanks to Jenson and his extensive knowledge on the XJs and how their brains process information, Danny had found staying in control of himself more manageable.

Thoughts of Danny and the conversations he'd had with Jenson consumed his mind for the entire drive home. He weighed up the pros and cons of telling Danny about his 'extra senses' and what that might mean. The thing Danny struggled hardest with was being so different. There was no getting away from it. His senses were so acute that he was often overwhelmed, and who wouldn't be in his situation? He could hear the tiniest noises and smell things that the rest of the world didn't even know had a scent. Jenson was probably right to keep this information from him. The thing he hated most was how nobody understood how he felt. He felt completely alone and different to everyone else, even though he was aware there were others like him. If he knew they all had a strange bond, that they 'sensed' each other, it would only serve to make him feel even more alone.

Frank reached for his phone to call Danny. The call connected and Danny's voice came through the speaker. "Dad! Are you on your way back already?"

"Yes. It was only a short meeting." He checked the time, it was almost 3:30 pm. "I should be home by 7:30 if the traffic is clear." He wanted to ask about Gemma, to ask if she was still there or if she'd mentioned anything about their meeting earlier that morning, but he was afraid to draw attention to it. Instead, he said, "What are your plans for dinner tonight?"

"Nothing much. We were just gonna order in, and then I was going to drive Gemma back home. Why?"

"Would you like to come home? Eat with us?"

"Erm... Dad, I'm seeing Gemma tonight."

Frank heard the annoyance in his son's voice. "Yes, I am inviting you both for dinner. I'd very much like to get to know your girlfriend a little better, Danny."

There was a pause. Danny seemed lost for words. "Oh... uh... yeah, sure. Thanks Dad." He sounded so taken aback, Frank felt a little ashamed that he had never even given the girl a chance before.

"Danny, how much does she know about you?" he tried to make the question sound casual, but this wasn't a casual type of question.

There was another awkward pause. It was obvious he didn't want to admit to telling her everything. "Danny?" he said in a more demanding tone.

"She knows. But honestly, Dad, it's okay. She's known for a long time..."

Frank let out a long exhale. He knew what Gemma had been hinting at earlier, but he didn't want to believe that his son would endanger himself by telling her everything.

"Dad? Are you okay?"

Frank could not answer that question honestly. He was so

far from okay it was unreal. He was seething, astounded that Danny would put his own safety at risk like this. His hands gripped the steering wheel so tight, his knuckles turned white, and his jaw clenched as he tried to keep the angry words inside. He tried to find some calm and reminded himself he was supposed to be building bridges with this girl. "Yes. It's good that she knows. It means we can have a proper discussion about things later," he said through gritted teeth.

"Okay. Right. Uh... Thanks, Dad." Frank noted the surprise in his son's voice. This wasn't the usual way these conversations went. Michelle would be so proud of him – he had listened to her for once.

"Just come whenever. We will order in. I'll let Michelle know."

They said their goodbyes and Frank sincerely hoped he could count on Gemma to keep her word and not let slip about their meeting earlier that day. All being well, he could keep her on his side for now, biding his time until they split. Then he imagined he would have to pay her a fortune to keep her mouth shut about what Danny had told her. He was pissed that his son had been so reckless.

Turning on the radio again, Frank shifted his attention back to the news. There was nothing new, they were still playing the same reports. Still spreading their lies, saying it happened less than 12 hours ago, saying that the escapees murdered 250 workers. Then came the official government representative claiming that they were doing everything they could to 'control' and 'minimise' this threat to public safety. And saying how there would be a full investigation into how human genetic testing could take place at all. The government wasn't planning to accept responsibility for the HGMR.

Frank shook his head in disgust. What else did the government lie about? The people were sheep, blind and controlled. The country was a mess.

As he drove, his thoughts turned to his past. The Poly-Gen site was so secret, people didn't apply to work there. The only reason Frank knew about it was because Janet had been plucked from death row to serve the HGMR. She had been sentenced to death for a crime of passion. She shot the man who had murdered their three-year-old son, Thomas. The offer of work in exchange for her life had seemed like a lifeline, an answer to their prayers. But once she was there, they forced her to do unspeakable things, things no person should ever have to do. She couldn't argue, she couldn't refuse, and if she didn't comply, she would have been back in prison, lined up for the next lethal injection. *And they would have had me killed, too,* he thought. There was no doubt in his mind this was why his wife had stuck it out as long as she did. Her love had never wavered, even when that place had sucked the life and soul out of her. The bitter thought left an unpleasant taste in the back of his throat.

Thinking of Janet always made Frank feel guilty. Guilty that he couldn't save her. Guilty that he loved his new wife, but he would never be over the death of his old one. Sometimes he yearned for his old life, when things were perfect, and he was George, and she was Nicole. He idly wondered what his life would be like now. Their son would be 26 years old, a perfectly average man. Maybe he would have children of his own. Frank liked the idea of becoming a grandfather. He would never get that from Danny. You don't make a genetically modified super soldier worth millions of dollars and then give it the means to reproduce.

Shaking his mind back to the present, he thought he better call Michelle to tell her about the dinner plans. She sounded pleased to hear he had invited Gemma; she'd been saying for a long time that he needed to give her a chance and that he was going to lose Danny if he didn't accept he was old enough to make his own choices. Of course, she was right. Danny used to talk to him. They would discuss every single decision together. But now Danny was his own man, he didn't need his advice or permission, and Frank's obvious dislike for the girl his son said he loved must be a factor in what had driven them apart.

Frank was becoming calmer and more hopeful as he approached home. He greeted Michelle and filled her in on his day, and it was comforting to know she wasn't overly concerned about the situation. "There are only eight escaped?" she asked.

Frank nodded. "Well, the chance of running into one will be slim to none then. Not here! We live in one of the most elite neighbourhoods in Harpton Main. Actually, one of the most elite neighbourhoods in New America. These 'X' people won't be able to cross the boundary without being discovered. They have no government issued ID!"

Frank hadn't looked at it that way. She was right. He expected they would increase security measures too. The reason the government had made it public and tried to incite fear and panic amongst its people was obvious. They were trying to drive further distrust between the classes. This was just another way to wage war on the casher and immigrant society, an insidious way to perpetuate the idea that people with no identification were not to be trusted.

It was only another hour before Danny and Gemma arrived. She looked unsure as she followed Danny in through the door and into their huge hallway. Frank remembered the one and only time she had been here before, and he had been less than welcoming towards her. He was determined to make more of an effort with her now. Surely, this was just one last act of rebellion from his son, and Danny would get bored with her soon enough, once Frank was more accepting towards her. Then he would find a new and more suitable girlfriend, one who had some sort of education and prospects.

Frank made small talk, but it was difficult. He didn't have a full picture of Gemma's situation, and there were vast differences in their backgrounds, but she seemed to try hard to keep things light and friendly. It was clear to Frank that she had indeed kept her word and not said anything to Danny about their discussion that morning.

Michelle was much better at making conversation with her.

She had a way about her that instantly put people at ease. Perhaps that's what made her such a good psychologist. Gemma got along well with Lyssi too. She seemed to know exactly how to interact with a fourteen-year-old. Asking her about boys and all about school and what it was like, confirming Frank's suspicions that Gemma had received no type of formal education whatsoever.

Lyssi was still very wary of Danny. They hadn't seen each other since his last 'incident', and he had terrified her. She spent most of the evening sitting close to her mother, barely looking at Danny, and once the meal was over, she retreated to her room, claiming that she had homework to finish.

"She'll come around," Frank said with gentle patience. He couldn't imagine how his son was feeling.

Danny's face was serious as he nodded. "She shouldn't have to. It should never have happened."

Michelle cast her eyes over to Gemma, then the two men. "Perhaps we should discuss this later..."

"It's okay. Gemma already knows everything," Danny said, in a tone that screamed 'don't start with me.'

Gemma's face turned a pale shade of pink as Danny grabbed her hand and turned to his parents, saying, "She's part of it now. She's in on it. We don't have secrets from each other."

Frank cleared his throat, "Well, since everybody is aware of the situation, you might as well hear what Jenson had to say," he said.

There was a slight shift in the atmosphere in the room as Frank spoke. A seriousness filled the air as Danny paid close attention to what Frank had to say. He gave little away about how the news of people like him being out in the real world was affecting him. His face remained passive and controlled as he listened. Gemma looked concerned but kept quiet. Frank wondered if she had anything constructive to offer, he doubted it very much. Still, he couldn't help but notice the comfort his son seemed to draw from the girl, he still hadn't released her hand, and was making gentle strokes up and down the back of it with his thumb as he listened to Frank retell the information he had learned.

Once the conversation turned back to lighter subjects, everyone seemed to relax a little, but it was getting late, and Gemma needed to be getting home.

"Thank you for coming Gemma. It was nice to see you again," Michelle said with a genuine warmth. "I hope we will see you again soon."

Gemma cast a hesitant look to Frank. He nodded and smiled in half-hearted agreement.

"Gemma, why don't you get in the car, I'll be there in just a minute," Danny said.

Danny turned to Frank as she left and said, "Thanks for tonight. It means a lot to me that you are giving her a chance."

Frank nodded. He didn't know what else to say. "I'll call you tomorrow, maybe we can grab some lunch? Unless you're busy, of course."

Danny nodded. "Sure. I'll see you tomorrow. Bye dad, Michelle. Um... will you tell Lyssi I said goodbye?" The pain and guilt were still there on his face. Frank had never felt so sorry for anyone as he did for his son right then. Michelle nodded and said she would, and Danny left, looking dejected as he trudged out.

"Well, that went well!" Michelle said, with a cheerful smile as she watched Danny drive away. "What has caused this sudden turn around with you and Gemma?"

"I just thought I'd take your advice that's all," he said, trying to arrange his face into an innocent expression.

She looked at him sceptically.

"Okay... I thought it would be better for Danny if I supported him, that's all. Jenson knows all about Gemma and I just... I'm the person he should talk to, not him. It's not that I don't trust him, but the way he talks, and the type of questions he asks... I'm not sure if he's just being friendly and trying to be helpful, or if his motivation for maintaining a friendship with Danny is more scientific."

Once he had said it, he knew it was true. Jenson was a family friend, and they owed him so much. And he trusted him... to a point. But Jenson openly admitted that his work came before everything else at Poly-Gen, and he had an inquiring mind. He seemed to have an unusually high interest in Danny's relationship with Gemma. *XJ5s weren't made to form close personal relationships.*

Frank decided it was better to leave out the part about trying to pay Gemma off to leave his son. Somehow, he didn't think Michelle would agree with that.

CHAPTER 5

*Friday 17th February
2102 (5 Days Ago)*

Poly-Gen Facility, Fairtock

XJ545-12 sat silently in her dark cell, waiting. Her eyes skimmed the dimly lit room, searching for some clue as to what the purpose of these orders might be. The door locks were still active, and the cameras were watching. There were others awake too. She could feel their same sense of trepidation swirling in the shared space of their connected minds.

Her orders had been given. At 1 a.m. she was to leave her cell and meet with her team on the third floor. As she sat perfectly still in the dark, waiting for 1 a.m. to arrive, she considered the reasons behind these orders. They had never ordered her to leave her cell during sleeping hours before. And they had never given her permission to go anywhere unaccompanied. They were always guarding her, watching her, controlling her. This seemed unusual, but she was not to question anything. Not ever. If they even knew she was thinking about the reasons behind the orders, she would be punished. Still, she continued to think.

If she tried to leave the cell unaccompanied, with no guard

to scan the door code and override the security measures, the security system would activate her compliance chip, causing her to be incapacitated and in extreme pain. However, if she failed to complete tonight's objective, they would most likely manually activate her compliance chip as punishment for failure to comply, and she would be incapacitated and in extreme pain, regardless. This must be a test. It wasn't uncommon for them to ask her to do things that resulted in pain or injury. The scientists liked to test their loyalty and make sure XJs would always obey orders, despite any risks involved. There were enough of them. She was expendable.

There was no clock in the small room, but XJ545-12 had an accurate sense of the passage of time. Lights went down at 9 p.m. and by her estimation, that was almost 4 hours ago. It would soon be 1 a.m.

XJ545-12 closed her eyes and tried to sense the others. It was impossible to say how many were awake and alert, but she knew she wasn't alone. She felt the others reaching out too, testing, just as she had, to see if anybody else had been chosen for this unusual task. A general feeling of apprehension swirled inside their shared consciousness, and suspicious feelings of uncertainty about what was to come. These were not new feelings; it was all she had ever known. Fear and uncertainty. Anxious nervousness, pain, and suffering. Her life had been the same since they first awakened her eleven years ago. They all worked hard at keeping these feelings to themselves and tried not to let them spill out into the shared space. Closing their minds and shielding their emotional and physiological responses to situations improved life for everyone.

Time ticked on, but still the door looked no different. The red light shone, indicating the door locks were still active. She could not leave. Her eyes travelled around the rest of the room, looking for anything that might indicate what the point of trying to leave might be, but it looked the same as always: small, no windows, one door. A small bed. A stainless-steel basin with a tap and a soap dispenser, and a small hand towel. To the back of the room, a stainless-steel toilet. Four cameras, one in each corner. There was nowhere inside the cell she could sit or stand without being in view of the cameras. As time marched closer, the feelings between the XJs ebbed and flowed until each one had themselves under control. A calmness rippled amongst them, even though team tasks were uncommon.

XJ545-12 stood and walked to the door then watched in silence as it let out a gentle click and the light switched from red to green.

Holding her breath, she gave a tentative push of the door, and waited for the searing pain to hit as her compliance chip became active. It never came, and she took a cautious step through the door, taking her time to absorb her surroundings. The corridor appeared to be the same as always. Plain, and empty, with cameras over every doorway. The other cells in this corridor were still sealed, the XJs here had not been chosen.

She marched with purpose towards the double door at the end of the corridor, though it was highly unusual to be afforded the freedom to walk alone, and XJ545-12 had been nowhere unaccompanied in her entire life. There were guards with their compliance controls, always. It felt so odd, but she couldn't allow these strange sensations to interfere with the task. All that mattered was completing her objective: reach the third floor and await further instructions.

At the end of the corridor, she reached an open and unguarded door. Another unusual occurrence – every door in the facility always remained locked. Each member of staff had special keys to open the doors (depending on their security clearance level) and codes to put in to allow the XJs to pass through the doors unharmed. As far as XJ545-12 understood, she should not be able to open or walk through any door unaccompanied, without being incapacitated. She thought back over her orders. Instead of direct orders, she'd been given codes to decipher to work out the directive. That was part of another test; one to test cognitive function. There is no use for an XJ who can't crack codes. She did a quick assessment of the evidence. *I deciphered the objective from the code. Leave my cell at 1 a.m. and arrive at floor three. The usually locked doors are open. My compliance chip has not activated. There are others awake and following the same orders.* She hadn't got it wrong, but something didn't sit right. *Where are the guards?* She tried to shake the thoughts away, fiercely reminding herself that independent thought and anticipating outcomes was not permitted.

Once through the door, she started on the plain grey metal stairs; the clunk of her feet created a rhythmic sound as she marched up each step. Even though the lights were dim, her vision was perfect. The dull and unmoving camera caught her eye as she passed by, and she stood watching for a second, perplexed. Was it broken? Had the others blinked as she walked by? She climbed the stairs quicker now. The cells were deep underground, and it was a long way up to floor three.

Once she made it to floor three, the almost magnetic-type-pull of the others told her which way to go. It was instinct; she didn't need to be told, but as she rounded the corner, it still surprised her how she was yet to see a single employee. No scientists. No guards.

Floor three was known as the diagnostics floor, and the layout differed from the labs and the cells underground. This floor had windows, but she knew better than to look. XJs did not have permission to look at the world outside. On this floor, they studied and tested the Ms. She had worked with an M on occasion and had had plenty of experience of the XFs. XFs were present for all experiments. Their main function, aside from overseeing security, was data collection and compilation.

Two XFs were manning the corridor. XJ545-12 stopped in front of them, arms by her sides, palms open and facing upwards, and stared down to the floor, as was normal procedure.

"Stand with the others," one ordered her.

She complied, walking across the corridor and around the corner to where there stood seven other XJ5s.

After a moment, both XFs joined the small congregation

of XJs. One of them was fiddling with a remote device that XJ545-12 did not recognise. Its purpose became clear after he pressed the button and a deafening siren sounded. XJ545-12 recognised the din as the sound of the escape alarm. A collective sense of dread filtered through the XJs. This must be an escape drill. They would all suffer in agony once the guards arrived with their compliance controls and incapacitated them.

"Let's go!" shouted the XF. He led the way out of the door at the end of the corridor. XJ545-12 didn't understand. The doors should be sealed now. An automatic lock down occurred whenever the alarm is sounded. Nobody can get in or out until they have contained the breach.

The general sense shared between the XJs was one of confusion, mistrust, and an ever-growing fear about what was happening.

The XFs led the way down the stairs at the far end of the corridor. The XJs followed their orders with blind obedience.

XJ545-12 arrived at the bottom of the stairs just in time to see the two guards at the next set of doors. They were accompanied by an M and the first guard shouted in an authoritative voice, "STAND DOWN," as he held up his compliance device and pushed the button.

There was a fraction of a second where each XJ5 held their breath, anticipating the agony that was to come, followed first by relief, then a mire of confusion when their chips didn't activate.

They had no time to process the collective disorientation before the M, who was standing between the two guards, took his opportunity to shoot. The guard's whole attention was on his handheld device. He pushed the emergency crowd control button, which should have incapacitated every XJ5 in the vicinity, with frantic repetition, desperate to make it work. He didn't even see the attack coming as M raised his gun and shot him straight to the side of his head. Without even a moment's hesitation, he rounded on the other, and one shot later, both guards lay dead, the contents of their heads spattered across the floor and over the desk.

The XJs stood, stunned. This was not meant to happen. This was never meant to happen.

M addressed the group of XJs. He spoke with an air of relaxed authority to his voice, but his body gave him away. This was a man under a great deal of stress. XJ545-12 could hear it in his pulse rate and smell it in the beads of sweat forming on his brow.

"Two guards are dead, and you are out of your cells," he said. There was a boldness and self-assured quality in his voice as he spoke. "Make the choice. Fight your way out and live, or they will kill you for this."

There was no discussion, no argument. The XJ5s collectively decided that attempting to leave was the only logical choice. The M was right, of course. There were humans dead, and XJs out of their cells, unguarded. It was obvious he had used them in this escape plan, but it was too late to halt things now.

The alarm still wailed with a deafening din, as M shouted over the noise to give them more information.

"We are going to make our way to Exit D. All doors on the route will be unlocked. No chip activators will be in working order. Almost all HGMR employees are on lockdown, meaning all doors in all other parts of the building are sealed. I suspect they already have techs trying to undo our tamperings. There will be guards on the ground floor, and guards at Exit D. You will need to deal with them swiftly. Their chip activators should be out of action. Once we have made it out of Exit D, we will run on foot past the perimeter. You will scale the fence. The voltage will be down. Once you are over the fence, you will run until you get to the second perimeter fence. Again, this will be offline, as long as we are quick. Once over that fence, you will run. I have two military wagons ready to go. If we get out of the compound and into the wagons, I will disclose the rest of the escape plan." He took a breath and looked around at each XJ5. "The formation I want is three XJ5s at the front, followed by the two XF's and myself. I want XJ's flanking either side of us and three in the back. Organise yourselves accordingly. Our success depends on the survival of the XFs. Make their protection your priority." It took only seconds for the XJs to work out their most efficient formation. XJs were designed to work in teams. They each knew their own strengths and weaknesses, and who outranked whom. Their additional senses and shared consciousness meant no outward communication was needed. The M looked at them once they had seamlessly arranged themselves and shouted, "GO. GO. GO."

There was no hesitation. They charged down the stairs and onto the ground floor, the three XJs at the front leading the assault. XJ545-12 was flanking XF31-03.

The first guards were downed without effort, and the doors were opened. They ran through, out into what appeared to be an entrance hall. A single security guard sat at the desk, his body quaking with fear as he frantically tried to communicate over his non-functioning radio. He had little time to react. He was dead before he'd even acknowledged the XJ's presence.

The M pulled open the door, and they all dispersed into the fresh night air. XJ545-12 had only been outside the facility two times in her life. The strangeness of being outdoors was both thrilling and terrifying. This was against the rules. She wasn't the only one to feel this way. The collective feeling was one of fear and uncertainty. There was no turning back now.

The facility was located in a deserted part of Fairtock, nothing but desert and wasteland, as far as the eye could see. The grounds spanned for miles. They ran until they reached the perimeter fence. Just as the M had promised, it was out of action. The XJs scaled the fence with ease; it took no effort for them to climb, but the XFs were tiring now. Their purpose was administrative duties, not physical feats such as this. The M was still in charge, yelling at them, urging them to hurry.

They continued into the desert and towards the second fence. XJ545-12 heard the gentle hum as she approached it. It was live. Each XJ waited and readied themselves for orders. If the M had ordered them to throw themselves at the fence and die, they would have done it without question or hesitation.

The unconditioned XFs were struggling to keep up. As they caught up to the XJs, they turned right and followed the fence along the perimeter, stopping in front of a grey box. Each produced tools and cables from inside their clothing. One held a small black device with buttons on it. XJ545-12 did not know how it worked, but its purpose was obvious.

M stood behind them shouting at them to hurry, as their hands worked feverishly, fingers dancing across the buttons of the device and inside the grey box. Eventually the green light turned dull, and the humming stopped. M ordered one of the XJs to grab the fence. He did it without hesitation, but nothing happened.

"Up and over. Now. Go. Go. Go!" M yelled. Everybody complied. XJ545-12 scaled the second fence with ease. She had zero knowledge of what lay beyond this point. Once they made it over, M directed them towards the wagons.

The sirens were still wailing within the facility, and now outdoor sirens had sounded too, to indicate a breach. Up ahead, they heard the chop chop chopping sound of helicopters, and blinding bright searchlights shone over them from above.

"Run. Go. GO."

They headed up a steep incline, scrabbling upwards, scuffing hands and knees, until they reached more flat land. The M directed them on, "Keep running, there is a road further on. The wagons are stationed there."

The XFs were struggling to keep up and M yelled, "Wait! I need them alive. We aren't leaving without them."

Without deliberation, without conversation, the XJs instinctively knew who would be best suited to the task of assisting the XFs. XJ545-12 held back and grabbed one by the right arm, as another XJ grabbed his left. They sped up, pulling him along, not giving him a chance to rest, or to tire. Another two XJs did the same with the other XF. It looked an impressive sight, the XJs executing a strategy in seamless perfection, without ever speaking a word.

A fleeting sense of accomplishment spread through the XJs, as the wagons came into view. One had a driver, one didn't. M was shouting, directing four XJ's into the first wagon. The driver didn't dally. As soon as the four clambered in, the engine revved, and the vehicle sped off down the dirt track and out of sight.

M was directing the others into the empty wagon. He ordered the XFs in the back first, then the XJs to follow, then climbed into the drivers' seat. He only allowed himself a second to recover before he set off. Aside from the helicopter still circling overhead, there were no other vehicles. It was a clear run to the main road, and he set off, speeding at full tilt.

The XJs sat in stunned silence. This was uncharted territory for all of them. The XFs may have been out of the compound before, but never without orders, and never unaccompanied. The XJs had rarely seen the outdoors, and they had never seen beyond the fence.

They were afraid. It wasn't a good combination; four of them in close quarters, each one experiencing fear. They all tried to keep a handle on themselves and shield their emotion from each other, but fear was an involuntary sensation that was difficult to contain, and situations involving overwhelming feelings of fear tended to escalate. There was one, XJ523-07, who was teetering on the edge of being overtaken. The XJs could all feel it; they were all in danger.

"Everybody okay in the back?" The M shouted back towards them. "XF talk to me, what's going on with them?"

One of the XFs supplied a brief explanation of how distressed the XJs would be right now, and how volatile the situation may become. He named XJ523-07 as being a potential danger.

"Get rid of it. We can't risk having them all in meltdown. XJs! Eliminate the threat."

XJ545-12 felt the panic surge from XJ523-07 as they all

rounded on him. He knew there was no point in trying to fight, he could not win. One opened the door, and the others grabbed him under the arms and hurled him out of the back of the wagon. XJ545-12 heard the thud as he hit the ground. As he fell from the moving vehicle, the fear and adrenaline peaked and pushed him over, out of his safe zone. The uncertainty of his situation, the new circumstances, the fact that he was now alone, and his team had turned on him had all played a part in his resulting meltdown. For a moment, XJ545-12 and the two other XJs were gripped by the tumbling blackness, dragging them down into the raging, red hot anger and were falling at speed into the dark abyss. They each tried their best to hang on and steady themselves as M kept driving. He sped up and as they left the fallen XJ5 behind, his pull lessened, and they were free of the immediate danger.

M drove in silence for the next 2 hours. He eventually slowed and came to a stop outside an abandoned building that stood in the middle of nowhere. All around, there were trees and grass fields. The sky was lightening. It wouldn't be long until the sun came up.

"Okay, XFs let's go. XJs, stay here."

XJ545-12 watched the three men leave the vehicle and enter the building. She could hear the whirring and buzzing sounds of electronics, and they were talking about deactivating tracking devices and termination cells. She knew the Ms were fitted with a termination cell. Many of the M's missions were completed away from the facility, in the real world. If any M should ever disobey an order, or go AWOL, the HGMR could activate it remotely, and he would be dead within seconds. The XFs were responsible for the maintenance and upkeep of the chip. They must know how to deactivate it.

M had prepared well for this escape plan. It seemed he had rigged this building up with all the equipment the XFs would need to deactivate his chip. She knew they were also removing his tracker. Her senses were so acute that even from inside the car, she could smell the blood and hear his grunts of pain as they pulled it from his flesh. She heard the plan of how they were going to scramble the signal and make it look as though he were somewhere else. According to the XFs, the helicopter couldn't have followed them. It was unmanned and sent out remotely because all the Poly-Gen employees were stuck on lockdown. The helicopter was only taking recordings of the escape. It was unable to leave the facility grounds. There was no way for the HGMR to track the M right now. For one thing, they were all on lockdown thanks to the XFs and their tampering with the security systems, but also, because they had tampered with the tracking devices too, and every single M was offline. It was a fail proof plan, one that had been executed with precision. Once they had completed their task of removing the tracer, and deactivating the Ms termination cell, he returned to the wagon.

"You." He pointed to the male XJ. "You and XFs will wait here until my contact arrives. He will take you to a city and what you do from that point is up to you. From the moment he drops you off, you will have your freedom. Any questions?"

The three XJs stared at the M. Freedom was not a concept they understood. No orders, no tasks, no experiments. They did not know what they would be without the structure and order of the Poly-Gen site. What was their purpose now?

M had walked around the back of the building. Hidden in an outhouse was a car. Different to the wagon they had just been riding in, it was silver and much smaller, with four doors.

"One in the front, one in the back," M said, pointing to the two remaining XJs.

The other went for the back door, leaving XJ545-12 with no choice but to take the passenger seat next to the driver.

M took a moment to thank the XFs. It was something that XJ545-12 had never observed happening before. Nobody had ever shown gratitude to any X, regardless of their type. She noticed how he shook their hands as though they were equals. She'd seen handshaking before, but never between human and experiment, and the M was human. Enhanced human, but still human.

M strode to the car and climbed in. He set off at once, speeding out towards the main road. The two remaining XJs sat in perfect silence and tried not to feel each other. Being in a confined space with only one other XJ5 was a strange, unnerving sensation. It was as if their sense for each other was being magnified. It felt uncomfortable and unfamiliar, almost painful. They were each concentrating hard on trying not to feel the other, while simultaneously trying to keep their own fear and apprehension in check and shielded from the other, to avoid meltdown.

The M drove for five more hours and still nobody spoke. XJ545-12 noticed as the surrounding scenery changed. She didn't look directly at it. Her head remained facing her lap, as was normal procedure, but her eyes surreptitiously darted to the side and her peripheral vision picked up details. She saw the sunrise and the sky change from a reddish hue to a beautiful blue, huge fluffy looking white clouds here and there. They were far from where they started now, no desert in sight. There were fields upon fields, farmland as far as she could see, and as they drove uphill, she could see small villages in the valley below.

M took a sharp turn and followed a country road into a small town. He slowed down and caught the eye of the XJ in the back. "This is your stop." He slowed to a stop and looked at the terrified XJ in the mirror. "Get out," he ordered her.

She didn't argue; she didn't know how to disobey, but XJ545-12 could feel her fear as she opened the door and climbed out. As she closed the door behind her, M sped away and the feelings of fear resonating within XJ545-12 lessened as he drove. Now she was alone. This was a new experience all together. Every feeling, every sensation, were all hers and hers alone. Since the day of her awakening, she had never been alone. She felt lost without them, but it wasn't a feeling she could process well, having never experienced it before.

"Are you okay?" M asked her. "Are you a danger to me right

now?"

"No." She only knew how to answer with clear and concise replies. She had no need for niceties.

"What's your name?"

She stared down at her knees, unsure of what he meant.

"Your identity," he clarified.

"XJ545-12." Her speech was robotic and unnatural.

"You're going to need a name, not a serial number. You're going to have to try to fit in and act like a regular human if you want to keep your freedom."

Her eyes slid across to take in his face, though she was careful to avoid direct eye contact. *Freedom.* The word sounded foreign to her ears. It wasn't something she had ever thought about. Her existence was for a purpose, and once she had fulfilled that purpose, they would discard her. She didn't matter. She was an item, a product with a product number. Freedom was never an option for her.

The M glanced over to her. "What was your number again?" She repeated her serial number in the same unfriendly, monotonous voice.

"Hmm. 5,4,5, 12. If you match those with the letters of the alphabet, you get E.D.E.L. Edel. That's a name. Or close enough, anyway. There are plenty of odd names out there in the cash towns."

She didn't speak or acknowledge she had understood what he was saying.

"Um... what's your name?"

"Edel," she said.

"Yeah, you're getting it." He smiled at her. "My name is William."

They drove along, but she did not know where he might be taking her. The stress of the day and the unfamiliar situation she had been forced into had been taxing. Her bones ached with lethargy, but she didn't know if she had permission to rest. She dared not ask. Questions were forbidden at Poly-Gen.

Eventually, M stopped in a small town. It was alien to Edel.

She had seen nowhere like it before. The buildings were small, not like the facility where she had come from, which spanned for miles and miles, all encompassed inside one building. The streets were dirty, something she had never seen before either. Poly-Gen was immaculate, she'd never seen litter or grime on the floor. It didn't smell the same here. She was used to the thick cloying smell of antiseptic and cleaning fluid, the kind that burns your nostrils as you inhale. There were new scents here, things she couldn't place, things she'd never smelled before.

William got out and pulled out a large black bag from the trunk of his car then closed the door with a dull thud.

He pointed to a building with a sign that read, 'Cityscapes Inn' in large letters. "Are you coming?" he said to her, not unfriendly, but with little in the way of patience.

She obliged, and silently left the car, awaiting further instructions.

"Okay, look. I know you're not exactly used to it yet, but you pretty much have your freedom now. I need you to stay here with me and protect me until I get to where we are going. After that, you are on your own, free. You won't answer to anyone at the HGMR, and nobody at the Poly-Gen site will know where you are. You're going to have to learn to fit in fast, though. I'm certain they will have overridden the system lockdown by now, and they will have all the trackers up and running. They will probably already know the location where the XFs removed my tracer. I am tired, I need to rest now. It's been a long couple of days for me. We are going in here," he pointed to the building in front of them. There was a flashing sign outside that said, 'Cash payers welcome.' "I am going to sleep. Can I count on you to keep watch? You protect me, wake me if there is trouble. If you suspect they have followed us, or they find us, we will have a chance of getting away."

She was staring at him, her expression never changed. Her face was plain and unsmiling, as though he hadn't just explained that she was now free to live a happy and pain-free existence.

"You have permission to speak now, Edel."

She kept up her silence.

"Okay. Well, I'm going to take that as a yes. We aren't in the best place for you to be out on your own here, you will fare better in a city. I am travelling to Harpton Main in the morning. It's another full days' drive from here, but if you stay with me and protect me until I get there, I will show you what to do and how to fit in. Here –" he opened the bag and pulled out some clothing. "Put these on. They are a little big for you, but they will do."

She pulled on the black hoody and black pants. He had provided some black socks too. It was only as she put them on that she realised how much her feet hurt. Shoes and socks were not a necessary requirement for XJ5s. The HGMR never intended for them to leave the facility. Her feet, like the others' who had escaped, were cut to shreds.

"Ready? Pull up the hood and cover your head. People aren't used to seeing females with shaven heads." He didn't wait for her to give him an answer. He walked in through the doors of the building, and she obediently followed, pushing all thoughts of exhaustion back from her mind. She had a task to complete. She would protect the M because that was her purpose now.

CHAPTER 6

Friday 17th February 2102

Cityscapes Inn, Elsom

There was a lot for Edel to notice as she followed William into the hotel. First, she was standing on carpet. It felt strange beneath her feet; soft and squashy. The smells here were different again, and the sounds. She held her breath as she tried to keep control of herself. Too much new information could overload her senses and force her into meltdown. If that happened here, everyone would die, including William. He said he would help her if she protected him.

She stood stationary behind him, listening to him speak to the woman behind the desk. She watched the wad of paper pass from his hand to hers and saw the woman hand him a card.

"Second floor, left at the top of the stairs." The woman spoke cheerfully, but eyed Edel with suspicion, as William set off for the stairs. Edel followed in silence.

Once they got into the room, William closed the blinds. Edel stood stationary like a sentry by the door as William used the bathroom and washed his face.

When he emerged from the bathroom, he looked at her. "You can relax a little. I don't think they will find us, but I need you just in case."

She continued to stand there, rigid, the same stony expression on her face. 'Relax a little' was not a term she understood. She looked like a statue, the only thing that gave her away was the way her body jumped and jerked with every new sound her ears picked up.

William sounded concerned as he asked, "Are you safe? Would you tell me if you weren't?"

Her eyes travelled across the room to him.

"Are you a danger to me?" he asked, with a little more urgency.

"No."

"Do you understand what freedom is? You can speak freely now and look directly at me. You can sit if you like or stand if you prefer. It's okay if you pace around, or look out of the window... You don't have to just stand there like that all night."

She heard the words, but she couldn't comprehend them. Her orders had been given. She needed to protect him while he slept. It only made her wonder if this was a test, to see if she would still obey.

William climbed onto the bed, but he didn't undress or get under the sheets. He looked in her direction a few times before he finally settled down to sleep and she could tell he was nervous of her, though she couldn't understand why. She had already confirmed she had control of herself.

The time was only 6 p.m., but William was sound asleep. He slept until 2 a.m. and woke with a start, his eyes fixed on her immediately, still standing in the same place by the door. She stood stationary, keeping up her guard, waiting and listening.

He pulled a bottle of water from his bag, and Edel watched him drink, her own sense of thirst grabbing at her throat. She counted the hours since she had last drunk any fluids. William held out the bottle towards her, but she made no attempt to take it.

"You must be thirsty XJ," he shook his head "Edel, sorry. Your name is Edel. Drink."

She took the bottle and drank, only because he had ordered her to.

"Are you tired?" he asked.

Again, she stood there, quiet and non-responsive. "Do you need to sleep?" he asked her again.

She was tired. But the question he asked was one of need. She could manage without sleep for days, if not weeks. She did not *need* to sleep right now.

"No."

He shook his head and laid back down on the bed.

Edel watched as he tossed and turned on the bed. After about an hour, he fell away into another sleep. It was a little after 5 a.m. when he woke and instinctively looked towards the door where she had been standing all night.

"Have you moved at all?" he asked, rubbing sleep from his eyes.

She didn't answer.

"You're going to have to get over this silence thing. That's going to give you away immediately. You better get comfortable talking, and quick, or they will find you, and I assume they will terminate you for escaping."

Silent outrage welled in her chest. She wanted to argue, to say that she hadn't intended to escape, that she had only followed his orders. She wanted to say she knew she had been used by him and the two XFs and that it should be him who was terminated. Instead, she remained silent. She had never given her opinion, and certainly never disagreed with a human before. The consequences of having independent thoughts at Poly-Gen weren't pleasant.

William checked the time. "Okay, stay here. I am going across the street to get something to eat. I will bring you something back." Then he looked at her quizzically. "What do you eat?"

She didn't understand. She ate what she was given, when it was given. It was always the same, plain and tasteless, but nutritionally balanced to provide her body with the correct nourishment. He gave a huff as he pushed by her and out of the door, aggravated by her continued silence.

Edel looked around the empty room. This was the first time she had ever been truly alone. She spent almost all her time alone, in her cell at Poly-Gen, but she was always connected to the others. She could sense them, feel them, and she was always being watched and monitored. She walked with slow, careful steps across the room towards the window and peeked through the blinds, testing her new freedom. The sun was coming up again and this time she looked at it properly. She had never seen a sunrise until yesterday, and she found herself mesmerised by the beauty of it. A feeling crept up on her she had never experienced before. She was choosing. She *chose* to walk here to the window. She *chose* to lift the blind and look outside. This wasn't an order. For a moment, she was frozen with a crippling fear of what they would do to her if they saw her. It took a second before she realised, they weren't watching. There were no cameras, no observations, no scientists. The heady feeling of choice and possibilities floated into her conscious mind, and she walked around the room, not because she had been told to, but just because she could. She was free to move her body.

She moved into the small bathroom. It was similar to her cell at Poly-Gen. There was a toilet and a sink, with a soap dispenser and some towels on a rail. She used the toilet, and then filled the basin, and washed herself. The soap smelled different; it was perfumed. Not unpleasant, but a shock none the less, when she could still smell the faint fragrance on her skin after she had dressed.

She heard feet shuffling outside her door and returned to her sentry position. William entered, carrying a small bag stuffed with food and drink.

"I didn't know what you would like to eat. I know you've only really had the same thing your entire life. I hope this is okay," he said, passing her a small loaf of bread. She took it but made no attempt to open it.

"XJ! Eat!" he ordered her.

She obediently opened the package and took a bite. She found the flavour and texture to be a shock. Taste was her most under-used sense; she had barely tasted anything before.

She bit into the bread, and her mouth began to water. It felt strange and spongy on her tongue and as she chewed it; she was surprised at how it seemed to ball up into a clump and stick to the roof of her mouth. She swallowed it and then fear rose in her chest. How much should she eat? Was she meant to continue or not? The instructions weren't clear enough, and she was terrified, completely unsure of the situation but unable to ask. The panic rose higher; she didn't know if she was doing right or wrong.

"XJ. You're not eating. You don't like the bread?" he asked.

She froze. Nobody had ever asked her if she 'liked' anything before. She didn't know. How did people know what they liked?

"XJ? – Edel?" he corrected himself. "It's okay. Eat if you're hungry. Leave it if you're not. Nothing will happen to you. Nobody is watching us. This isn't a test." He spoke to her in short, easy-to-understand sentences. "Why don't you sit down? You've been standing all night. You must be tired. Your legs must ache."

Her legs were fine, but she sat because he told her to and took another bite of the bread. He passed her another bottle of water, and she took it wordlessly.

"You understand you may drink that water whenever you please? I don't want to have to tell you to drink. That is your choice," he told her.

They ate in silence and when they had finished, he said, "We need to leave, I have to get to Harpton Main. I have a train to catch."

Edel didn't know what a train was or why he needed to catch one. She continued her silence, but William seemed to have become used to it. He collected his things, stuffing the food into his bag, and gestured for her to follow as he opened the door. She followed him out into the hall and down the stairs then watched in silence as he handed the key to the person behind the desk. Edel followed him out of the building and watched as put his bag in the back and opened the driver's door to get in.

"I shouldn't need to instruct you to get into the car," he said, a touch of annoyance in his voice.

She dropped her eyes to the floor as the confusion hit, and she walked around the other side of the car then climbed in. This was all so unfamiliar. She didn't know how to behave.

The drive was long and Edel felt exhausted, but she dared not close her eyes or rest for a second. William had given up trying to talk to her for the moment, but there was plenty of other information for Edel to take in, even with her eyes cast down to her knees. It began to rain, and she found it fascinating. She watched from the corner of her eye as the drops ran down the windows and colours deepened outside. It changed the scents too, as if the rain had released new fragrances with new depths. She saw the changes as they drove from rural villages to vast spaces of nothingness, to built-up cities brimming with people and buildings and cars.

"We need to switch cars again," he said, after a few more hours had passed. "We're almost out of fuel, and you need digital money and ID to purchase it. I have my ID, but once they run it through the system, it will give away our location. I have a new car set up ready to go." He pointed to a storage unit with large, corrugated shutters. He continued to drive, circling the storage unit twice before coming to a stop a few hundred yards away. He got out, and she followed in silence. The rain had stopped again, but the fresh puddles on the ground interested her immensely. She wanted to inspect them, to touch them with her fingers, but she didn't dare stop or slow down. She kept pace with the M. He punched the code into one of the storage lockers and lifted the shutter. The car was similar to the one they had been driving in, silver, with four doors. He opened the driver's side and slid in, offering her an impatient scowl as she stood motionless, waiting for her instruction to do the same.

Edel stayed vigilant on the drive. She watched the sky turn darker, and the rain fall once more. Faster, heavier.

"Looks like this has set in for the day," William said, pointing to the sky.

Edel's eyes followed his finger as he pointed, but she didn't respond, and William seemed to give up trying to make small talk after that.

Eventually, she saw the signs for Harpton Main, and the scenery outside had changed again. There was a coastline view from her window, and she had never seen such a huge expanse of water. The waves looked dark and dismal as they rolled roughly and smashed into the rocks below. She craned her neck to see, then checked herself with a jolt of shock. That was against the rules. The panic hit her hard. How had she been so quick to forget herself? She chanced a look at the M, then realised that she not only had permission to see, but the choice, too. She was free to look if she wanted to.

She couldn't bring herself to stare back out of the window. She still didn't fully believe it, and expected that at any moment, he would reveal the true purpose of the last two days and drag her back to the Poly-Gen facility.

William turned on the radio to check for any news on the breakout as they drove into the city, but there were no reports.

Edel had never seen anything like the tall, narrow buildings, reaching up, high into the sky. It was busy, crawling with people and traffic, and she found it too much to take in at once. Too much movement, too much noise. It was distressing to see so much happening all at once. She didn't know where her attention should be and her eyes darted from one thing to the next, her head jerking in all directions, as the noise and the colours and the way things moved assaulted her senses.

William looked across at her as if he could sense her tension. Switching off the radio, he spoke in a quiet, soothing tone and asked her, "Are you okay?"

She didn't know how to express her discomfort. The idea of forming a sentence was difficult right now. Her brain was processing too much. William didn't wait for an answer. He drove out of the city centre and into a quieter place, pulling up in an alleyway, out of the hustle and bustle. The engine stopped, and the motion of the car had stopped too. There were fewer people here, less movement, less light, less noise. She listened to the rain bouncing off the roof of the car and calmed herself. William didn't speak or rush her. Only once she appeared to have returned to normal, did he speak, and ask, "Am I safe?"

"Yes."

"Was I safe, before?"

She didn't answer. She didn't know.

"Edel. We need to go into the city centre. I have some documents I need to collect."

She wasn't looking at him; she was staring down at her knees.

"Can you handle it?" he asked her.

"Yes."

"Edel. This isn't a test. This isn't a controlled environment. If you can't handle this, I need to know now. If you lose control of yourself, there will be no way for me to stop you or to protect myself."

She continued to stare at her knees, the same plain, expressionless look on her face.

William hesitated before starting the car up again. He looked across at her, but she didn't acknowledge him. He let out a sigh and started the engine again, pulling out of the tiny side street and back into the hustle and bustle of the city.

She was doing a better job now, but her head jerked in small, sharp movements from side to side and her eyes darted from one thing to another.

William pulled into a parking space at the back of an office building. "I will only be a few minutes," he muttered as he left.

She sat in the car and gathered her thoughts. This was an odd feeling. She was alone again, completely alone. She watched the people outside, walking along, oblivious to her. It made her wonder what their lives were like. What did it feel like to be free? She didn't know.

William returned shortly; his new ID concealed inside his jacket.

"Look, I've got a little time to kill before I get the train. Let me take you to the cash zone, I'll show you what to do. Here –" he reached into his pocket and produced a wad of cash, all bundled up and handed it to her. "This is money. You can exchange it for food and drink. It's not much, but it will help you get started." He explained the value to her and how it worked, then he set off driving again, taking her into an area that was very different to the city where they had just been. It was just as busy, but it was dirty and scruffy. The people were scruffy too, and the buildings were crumbling. "Stay in the cash areas, they will be the safest places for you. Nobody here has any identification," he said.

He pulled into a back alley and pointed in the direction she should go. "They call this area Gromdon. Further down that way are the slums. There are a lot of abandoned buildings and quiet places you can hide in if you need to." He looked at her and smiled. "Well, you made it. Freedom!"

Anxiety rippled through her body. This was the unknown.

"Edel." He looked at her with a kind and patient smile. "Thank you for staying with me. Thank you for helping me."

She didn't know what to do or how to react. Nobody had ever given her gratitude before, and it felt strange to be thanked for performing her duty. William reached into the back and pulled out a bag. He filled it with their leftover food from the morning and a small medical kit. "Here, take this, it might be useful." He passed it towards her.

She took it in silence. She had no knowledge of what to do, or what to expect.

"It's time," he murmured, as he gestured to the door.

She obliged obediently, opening the door and climbing out into the rain.

"Good luck."

A sense of panic engulfed her as he drove away and left her.

She was in an unfamiliar environment, without instructions, with almost no knowledge of how things worked. She was exhausted; it had been close to three days since she last slept.

She wandered into the cash town with no real idea of what she should do or where she should go. There was too much noise, too much for her senses to take in. She knew she needed to find somewhere quiet, try to avoid too much stimulation. She walked until she came across a broken and falling down building. There was a hole in the roof and the windows were all smashed in, but it would suffice for a resting place until she could get control of herself and work out a plan.

She entered the abandoned building and sat in the corner on the cold, damp floor, avoiding the hole in the roof, and tried to ignore the icy draft. She decided her priority was sleep, knowing exhaustion was hindering her decision-making skills. It would be better to make a plan after she had rested.

Her clothing was mostly dry, just a little damp from the rain, but her socks were soaked through, and her feet were cold. She removed them and pulled the ends of her pants down over her feet to keep them warm. She considered what she was doing. Nobody had instructed her to do this, it was an act purely for comfort, something she would have been punished for at Poly-Gen. Comfort was never a factor in her existence.

She opened the bag the M had given her and took a drink from the water, leaning back against the damp wall, then closed her eyes. She slept for a long time. The stresses of the last three days had taken their toll on her, and she was more drained than she realised.

For a moment, she felt disoriented when she awoke. Her body was cold as she pulled herself up and tried to work some movement back into her stiff joints.

She was alone, there were no others near her. What an odd feeling! She had no direction, no orders. She did not know what she should do. What did people do? She assessed her immediate needs. She was thirsty, hungry, cold. She needed to urinate. The last was the most pressing, but she had no idea where she might find a toilet. She had no choice but to relieve herself in the corner of the empty and broken-down building.

She drank from the water bottle the M had given her and once it was empty, she discarded it, thankful there were another two bottles in her bag. There was food in the bag too, a package that looked like the bread the M had given her before but cut into triangles with something between the two slices. She bit into it with caution, and again, the shock of the flavours took her by surprise. Her mouth watered. She found it unpleasant, even uncomfortable, but she knew she had to eat. The more she persevered, the easier it became. The unusual sensation of tasting something new became more manageable as she pushed through the urge to remove it from her mouth.

She moved on, knowing she couldn't stay in this dilapidated building forever. She needed to learn about her surroundings.

She took a steadying breath and peered outside the entrance. The rain had stopped, but there were puddles on the floor and the walkways were soaked. She couldn't see much point in pulling on the wet socks, they wouldn't be much use.

Back out in the streets, there were lights and noise everywhere. Flickering illuminated signs, advertising food and drink and loud banging beats and shrieks of laughter. It was a lot to take in, but the sleep had done her good. She still felt in control of herself.

She froze in fear as she took in the people ahead, unable to decide if they could or would hurt her. The only experience she'd had of other humans so far had not been pleasant, and she was painfully afraid of them. She stood back against the wall of a building and let them pass, but she found the sound of their laughter intriguing. They passed by without incident and she slipped by unnoticed, wandering into the night, without a purpose or even a hint of an idea of what she should do. She slumped into a doorway in a quiet alley and waited for the night to pass.

She watched as the sun rose again, the darkness subsided, and the black sky changed to a steely grey.

She was still hungry as she watched the people, paying attention to how they interacted with one another and observed as they entered shops and cafes then left with food and drinks. She understood that was what the cash was for, but she didn't know how to purchase anything, and the idea of speaking to another human was a terrifying prospect. She had never initiated a conversation in her life, let alone asked an unprompted question.

Hours passed, and she continued to watch and learn. She was still cold, but it was nothing she hadn't lived through before. She was still hungry, but her experience at Poly-Gen had taught her she could live without food for weeks. The rain fell again, and it made her wonder if the weather was always like this. She had walked all day and was far from where she'd started now. She could find her way back if she wanted, but what would be the point? Instead, she walked on, and found another place, like before. Empty, broken, and damp.

The dampness of her clothing wasn't helping her to remain warm, but there wasn't a lot she could do about it. She opened the bag and ate the rest of the food that the M had left her and drank some water; she was down to her last bottle now. Tomorrow, she would have to use the cash to purchase more, and the thought filled her with dread. She settled down to sleep, hopeful that tomorrow she could navigate freedom better. The experiments at Poly-Gen may have been awful, but they would always end, eventually. There didn't seem to be an end in sight for this. Freedom wasn't something she had ever yearned for. She'd never dared to dream of it. Poly-Gen was all she'd ever known. It was a miserable and painful existence, but it was her purpose. It was what she was made for.

She woke as day was breaking. The rain had stopped again, but the sky still looked full and angry. She knew little about weather, but it didn't look like it had done raining. The day passed in a blur. She was lost and alone, and clueless about what she was doing. Was this life now? Was she expected to wander these strange streets, lost and alone, for the rest of her life?

She continued, searching the area for places to stay, to rest, to hide. It had been two days since the M had dropped her here, but nothing was getting easier. It was all too unfamiliar, and she was dreadfully afraid.

She was still hungry. She hadn't yet plucked up the courage to speak to a human and try to spend the cash. The reality was, she had only eaten a small loaf of bread and a sandwich since the escape four days ago. This wasn't enough to keep her functioning at optimal performance, but she had survived a lot longer than this without food. It wasn't a priority right now and interacting with the other humans was a such terrifying prospect, that she decided it could wait until morning.

She found another place to stay. This place was smaller than the others. No bigger than a hut. Its roof was intact, and the door was too. She could tell the small building was empty as she approached.

She pushed open the door and settled down on the floor to sleep, wedging her body up against the door to stop any intruders entering unnoticed. Sleep came easily. It was never an issue for her. She could sleep if she was instructed, she could stay awake if instructed, too. When she slept, her body would enter a relaxed state and only her base instincts were active, allowing her body and mind to switch off, but allowing her to remain aware of potential dangers. She felt nothing during sleep. She would close her eyes, and although when she woke, she would have an accurate sense of the passage of time, she couldn't tell anything about sleep itself.

CHAPTER 7

Wednesday 22nd February 2102

*Gromdon Cash Slums,
Harpton Main*

Edel awoke the next morning, and nothing was different. The sense of the unknown was upon her again, and it was an uncomfortable feeling to process. Feelings in general were a new experience for her. From the moment she was awoken, eleven years ago, she had been expected to close her feelings down. It was a system that benefited the entire XJ5 product as a whole. It was easy to close off when others around her were closed down too, and every sensation or feeling or emotion, was collectively dampened down and snuffed out, to protect the hive mind. But it was proving difficult to block her feelings out by herself now. They crept up to the surface often and took her by surprise. The gripping, crippling fear, and the uncertainty of everything that was in this strange new world bubbled up and she didn't know how to manage it alone.

She was still getting used to living without the shared consciousness of the others. The involuntary sensations they shared were never pleasant, there was always a dull sense of fear, mistrust, and anxiety, but she missed it all the same. She felt strangely empty without them.

She left the small building and went out into the stinging cold rain once more. She pulled up her hood over her head, but she was still soaked within minutes. Her wet clothing stuck to her skin as she moved through the alley, and her bare feet throbbed from the cold.

The sound of men approaching took her by surprise, and shame engulfed her as she tried to hide. She had never hidden from anything before unless she had been instructed to do so. It was absurd, really. She was stronger, faster, and more intelligent than any human.

She wasn't hidden from view, but crouched in a doorway, trying her best to shrink into herself and go unnoticed. She stayed quiet, hoping they would pass her by.

The two men staggered by her. She recognised the smell that lingered around them as alcohol. They appeared to be holding each other up unsteadily.

Edel rose from the floor as they reached the other end of the alleyway, but the two men seemed to have changed their minds about which direction they were headed. They turned back and spotted her as she made a move to crouch again, hoping she would remain unseen.

The larger of the two men began to laugh. It wasn't the same laughter she had heard before in the streets when she had first arrived. There was no lightness to it. It sounded quite sinister, and a chill shot through Edel. She knew she was being irrational. They couldn't hurt her, not really. She, on the other hand, could take them with ease. They were no threat to her.

The one who laughed tapped the other man on the arm and pointed at her. "Look here, Len. Our luck's in after all."

The other man followed his friend's gaze and laughed, too. "Aww don't be shy, sweetheart. Why don't you come out from there and let me have a good look at you?" His gravelly rasping voice made the hair on her arms stand up.

Edel could not place the look on his face, but she didn't like it. Her senses were snapped onto high alert, forcing her to notice everything about these men. The first was overweight but looked to be strong. He would be slow to move, but she would need to exert some force to overpower him. He wasn't a direct threat, except he was armed with a knife, she noticed. His heart was beating at a healthy pace, and he did not seem stressed by the current situation. The same information was true for the other one, Len. He was smaller than the first man, and she estimated he was in better physical condition. Possibly quicker and stronger than the first, but still no real threat.

"I bet you'd like to earn some cash, wouldn't you?" the first man leered at her.

They both made their way forward. "You don't need to be scared. We won't hurt you… if you cooperate." He let out that same, mean sounding laugh again.

Edel froze. She knew she could handle these two men, but she couldn't push through the decade worth of conditioning she had been through at Poly-Gen. Pain was an everyday occurrence. She expected it. It was her duty, her responsibility, to put up with it and allow the humans to hurt her, to test for weaknesses and see where improvements needed to be made in the XJ formula. She wasn't allowed to resist, or to stop them. The idea of freedom hadn't fully sunk in, and she adopted her usual submissive position, standing in her passive posture, eyes cast down to the floor.

The one named Len was speaking now. "Lift up your shirt. I wanna see those titties. See what you're worth," he growled at her.

The other man was still leering at her. "What's the matter? Cat got your tongue?"

She couldn't answer. She wouldn't dare. She continued to stare down at the floor, reminding herself these men were not her superiors, and telling herself if they came any closer, she would defend herself.

She was organising her thoughts and telling herself that they were the ones who should be afraid, not her, when another man seemed to appear from nowhere. She hadn't been paying enough attention. With the stress of this new situation, she hadn't even heard him approach. She wasn't functioning properly. Too much new. Lack of sleep, lack of food. It was all affecting her cognitive ability.

He stood further back from the two men, but he shouted across at them, telling them to leave her alone.

Confusion hit Edel at once. This new man was like the others, unclean and smelled of alcohol. He came closer, and they exchanged words. She understood the words but not really the meaning behind them; she was unsure of the situation. It seemed that the new man was trying to help her, but she didn't understand why. No human had ever helped her before.

It happened quickly; the new man shouted at the two men in front of her and the one named Len lunged forward knocking him to the floor. They both stood over him, kicking and punching. Edel heard ribs cracking and the man on the floor was gasping in pain. He had curled up on the floor in a vain attempt to protect his body from the attack and appeared to be on the verge of losing consciousness.

Edel's primary objective had always been to protect human life, unless otherwise instructed, and this human was about to die. She saw the first man pull the knife from his pocket and intervened just as the knife made contact with the man's abdomen. The man was caught off guard by how strong this small and fragile looking girl was. She didn't hesitate. She grabbed his wrist with both her hands and stepped past him, under his arm and crossing in front of his body, positioning herself at his other side, then turned the knife upwards, and bent his arm at the elbow and thrust it forward, using his arm to slash his own throat in one sharp, deadly movement. It took less than a second, and the other man had no idea. He was still standing over the unconscious man, gleefully kicking him.

The first man's eyes were wide in horror as his hand went up to his throat and he tried and failed to catch the blood that was pouring from the open wound in his neck. He fell to his knees, choking and spluttering. The second man looked around, startled by these sudden developments. It took a second before he realised his friend had had his throat slashed, and the girl stood behind him was holding the bloodied knife.

He backed up almost immediately, and Edel heard the already rapid beat of his heart increase further as the smell of his fear filled her nose. His hands were held out in front of him in a gesture that suggested surrender, but Edel didn't care. The man was shaking his head and whispering the word *please* to her, but it fell on deaf ears. She didn't waste any time; she killed him in the same way as the first, slashing the knife across his exposed throat, so quick the man had no time to react. It was a clean and efficient kill.

The blood pooled around her bare feet and mixed with the rain, turning the puddles red and causing a crimson river to run into the gutter. She dragged the unconscious man across the wet floor and into the empty building across the other side of the alley where she had spent the night before. It may be dirty, but it was dry and unoccupied.

She laid him in the recovery position and went back to the alleyway to retrieve her bag, which she had left in the doorway when the two men had approached her.

She decided she should conceal the two dead men. People would be looking for her by now, and she didn't want to draw any attention to herself.

After a quick sweep of her surroundings, her eyes rested on the large refuse bin at the other end of the alley, overflowing with rubbish. This would be the best place to conceal the bodies if she could make room.

She worked swiftly, dragging the two men across the floor with ease, leaving streaky trails of blood across the concrete. She emptied out the top layer of trash. There were a lot of rotting foodstuffs in there, and the smell was putrid.

Underneath the rotting food, she found a large, filthy sheet and some large flat-packed cardboard boxes, and pulled them out too, unfolding them. She grabbed the first man under his shoulders and hoisted him into the bin with ease. The second one was every bit as easy for her to lift, but there wasn't a lot of room. She had to climb in and adjust the bodies, snapping the legs of the taller man and bending them in an unnatural manner to conceal him and make him fit.

When she had finished, she piled the rubbish back on top to hide the dead men from view and took the cardboard sheets, laying them over the bloody trails where she had dragged the bodies across the ground. Bringing the filthy sheet of material to a large puddle across the other side of the alley, she used the rainwater to clean the blood from her face, hands, and bare feet, trying her best to wipe it away, mopping up what she could from her clothing. Thankfully, the clothing the M had provided was all black, so the blood didn't show in an obvious way. It wasn't perfect, but it would do. Next, she carried the sheet and deposited it in the bloody puddles, where the murders had been committed. She hoped it would absorb enough of the blood to go unnoticed. After all, nobody was looking for those men yet.

She returned to the unconscious man and lifted his shirt to get a good look at the injuries he had sustained. There was some bruising, and inflammation, possibly fractured ribs, but the knife wound wasn't deep enough to cause any substantial damage. It would need stitching, though.

Opening her bag, she pulled out the small medical kit the M had given to her and began to clean and patch him up. She worked methodically; the stitches were perfectly neat and looked as though she may have spent her life stitching up patients. Though, in truth, this was her first time. She didn't know how she knew half the things she knew; she just did. The information was already there, implanted in her head, during the ten years in stasis, before her awakening.

She searched her bag again and found something for the pain and some water for when he awoke. There was nothing to do now but wait to see if she had completed her objective of protecting this human's life. The familiarity of following her original primary objective felt strangely comforting in this current chaotic and abnormal situation.

She thought about the two men in the alley. She hadn't protected their lives; she'd taken them instead. Back at Poly-Gen, that would have been enough to have her terminated, or at the very least tortured, but she wasn't there now, and those men posed a threat. They were armed, and they attacked first. She felt no hint of remorse or guilt. Killing those men was a logical choice, and she was satisfied with the decision she had made.

She repacked her bag, then settled down on the floor by the door. It would be the best place to rest. She could intercept any humans trying to enter, and she could make a quick exit if needed.

Edel waited patiently, sat like a statue, her back was rigid and straight, she didn't slouch or lean against the wall. She continued to watch the unconscious man, monitoring him, listening to the steady thrum of his heart. It was a normal rhythm, and his breathing was slow and relaxed. He didn't appear to be in any sort of distress, but he was taking longer to wake than she had anticipated. It had been almost 20 minutes, and she wondered if perhaps his injuries were more serious than she first thought, but then, considering the smell of him, she decided the alcohol would be a factor in his recovery time.

Eventually, his breathing changed. He took a deeper breath, and his eyelids began to twitch. She waited patiently for him to open his eyes.

He made a groaning sound, and she wondered how much pain the man was in. Crouching beside him, she gently lifted his head and held the bottle to his lips and said, "Drink."

The man blinked in confusion, but obeyed her instruction, taking a deep drink from the bottle. She gently set his head back on the floor and moved back towards the door.

It took a few minutes for the man to come round to his senses. He eventually rolled onto his side and pushed himself into a sitting position, wincing in pain as he manoeuvred his injured body.

Edel laid out the pills next to the water and said, "Take

them."

The man looked first at her, then at the pills. "Thanks," he muttered. He reached for the bottle, poured two pink tablets into his hand and took another long drink. He seemed to be a little more focussed now as he looked at Edel and asked her what happened to the two men. When she didn't answer, he pressed her again, asking if they had hurt her.

"No," she answered.

He didn't badger her for more information. He seemed far more concerned about his stitches. She confirmed she had stitched him, and that she didn't think it was in any way life threatening.

The man pulled himself up from the floor and stood to face her. She recoiled with a slight repulsion as he held out his hand towards her. She had seen this gesture before, but she didn't know what it meant. Physical contact wasn't something she was used to – nobody had ever touched her skin without meaning her harm. She would not offer herself to this man willingly, in any way.

"My name's Jay. What's yours?" he said.

Alarm bells rang inside her head. J. J was not a name, J was a letter or a code. Her immediate thoughts were that he could possibly be some other experiment. There were other sites, other programs. He could be looking for her. She took her time to think it through. This man wasn't special. He was unconscious a few minutes ago, after taking a beating from two older and unconditioned men, and he smelled of stale alcohol. There was nothing extraordinary about this man. He was just a man.

The man appeared to have given up on the idea of touching her, for which she was thankful, but he was still expecting an answer to his question. "Edel," she blurted out. It felt strange to have a name. To say it out loud to a stranger, a human who didn't seem to have any idea who or what she might be. He fiddled with his pockets and then produced a plastic card with his photograph and personal information printed on it. She read the name Jaydon Powell. J was short for Jaydon? He *did* have a human name.

He was talking to her in a way she'd never been spoken to before. Gently and kindly. He seemed to make an effort not to frighten her. She didn't know what to make of it all. Then he offered her food and a place to get warm. It was an easy decision – if she went with him, she could see how he interacted with other humans. She would learn what to do with the money the M had given her. He was injured; he had no idea who she was, and he was alone. He was no immediate threat to her, and he was her best option right now. She looked up at him, still not quite able to find her voice, and nodded her head.

Edel held her breath in fear as Jay opened the door. He would surely notice the differences in the alleyway. The smell of the blood, and the sheets of cardboard strewn across the floor. She watched as he stepped outside. She couldn't believe he didn't notice anything. He seemed so oblivious to it all.

Jay led the way, and she blindly followed him, always walking slightly behind, never by his side. Even though she knew he wasn't a danger to her, the fear of humans was still very real.

The man tried to talk with her many times, but she didn't know how to respond. She decided silence was a safer option, and he eventually seemed to give up trying to make her speak.

As they walked, Edel noticed a change in the world around her. There were more people, more buildings, more traffic. More to take her focus and bombard her senses. She tried hard to concentrate only on her task, which was to follow this man and learn how to act 'human', but it was difficult. She noticed everything, every noise, every person. Every colour, every fragrance. Her head jerked to face the direction of every new sound her ears picked up, and her gaze fell upon everything that moved.

Their journey continued in silence until he suddenly stopped and pointed out that she had nothing covering her feet. *He only just noticed that?* She knew humans didn't take in information as readily as XJs, but this man seemed to lack any observational skills whatsoever.

The man took off his own socks and handed them to her, telling her she would need to wear them. She didn't question it, she just pulled them onto her feet. They felt warm and damp, and they didn't smell pleasant.

They continued to walk. She still could not bring herself to speak to this man. Too much new was still overloading her senses, but she was holding it together.

They crossed the road and into the park. The grass was wet, and it soaked into her socks, chilling her feet again. She ignored the discomfort. It was nothing to her. She caught sight of the man at the other end of the park, wearing clothing very similar to the guards at Poly-Gen and recognised it as an authoritative uniform. He was also armed, and he had a radio communication device. She could hear him speaking, even with the huge distance between them. "Possible unauthorised citizens in a no cash zone. I'm going to ID." The man started walking over to them, and the panic rose in Edel. Another human. She didn't want to have to interact with another human.

Jay spoke to the man and showed him his identity card, while Edel tried to shrink into herself and hope that she would not have to communicate.

"Miss, are you here of your own free will?" Her heart rate increased rapidly as he spoke to her. The man had asked her a direct question. She must provide a direct answer. Those were the rules.

"Yes." She looked down at the ground as she spoke. The man nodded and stepped aside to allow them to pass. Edel followed Jay in silence, still barely daring to breathe.

The stress of being questioned by a uniformed man had sent her adrenaline pumping again. She was stressed, and she wasn't coping well. She couldn't control the way her head twitched and jerked, and her eyes shot from one thing to another. She was on high alert now, checking for dangers everywhere. The information was being taken in as quickly as it was supplied, but her brain wasn't processing everything, and it was becoming impossible to keep up. This was going to become a dangerous situation if she couldn't get hold of herself.

They walked on, and the man seemed uncomfortable as his eyes swept across the large building in front of them. Edel eyed it too. There were young adolescents standing in small groups, talking and laughing. They were all dressed the same, and Edel wondered what it meant. The man caught her eye, and she averted her gaze with one rapid movement. She shouldn't be looking at things that didn't concern her.

The man came to a stop in front of a tall building with a small set of steps that led up to huge double doors. He walked up the steps and pulled the door, holding it open for her, and she held her breath as she passed by him, nerves threatening to overtake her as she followed him up the stairs and into his apartment.

Her eyes took in the chaos in front of her. She had only ever known order and cleanliness before now, but this was madness. There were items of clothing all over, there were food containers and plates and cups, empty bottles and cans laying over every surface. It smelled, but not unpleasant, just not the extreme smell of disinfectant she was used to. Until this point, she had assumed all living spaces were the same.

Jay was speaking again. She heard him, but there was too much to take in to understand what he was saying. He was pointing to the door at the back of the room. Her eyes followed his finger as he muttered words about getting warm and dry, and before she knew what she was doing, she was blindly following him to the room, unable to decline his offer. She watched silently as the man turned on running water and told her to leave her clothes by the door, then he left and closed the door behind him.

She took a moment to collect herself and try to think what was expected of her now. She hesitated before extending her hand under the stream of running water, but once she was satisfied the temperature wasn't enough to cause her any damage, she removed her blood-soaked clothing and dumped it into the base of the shower, attempting to wash them clean. The man did not need to know she had murdered anyone.

Taking her time, she stood still and took a deep, steadying breath, trying to process the most recent events. She was pleased to be inside, away from the noise and the people out in the streets. She hadn't realised how stressful it would be, to be exposed to such a barrage of new sensations all at once, and it was all she could do to keep herself in check and not fall into the madness of meltdown.

She closed her eyes and concentrated hard on trying to block out her senses and bring on a sense of calm. It was a skill she had learned early in life and proved to be invaluable in situations like this.

She felt oddly alone as the world went dark and quiet around her. A feeling of complete solitude and isolation crept in. She found it neither pleasant nor unpleasant; it was just new and unfamiliar. She'd always had the sensation of others swirling in her consciousness. Every feeling and reaction to every situation from now on would be her own, and hers alone. The others weren't part of her anymore.

The steam filling the bathroom gave a calming sensation, and the heat rising from the shower was taking the chill from her body. She reached in and squeezed the excess water from her clothing. They still ran red as the water was squeezed from them, but they were cleaner than before. She deposited the clothes in the sink to drain and stepped into the shower.

She gasped as the firm stream of hot water hit her body. Another new sensation. She allowed herself to open her mind a little to allow the feelings to penetrate. It felt good. She stood still, facing the shower head, allowing the water to hit her chest and fall over her body, instantly warming her up. The steam was rising, and she breathed it in, another unfamiliar feeling as it caught in the back of her throat and inside her nostrils. She leaned forward and bent her head under the stream of running water, relishing the feeling of the water running down her face then dripping off the end of her nose and chin, then quickly panicked. *Was that allowed? Should I have done that?* Enjoyment wasn't something she was allowed to feel. Her head jerked up to look for the scientists, even though she knew they weren't there. She recovered herself, breathing in deep and exhaling slowly in an attempt to calm herself down. This was not an experiment. This was not a test.

She wondered how long a person should spend in a shower. What would happen if she spent too long? Or not long enough? Would she be punished for not doing it right? Was that man, Jay, able to hurt her in some way? She doubted it very much, but she had spent her life being tortured by humans, and the fear they instilled was deeply rooted in her.

She thought about Jay. He had tried to help her before, at least that's what she thought he was doing. The two men had intended to cause her harm. Everything about their body language was threatening, and one of them was armed with a knife. She wondered why this Jay man would want to help her. Nobody had ever tried to help her before. Even during the escape, she was used as a tool. Nobody was helping her to get out.

She turned her attention back to the task at hand. The shower was turning out to be a very pleasant experience, and she hadn't had many pleasant experiences in her life so far. She scrubbed her body with her hands and rubbed the stubbly hair on her head clean. There was soap, but she didn't know if she had permission to use it. She left it untouched.

She rubbed her feet and picked out the small stones and dirt fragments that had become embedded in her soles from her lack of shoes.

The shower had somehow cleansed her mind as well as her body. She felt a sense of being renewed and refreshed and somehow stronger and more in control. Her mind was able to process her senses a little more steadily, rather than everything being so jarring and painful to experience.

She was clean now, and warm, and really had no reason to continue standing under the water, no matter how pleasurable it may feel. It was as she switched off the water that it hit her how she didn't know what she was supposed to do next. She held her breath and waited for the rising panic to leave her body, assessing the situation in a logical way. Jay had said he would give her some clothing, but how could she ask him? Was it okay to speak now? To ask questions? Punishment for failing to adhere to the rules was severe, and extremely painful. To say she was afraid to speak, even though she was now free, was an understatement.

There was a gentle knock at the door, and it made her jump. She'd been so busy closing off her senses to keep her mind calm, that she hadn't heard him approach. The shock of being brought back to full alertness so suddenly sent her heart racing and her adrenaline pumping again. She didn't have time to calm down before he was speaking to her.

"Edel? Um, I've got a towel here for you. Sorry, I forgot to leave you one before." He opened the door a crack and his hand appeared clutching the towel. She wondered why he was still on the other side of the door. Privacy wasn't something she had ever been afforded. She didn't even realise it was normal.

She took the towel and wrapped it around herself and then heard him knock again. "um... do you have your clothes?"

She tried to answer him, but the words wouldn't come. How could she tell him that the clothes were wringing wet, because she'd put them in the shower to wash them clean? He was expecting them to be a little damp at best. Again, she reminded herself, this man could not hurt her. It didn't matter how many times she told herself that fact; the fear remained.

He knocked again "Edel? ... are you decent?"

She didn't understand that question. Decent? What did that mean? She stayed silent. A second later the door opened again, just a crack, and Jay's head poked through. She noticed his expression change as he took in her appearance. His eyes lingered too long on her head, and she knew without a doubt that it was her hair. Other women had hair. Long hair, not cropped short and buzzed off with an electric razor. This was the reason the M had told her to keep her hood pulled up since leaving the facility. Then she caught his heart rate. It just increased a lot. The smell of him changed rapidly. She knew it was fear; it came off him in waves and she followed his gaze. His eyes were fixed on the stamp of her wrist, the bar code etched into her skin with the code XJ545-12 printed below.

She noticed these changes in less than two seconds. Jay had barely stepped foot in the bathroom before he caught sight of her stamp. His eyes averted almost immediately, but she knew rapid eye movement was a normal human reaction to surprise, and he would look back at her within the next second. She adjusted her position, hiding her left arm behind her back, while grabbing the wet clothing from the sink and roughly shoving it at him to take his attention elsewhere.

He took them automatically, but his eyes, as she suspected, were searching for her other wrist. She heard his heart rate increase again, pumping harder and faster, and the subtle changes to his breathing. The fear was radiating off him, so much she could taste it in the back of her throat. *He knows.*

It wasn't difficult to work out how he knew. She could hear the news report in the background. They were giving descriptions of the missing XJ5s, the XFs and the M. They were talking about bar codes on wrists and necks, and they were talking about how dangerous they were.

Edel wasn't certain what she should do next. The HGMR had finally made a move. They were trying to reclaim their property.

CHAPTER 8

Wednesday 22nd February 2102

Jay's Apartment, Helstain, Harpton Main

A lump appeared in Jay's throat as he took the clothes from the girl and saw the strange markings on her left wrist. He felt uneasy, panicked even. What the hell was this? He tried to convince himself he was getting worked up over nothing. His mind was playing tricks on him. It was only because he had just seen the news report.

Jay let out a small nervous laugh, trying to shake these crazy thoughts from his head and said, "I'll get you something to wear until these are dry." He backed out of the bathroom, not quite daring to take his eyes off the girl and tried to pull the door closed.

Her hand jutted forward with unnatural speed, stopping the door from closing, and Jay let out a shriek of surprise. The way she moved was too sudden, too quick!

An intense fear gripped Jay. There was no denying it, she was one of *them*. He dropped the wet clothes in a heap at his feet and scrambled backwards from the doorway, trying to get out of her reach.

He wasn't crazy – she really was what he feared her to be.

How had he invited one of these things – one of these human weapons – into his home? He continued to scrabble backwards, his panic rising to an unmanageable level.

"Don't hurt me!" He almost screamed the words at her in a blind panic. He couldn't recall ever being so petrified in his life. He stepped backwards again a few more paces until he was out in his main living space, but she matched every step he took, closing the gap between them. His leg caught on the corner of the coffee table as he took another step back and he fell to the floor, landing in an awkward heap on his hip, the pain in his already bruised and beaten body momentarily taking his breath. She stood over him, staring at him with a harsh and unfriendly expression.

"Please," he whispered, "I was trying to help you."

The girl looked at him with her unfriendly eyes. She was terrifying.

"Why?" she demanded. There was nothing but hostility in her voice. Everything about her demeanour screamed murderer.

"You helped me. Why would you help me if you were just going to kill me, anyway?"

The girl stayed silent, regarding him with the same cold expression. Jay noticed how unnaturally still she was, almost like a statue. She made no noise, there was no movement when she took a breath. She didn't even seem to blink as often as a normal human.

"I won't tell. I swear I won't tell anyone. Please! Please, just let me go. You don't have to kill me. I swear I won't tell," he begged her.

"You will." The way she spoke was monotonous, almost robotic. She took another step forward, closing the gap between them once more and he shook with pure terror, knowing that if she wanted to, she could kill him right there on the floor.

Jay looked around the room in a frantic panic, desperately trying to draw inspiration from somewhere, anything that could possibly save his life.

"I can help you! Please, I can help you," he blurted out at her. She seemed taken aback by his offer. She hesitated, and he seized the opportunity to talk his way out of this terrible situation.

"You don't fit in. You are so different. People will be able to tell immediately. They're looking for you. They will catch you because you stand out. It's obvious you're different."

Jay's heart was in his throat, and he held his breath as she seemed to consider what he was saying. He gave his begging another desperate stab. "You can stay here. I will help you fit in. I will show you. Just *please*, don't kill me."

His limbs seemed to turn boneless with relief as she gave him a single curt nod and stepped back from him, though she continued to stare at him with the same unfriendly look in her eyes.

Jay slowly raised his shaking body up from the floor, wondering what the hell he was meant to do now. He made a mental note to never offer help to a stranger again.

The hours that followed were the most tense and uncomfortable of Jay's life. He made his way to his bedroom on shaking legs and collected the clean sweatpants and t-shirt he had intended to give to her. He was unnerved to find she followed him. She never left more than two or three feet between them, and he had the sinking feeling she wasn't planning on letting him out of her sight for a second. He handed her the clothes and to his surprise; she dropped the towel and donned the clothing without hesitation.

Jay averted his eyes as soon as the towel fell to the floor, but he couldn't help seeing. Her body was covered in scars, some looked like operations, others seemed to have been inflicted intentionally, some looked more like burns. She didn't seem to care that she had just been standing naked in front of him. Embarrassment and modesty must not be something she was used to.

He left the bedroom, and she followed, never taking her eyes off him. The tension rose as the silence grew around them until she eventually spoke.

"Give me your door key." Her speech was abrupt and unfriendly. He didn't dare argue with her. He walked across his living space to the kitchen counter where the key had been left and held it out towards her with trembling hands. She took it and abruptly turned, locking the door, and pocketed the key in silence. The feeling of dread crept higher up Jay's chest. He was trapped. There was no way out for him now.

Jay didn't know what to do, what to say, or how to act. He was scared to put one foot wrong in case she changed her mind and decided to kill him. He stood in the same spot, by the kitchen counter where his door key had been so casually lain. His arm rested on the side to support his weight – his legs weren't able to manage on their own.

Jay felt the vibrations of his phone buzzing in his pocket. He always had the volume down; it never rang out loud and feelings of safety bubbled up under his skin. He had a phone.

Jay had no idea that the strange girl could hear it vibrating. She held out her hand and stared at him. "Phone," she demanded.

With no choice but to hand it over to her, the feeling of being trapped increased tenfold. Now he had no way to escape, and no way to contact anybody for help.

The news report was still playing in the background. Jay couldn't stand to hear it anymore, but he didn't want there to be nothing but this awful, uncomfortable silence either. He left it playing and tried not to listen to how dangerous these escaped murderous experiment-people were.

Jay had never felt so unsure of himself. He didn't know what to do or how to act. All he could do was stand aimlessly in his kitchen and try to act natural. Edel hardly spoke, and when she did, she wasn't friendly. Jay wouldn't even dare look at her. He kept glancing at her from where he stood, but his eyes would always dart away before he dared allow them to rest on her face.

The hours wore on, and nothing about their situation

changed. Jay had worked up enough courage to walk to his dining table and sit down. He was now sitting at the table with his head in his hands, silently hoping, praying, wishing, begging any entity who might hear his pleas. He wasn't a religious man, but he had never been so desperate for a miracle.

Edel stood at the wall, still guarding the door. She hadn't moved for hours; she kept her watchful eye on Jay.

Jay's headache had returned. He knew it was a mix of the hangover, the stress of this situation and the fact that the effect of those magic pills she had given him earlier had started to wear off. He sat, nervously picking at the skin on the edge of his thumb. It was becoming sore, but he couldn't stop. He needed something to focus on, anything to keep his mind occupied and stop him worrying about how much longer he would be kept prisoner in his own house. At least he was alive right now... she could change her mind at any moment and kill him.

Jay noticed how, even though she held all the power in this situation, she was still incredibly jumpy. She seemed to flinch at every noise, and her head would jerk toward every sound she heard. Other than these tiny nervous movements, she was motionless, almost like a statue. She never shifted her weight or slouched. She never paced or leaned back against the wall to support her weight.

Jay couldn't take it anymore. He needed to get up and get away from her, but he didn't know how. He was hungry, thirsty, and he needed to pee. It took him a little longer to psych himself up. He didn't know if she would hurt him if he made any movements.

Slowly, he eased himself up from his chair without looking in her direction and tried to be as casual as possible as he made his way to his bathroom. Her eyes followed him across the apartment, but she made no attempt to follow or to stop him.

Jay let out a long sigh of relief as the door closed behind him. It felt oppressive to be under her constant scrutiny. He checked his watch, and it came as no surprise to find it was almost

4 p.m. He had been sitting in that uncomfortable silence for hours. It felt like an age since he had brought this girl into his house.

He used the toilet and washed his face, trying to freshen himself up. He brushed his teeth just to make himself feel more like himself. It didn't work, but at least he had removed that awful stale taste in his mouth, caused by three days of heavy drinking. He took several deep breaths, knowing he had to go back out there, where she would continue to glare at him and make him uncomfortable.

She was standing in the same spot, eyes pinned on the bathroom door, waiting for him to emerge. She didn't appear to have moved at all, and Jay wondered how her feet and legs weren't aching. Her eyes followed him as he walked back across the floor of his living room and back into his kitchen. He slumped into the same chair he had been sitting in before, not quite daring to change anything.

He sat for another few minutes, then discreetly checked his watch again. Time seemed to have slowed down. It felt more like twenty-five minutes to have passed, not five. Hunger gnawed at him, and he decided that if she allowed him to use the bathroom, then she probably wouldn't stop him from using the kitchen. He sat a few more minutes, weighing up the likelihood of her stopping him from moving, but since he was desperate for something to drink too, he decided it was worth the risk. Calmly raising himself up from the chair, using the table to support himself, he walked to his kitchen, trying his best not to draw attention to himself with every movement he made. Not that it mattered. She was still staring at him. She hadn't taken her eyes off him since he had found out who she was. Almost as though her sole purpose in life was to guard him and make sure he didn't move.

He pulled a glass from the cupboard, filled it with water and took a long drink. His thirst wasn't satisfied, and he refilled the glass. Then a thought hit him: the girl was probably thirsty too.

He filled another glass and slowly approached her, holding

the water out towards her with shaking hands.

She looked at his face, but she didn't make eye contact as she took the water in total silence. No murmur of a thank you or any ounce of gratitude left her body.

Jay saw how she held the glass but didn't drink from it. He returned to the table and sat with his own drink, watching her out of the corner of his eye, as she lifted the glass to her lips and took a cautious sip.

Jay couldn't stand the silence anymore. If she would just talk to him, it would be something. If she could reassure him that she would not snap and kill him at any moment, or if she told him what behaviour was acceptable. Was he allowed to walk around his house? Was he allowed to go to his room? Without much thought, he blurted out, "Are you hungry?"

He was gaining confidence around her now, having already been to the bathroom and to the kitchen, and she hadn't stopped him from doing either.

The girl didn't answer his question, but he got up from the table regardless and walked to the kitchen in search of something to eat. There wasn't a lot. He hadn't been shopping for quite some time. Since Tanya's anniversary had come closer, he had lost his appetite for anything solid.

Half a loaf of bread was sitting open on his counter, and he opted for toast. The bread was a little stale and had seen better days, but it would taste okay toasted.

Jay busied himself in the kitchen, deciding to toast all the remaining bread just to give his hands something to do, and give his mind something else to focus on. When he had finished buttering all the slices, he pulled two plates from the cupboard and divided the toast between them. Nerves got the better of him as he carried them to the table and set one down at the end closest to the girl. His legs were like jelly as he carried his own plate across to the other side, as far away from her as possible.

Her eyes travelled across the room and settled on the plate of food closest to her, but she made no attempt to move, speak or eat. She kept her silent watch.

"Are you going to stand there all day?" Jay snapped. His own bravery took him by surprise, but it had no effect on Edel. She remained silent.

"Why don't you speak?" he asked her. There was an undertone of annoyance in his voice, and he silently cursed himself for his stupidity. What was he thinking, trying to rile her or get a response out of her?

Jay ate his toast in silence. Hers remained at the end of the table, untouched.

"I'm going to bed," he blurted out. The words came from his mouth without thinking them through. It was only 6pm, and although he was tired, he knew there was no way he could sleep. What if she insisted on following him to his bedroom and watching him while he slept?

"You are welcome to sleep in the spare room," he added, pointing to the closed door next to his open one, and hoping she would take the hint.

He got up, praying she wouldn't follow him. She stayed where she was, and relief flooded his body with such force, he almost cried. He had made it to the bedroom door, hand poised on the handle. He was just about to disappear through it when she spoke to him.

"I will kill you if you try to leave. I will kill you if you tell anyone I am here."

Jay couldn't respond. The only words she had spoken to him since she had been here were ones threatening his life. He closed the door behind him, attempting to feel like he was away from her, and collapsed onto his bed. His room was cool and dimly lit, the blinds had not been opened since before his three-day drinking adventure.

Jay lay shaking, the fear kept hitting him in waves. He wondered if he was experiencing shock, or if this was what it was like to have an anxiety attack. He tried to calm himself, taking his time to breathe deeply and remind himself that at least she wasn't inside this room with him.

There was no way he would be able to sleep. What would

stop her from coming in and killing him while he slept? He tried to tell himself that if she wanted to kill him, he would be already dead, but those thoughts were not as comforting as he had hoped.

He idly tossed around the idea of waiting until she was asleep and climbing out of his bedroom window, but his apartment was on the third floor. Even if he survived the fall, it wouldn't be easy to get away. She would kill him.

He was trapped. He laid awake for hours, unable to switch off. There was no noise to be heard, save for the quiet ticking of the old-fashioned clock on his wall and his mind raced in circles, the same thoughts intruding on him over and over. *What is she doing? What is she thinking? Am I safe? Will she kill me?* The hours ticked by, and he did eventually drift off into a fitful sleep.

Thursday 23rd February 2102
Jay's Apartment, Helstain, Harpton Main

Jay awoke the next morning and rubbed his face and tried to think straight. What was he meant to do? *At least I'm still alive,* he thought. It was almost 8 a.m., and he had absolutely no desire to leave the safety of his bedroom and face the girl, but he knew he couldn't spend the day here either. He wasted another hour of his day worrying before he eventually plucked up the courage. He could hear no noise from outside his closed bedroom door, and he was unrealistically hopeful that perhaps she had left. Maybe she had gone while he was sleeping, and he could just continue with his life and forget all about her. He knew deep down it wasn't true. She wasn't going anywhere.

It took a few tries to work up his courage, but he finally left his bed. Holding his breath and praying she wasn't around, he gently opened his door. It was absurd to be sneaking around his own house, but he was terrified to make too much noise or any sudden movements.

He spotted her immediately. She was standing in the same place by the door. It looked as though she hadn't moved all night. The water and the toast he had given her had gone, but aside from that, nothing had changed.

"Morning," he said, casting a tentative look in her direction.

She didn't react, so Jay scuttled off to the bathroom and decided he needed a shower. Once he was in his bathroom and knew she was unlikely to follow him, he breathed out a sigh of relief.

Jay took his time in the shower. He washed his hair and shaved his face in an attempt to ready himself for whatever today might bring. He should have been at work today. This was his fourth missed day in a row, and he knew he was in big trouble. At the very least he needed to contact them, but she had his phone. He wondered if she would allow him a phone call. But how could he ask her? She was terrifying.

He ambled back to his room, taking as long as humanly possible to get himself dressed. Once he was clothed in his black jeans and plain blue button-down shirt, he decided the only thing to do now was to make some coffee and try his best to act normal. She wore the same passive expression on her face as her eyes followed him across the room. Her cold, grey eyes were the only part of her that moved, the rest of her body remained perfectly still. It was unnatural.

Jay busied himself in the kitchen. He made two coffees and asked her, "Do you take sugar?"

Her expression momentarily changed to one of fear. It seemed that question had upset her, but she was quick to recover herself, and the plain, stony face returned. Jay wondered if she had even heard him correctly.

He placed the coffee on the table next to the empty plate that was there from the previous night. "There's sugar over there if you want it," he said, pointing to the canister on the work surface.

There was no answer, and the silence was hard to stomach. She gave no response to any of his attempts to communicate, and he didn't know if he could cope with another day like yesterday. A day in complete and uncomfortable silence while anxiety threatened to engulf him as he feared for his life.

Jay poured himself a bowl of dry cereal. The milk was not within its usable date, but he gave it a tentative sniff anyway. He quickly decided against it and sat down, picking at the dry cereal with his fingers, offering nothing else to the girl.

He took his time, picking at the cereal and sipping his coffee, noticing how hers was left untouched on the table. When he'd finished eating, he cleared the plates from yesterday and washed up his dishes, trying to work up the courage to speak to her. "Um, Edel?"

She seemed to startle at hearing her name, and he wondered if it was even her name at all. She was looking at him, her eyes boring into his head, but she didn't make eye contact. Her eyes fixed on his lips as he spoke.

Jay wasn't sure how to continue. He took a nervous intake of breath and tried to quell the anxiety. "I need to use my phone. I need to contact my work."

Her eyes narrowed, and she looked to be considering what he was saying, though she still made no response.

"People will expect me to be at work today. They will try to contact me. I need to let them know I won't be able to make it today." He spoke in slow and concise sentences, as though maybe she didn't understand. "Please, Edel, I can't afford to lose my job."

She was still staring at him. "What is the purpose of your job?" Her speech was sharp, it sounded harsh to Jay's ears.

Jay was momentarily taken aback. He wasn't expecting a response at all. "I'm a manager at a warehousing firm. I handle stock and distribution."

"But what for?" She asked. "What is the purpose of work?"

Jay took a step forward, and the girl seemed to flinch. It seemed she was every bit as afraid of him as he was of her. It made no sense.

"I'm sorry, I'm not sure what you mean... do you mean why

do I go to work?"

"Yes."

"To earn money. To pay for things." It had only just dawned on him how she really had no knowledge of the world. When he said he would help her fit in, he only meant that she was strange, and it was obvious she was different. He explained in simple words, as though he were addressing a five-year-old.

"I get paid to work. I spend the money on food, and bills, and rent. If I don't go to work, I don't get paid. If I don't get paid, I can't live in this house, or buy any food."

She didn't answer, she only continued to stare at him.

"Do you understand?"

"Yes."

"Then, can I please have my phone? If I don't call in, I might not have a job to go back to."

She handed the phone to him. "Only speaking. No writing."

Jay gulped. Clearly, she wanted to be certain what was being communicated between him and whoever he spoke to.

Jay dialled the number for Maarku. If anyone could get him out of trouble, it was his best friend. They had covered for one another so many times; Maarku owed Jay big.

"Maarku, it's me," he said as his friend answered the phone.

"Jay! Where the hell have you been, man? Glasby's going ape. You've not shown up for four days. Even Mr Johnson has been trying to get hold of you."

Jay tried not to panic.

"Um, look, I'm sick, okay? Just tell Glasby I'm sick. Tell him I'm in the hospital or something. Tell him I'll be back after the weekend."

"You'd better be sick, Jay! You know he's gonna want to see your medical record. You can't tell him you've been to hospital if there's no record of it."

"Okay, okay. No hospital. Just tell him I'm sick then. Just tell him I'll be back on Monday."

"Okay, so where have you been, really?"

Jay couldn't answer. He saw Edel tense as Maarku spoke. He

was certain she could hear both sides of this conversation.

"Jay. C'mon! If I'm covering for you, I need to know why. Are you in some sort of trouble? You were pretty drunk last time you called me..."

Edel was tense. She looked like she was poised for an attack. Jay was struggling to sound normal on the phone.

"Okay, look, I got drunk. I got into a fight. I got arrested. They've banned my cards and everything. And I've been in a mess, but I'm okay now. I'm going to get my shit together and I will be in work on Monday."

"Why can't you come to work today, Jay?"

Jay looked at Edel. He didn't know what to say, or how to stop Maarku asking questions. The silence drew on for a long moment, until Maarku eventually said in an exasperated tone, "Right, whatever. You owe me big! I'll come by later and make sure you're okay."

"NO!" Jay shouted down the phone in panic. He recovered himself and said more calmly, "No, really, I'm fine. I'll see you Monday."

He clicked off the phone and slumped into the chair. Hearing his friend's voice had been comforting. But now he was gone, Jay felt alone and afraid again.

Edel was standing in front of him, hand outstretched. "Phone," she demanded.

Jay swallowed. "I still need to use it," he said, trying to sound confident. "There are emails I need to reply to, and things I need to do."

Her hand was still outstretched, and her face said not to argue with her. He reluctantly handed over his phone for the second time.

The rest of the day passed much the same as the previous one. Every feeble attempt he made to speak to her got no response. He paced around his apartment, like a trapped animal, desperate to get out. Until this week, he had never realised how much he hated being cooped up inside.

Edel never took her eyes off him, not for a second. She even forced him to accompany her to the bathroom. She didn't seem to have any qualms about peeing in front of a stranger.

His stomach rumbled with hunger, and he found some old potatoes. They were covered in little sprouts and looked less than appetising, but he didn't have many options if he wanted to eat. He cooked them in the microwave and offered her one. She stood in the same place as always, her food left untouched, and Jay ate in silence, wondering if this would be his last meal.

He eventually went to his room and again prayed she wouldn't follow. She never did, and he remained in his room, trying his best to forget she was out there. He didn't leave his room again for the rest of the day, except for one trip to the bathroom before he tried to settle down to sleep. She was still standing in the same spot. It was like she was a machine or something. How could a person stand for two days straight, perfectly still, perfectly silent? Jay noticed how the food he had left vanished. She needed to eat. Surely that meant she needed sleep too.

He laid in bed and tried to sleep, tossing, turning and rolling around. When that didn't work, he got up and looked out of the window, still idly thinking of escaping through it. He wandered around, pacing up and down but not daring to leave his room. He didn't want to look at her. She never let him have his phone back, and she gave no indication of whether anyone had called. If Jay wasn't so fearful for his life, he would be very worried about his job right now.

CHAPTER 9

Thursday 23rd February 2102

Danny's House, Helston, Harpton Main

Danny shoved his way in through his front door and it slammed behind him with a dull thud. The constant news updates about the recent escape from the Poly-Gen site were getting to him. The reporters didn't paint the human experiments in a good light. They said they were not human, that they were unfeeling, uncaring, and emotionless. They were dangerous, unstable, and should not be approached under any circumstances. Danny couldn't help wondering if that was what he was – dangerous and unstable. Was he the same as them? He certainly felt it sometimes. He knew he was different from everyone else, and when he allowed his temper to get the better of him, he was dangerous. His dad, Gemma and Lyssi could all testify to that.

He could hear the voices of Tony and his friend Billy talking and laughing as he moved through the house. Tony was always inviting his friends here, and Danny rarely minded – it was his house after all. But it would be nice if he could come home and not have people in his personal space. Tony was overly sociable and didn't understand how Danny just needed solitude sometimes.

He made his way through the house and found them in the living room. They were laughing, and the atmosphere was easy, but it did nothing to lift Danny's foul mood. He greeted them as politely as he could manage and disappeared into the kitchen, hoping he would be left alone. He thought Tony would take the hint, but the two men followed him, trying to include him in their conversation.

They had been arguing about the cashers, and how they should (or shouldn't) be given financial aid. Danny stared at them sullenly. He wasn't in the mood for a political debate, not with everything else that was going on.

"You don't know what it's like Billy, you've never even stepped foot in Gromdon!" Tony said, shaking his head.

Billy gave a derisive snort. "It's not like people can't work, even if they have no identification. There's always work. They're just lazy."

"Huh. You don't know what you're talking about, Billy. Did you forget I grew up in the slums? I've seen first-hand what life is like for them. If it wasn't for Patricia and Graham adopting me, I'd still be there! The cashers aren't afforded the same opportunities as everyone else, and you know it."

"Well, they shouldn't be! If they wanted to live here, they should have gone through the proper channels and arrived legally! Or they should have stayed where they were."

"Their countries don't exist anymore, Billy. How could they stay where they were? My family was from England. It's not even a country anymore. Danny's girlfriend's family came from Ireland. It's entirely uninhabitable now. People CAN'T live there. Just think about what you're saying for a minute."

"Woah, woah, Danny? Your girlfriend was a casher?" Billy asked, sounding surprised that someone of Danny's social standing would date someone who used to be poor.

Danny turned to him and said, "IS a casher, not WAS!" His usual placid and friendly tone had vanished. He wasn't in the mood for racism, or the usual classist bullshit he encountered whenever people found out about Gemma.

"Seriously? She's not like, real poor though, is she? She's not from *Gromdon*!"

"Billy, I'm from Gromdon!" Tony cut him off short before he could offend Danny any further.

Billy dismissed Tony's words with a wave of his hand, "Yeah, but you were adopted when you were a kid, so you don't count. You're legit now!" He turned to Danny and said, "What are you doing with a casher from Gromdon? You could have any woman you want!"

"Yes. And I want Gemma."

A tense silence followed. Billy seemed to have realised that he had crossed a line. "I didn't mean anything by it." He gave an apologetic shrug and changed the subject. "Hey! What about the news about those escapees from that genetic research facility? I mean, how crazy is that?"

Tony caught Danny's eye, and they exchanged a tense and uneasy look. Billy carried on, completely oblivious, relishing the scandalous nature of this story. "They're meant to be crazy. Like psycho's or something! They reckon they don't have feelings or feel pain and will kill you as soon as look at you!" he sounded so animated and excited; Danny felt bile rise in his throat as he listened.

"I'm sure the news is just sensationalising things," Tony said. "I bet they're not like that at all."

"Yeah, right!" Billy said, rolling his eyes. "The news says they were created as a prototype for war. They're soldiers, but they aren't human. They don't have any human rights, so they've kept them in cages all this time and now they've got out, they're crazy!"

Danny could not bring himself to even try to contribute to this conversation. He couldn't be sure how much was true and how much was media frenzy, but he didn't want to think about what they were. *What he was.* He barged past the two men and disappeared into his room.

"What's up with him?" Billy muttered to Tony as he left.

"Hope I didn't upset him about his girlfriend. I didn't know she was a casher."

Danny was thankful when he heard Tony suggest leaving and going out for food. He waited until they had left before he came back downstairs and fixed himself a sandwich.

He was still stewing about what had been said before. All of it: the jibes about cashers and the insinuation that he could 'do better' than Gemma. As if the fact that she wasn't an official citizen of New America made her somehow worthless. And of course, he had been riled by the discussion about the escapees. He'd been trying his hardest to think of anything else since the news broke, but that was impossible! He had been dreaming of it. Dreaming of being locked in a cage while men in white coats poked and prodded. Dreaming that people were running from him in the streets and the police had him surrounded. He had been permanently on edge since he heard the news.

Danny sat on the sofa, in the dark and the quiet, trying to bring himself to finish eating. Not that he was hungry, he just knew that he ought to eat. He didn't know how long he'd sat there, lost in his thoughts, but he wasn't feeling any better, only worse. More anxious and annoyed. He heard Tony approaching well before he made it to the door, and he had intended to get up and hide out of the way, but he couldn't seem to motivate himself to move. At least Tony had left Billy behind and had returned alone.

"Sorry about Billy, he just doesn't get it, he doesn't know what it's like for cashers," Tony started as soon as he entered the house.

"Why do you hang around with him? He wouldn't want anything to do with you if you still lived in the slums!" Danny said.

"Neither would you. It's not as though our paths would have crossed if we weren't put in school together."

Danny felt his annoyance peak. "Maybe not, but I would still treat you with decency if I met you. Not like Billy. He thinks he's automatically better than everybody outside of Helston," he snapped.

"It's not just Billy. Everyone thinks like that in Helston!"

Danny couldn't understand why he was defending that idiot. "*I'm* not like that."

"Yeah, well, you're not like everybody else, are you?"

It happened so fast, the blinding anger, the inability to think clearly. He didn't quite know what he was doing as he grabbed Tony by the shoulder and slammed his body into the wall. He could hear screams, hear his friend pleading. The distant sound of begging rang in his head, but he could not seem to acknowledge it. It came on fast, but he knew he was in the grip of another episode. He wasn't in control of himself at that moment, but he was aware enough to know he didn't want to hurt his friend. His fist came back, and he drove it forward, purposely missing Tony's face by mere millimetres, his knuckles smashing into the wall with a sickening thump. Tony yelled, a terrified scream escaping his mouth. Danny dropped him to the floor and hissed at him through gritted teeth, "Get out."

Tony heaved himself up from the floor as quickly as he could and bolted through the front door. Danny didn't have time to worry about his friend, or why this kept happening. What little control he possessed had deserted him. His head lurched forward involuntarily and slammed into the wall, and his fists came up and he pounded it over and over again. He could hear screaming, a type of blood curdling noise that sounded almost inhuman and was unnerving to listen to. It took him a moment to realise the noises were coming from him. He screamed harder with this realisation, but the confusion in his brain, and the vague knowledge that he didn't like the strange wailing sound, made him hurl his head forward again, smashing it into the wall, leaving bloody marks on the crisp white finish. He spun around and saw the black glass coffee table, and his arm smashed through it, shattering the glass. The pain was somehow soothing and satisfying, but it wasn't enough. He picked up the chrome table leg and whacked it down over his own thigh with as much force as he could muster. Again, and again, the pain somehow easing the rage within him. He turned once more to the wall and slammed his head into it, like a madman, still screaming. Still raging, yet still needing the noise to stop. He lifted the leg of the table again, and turned around, coming face to face with the TV. The table leg smashed into the screen, and he ripped the television from the wall and threw it across the room. It sailed into the large ornate mirror hanging on the back wall and it shattered into a thousand pieces. The noise was enough to jar his senses. He took a sharp breath. He was seeing sense again. The blind insanity was lifting, and he could see through the hazy fog.

He took in the devastation in front of him and fell to his knees, exhausted and confused. He tried to remember, but nothing made sense. What had caused this? Who was here? Had he hurt somebody? He took in his surroundings and realised he was at Tony's house. No, his house. He lived here now; he remembered. He couldn't think straight, he couldn't remember, and he was so unnaturally exhausted. His body ached, his limbs seemed so heavy, and his senses were dulled, fuzzy like his brain just couldn't process anything. He stayed on the floor a while until his body decided to work, drifting in and out of sleep.

When he woke, he took in the broken room and knew without a doubt he had caused this, though he had no memory of doing it. He tried to think back to the events of earlier; Tony was here before. And Billy. Billy had made him angry. He put his hands to his head and tried to remember. Had he hurt Billy? He could see streaks of blood on the wall, but he didn't know who it belonged to. He noticed the holes in the wall, and the pain in his knuckles seemed to sing to him. The memory of hitting the wall assaulted his mind, and Tony's terrified face flashed before his eyes. He searched around in a frantic panic, hoping with everything he had that he wouldn't find the body of his friend.

He was coming back to himself now, his cognitive functions were returning, and his thoughts were becoming more ordered and less chaotic. Slowly, he raised himself up from the floor and searched the rest of the house. The damage had been confined to one room, and there were no bodies, so it was safe to assume he hadn't hurt anybody. Tony must have escaped before the full effect of the episode happened.

Danny sat on the floor with tears starting to form. Why did this keep happening? What was so wrong with him that he couldn't control his temper? The things that were being said about the escapees – that they were dangerous, that they were crazy, were they true? Was it true for him too?

In that moment, he hated everything about himself and what he was. He tried so hard to be like everyone else, but he wasn't. He was a monster.

For a long time, he sat on the floor, wishing he was somebody else. Hours passed and he couldn't bring himself to move. It was getting light outside before he realised, he hadn't even checked on Tony. He berated himself further for being so caught up in his own self-pity that he hadn't made sure his best friend was unharmed.

He checked his phone, but there were no messages or missed calls. At least that meant nobody else knew about it. He didn't know how he could explain to his dad that it had happened again. He'd promised after what happened with Lyssi that he would keep control of his temper. If Tony wanted him to leave, he'd have nowhere else to go. Michelle wouldn't have him back in the house, not while Lyssi lived there. And he couldn't blame her.

He didn't have the guts to call Tony. He texted him instead.

< Are you OK? >

He didn't know what else to say. "I'm sorry I lost my temper and almost killed you," just didn't seem like the sort of thing he could say in a text.

A moment later, his phone pinged. The message read,

< Yeah. I'm fine. Are you OK? You really scared me. >

< I know. I'm sorry. Can we talk? >

< I'm not coming back until I know it's safe, Danny. >

Danny had nothing to say. He wanted to tell his friend that it was safe, and he wouldn't hurt him. But was it ever safe?

< I'm sorry. >

was all he could manage.

Danny started cleaning up the mess he had made and then called Gemma. She could instantly tell something was wrong. He didn't want to tell her at first, but she managed to coax it out of him.

"Do you want me to come and help?" she asked. "I can get the train to Branley, it only takes an hour to walk from there to Helston."

Danny smiled. These were the reasons he loved Gemma so much. These were the things that made her worth her weight in gold. It would take her almost two hours to get here, and she would have to walk such a long distance in the cold, in an area she had no legal right to be in. If she was stopped by the border police, they would arrest her, maybe even beat her. Yet, he knew it wasn't an empty offer. If he asked her to, she would do it without hesitation. Anything to make him feel better.

Of course, he couldn't take her up on her offer. He gracefully declined but promised he would see her later. She offered to meet him at the restaurant where she worked. Again, he smiled and shook his head. She would never allow him to meet her at home. She was too ashamed of where she lived to allow him inside. Plus, he knew it caused arguments with her brother. Craig hated that she was dating a rich guy from Helston.

After Danny had cleared up the debris, he went to see his dad. He had hoped for some sort of comfort or understanding, but as usual all he got was lectures.

"You can't keep doing this, Danny. You need to learn to control your temper. What's going to happen if you kill someone? What if you killed Tony?"

He went on and on and Danny felt worse for it. No matter how many times he tried to explain, he couldn't make anyone see that he couldn't help it. He hated himself so much for how he acted. He knew he should be able to stop, or not get so angry in the first place. And he tried. He really did try, but whenever it happened, it was like something else took over, like he had no control.

"Where is Tony now? Have you spoken to him?" Frank asked.

"I texted him." He felt so unhappy, but Frank didn't offer any sympathy.

"You need to sort it out with him, Danny. It's not like you can come home. Michelle would never allow it, and Lyssi is still afraid of you."

Danny's heart sank even further.

"Do you want me to call him and try to explain?" he offered begrudgingly.

Danny could only imagine how that conversation would go. *'Danny is different. Danny is dangerous. But please don't worry, he doesn't mean to hurt you. Oh! And don't kick him out because he is too dangerous for us to have at home...'* It wouldn't surprise Danny in the slightest if his dad tried to offer Tony money to keep him. Money fixed everything as far as Frank was concerned.

"No. I'll talk to him myself," he muttered, and got up to leave, wishing he hadn't bothered coming to see his dad in the first place.

He thought about confiding in Jenson, but those were never easy conversations to have. What he needed was someone to listen and understand, not someone to ask endless science-based questions. Jenson was nice enough, but he always made Danny feel like an experiment instead of a person. Shaking his head, he reminded himself that to Jenson; he was a science experiment!

He left his dad's office feeling worse for the visit. He had pretty much exhausted his options of people he could talk to. He couldn't speak to Michelle, she wouldn't understand, and he was hoping his dad wouldn't tell her about this, anyway. Lyssi would find out, and it wouldn't do much to ease her fears if she knew that even his own best friend wasn't safe.

He decided to go into the city and buy replacements for the furniture he had trashed. At least that was something he could fix.

A few hours later, his house looked like new, except of course for the holes in the wall where his fists had gone through. He would need to hire a plasterer to fix that.

There was nothing else to do except apologise, properly. He picked up his phone and dialled, holding his breath as he waited for Tony to answer.

"Danny. Hey."

"Tony. Are you okay?"

There was a slight pause before he heard his friend exhale and say, "Yes. I'm okay. Are you okay?"

"No, not really. Tony, I'm so sorry. I never meant to, I would never…" he trailed off. The fact was, he couldn't say what he would never do, not with certainty. He wasn't in control of his actions when things like that happened.

"I know, man. I know. Look, are you at home? I'm coming home and we can talk about it, okay?"

He ended the call and Danny had nothing else to do but sit and nervously wait. Tony knew everything about him and had for a long time. He had witnessed a meltdown before, when they were younger, but Danny had never attacked him before. He hoped Tony could fill in the blanks for him – he still didn't understand what had caused this last episode.

Tony arrived half an hour later, and Danny didn't even know where to begin. He was so ashamed of himself. The atmosphere between them was uncomfortable, maybe even frosty. Tony seemed on edge and Danny couldn't help but notice how he lingered in the doorway, as though he was too afraid to come inside.

"Are you feeling better?" he asked, from the other side of the room. Danny knew that was code for 'Are you safe to be around now.'

He nodded. Tears filled his eyes and there was a begging to his voice as he apologised again and again.

"I don't know what happened, I usually get more warning than that. It's just been so hard these last few days, with the news about the escape and I've been so on edge. I know it sounds like excuses, and there are no excuses for hurting people. I'm just so sorry it happened. I don't want to hurt people. I don't want to hurt you."

Tony walked forward and embraced his friend, clapping him on the back. "I know man, I know you don't, and I know you didn't mean to. That doesn't make it any less frightening, though. I thought you were going to kill me! I mean, when your fist came at me, I thought that was it for me."

Silence fell, then the sudden, uncomfortable realisation that they were still hugging, and Danny was crying. Tony cleared his throat and clapped Danny on the back again as he stepped back from his embrace.

"I know that's not what you want to hear, but I can't stand here and pretend that you didn't scare me yesterday. There was no warning! I knew you were in a mood or whatever, but I didn't think you would try to kill me. I mean, what did I do?"

Danny was quiet for a moment. "I don't remember."

"Oh. Well, that's super helpful!" Tony said, sarcasm dripping from every word. "I thought you had a photographic memory or whatever? You never forget anything. You remember things you didn't even know you knew."

Danny looked down. "Normally, that's true. But after something like this, I don't. When it's over and I come out of it, I don't remember what happened, or what caused it. And I can't think straight after. It's scary sometimes. I don't remember what happened yesterday. All I know is, Billy was here and, were we arguing about Gemma? And then I have hazy memories of you, and me almost hurting you. But I don't know what happened. I was hoping you could tell me..."

"Oh. Right... well, you were upset about Billy and his views on cashers. You said he was elitist and were asking why I have anything to do with him, and I pointed out that we wouldn't have anything to do with each other if I was still a Gromdon grot. Then you said something like you would still respect me though, and I said you're not like everybody else."

Danny closed his eyes. He remembered the feelings of anger and shame as his friend reminded him he was different. He felt the anger surge in his chest again and his hand closed into a fist. "That was it," he said flatly. "That was what caused it. I already know I'm different, Tony. I don't need reminding of it."

Tony stared at him. "I didn't mean it like that! I meant, that not everyone with your money or upbringing is as respectful to cashers. Jeez! You almost killed me because I said something, and you didn't like it?" He put his hands up to his head. "Danny, we've been friends for seven years. I know you told me before about these meltdowns, but I didn't think that you would ever attack ME! How do I know it won't happen again? How do I know that next time it won't be my head through the wall? There was no warning! I don't know if you are safe to be here. If *I'm* safe with you here."

Danny couldn't bring himself to answer. The truth was, he didn't know if Tony was safe either. He looked down at the floor, his shoulders rounded. He felt so alone, and so very guilty. "Do you want me to leave?" he asked, full of dread that Tony was going to kick him out. He really would have nowhere else to go.

"No," Tony shook his head. "But some sort of warning would be helpful," he sighed.

"Are you afraid of me?" he asked, though he wasn't sure he wanted to know the answer.

"Not right now. Now you're just my friend, and you're upset, and I want to make you feel better. Yesterday, you weren't my friend though. Yesterday, well to be truthful, Danny, you were terrifying! I mean, you didn't even look like you."

"I didn't mean –"

"I know!" Tony cut him off, holding his hand up in the air. "Look, we're going round in circles now. I know you didn't mean to; I know you say you can't help it. But you're going to have to help it if you want us to be friends. If anything like that ever happens again…" He couldn't finish his sentence. But they both knew what he was saying.

Danny nodded, and Tony walked by him and disappeared into his room. He closed the door behind him, leaving Danny to wonder if he really was forgiven, or if Tony was just too afraid to speak his mind.

Tony didn't emerge from his room for the rest of the day, which did nothing to quell Danny's fears. After a while, he decided to go to the restaurant to see Gemma.

Danny entered the restaurant, and the sight of Gemma eased his anxious mind immediately. She was busy and hadn't noticed him yet, and he took a moment to watch her. She always smiled and was always pleasant to people, even though they treated her like she was worthless. People were mean and disrespectful towards her, as if the fact she held no form of identification somehow made her insignificant.

He ordered a drink while he waited for her shift to finish, and chatted a little with Terri, one of the other waitresses. She always made pathetic attempts to flirt with him. It was sad! He knew she couldn't understand what he saw in Gemma, and it was laughable how jealous she was. Her face turned sour when Gemma approached, wearing her coat.

"Hey!" she greeted him, leaning in for a kiss on the cheek.

They left together; Danny's arm draped over Gemma's shoulder. Terri watched with a look of envy, no doubt wondering what was so special about Gemma that she was dating one of Harpton Main's richest legitimates.

Danny walked her home. It was easier than driving. Cars were an unusual occurrence in Gromdon, and Gemma didn't like to draw attention to herself.

Being in her company was easy, and the stresses of the last two days ebbed away as he listened to her beautiful voice and breathed in her soothing scent.

They talked as they walked, and she asked him about what happened with Tony. It was funny, but the things he had been searching for all day, he found in Gemma. She was understanding and accepting, she listened to him, and she was sympathetic. She didn't tell him he should control himself better – she fully accepted and believed him when he said he couldn't help it. And she didn't show any fear of what he was or what he was capable of. She loved him for who and what he was. Not what he ought to be.

They arrived at her house, and she lingered outside a while, leaning against the wall.

"Thank you, Gemma. You always make everything better."

She shook her head. "I didn't do anything!" She sounded so surprised.

"I love you, you know?"

"I do. I love you too." She leaned into him, and he hugged her to his chest, planting a gentle kiss on top of her head.

She left him at the door, still too ashamed of her meagre home to invite him inside. He had told her so many times that it didn't matter what she had or didn't have. It was HER he was here to see, not her house, but she would never relent.

He wandered back towards the restaurant, feeling renewed. He felt in a much better place now and felt much more confident that he could tackle his problem with Tony. He didn't know how she managed it, but he loved her for it.

CHAPTER 10

Friday 24th February 2102

Jay's Apartment, Helstain, Harpton Main

It was a relief to take the weight from her feet as she eased her tired and aching body into the chair. Keeping her eye on this Jay person was proving to be a difficult task. She didn't trust him and was certain he would report her to the authorities as soon as he got a chance. She also knew she couldn't keep him here, in this small place, forever. He'd already expressed he needed to work. That meant he would be missed. People may come looking for him, and this thought troubled her.

She heard him moving and walked back to her sentry position by the door, even though it made no sense when she held all the power in this situation. Still, the fear of sitting without being given permission was a terrifying prospect. It was absurd to think it, when there was nothing he could do to her, but she still dared not be caught using his furniture, as though she were his equal.

"Good morning," he spoke to her as he emerged from his room. She didn't know what he expected her to say, but it seemed he was waiting for a response. She stared at him, noticing how her continuous silence and lack of communication set off his stress response, but she couldn't understand why.

"Did you sleep?" he asked her.

Her heart pounded in her chest. Did he know she had slept? Just for a short time, less than thirty minutes, but she had no permission to sleep.

"Do you want some coffee?"

Confusion hit her at once. She couldn't understand why he was treating her as though she was his equal. She looked at him through narrowed eyes, suspicious of his intentions, but she couldn't bring herself to answer him. How should she know if she wanted coffee or not?

She watched him busy himself in the kitchen. He made two cups of coffee even though she hadn't answered his question, and he carefully placed one on the counter beside her.

"Um, did anybody call for me yesterday?" His voice did not sound confident when he spoke.

"No."

"Um, Edel, I'm going to have to use my phone. I need to deal with some work stuff."

He was looking at her with fearful eyes; she noticed how his body was showing signs of stress. He was still afraid, but he was getting braver. So far, he had been too afraid to talk, or to get close to her, but his confidence was growing. She knew they would need to communicate with one another if she wanted him to help her, but every time they spoke, and every minute she spent in his presence without threat, was time for him to become less afraid. If she didn't keep him sufficiently afraid of her, what would stop him from contacting the authorities?

She still hadn't answered him.

"Why don't you speak?" he asked. There was a slight tone of anger to his voice, diluting the fear. This wasn't good. He was already becoming less fearful around her.

The silence drew on, and he spoke with caution as he asked, "Are you going to allow me to leave the house today? We need food, and I need to go to the bank to reinstate my digital banking."

She still didn't answer. She knew she couldn't keep him confined here forever, but how could she allow him to leave? He would surely inform the authorities at his first opportunity.

"Edel, please. You can't keep me prisoner forever. Please, you've got to allow me out."

She was still yet to answer him, unable to think what to do for the best. Her mind worked at speed, weighing up her options, until the sound of footsteps approaching the door outside interrupted her thoughts. A loud knock followed, causing Edel to jump with fright. She turned on Jay, a look of pure accusation on her face.

"Jay! Jay!" The knocking continued and was accompanied by the cheerful voice of a young girl.

Edel looked at Jay and saw the fear in him increase. His face turned ashen, and his heart beat faster.

"Jay, are you home?" the voice of the young girl called to him.

Edel stood in front of the door, readying herself for attack.

"Please, don't hurt her. She's just a kid." She could hear the begging in his whispered tones. "Please, let me get rid of her. I'll tell her to go away."

Edel offered a single nod and took a step to the right, positioning herself behind the door, still close enough to grab him should he try to make a run for it.

As she peered through the gap between the hinges of the door, she saw a young girl, no older than thirteen at a guess. She knew she would need to remember this girl, and observed her fastidiously, taking in every ounce of information. The girl had long, dark, curly hair and big lips that looked as though they had been painted. She wore a green blazer with the emblem of a sword pointing down through three coloured rings, and the words St Mary's printed underneath.

A flicker of recognition sparked in Edel. They had walked past a large building with children outside, wearing the same clothing. The same emblem was flying from flags outside the building. That must be where she lived. Edel's eyes flitted to a small, framed photograph of the same girl displayed on the shelf in Jay's kitchen. This girl was important to this Jay person.

Edel listened to the exchange between Jay and the girl. He was apologising, telling her he had forgotten their plans, and he was sick. "Gabriella, I will make it up to you when I'm feeling better. I'm really sorry to let you down."

Edel noticed the ease with which this man could lie. His face stayed passive and didn't change colour. He didn't seem to have any increase in perspiration, and his heart rate didn't increase. Although, since he was already under stress, she decided that observation wouldn't be a fair or accurate test.

She noted his sigh of relief as he closed the door and leaned his forehead against it with closed eyes, but she didn't understand the gesture. She stood stationary for a moment before working up the courage to speak.

It wasn't easy. She wasn't used to asking questions, or speaking without permission, but it was a barrier she would have to push through, if she was going to get anywhere with this human.

"You care for that girl." It was more of a statement than a question.

He seemed startled by her sudden bout of speech, and he turned to look at her with a face full of confusion. "Yes."

"Who is she to you?" Edel asked. Her speech was aggressive and to the point.

"She's just a girl that I help. I sponsor her to go to school and pay for her place at the children's home," he said, with an unsure frown.

She offered him a single curt nod while she considered what this meant. She didn't know the term "sponsor" or "school", but the children's home must be where she lived. If he was helping her, then he must care for her. And in her experience, people would do almost anything to protect the people they cared for, especially children. Back at Poly-Gen, if she had to extract information, or perform interrogations, people would give up their secrets far quicker if the lives of children were threatened. People always begged harder for the lives of their children than for their own. This behaviour was a mystery to Edel, but she accepted it as a human norm.

Psyching herself up for the threat she was about to make, she looked at him and said, "You are safe now. No matter who you tell, or what you do, I will not kill *you*." She stared at him with cold, hollow eyes and continued. "I know where that girl lives. I know her name, and what she looks like. She will die if you betray me."

Edel noted how the man's heartrate skyrocketed, and his stress response elevated. This was the effect she had been anticipating.

"Please! She's just a kid. She's got nothing to do with this. Don't bring her into this, she's no threat to you," he pleaded with her.

"You are a threat. If you care for her, you will help me. If they come looking for me, I will kill her before I do anything else." She glared at him with determination in her eyes. This was easier than she had expected. "You help me. Or she dies."

Jay was stunned. "I will... I was... please don't hurt her."

Edel walked away from him. It was the first time she had turned her back to him since they met. She was satisfied with how things were turning out: Jay would always fear for the life of that child, but since he no longer needed to worry about his own life coming to an abrupt ending, they should find it easier to communicate with one another now.

There was no doubt in her mind she was right about this. The fact she had left him by the unlocked door, but he had not tried to leave, confirmed it. She assumed the dread of her threats against the young girl is what kept him in his place.

She held his phone out to him in silence. He stared at her with a bewildered expression as he took it from her, as though he didn't know if she was serious or not.

The hours passed, and they hadn't spoken to each other

since Gabriella left. Doubts and fear forced their way into Edel's mind. The brief period of bravery she had experienced before had vanished, and she had reverted to feeling unsure and afraid. She was too fearful of humans and too used to obeying orders to give any.

Jay eventually broke the uncomfortable silence. "Edel?"

Her eyes travelled towards him, and he seemed to shrink under her intense stare.

"Um... I need to sort out my banking, and we need groceries... um... can I go now? Am I allowed to leave?"

"Not alone," she answered in her usual unfriendly and abrupt speech.

"You want to come with me?" he asked, dismayed.

She nodded her head slowly.

"Right..." he said uncertainly, as he looked her up and down. "We need to get you some clothes that fit, and some shoes."

She hadn't thought of that. She should try to blend in with the humans.

"Um... here." He handed her a plain black hoody and a pair of fresh socks then told her to cover her head with the hood.

The idea of leaving this place of safety was unnerving. Outside, there were many humans, many new noises, smells, and sensations. Too much to take in at once. She had barely slept since her arrival, and too much could push her over the edge. She remembered how close she came to meltdown as she walked to this place three days ago.

She silently followed him out of the door. If he was afraid, he didn't show it. He did a good job of pretending everything was normal as they walked down the street together and she tried her best to remain calm, but every sound had her head spinning.

Jay stopped outside a posh looking, glass fronted building and turned to look at her. "Edel, you can't come in here without shoes. They will think you are a casher. Cashers aren't allowed into the mainstream banks."

She narrowed her eyes, feeling her uncertainty and suspicion grow. "How long will you be?"

He shook his head. "Not long. It should only take a minute or two to get my cards reinstated."

She fixed him with her cold stare. "I can hear everything that is being spoken about inside that building. I will know if you tell them about me."

He didn't have any answer to that. She didn't know if he was planning to get help or not, but if that had been his intention, he would be having second thoughts about it now.

She waited outside and listened to everything. He was right about it not taking long; he was in and out in a few minutes. He didn't speak a word to anyone about her, and nobody suspected a thing.

Next, he led her to a shoe shop and ushered her inside. "What's your shoe size?"

The question sounded so casual, and panic hit her out of nowhere. She did not know the answer to this question. She swallowed hard and looked to the floor, awaiting the searing pain that would surely follow her ignorance.

"Edel?" He reached forward as if to touch her arm, a look of concern on his face. She jerked herself out of his reach before he got close to her. It wasn't intentional, it was more like an involuntary impulse.

He frowned at her, and asked again, "Your shoe size? What is it?"

Edel could not answer. She didn't know the answer.

Jay seemed to realise. "Have you ever owned a pair of shoes?" he whispered to her.

Without waiting for her answer, he pulled a sizing gauge off the wall and told her to put her foot in it. He measured her feet then asked, "Do you see anything you like?"

Edel didn't understand the question. She stared at him with a blank expression.

He looked around the shop and picked up a pair of black flats in her size. "What about these?"

She couldn't even bring herself to look at them. *What about them?* She wondered. What exactly was he asking?

He let out an exasperated exhale. "Try them on," he said. She obeyed and slipped them onto her feet.

"Do they feel okay?"

She didn't know what to say. She didn't know how shoes should feel. It felt strange having her feet encased inside something solid. It was a new sensation, but beyond that she had no opinion on it. Her silence seemed to irritate him, but she didn't understand why. Her whole life had been mostly silent.

"Right!" he said in a huff, more to himself than to her. He held out his hands for the shoes, and she obliged, peeling them off her feet and handing them over. He marched up to the counter and paid for them, declining a box. "She wants to wear them now," he said to the cashier, without much more explanation.

They left the shop and she followed him into a convenience store. She observed Jay as he picked up a basket and started haphazardly shoving items into it.

"What do you like to eat?" he asked her. Again, he sounded so casual.

She stared at him. How was she supposed to answer that question? She didn't *like* to eat anything. She wasn't supposed to have any opinion or preference about what she ate. The food had been plain and bland at Poly-Gen, and most of her nutritional needs were met with the green juice they served her with each small meal.

He let out another huff and puffed his cheeks out. "You're not making this easy, are you?"

He filled his basket with pre-packaged convenience food and bread and milk. She watched in silence as he paid for the food and followed him out of the store without a word.

The streets were busy as they walked back to his apartment, and she was finding it difficult to remain calm as her senses were bombarded from every direction.

"Um.. Edel? Uh, is everything okay?" He sounded uneasy, and she turned to look at him, unsure of what he was asking.

"You seem jumpy... you said you wouldn't hurt me, but you don't seem... You don't look okay," he choked out. She could sense the fear emanating from him, taste it even.

"I won't harm you. I am stable," she said, her robotic voice doing nothing to help him relax.

A car honked its horn as it passed them, and she spun around with unnatural speed, her heart in her mouth, startled by the sudden assault on her ears.

Jay let out a startled yelp as her body coiled up in reflex. "Sorry," he muttered, "you made me jump." He let out a nervous laugh.

Edel glared at him, unable to understand the laughter that just escaped his lips.

They arrived back at his apartment, and he put away the shopping.

"Hungry?" he asked.

She was, but she couldn't bring herself to admit the weakness. Did it matter if she was hungry?

"Edel. Why do you never answer?" he asked her. Her eyes fell to the floor. How could she explain?

"Here," he approached her with caution, holding out the cup of instant noodles he had made.

She made no move to take it, so he placed it on the table, and made another for himself.

"Eat it while it's hot."

She obeyed the order. It was all she knew how to do.

"Sit down," he told her. Again, she did as she was told.

"Right," he said more to himself than to her. He stared at her thoughtfully. "Do you like the noodles?" His head tilted to the side as he paid close attention to her face. "You don't like questions, do you?"

The fear grew. He knew she was afraid. Showing fear was not allowed. Not ever.

"It's okay," he said, holding his hands up in a gesture she recognised as surrender.

He seemed to be much more relaxed since leaving the apartment. He kept trying to talk to her, and she found it unnerving. Her plan seemed to have backfired spectacularly. The small amount of power she held before had swung the other way. He no longer seemed so afraid of her, but she was still beyond terrified of her new situation.

"That is your room now," he pointed to the closed door beside his own bedroom. "There is a bed in there, and all the things you will need. You already know where the bathroom is. Towels are in the cupboard over there," he pointed to another door close to the bathroom. "Um, make yourself at home, I guess." He shrugged and smiled at her, leaving her confused by what he meant. He left the table and wandered to the kitchen and pottered around it, but not in the same nervous way he had the first day she had been here.

Edel stayed where she was. Like a statue, she watched Jay and tried to understand how he was suddenly so calm in her company. Had he taken what she said at face value? He was no longer the one in danger, so he was no longer afraid? She hadn't expected this. She had assumed he would still be wary of her.

"So...." he turned to look at her and her heart kicked up a gear. "You don't have to sit there all day. You can move." He said it in such an offhand way, as though he were speaking to a guest, not his captor. He gestured to her bedroom door with his open hand. "Why don't you go check out your bedroom?"

Her eyes travelled in the direction he was pointing. She stood without speech and walked towards the room, but she noted his sigh of relief as the door closed behind her. She couldn't make sense of him. Was he afraid or not?

She looked around the room. It was small and plain like her cell at Poly-Gen, but there was a window she noticed with amazement. She tentatively walked towards it and looked out into the street below. She could hear Jay talking on the phone, and listened with interest, but he gave nothing away about his current situation. He was apologising and promising to make up working hours. For now, it looked as though she was safe.

He really was going to help her.

Edel didn't leave the room for the rest of the day. She sat in silence and switched off her mind, listening only to Jay's movements to make sure she was still safe here. She allowed no thought or feeling to penetrate her mind, and even as the day turned to night, she still did not move. This is how she was expected to be. This was familiar to her. It was all she'd ever known.

There was a gentle knock on her door, and she almost jumped out of her skin. She dared not move, as ridiculous as it was.

"Edel? Uh, may I come in?" The door opened a fraction, and he peeked his head through the crack.

"I'm going to bed. Do... do you need anything?"

She could not understand him. What would she possibly need? He didn't react to her silence, he only nodded his head and offered her a weak smile. "I just thought I'd check. Help yourself to whatever you want," he said. He took a sharp intake of breath, and she could tell his next words were something he was afraid to speak. "Pl – please don't come into my room," he stuttered. "I er... it's just... please don't." He closed the door, and she heard his long, slow exhale as his own door closed with a soft click.

He was still very much afraid; she decided. She could tell he was having trouble sleeping as she listened to him toss and turn and sigh in his bed. It wasn't until she heard his long, slow, rhythmic breathing and gentle snores that she finally allowed herself to sleep.

She awoke the next morning and she could tell Jay was still sleeping. She felt better today. A full night's sleep and a solid six hours of sitting in the quiet had reset her body. She rose from the bed and made it up, then, not knowing what else to do, she continued to sit.

She heard Jay wake and listened to his movements. He made a drink; it smelled like the coffee he had given her before. It seemed he did this each morning. She listened to him walking around the apartment. Then came the sound of the shower running. She heard his bare feet pad back past her room and into his, then the shuffling sound of clothing being unfurled and worn. Next, she listened to him walk back to the kitchen and the scent of something burning hit her nose.

Edel did not move from the bed. She did not know if she should. Did she have permission to leave this room? Hours passed, and she still hadn't moved. She heard the knocking again, and she tensed up.

"Are you awake?" he spoke gently. "I've made you some coffee. Come out if you want it."

She didn't know what to do. She knew she couldn't stay in this room forever, even if she wanted to. Hesitantly, she opened the door and walked with careful and controlled movements to the table where the hot drink was waiting. Truth be told, she didn't like the taste. She wasn't used to drinking hot liquids, and it was a strong flavour she had never tasted before, but she didn't know how to refuse things. Refusing anything had never been an option before.

"Did you sleep well?" Jay asked from behind her. She spun around at an inhuman speed, causing Jay to almost scream as he took a step back away from her, hyperventilating.

She stared at him, unable to understand what he was asking, and why she had startled him.

His hand covered his mouth as he recovered himself and breathed normally again. He was looking at her as though he had something to say.

"You don't speak much," he said.

She didn't answer him. It was more of a statement than a question, anyway.

He cocked his head to the side and looked at her face. "It would help me if you would talk."

She still had nothing to say.

"How can I help you if you don't speak to me? How can I know what you need?"

She swallowed hard. How could she explain even she didn't

know what she needed?

"Look, I agreed to help you. And I will. But you need to talk to me. We need to start trusting each other."

"Yes," she said.

"Yes, what? Yes, you trust me? Yes, you will talk more? Yes, you agree with me? What?" His voice sounded angry or frustrated.

She tried harder to get her words out to him. "I will try to talk. It isn't easy."

"Will you answer my questions?" he asked.

She was doing a terrible job of showing willing. She just didn't know how to talk to a human. To anyone, really.

"Will you at least try?" he asked her.

She gave a nod. It was the best she could manage.

"Yesterday, when we went out. You were acting strange. It was the same as the day you came home with me. You were jumpy, and your body was twitching. Why? You looked dangerous."

"Too much new," she said, as if that was a complete and detailed explanation.

"Too much new?" he repeated. "What was new to you?"

"Everything. I have always been inside. Never outside."

She didn't understand the sorrowful expression on his face, or the way his hand went up to cover his mouth. "Never?" he whispered.

"Two times, I saw the outside."

"I'm sorry," he said to her.

He looked at her for a long time, a look on his face she had never seen before. It was a look of deep sympathy and sorrow that a person could be abused in such a way. Although, she didn't understand what it meant.

"You can now," he said, emotion hindering his words. "You are free now."

If only it were that simple, she thought.

CHAPTER 11

Sunday 26th February 2102

Jay's Apartment, Helstain, Harpton Main

The following day passed much the same as the previous one. Edel stayed in her room for most of it, and for that, Jay was thankful. He made food for her whenever he ate, and drinks too, which she would leave her room for, but aside from that, and seeing her come out of her room to use the bathroom once, he saw nothing of her all day.

Jay still couldn't fully relax with her in his house. He walked on eggshells, afraid to put one foot wrong, and the fact she still didn't speak wasn't helping to relieve his stress. Though, she seemed happy to keep out of his way, and happy to be told when to eat and drink. He wondered if she would eat at all if he didn't make something for her.

Jay had been arranging his return to work for most of the day. They had given him a disciplinary hearing for missing so many shifts with no explanation and Mr Johnson, one of the company directors, wanted to meet with him. The thought of it set his nerves on edge. He didn't know if he would still have a job after Monday. He turned in early for the night and tried not to obsess about it. There would be other work, even if he had to work a cash job until he found something more suitable.

The following morning, he got himself up, showered and ready for work, and kept telling himself things would be okay. He was dressed in his smartest grey suit and was grabbing another coffee when he spotted her out of the corner of his eye. She stood motionless behind him, and he jumped once he realised she was there. *Why does she just stand there and not speak?*

"Morning," he called, as casual and upbeat as he could manage. He didn't know why he bothered. She never responded, she only looked at him with the same plain expressionless face.

"You are leaving." It was more of a statement than a question.

He wasn't sure what to make of her words. He swallowed down his apprehension and said in a calm voice, "I am going to work."

"If anybody comes for me, I *will* kill her." Her tone was not friendly, but not threatening; it was more like she was stating a fact.

Jay swallowed the lump in his throat. He hadn't intended to tell anyone about his unusual house guest. If he was honest, he would rather try to forget she was here.

"I won't say anything to anyone. I thought we were going to trust each other."

"When will you be back?"

This question took him by surprise. Was this it now? Was he still a prisoner in his home, except now he had permission to leave for work? Would she always want to keep tabs on him and know where he was at all times, and when he would be home? He didn't think he could handle that.

"I'm not sure. I won't be done until evening. I have a lot to catch up on. I might be late." *Or I might be home within an hour if they fire my ass.*

She didn't push the subject. She returned to her room without another word, and Jay left a moment later. He felt much better for it. Being in her company was tough.

Maarku was waiting for him as he pulled into his parking space, and he bombarded him with questions as soon as he left the car.

"Where have you been? What's been going on? Glasby's been throwing a fit!"

"I just needed some time," he said defensively. "It was Tanya's anniversary last week…"

"Oh man, I'm sorry. I didn't think. I had no idea."

Jay shook his head. "It's okay. It doesn't matter." He hated himself for using his dead girlfriend as an excuse. Although it was sort of true, for the first three days, anyway.

"Are you off the booze now? You were pretty drunk when you called me before."

"Yeah. I haven't had a drink since Wednesday."

"That's good, because I think Glasby's planning to test you!"

It wasn't uncommon for random substance tests to be given at work. At least he had touched nothing since Edel had fallen into his life.

"So… You have a few bruises…" Maarku said with raised eyebrows.

"I got into a bit of trouble. It's nothing to worry about," he shrugged, trying to feign nonchalance.

"What kind of trouble?"

"It's nothing." He walked forward, trying to escape Maarku's questions, and winced in pain as he pulled open the heavy door to the building, a reminder that he was still not fully healed from taking a beating in the alley a few days ago.

Maarku stared at him through narrowed eyes, but he asked no more questions.

Jay walked straight to his office and tried to ignore the sinking feeling in his chest. He got his head down and started working through his emails, but it wasn't long before Glasby found him.

It wasn't as bad as he expected. He got bawled out and Glasby shouted a lot, but Jay had always been good at apologising, and acting contrite. He had a talent for embellishing the truth, and Glasby left feeling more sympathy for Jay than he deserved. For now, his job was safe, and he felt a monumental amount of relief. That was until Glasby announced that Frank Johnson was taking time out of his busy schedule to see him today.

"Mr Johnson is coming in today to speak with you, Powell. I hope you are prepared to beg for your job. I doubt he has much in the way of sympathy. He is all about productivity."

Jay's shoulders sagged with the weight of stress again. He just might lose his job today, after all. He knuckled down and cleared as much of the backlog as he could. Maarku had covered for him and dealt with most of the problems, but Jay was left with a staffing issue: they had lost another stock checker in his absence.

Spending hours tucked away in the lonely electricals stock room, doing monotonous work, wasn't a pleasant job, but surely, they could find someone who would stick it out? Losing a stock checker meant the pickers would be short-handed and if the pickers were short-handed, then productivity would be down, and they would likely pin it on Jay and his unauthorised absence.

Now he was getting back into his normal rhythm of work, he felt himself relax and Edel had barely crossed his mind at all. It wasn't until he broke for lunch that thoughts of her invaded his head. Would she have eaten anything? So far, he had provided all her meals. He didn't understand why she didn't look after herself.

Frank Johnson arrived at the building after lunch to meet with Jay. Frank had his own office at the top of the building, but Jay had never seen inside it before, because Frank rarely visited the warehouses. His real office was in one of the large skyscrapers at The Grid. Those buildings screamed money and success. It didn't fill Jay with confidence that he was lowering himself to come here, just to see him.

"Good afternoon, Jay, take a seat." Frank said in a business-like tone, gesturing to the chair on the other side of his desk.

Jay shook his hand and sat, not knowing how to act in this meeting. There were no other people here, no HR people, no employment law people, no witnesses, no moderator and nobody to take the minutes. It looked like if he was going to be fired, they weren't planning to do it lawfully. He wouldn't stand a chance at an appeal.

Frank began by introducing himself, as if Jay didn't already know who he was. He started by referencing Jay's good qualities and his positives for work. Then he got straight to the point and asked him about his previous absences and his alcohol consumption.

Jay couldn't help becoming defensive. He argued his case, saying how he had been a model employee for the last twelve months. Instead of keeping his cool, he got angry and began shouting that he worked his ass off for this company, was never sick, tried not to be late (he was always late) and handled a lot of shit they did not pay him for. He knew he wasn't doing himself any favours, but he couldn't help himself. All the stress of the last few days came pouring out, and Frank Johnson got the full force of it.

Frank sat and took Jay's outburst. He didn't silence him or interrupt. When Jay came to the end of his tirade, he was panting, and angry tears had sprung up in the back of his eyes. Jay wasn't much of a crier, and he felt embarrassed that tears were present. Who cries in front of their boss during a disciplinary hearing?

Frank sat back in his chair and puffed out his cheeks, slowly blowing out his breath.

"Jay, you are a valuable employee. I see your worth, and the other members of staff speak highly of you. It might surprise you to learn my reasons for coming here to see you today. My intention isn't to remove you from the staff force. I came to offer you some support."

Jay looked up at him, perplexed.

"May I speak candidly with you?"

He nodded, unsure of what was likely to come next.

"What we speak about in this meeting will remain confidential. I do not share private information about myself lightly."

"Yes, Sir. Of course."

Frank nodded. "My wife was an alcoholic. She struggled for years. She tried hard to beat it, but it had her gripped. It's a terrible, evil disease, Jay. I have looked over your file, and I understand the sporadic absences and the marks on your record are due to alcohol and substance misuse. I'm not here to judge you for it, I'd like to help."

He reached forward and handed a card across the table. It was for addiction therapy.

"Did this help your wife?" Jay asked.

Frank shook his head. "My wife never conquered her addictions. She committed suicide eleven years ago," he said. There was a hardness to his voice that Jay didn't know how to react to.

"Oh... I'm so sorry." Jay started to say, but Frank cut him off.

"It was a long time ago, and I didn't come here for sympathy," he said, brushing off Jay's words. "I came because if I can stop what happened to her from happening to you, then I want to help."

Jay swallowed hard. He could deny he had a problem. As far as he was concerned, he didn't have a problem. But there were so many instances of him drinking to excess, to block out Tanya, and even before that, trying to deal with the demons of his childhood and less than ideal upbringing. He had been in trouble so many times before. He couldn't find any words. Instead, he took the card from Frank's hand and pocketed it. He had no intention of calling the number, but told himself he would try harder, and not drink to excess. Perhaps he ought to adopt a 'never drink alone' policy.

"I'm sorry, Mr Johnson. I know I've been unprofessional."

"Yes. You have," he said, pinning him with his intimidating stare. "I don't want you to leave here thinking you aren't in trouble. We will be watching and monitoring you from now on. Consider this your final warning. You have a lot of potential. Get some help. Get yourself together and show me I'm not wrong about you."

"Yes, sir."

They shook hands again and Jay walked back to his office, feeling a strange mix of both shame and pride. He'd spent his entire existence coasting through life without applying himself, but his boss thought he was worth keeping. He had to show him he was.

Jay was feeling so much better about everything until he got in his car and started for home. He hadn't worried about Edel all day, but now he was on his way back home, the anxiety built. Had she been in her room all day? Or had she ventured out? Maybe she had left the apartment… maybe she had left and would not come back. He shook his head at the hopeful thoughts. There was no way he would ever get that lucky.

He took a few moments to calm himself and organise his thoughts once he had pulled into the underground parking. He didn't want to see her or walk on eggshells around her. She still terrified him.

He swallowed hard, and steeled himself, pushing open the door to his battered old silver car. He traipsed up the stairs, dragging his feet, taking his time, whiling away the minutes.

She was nowhere to be seen when he entered the apartment. Her bedroom door was closed, and he heard no noise coming from her room.

"Edel? Are you home?" He could have kicked himself. Why the hell did he just do that? He was hoping she wouldn't answer. Praying she had left while he was at work.

He had no such luck. He heard the shuffling of feet on the other side of the door, and it slowly opened. She stood facing him, her plain looking, unsmiling face staring back at him.

"Hi," he said, smiling at her and trying not to sound nervous. She didn't respond, she just looked at him.

"Um…" he really should have thought this through. "Have you eaten?" he asked. It was all he could think of.

Her face changed a fraction, she looked momentarily afraid.

She looked down to the floor as she answered a solitary, "Yes."

"Oh." It surprised him to hear it. He looked at her, her body language was so passive – she was staring at his feet, her arms dangling by her sides, palms facing up.

"Does this mean you won't be wanting any dinner with me? Or do you mean you ate earlier?"

She continued to stare at his feet.

"Okay..." he said. "Great talking to you, as usual." He bit his tongue, wondering why the hell he was baiting her. She was a lot less terrifying when she was like this. If anything, she seemed to be more afraid of him.

She didn't move, and he eventually backed away from her to his room to get changed. He took his time, hoping that she would have retreated into her own room before he was done. He was disappointed when he emerged to find her still standing in the same awkward, passive stance, almost as though she needed permission to move.

Jay gave her a sideways glance as he hurried to the kitchen. He needed something quick and easy tonight. After a hasty search of his freezer, he pulled out a frozen pizza. He couldn't help himself – he couldn't just cook for himself. He pulled out another of the same and shoved them both in the oven together.

"I hope you like pizza," he called to her from the kitchen. He saw how she jumped as though he had just burned her.

"Edel?" he spoke her name, and her eyes lifted from the floor to find his face. It was unnatural the way she did it. No other muscle moved. "Uh..." his words wouldn't come out. "Uh... why are you standing there like that?"

Her eyes fell once more to the floor. She seemed to tense up, as though she was waiting for some sort of pain and a deep sympathy filled him. It was as though she had no idea how to communicate at all.

"Why don't you sit here?" he asked her, as he slid a dining chair from under the table. Her eyes lifted from the floor once more and settled on the chair. She walked with careful steps across the apartment, eyeing Jay suspiciously. He waited until she was seated before he pulled out his own chair and sat directly across from her.

"What did you do today?" he asked her. The look of fear was back on her face, as she seemed to search for words. He tried a different question. "Did you go outside?"

"No." The answer was instant. She seemed more able to give direct yes or no answers. He decided closed questioning would be the best way forward.

"Did you watch TV?"

"No."

He thought for a minute. "Did you read?"

"No."

It dawned on him that she may not know how to read. He asked her, "Um. Do you know how to read?"

"Yes."

"Okay, what else…. Um, you said you ate. What did you eat?"

The fear again. She looked so distressed. "Bread."

"Just bread?" he asked her, making a face.

"Yes."

He was relaxing around her again. She seemed far more afraid than he did right now. He leant back into his chair, considering her. She already promised she wouldn't hurt him. She promised he was perfectly safe.

"Do you want a drink?" he asked her.

She looked down at the table and didn't answer.

He stared at her for a moment. Then he asked, "Edel, are you thirsty?"

"Yes." It was almost a whisper. An almost shame filled, terrified sounding response.

"Help yourself." He pointed to the kitchen behind her. "Cups are in there." He pointed to the cupboard. "There is juice in the fridge, or water, or soda."

She seemed to be frozen.

"I'm not planning to be your maid, Edel!" He bit his tongue and tried to quell his fear. What the hell was wrong with him?

Why was he always like this? He took a breath and tried again, without the sarcasm. "If you want a drink, get one."

She rose from the table and turned robotically towards the kitchen. Her movements were slow and precise. She poured herself some water, returned to the table and hovered for a second before finally deciding to sit. She seemed to be torn, having some sort of mental stand-off with herself about whether to drink the water.

Jay pulled his phone from his pocket, checked his emails and saw how she waited until he was busy before she dared to drink the water.

For the next few minutes, he fiddled with his phone, seemingly ignoring the strange girl in front of him. He wasn't though – he was observing everything. She did not move. Her body was statue-still; she did not slouch, tap her feet, or swing her legs. Even her chest barely moved as she silently drew breath. If she didn't make him so uncomfortable, it would be easy to forget she was even here.

Jay turned his attention back to the food. He removed it from the oven, plating it up and returning to the table with it. He slid one towards her and saw her look at it questioningly.

"Never tried pizza before?" he asked her, smiling.

"No."

He picked up a slice and indicated for her to do the same. They ate in silence until Jay spoke to her, "What do you think? Do you like it?"

There it was again; that look of fear on her face. Then her eyes fell downward to the tabletop.

"It's fine if you don't!" he said, laughing a little. It wasn't the best pizza he'd tasted, but it was cheap and quick to cook.

Jay continued to eat, and she copied, matching his pace. In the last hour, his feelings had shifted from being massively afraid to feeling sort of sorry for her. She didn't seem to have any ability to communicate, and it was obvious she was nervous and afraid. It made no sense. If everything they said on the news report was true, she was supposed to be dangerous.

"So, you just sat all day? Except for when you ate some bread?" He picked up where the strained conversation had left off before.

She still wasn't looking at him. She stared down at the table.

"Edel, it's not a trick question; there aren't any wrong answers here," he said, trying to work out why she wouldn't, or couldn't respond to him.

"Yes," she answered his question.

"You sat, all day? And did nothing?"

"Yes."

"Don't you get bored? Or lonely?"

"No."

"Okay!" he said in a voice that indicated he thought she was either lying, or crazy.

He cleared the plates and threw them in the sink to soak, then he busied himself again with work emails. He was far more relaxed with her in his home now, not nearly as uncomfortable as he had felt just one day ago, even though she continued to sit stock-still. She didn't move at all. Even when he'd finished his work and went to bed, she still hadn't moved.

"Um, I'm going to bed now, Edel. I will see you tomorrow, okay?"

"Yes."

He shook his head as he wandered toward his room, wondering if she would still be sitting there in that exact same spot in the morning.

The next morning, Jay got up and showered as normal. She was not at the table and her bedroom door was closed. She must have gone to bed at least. He wasn't nearly as sure of himself as he was last night. He was relieved she remained locked away, out of sight, and he didn't have to see her before he left for work. He didn't want to make awkward, strained conversations, or wonder if she was going to hurt him. Counting his blessings, he hurried out of the door, thankful he didn't have to interact with her.

When he returned, she was still nowhere to be seen. She had

been on his mind all day, like a problem that just wouldn't go away. There was no solution. He couldn't just ignore this and hope it would sort itself out.

He decided to knock, telling himself that last night hadn't been so bad. Besides, they would have to get used to each other, eventually. It's not like she was going anywhere.

"Edel? Are you in there?"

Just like yesterday, she opened the door and looked at him with frightened eyes.

"Come and sit with me," he said.

She followed him out of the bedroom and sat at the table again, in the same spot as yesterday. He questioned her again on her activities of the day, but she didn't give him any more than yesterday, and only spoke yes or no answers.

They seemed to settle into a bit of a routine after that. Each day, Jay would leave for work, and when he returned, he would make food, and try to talk to her while they ate. He wasn't getting far with the conversation. She never offered more than her one-word answers, but now he was becoming used to her presence, he found he was looking forward to seeing her. As the weeks passed, he had started to tell her all about his workday when he came home, and even though she never had anything to offer, it was a welcome change from being alone.

It surprised him to find her sitting at the table when he left his room one morning. She wasn't doing anything, but he noticed she had made herself a hot drink. This was a first: In the five weeks she had been living with him, she'd never helped herself to anything before.

He walked past her and into the kitchen. She never acknowledged his presence, although Jay was certain she knew he was there. He made his coffee and set about searching for his phone. He spotted it on the table, and without thinking he reached over Edel to grab it, supporting his weight on her shoulder to steady himself.

It was almost instantaneous, the way she spun around and stood, lightning fast, simultaneously grabbing him by the throat and slamming his body up against the refrigerator. His feet were a few inches off the ground, but she held him with ease, even though he was a foot taller than her and considerably heavier.

Jay wanted to scream, but he couldn't make a sound. She was choking him, but even if she wasn't, he would have been too terrified to speak. She held him there for what felt like an eternity to Jay but was actually less than 20 seconds.

She was almost panting. She concentrated hard on gaining control of herself and loosened the grip of her fingers around his throat. She lowered him to the ground and set him on his feet.

He coughed and brought his hands up to his throat, massaging the area where her hand had just been.

She stood in front of him, staring down at his feet. The silence between them seemed to stretch on, and she eventually looked up at him with wide eyes. Jay still had his hands around his throat, not daring to speak or move at first, until she backed up a step and set some distance between them. He had been holding his breath, but as she moved back, he let it out in a slow and controlled exhale. He closed his eyes and allowed the back of his head to rest on the door of the refrigerator but winced as his head made contact with the hard surface.

"Are you injured?" She was guarded when she spoke. It wasn't a question that contained even an ounce of sympathy.

Jay gaped at her open-mouthed. "What do *you* think? You're the one who just flipped out on me. I thought you were going to kill me," he said, the mixture of anger and fear getting the better of him.

She remained silent.

"What made you hit me? Did I make you jump? There's no way you didn't know I was there. You said your senses are more acute than any human's. It's not like you missed me. I walked right past you." He continued his angry rant, even though he was still afraid she would hurt him again. She could kill him with ease, but he couldn't seem to shut up.

She continued to stay silent.

"Oh wonderful! More long and awkward silences! Can I expect to get slammed into the appliances every morning then? Or is today just extra special?" His voice was dripping with angry sarcasm, and he wanted to bite his tongue off. Now would not be a good time to goad her.

She spoke slowly then, a space between every word, as if she were addressing an idiot.

"Are. You. Injured?"

"No. I'm fine, I'll be fine," he snapped.

She turned and walked away, disappearing into her bedroom, and closing the door behind her. She didn't come out again before Jay had left for work, and he was grateful for it.

***

Edel was nowhere to be seen when Jay returned. He had spent the day out of the way, with his head down, trying to avoid his colleagues in case they noticed his injuries, but now he was home, he loosened his tie and unbuttoned the collar of his shirt and examined the damage. There was a large, ugly purple bruise around his neck, and it was painful to touch.

He had spent the day worrying about his current living situation. Some days he thought he could manage – he had kept out of her way by working every hour of overtime he could, he hadn't taken a day off since he returned to work. And she stayed locked in her room most of the time and he could pretend she wasn't there. But then today happened, and it really hit home how dangerous she was, and he was anxious.

After spending all day thinking and worrying about it, he had decided his best course of action was to talk to her, trying to be as direct as possible. He knew it wouldn't be an easy task. She rarely spoke and needed A LOT of coaxing to answer even basic questions.

He took a few deep breaths to steady his nerves and decided there was no point in waiting. He gave a tentative knock on her bedroom door and spoke her name. When he prized the door open a little and pushed his head through the gap, he found her sitting rigid, with her back straight, staring at the blank wall. Only her eyes shifted to look at him as he entered the room.

"Can I talk to you?"

She didn't answer him, but she kept her gaze steady, so he knew she was listening.

"Please, can you come out here and talk to me?"

She nodded and rose from the bed, following him out of the door. He sat opposite to her at the table and tried his best to control his nerves. He took a few deep breaths and worked up his courage, then began, "About what happened earlier... Edel, what happened?"

She swallowed hard and looked at him. He could tell she was trying to organise her thoughts, but she was taking too much time and he was getting impatient.

"Edel?"

She was still thinking and not speaking.

"For God's sake, Edel! Will you please just TALK to me? You scared me this morning. You hurt me, and I need to know why? I need to know it won't happen again." Jay's exasperated outburst took them both by surprise. He knew that getting frustrated with her would not help, but she seemed to be being deliberately difficult. He brought his hands up to his head and rubbed his face. "I'm sorry Edel, I just... I think this is hard for both of us." He took another deep, steadying breath.

"Yes," she said.

"Yes, it's hard for you? To talk?"

"Yes."

"Why?"

There was another long pause, before she quietly and tentatively said, "I've never had the freedom to speak."

Jay had never considered they may not have allowed her to speak when she was at the facility. A deep sympathy settled around him,

"Can you tell me why you attacked me?"

"You touched me. I didn't know you were going to do that."

Jay thought back to this morning. He had placed his hand on her shoulder, but it was just an innocent action. He just needed to steady himself, to reach across the table.

"You almost killed me because I touched your shoulder?"

She looked at him, and he understood she was thinking now, trying to put her words together. He held her gaze and waited a little more patiently this time. She eventually spoke, the same apprehension in her voice as she said, "Nobody has ever touched me without hurting me."

"Not ever?"

She didn't answer.

"Not even when you were a kid?"

She didn't answer. It didn't look like she was even trying to answer. She had closed down, and he knew she had no intention of answering these questions.

"But I won't hurt you. I *can't* hurt you," he persisted. He'd just about given up on getting any more out of her when she spoke again.

"My body is different to yours. It responds on instinct. My senses associate physical contact with pain. The physiological responses aren't something I can control easily." Her speech was abrupt, almost robotic. The sentences were short and simple. It was obvious she didn't find it easy to speak so many words at once.

"So, you're saying you didn't mean to? It was an accident or a mistake or whatever?"

The word 'mistake' seemed to set her on edge. Jay saw how she visibly changed in front of him into someone who looked to be terribly afraid.

"Edel, what's the matter?" he asked her. There was a look of shock on his face as he took in her terrified expression.

She couldn't answer this time. And he let it go, feeling a deep amount of sympathy for her. He hadn't given much thought to how mistreated she must have been, but she had just admitted to never having been touched without someone intending to cause her pain. That was a monumental amount of neglect or abuse. There was no wonder she was so nervous around people.

"It's okay. It's okay," he soothed. "We can keep working on the talking thing. You'll get better." He smiled at her, hoping she would understand that he didn't want her to be afraid of him, any more than he wanted to be afraid of her.

She kept her silence.

"See! That's much better," he laughed sarcastically as he got up and walked away.

CHAPTER 12

Monday 3rd April 2102

Jay's Apartment. Helstain, Harpton Main

The following morning, Edel didn't dare come out of her room. She didn't know how she was supposed to face Jay after her unprompted attack yesterday. The fear she experienced when he touched her was immense and unexpected, and she had momentarily lost control. She didn't mean to react the way she did, but she couldn't admit to her mistake. When he questioned her on it, the simple word 'mistake' set her heart racing. XJs do not make mistakes! Mistakes are punishable. Mistakes cost lives. Mistakes cause untold amounts of pain and suffering. She sat on the bed, waiting for him to leave for work.

As time drew on, she realised something was different. She had become accustomed to Jay's usual morning routine. He was normally in the shower by now, but she had yet to hear him move from his bed. She listened to his rhythmic, relaxed breathing and concluded he was still asleep. This change in routine threw her. She liked to know what to expect and couldn't understand why things were different.

She sat for another hour and waited, trying not to worry

about why things were different. He woke, and she heard his bare feet padding across the floor and into the kitchen, followed by the sounds and smells of coffee being made. She heard him approach her room, then the soft knocking of his hand against her door.

"Edel? Are you up?" his voice was soft and calm, but it did little to put her at ease.

"Yes," she mumbled and got up to open the door. Jay was pushing the door open as she approached it, and she caught his eye as he peered in through the gap.

"Hey!" he greeted with a casual smile. She didn't know what the correct response was, so she remained silent, staring at him, wondering what it was he wanted.

"You want a drink?" he asked.

She looked down and adopted the passive stance. *Yes*, she thought. But she had no idea how to voice a want. She wasn't supposed to 'want' anything.

"Come, sit with me," he gestured to the living area. She followed his hand with her eyes, then looked back at him, unable to understand why he was being so nice to her. No human had ever been nice to her before.

She followed him out of the room and sat at her usual spot at the table.

"It's my day off today," he said with a casual smile. She understood it meant he wasn't working today.

"So, what do you want to do today?"

Fear and panic erupted inside her. She had no idea what he could mean. She chanced a glance at his face to see if his expression would shed any light on what he was asking her, but as her eyes met his, nothing was any clearer. There was no single right answer to this question; it was a question with endless choices and possibilities, and choices were prohibited.

"What's the matter?" he asked, looking at her face. "Edel? Why don't you answer me when I talk to you?"

Her head dropped again into the submissive pose. It was ingrained into her; she couldn't help it. She noticed, though, that this Jay person was not angry with her. He was smiling at her with his head cocked to one side. Patience was something she had rarely experienced from a human.

"Edel? I thought we were going to trust each other. I'm trying my hardest, but it's hard for me when you won't speak to me."

She couldn't bring herself to answer. She didn't know what she should say.

Frowning, Jay said, "You need my help to fit in. You need to communicate with me."

She only continued to stare at the table.

"Edel," his patient voice broke her silent concentration. "You told me yesterday, that you're not used to being able to speak. I am trying to understand how hard it is for you to talk, but you have that freedom now. You can speak to me."

He was quiet again for a moment. When she still didn't answer, he peered at her more closely and said, "Edel, do you understand what I am saying to you?"

"Yes," she answered, finally finding her voice. Yes and no answers were much easier to give. They required no thought; they were simple.

He narrowed his eyes and poked his tongue out between his lips. "Do you find it easier to answer direct questions?"

"Yes."

"Can you tell me why?"

She swallowed hard and prepared herself for her next words. "There is only one right answer." She hoped he would understand, but the look on his face was one of confusion. He didn't ask any further questions about it; instead, he said something that threw her off guard straight away.

"Have you left this apartment since we went shopping?"

"No," she said, wondering why he thought she would leave. There were people outside, and too much of the unknown. She wanted to stay away from people as much as she could.

"Let's go out. I'll take you for coffee," he grinned at her.

Fear enveloped her. He wanted her to leave this place. She

had begun to feel safe, enclosed in this apartment, shut up in her room, away from the world. It had been almost six weeks since her escape and nobody had come looking for her, nobody knew she was here, except Jay. He seemed to know what was going through her mind, and he coaxed her with a gentle voice, "You can't stay shut away in here forever."

It's not like she would or could refuse to do what he said, anyway. Those first days of bravery had vanished, leaving nothing but abject fear, even though she knew he couldn't hurt her. Humans terrified her.

"Put your shoes on," he instructed.

An instruction was something she could not ignore. She stood robotically and walked to her room. She slipped the shoes onto her feet and returned to Jay silently, awaiting further instructions.

A moment later, they were ready to leave. He walked through the door, and she followed in silence, desperately trying to keep her apprehension in check. This was difficult, but she must not let it show. Fear was for the weak.

He led the way down the stairs, and she matched his pace, walking by his side. He seemed at ease and was showing almost no signs of stress.

Edel found the act of movement soothing. She was used to spending hours alone, sitting in a closed down state, not thinking or feeling, but she was always glad of the opportunity to move out of her cell. She found if she did not burn off her energy, an uncomfortable, nervous buzzing sensation would start pulsating through her body. It wasn't until they began walking that she realised how much energy she needed to expel. She wished she could run. Then she pushed the want from her mind and snuffed it out. Wanting and wishing for things was not what she had been designed for.

The outside world assaulted her senses as they emerged into the busy street. Traffic zoomed by and there were people in every direction. Edel couldn't help how her head jerked left and right toward every sound.

Jay continued walking, occasionally glancing at Edel with a nervous expression. He crossed the road, and Edel obediently followed. They entered a small cafe, and Edel's senses were assaulted by many new sensations. She couldn't control the way her head jerked and moved to face every sound. Her eyes could not focus on just one thing at a time.

Jay was looking at her, unsure of himself. "Edel? Are you doing okay?" He was smiling at her, but she could smell his fear.

"Edel?" he said, with a little more urgency.

She locked her eyes to his lips as he spoke, trying to ground herself.

"Um, sit down." He gestured to an empty table. She sat and tried to take in her surroundings at a more manageable pace. She closed her eyes and took in the sounds and smells first. There was a lot to process, and she hoped her body wouldn't betray her. A meltdown would be catastrophic.

"Uh, Edel, are you okay?" He sounded worried. She could smell the stress coming off him in waves. Her eyes sprung open, and she saw his nervous face peering at her.

"What are you doing?"

The answer wouldn't come right away. She needed a moment to adjust to her new surroundings and forming a sentence right now was one thing too many to concentrate on. She allowed her eyes to close again.

"Why are your eyes closed?"

She could hear the urgency in his voice. For some reason, closing her eyes was distressing him in some way. She took a breath and said, "It helps me to process properly."

He didn't have an answer to that, but he didn't seem any less afraid. He remained silent until she eventually opened her eyes again, then he asked her, "What do you want to drink?"

Panic smashed into her. How was she supposed to know what she wanted to drink? Her voice seemed to freeze in the back of her throat.

"Edel, what do you want?" he asked again.

How could she make him understand? She'd never had a choice about anything before. She didn't understand how people knew what they wanted. Never mind the fact that this was her very first experience of anything quite like this. She didn't know so many drink options existed, and she had no idea what any of them were.

"Are you thirsty?" Jay asked, his tone was more aggressive this time, his annoyance at her continued silence showing through.

Edel's automatic submissive response won out, she cast her eyes down to the table as she answered a single, solitary "Yes."

Jay swallowed, and asked with a little more patience, "Then, what do you want to drink?"

She couldn't look up from the table, the fear was too much. He'd asked her an impossible question, one with no right answer. Her insides knotted together as she awaited the punishment she would surely receive for not being able to answer his question.

The waitress approached and Jay seemed to have given up waiting for Edel to choose. He ordered two of the same, some fancy caramel latte from the specials board.

The silence drew on, and Jay seemed to grow more uncomfortable. He pulled his phone from his pocket and started typing on it. Edel sat still as a statue, not knowing how else to act. She occasionally glanced around at the other humans in the room, discreetly observing them to learn how they interacted with each other.

The waitress returned with their drinks, and Edel noticed how at ease Jay was with her. He laughed as he joked with her about the weather. Edel listened to it, perplexed. She hadn't heard much laughter before in her life, and she didn't understand the concept of humour.

"What are you thinking about?"

Edel's body jolted in shock as he spoke to her. Nobody had ever asked her that question before. Her thoughts were private, for her alone. She wasn't supposed to have independent thought, or at least if she did, she was never meant to communicate them unless instructed.

He sighed and leant back in his chair. "I thought we were going to trust each other."

She heard his words, but she couldn't respond. She was trying, but trust didn't come easily.

"Ugh! Edel! Please try. Be honest with me. You are not there now. You have freedom now. You have choices and you are allowed to speak and think and form opinions. You are allowed to voice them. Please, tell me what you are thinking."

He was right, she knew. So far, this man had kept his word. He had been kind to her, and he had helped her. She wanted to trust him. She took a deep breath, and looked at his face, forcing herself to make eye contact. "It's very busy in here," she said.

Jay scoffed at her, "What? There's like five people! How is that busy?"

She didn't know how to continue. All her life she had never contradicted or disagreed with a human. But really, what could Jay do to her? She reminded herself that he couldn't hurt her. He would be too weak, too slow, too clumsy. She could snuff out his existence without even breaking a sweat. She drew breath, aware that she was still sitting in silence, and spoke. "There are thirteen people here, fifteen including us."

She said it in such a matter-of-fact manner that it surprised her to see Jay look around the room and count.

"I only count nine, including us," he said, frowning.

Was he questioning her? That had never happened before. When an XJ gives a fact, it is a fact, without question or exception. Usually, whatever answer she gave to any question was taken at face value. XJs do not make mistakes.

She swallowed down her fear and forced herself to disagree with him. "There are two in the bathroom, three staff, and one smoking outside. He will be back in a minute – he left his jacket on the chair."

Jay's eyebrows raised up as he considered what she had noticed. "Okay, but how is that too much?" he asked.

She was gaining confidence now, and answered with almost a whisper, "It's all too much. I can hear them – their conversations, the clinking of cups and cutlery. The sound of chewing. I can even hear their hearts beating in their chests. Then there are the coffee machines, the humming of the lights, the sounds of the toilet flushing and the noise of the hand driers in the bathroom. The smells – too many to name. Too many I've never experienced before. People, the scents of their perfume and the fragrance of the food and drinks. The cleaning solution they use to wash the crockery. The movement of the people, it catches my eye and steals my concentration. There is a lot to take in here."

She stopped and took a breath, awaiting the pain that would surely come from speaking so freely. That was the only time she had vocalised a thought in her entire life, and most likely the most words she had ever spoken in one go.

Jay leant back in his chair and shrugged and said, "Then don't take it in. Just ignore all that. Relax and drink your coffee."

If only it were that simple! She didn't answer him at first. How was anyone meant to ignore all this stimulation on their senses? It took a moment before she realised, he didn't understand. Normal human senses were nowhere near as acute as her own. She took a moment to work up her courage and tentatively asked him, "When we walked in here, what did you notice?" She braced herself for punishment. Questions were forbidden at Poly-Gen. XJs do not ask questions, only obey orders.

Jay shrugged. "I noticed it's fairly quiet, and they accept cash in here. What did you notice?"

Her answer came immediately this time. "As we walked in, I did a head count and saw how many men, women and children were here. I judged the approximate weight of each person and determined who could be a possible threat. I noticed how many members of staff are here, and where the emergency exits are located. I located the cameras and noticed the telephone behind the counter. I noticed who is definitely armed, and who has the potential to be armed. That man by the counter has a heart condition. I can hear its irregularity as it beats. The two women at the back of the room are speaking a language they think nobody else here understands. I noticed all this before you had even closed the door."

Jay stared at her as though he was looking at an alien from another planet.

"This is what it is to be XJ5. It isn't something I can ignore."

Jay gaped at her open-mouthed. "You're doing really well," he murmured. "I can't imagine how alien all this is to you."

Edel was stunned. Nobody had ever said a single encouraging word to her in her life. Not knowing how to react, she slipped back into silence for a long while, and Jay seemed to be lost in thought.

Taking a deep breath and working up her courage, she brought the cup to her lips and took a sip. It differed vastly from the coffee Jay had given her before. It was thick and creamy, and the intense sweetness took her by surprise. Having tasted nothing so sweet before, it was almost painful as it hit her taste buds. She tried to swallow it down without drawing attention to herself, but her face must have given her away, because Jay let out a sudden bout of laughter. Shock stopped her in her tracks. She swallowed the liquid in her mouth and stared at Jay, trying to understand the laughter.

"I'm sorry." He was still laughing at her. "I guess you don't like caramel latte!"

Edel froze in terror. Openly disliking something was a punishable offence. She was expected to push through pain, torture, and unpleasant experiences, without complaint. No matter what, it was her duty to keep going. Never give in.

She swallowed hard and waited. The pain of the compliance chip never came, and she realised again that Jay could not hurt her.

He seemed to realise something was wrong. "Hey! It's okay. You're not in trouble. It's fine, don't drink it if you don't want it." He was being so kind, so patient. Not knowing what else to do, she reverted to silence.

She noticed how relaxed Jay had become. His breathing was smooth and rhythmic, his heart beat at a constant pace. He wasn't finding her nearly as frightening as he had when they first met.

"Can I ask you something?" he asked. She stared at him, unable to understand why he was asking permission to ask questions.

"Yes."

"Before, when we were walking here, you looked… odd," he managed to get out. She didn't understand what he meant, and after another moment of silence he elaborated, "You seemed jumpy. You sort of looked dangerous. You had me worried for a moment."

She was still waiting for the question. She hadn't realised that these series of statements were his question.

"Edel?" He pushed on, gazing at her face with interest.

"There were a lot of new sensations. Things I've never experienced before," she said. She couldn't admit that it was difficult for her.

"But you looked mad, like insane mad. I guess I'm asking if that's the sort of thing I should worry about?"

"I was in control."

"What do you mean? In control of what?"

"Of myself. I won't hurt you, as long as I'm in control of myself."

Jay did not look comforted by this information. His frown set deeper on his brow as he asked, "What happens if you're not in control?"

Edel realised he had no knowledge of meltdowns, what they were, or how they worked. She didn't know how to answer his question. The truth was, if she lost control, he wouldn't be safe. Nobody would be safe.

Jay didn't push for an answer, and after it was obvious she would not offer a response, he shook his head and said, "Will you be alright walking back home?"

The word 'home' sounded foreign to her ears. "Yes." she answered, hoping it was true.

"Are you ready to leave now?"

Her eyes glanced to the unfinished coffee she was still yet to drink, then darted back to Jay, but she was unable to ask the question.

"Leave it. It's obvious you didn't enjoy it!" He smiled as he spoke to her. "I've got a few more questions. Would you mind trying to answer them?"

She wondered again why he was being so nice to her. It was unheard of for anyone to ask her nicely for anything. "I will try."

He spoke to her as they left the little cafe. "Why did you help me?"

She stared at him for a minute, trying to put it into words. "My primary objective is to protect human life. Your life was in danger. Those men were armed."

Jay hesitated a moment. "I thought you were meant to be some sort of weapon, not a protector. All the news reports say you're dangerous."

"I am both. If I am instructed to kill, I kill. If I am instructed to protect, I protect."

"But there were no instructions on that day. So why did you help me?"

There was a pause, she was trying to work out how much she should say.

"You can tell me, Edel. I won't hurt you, remember?" he encouraged her.

It took her a moment to organise her thoughts. Her speech sounded wrong as she talked in short, abrupt sentences. "You were trying to help me. Then, they hurt you. They were armed. They were going to kill you. Their intentions were to hurt me, too. I didn't give them the chance."

Jay stopped dead in the middle of the street and stared at her. "What happened to them?".

"I killed them," she said bluntly.

Jay's face turned ashen, and the pace of his heart picked up. Had this information come as a surprise? She wondered what he was expecting her to say. She couldn't understand his fear response to her admission of murder. They were a threat to his life. To her mind, he should feel safe, not afraid.

"You killed them?" he repeated, the shock ringing clear in his voice.

She was uncertain of herself now. Killing humans without a direct order was the worst atrocity an XJ could perform. Jay was clearly having some sort of emotional reaction to finding out the men had been killed. She stood, staring at him, waiting to see what her punishment would be.

"You can't just kill people, Edel." He set off walking again, and she blindly followed him. "They weren't good men, and they wanted to hurt you, but you can't kill people. Promise me. Promise me now, you won't kill anybody." His body was shaking, displaying his fear or displeasure. Or both.

She didn't answer right away.

"Promise me, Edel, or the deal is off. I don't want to help a killer. You've got to promise you won't kill anyone else."

She nodded. Killing people was nothing to her. She didn't take pleasure in it, but she didn't feel remorse or guilt either. She did only as instructed.

They walked back up the steps to Jay's apartment building in silence.

"Well, what now?" he asked as they entered through the door.

She turned to look at him, wondering what he meant.

"We've only been out an hour, Edel. What else do you want to do today? Edel? Why is it so hard for you to answer a question like that?" he asked, after she had been standing in silence for some time.

"I don't know the right answer to your question," she admitted.

He frowned. "There isn't a wrong answer! What are you

not understanding about freedom? You can do whatever you want."

How do people know what they want? she wondered.

"Was there anything about our outing today that you enjoyed?"

Her blank expression gave her away. "How can you not know if you liked something or not, Edel?"

She swallowed her fear. She was becoming braver in this humans' company. "How do you know if you enjoyed something?" she asked, full of wonder.

He seemed flummoxed by her question. "It makes you happy. It brings you joy. If you enjoy something, you will choose to do it again."

She was lost in thought. Being outside was overwhelming, but exhilarating. There was so much she had never seen or experienced before. She would like to do that again. The act of walking had been calming. She needed to move her body more. She knew it would settle her anxious mind.

"I think I enjoyed the walking," she mumbled and swallowed, as the fear smashed into her like a hurricane.

Jay smiled at her and shook his head. "Well, it's obvious you didn't enjoy the coffee." He laughed again. Her eyes were wide with confusion as she watched him disappear into the bathroom, chuckling to himself as he walked away. She retreated to her bedroom, staying there for the rest of the day and tried to make sense of this strange day.

He didn't bother her. Whatever he was doing, he was occupied, and he seemed completely relaxed. She eventually heard him leave and felt her stress lift once she was alone again. She waited until she was certain he was gone before she emerged from the safety of her room, then helped herself to water and paced up and down, trying to expel some of her pent-up energy.

Jay returned after a couple of hours. She had already returned to her room, but she heard him enter. He called out to her, "Edel, I brought dinner."

She peeked out from her door. "Come on! It's good. It's Chinese food," he said, reaching for plates. They ate, and he chatted amicably to her, though she had nothing to add to his stories. He smiled as he showed her a bag of clothing he had picked up for her from a charity place. "You can't get by with just one set of clothes, Edel," he said.

She stared at the bag, a bewildered expression on her face. She didn't know what to say.

"Are you gonna help with the dishes?" he asked once they had finished eating. "Come on, I'll show you."

He continued his mindless chatter as he showed her how to wash up. "So, you enjoyed walking outside?"

She tensed up, wondering why he would bring up her admission that she had experienced enjoyment.

"Don't look so worried, Edel! It's good. You are allowed to like things."

She swallowed and nodded her head in agreement, though she didn't fully believe him.

"I was wondering if you would like to go for a walk with me now? It's dark outside. Things look different."

"Yes."

He smiled at her short, one-word answer.

A little while later, they were out in the street again. The traffic was lighter, almost no cars, and the streets were lit. He was right; it did look different in the dark.

"Are you doing okay?" he asked.

She could tell he was wary. Her head jerked at every noise and her eyes darted in short, rapid movements as she took in the sights.

They wandered past a bar, music was blaring out through the windows, and she stopped dead, almost hyperventilating.

"You don't like music?" he asked her. "It's okay, it's okay," he said in a panicked voice, turning back the way they came and walking away from the noise.

He crossed the road and walked towards the park. It was dark, but there were lights illuminating the path that ran through it. Once they were at the entrance, and it was quieter, he quizzed her on her bizarre reaction to the music.

"You seemed afraid back there. Did the sound of the music scare you?"

She forced herself to look at him, but she could not answer. She knew he was trying to communicate with her in a way she could handle. Direct questions were easier, but admitting fear was not.

"Edel? Have you heard music before?"

"No. Not until I was free."

"And, you don't like it?" he pressed on.

"There are a lot of sounds at once. I can't make sense of it. It hurts me."

He was looking at her like she was insane. "It *hurts* you?" he asked, in a tone that suggested he didn't believe her.

Her eyes took in the vast open space in front of her. She'd never seen anything like it until the M ordered her to leave Poly-Gen. It filled her with a strange sense of wonder and possibility. The smells of the grass and the trees and the sounds of insects in the overgrowth around the surrounding edges were intriguing. A man wearing illuminated strips on his clothing jogged by them into the dimly lit park. Edel watched him run, feeling a pang of want for herself. If she could move her body, and exhaust some of her energy, she would be calmer and more able to function.

"What are you thinking about?" Jay gazed at her intently.

There it was again – that question. And it wasn't an accusatory question either, he wasn't angry that she had been thinking.

Her eyes travelled to the man. How could she tell him she wanted to be running like him?

He followed her gaze. "Are you worried about the jogger?" he asked.

"No."

"He's not running away from anything, he's just running," he tried to reassure her.

"Yes. Running is good."

"You like to run?" he asked, with an unsure voice.

"It helps." She offered only that, and he didn't push for more.

"You can run. Run, if that's what you want to do."

She turned to look at him. There wasn't enough information in his instruction. Run where? How far? How fast? How long?

"Edel, I'm trying to understand what you need, what you want. Can you help me? Can you talk to me?" he asked, after she had been standing, staring into the darkness for a while. "Do you want to run?"

She swallowed hard. "Yes."

"Then what is stopping you?"

She was almost shaking with fear. She couldn't admit that she didn't know, what if she should know?

He tried a different approach. "Can you find your way back home by yourself?"

What kind of stupid question is that? "Yes."

"Okay. How about if I go home, and you figure this out by yourself? Just come back when you're done!" He shrugged.

Her eyes were wide as she tried to understand what he was saying. He was giving her freedom to come and go as she pleased. She didn't answer to him, or to anyone. The thought that this was some sort of trick flitted across her mind, but he seemed so eager to help her, she wanted to believe he would not turn her in. After a moment of consideration, she decided to take this opportunity, but she would not exhaust herself. She would not give him enough time to alert the authorities. Her head moved up and down in a slow nod, as she accepted his offer.

"I'll see you at home then, okay? It doesn't matter where you go but look out for border patrol. You have no ID, and this is a casher-free zone. You remember the first day we met? The guy in the grey uniform? Avoid the grey uniforms."

She nodded again and then watched as he turned and strolled away.

She set off, a feeling inside her she had only experienced once before – The day she escaped from Poly-Gen. It was exhilarating, exciting, and breath taking all at once. She was free. Truly free right now. She had no objectives, no targets to meet. No direction to take. She could run until she WANTED to stop, not until she was so exhausted, she had to stop. There were no scientists timing her, or pushing her, or hurting her to see if she could keep going through injury. Choices were a heady feeling.

She felt better almost as soon as she set off. The built-up stress of five weeks in the small room in Jay's apartment was being released. She dared not stay too long; she circled the park, keeping close to the footpaths. Once she was across the far side, she sprinted back as fast as she could. Finally using her muscles felt good.

She slowed to a walk as she approached the entrance to the park. Her breathing was steady, you would never know she had just sprinted half a mile. She hadn't even broken a sweat, but she felt both calm and energised.

The calm feeling didn't last long. Her nerves were already creeping in as she made her way back to Jay's apartment. Would he have expected her to stay longer? Or what if she had taken too long? She hadn't pushed herself to breaking point. Would he send her back out and force her to run until her lungs burned and her legs gave up?

She reached the door and gingerly pushed it open, the fear of what was waiting inside growing in her chest.

Jay was sitting on the sofa, watching the TV. He looked up from where he sat. "You're back," he smiled. She didn't have an answer, she just stared at him, wondering why he would state something so obvious.

"How was it?"

Again, she didn't have an answer. She had no idea what he could mean.

"Did you enjoy your run?" he tried again. He met her blank expression with a small, patient smile. "Would you choose to do it again, another time?"

"Yes," she answered, knowing she would do that again if she had the choice.

He smiled at her. "Then you enjoyed it. You can go again whenever you want, Edel. You have the freedom."

She nodded and walked to her room. It was starting to sink in now. Freedom! Choices. Possibilities.

She slept well and woke refreshed. The act of running the day before had helped her immensely. She listened to Jay's movements in the kitchen, and the familiar sound and smell of coffee being brewed. She peered out of her bedroom door, hesitating, still unsure of how much leeway she had.

"Morning!" He walked toward her and handed her a key. "Here. Make sure you lock the door if you go out today."

She stared at the small silver key in her hand, and then looked at him, unsure if she had misinterpreted what this meant.

"It's okay," he said. "You don't have to leave the house, but if you WANT to, you have the freedom to come and go as you please."

He grabbed his jacket and headed out the door. "I'll see you later – if you're home!" He laughed cheerfully as he left.

Edel settled into a sort of routine after that. She would see Jay in the morning before he left for work. She would spend most of her day in her room, doing nothing, then when he came home, she would eat with him, and listen to him talk about his day. Then she would run. She found she looked forward to it every day, and after her run, she would use the shower. It was a luxury she had never been afforded before and another thing she looked forward to each day. On days where Jay didn't work, he would take her outside with him, usually to a cafe.

As the weeks passed, she was becoming more confident and embracing her new life. She still didn't talk much, and Jay still did almost everything for her, from cooking, to washing, to grocery shopping, but she was learning every day. She found she looked forward to seeing him when he returned from work. He didn't frighten her as much anymore, and he didn't seem to be afraid of her either. She was beginning to trust him.

CHAPTER 13

Saturday 22nd April 2102

Helstain Club Scene

Danny and Tony made their way through the busy club. Danny had agreed to come and celebrate his friend's birthday, but he'd had more than enough now. It was hard to cope with the noise, the flashing lights and the sheer amount of people compacted into this one confined, sweaty space.

He was wearing his shades, even though it was late at night and the sun had gone down hours ago. He never left home without them and his trusty pair of earplugs that emitted a quiet hiss of white noise. These items were invaluable for blocking out the world around him and drowning out background noise. He could still hear Tony, or anyone else speaking directly to him, but he found it easier to focus when he wasn't constantly assaulted by every tiny sound.

They walked out into the fresh evening air and climbed into the cab that was waiting for them.

Danny removed the earplugs, and Tony waited for his friends' ears to adjust. If he spoke now, it would sound too loud and be a shock to Danny's ears. Unfortunately, the driver of the car did not know this information.

"Where to fellas?" he called from the driver's seat.

Danny flinched as his hands shot up to cover his ears, and Tony, who was quite inebriated, fell about laughing. Danny couldn't help but see the funny side too. He smiled, feeling thankful his best friend had forgiven him for what happened a few weeks ago. All he cared about was that his friend wasn't afraid of him.

"Helston," Tony yelled from the back, causing Danny to grab his ears again. "Whoops! Sorry man!" He was laughing again.

Danny gave the driver the correct address, and they set off. His ears had adjusted now, and he was calming down from the crowd.

"Thanks for coming tonight, Danny. I know you don't really enjoy clubs," he said, pushing his long hair out of his eyes.

"I wouldn't miss your birthday! Besides, it was fun. I had a good time."

They talked a little about their evening and how and why Tony was on his way home alone instead of following home the guy he'd been chasing all night. Tony was drunk and as they talked, he was becoming increasingly sentimental, telling Danny how much he loved him. Danny, good humouredly, threatened to punch him. And Tony laughed even harder.

"I mean it!" he wailed, throwing his hands in the air with a dramatic flair. "You're my best friend!"

"So do I!" Danny threatened with a smile, curling his hand into a fist, and shaking it at his friend's face.

It wasn't a long journey to Helston, it was only the next district, but Tony had already lolled his head back against the backrest and his eyes were beginning to close.

Danny poked him hard on the arm, "I'm not carrying you inside, Tony!" he joked.

Tony opened one eye and mumbled something incoherent. Danny only smiled and shook his head, thinking how he might actually end up carrying his friend to bed tonight, and how it wouldn't be the first time.

He allowed Tony to drift off into sleep, and leaned back into his seat, staring absent-mindedly through the window, calming down from the stimulation of the club.

Danny sat up with a jolt of surprise. The calm he had just been experiencing vanished and was replaced by a surge of panic, as a strange sensation he had never experienced before came over him. It felt like a vibration inside his body, deep inside his bones. A throbbing, pulsating sensation. It wasn't painful, but the unfamiliarity of it was unsettling. He held his breath and tried to work out what was happening. He placed his hand over his chest, trying to determine if his bones really were vibrating, or if there was a more logical explanation for this bizarre feeling. The vibrations moved and swelled until he felt them through his entire body, and his head seemed to almost buzz.

It frightened him, as his head automatically turned to face the window. It wasn't a conscious choice, but he couldn't look away. He stared out of it, desperately trying to see what was out there. He couldn't explain it, but over there, in the direction his head was facing, there was *something* there. There was nothing to see, only high-rise buildings and apartment blocks, and he tried to tell himself he was being ridiculous. Even so, his eyes continued to search.

Out of nowhere, a terrible fear gripped him. His heart raced in his chest, and his hands curled into tense, tight fists as he tried to breathe through the terror. His eyes continued staring through the window, but there was still nothing to see.

The car continued on, and the fear lessened, then vanished, as quickly as it had appeared, almost as if the feeling had been erased. But Danny still felt an overpowering need to see. He craned his neck in an unnatural way as he tried to see behind him, unable to tear his eyes away, almost as if he was being pulled by a magnetic force. As they drove, the vibrating sensations lessened until he could no longer feel them, and he found he had full autonomy over his body again. He turned his head and looked around himself, examining his hands and arms, trying to see if there was anything different about his skin.

What the hell was that? It felt like nothing he'd ever experienced before. He looked across at his sleeping friend and wondered if it was something that happened to normal people. Maybe it was something perfectly normal, and he'd just never experienced it himself before today. Hadn't Tony tried to explain anxiety in that way? The way his chest shook, and feelings of fear would rise from nowhere? He could use someone to talk to about this, but Tony would be no use right now.

The driver pulled up outside their house and Danny dragged Tony from the car. Once inside, he tried to talk to him, but he didn't get far. Tony was drunk and making very little sense.

Danny thought about calling Gemma, but it was late, and she had been working. Not that he thought she would mind, but he hated to bother her and interrupt her sleep. She never complained about having to work such long hours, but she must be tired.

He assessed his body one more time. There was nothing at all to indicate anything was wrong, and he was starting to wonder if he had imagined the whole thing. Perhaps it was a reaction to the alcohol? He had drunk more than usual, but he didn't feel intoxicated.

He considered calling his dad, but no doubt he would end up with a lecture on why he shouldn't drink alcohol. He certainly wasn't in the mood for another lecture on how different he was or how dangerous he might be if he got drunk. Besides, his mother had been an alcoholic, and as a result, Frank rarely touched the stuff himself. He couldn't discuss this with his dad.

He picked up his phone and dialled Jenson's number before he had time to talk himself out of it. If anyone could give him any inkling on what he had experienced, it would be Jenson.

"Hello?"

Danny regretted calling already. This guy was in his late 50s. He didn't need people calling him in the middle of the night.

"Um, Hi... It's Danny, Danny Johnson," he said, trying not to feel stupid for wasting Jenson's time.

"Danny? Is something wrong?" he asked, sounding a little panicked.

"No, not really..." Now he had made the call, he had no idea what he should say. It seemed ridiculous to be getting so worked up about a 'feeling'.

"It's 2 a.m., Danny. What is going on?"

"I'm sorry, I shouldn't have bothered you." He was about to end the call, but Jenson continued talking to him.

"Danny, you wouldn't be calling me at 2 a.m. for no reason. What's going on?"

He deliberated on if he should say anything. He felt foolish for getting so worked up. "Um, something strange happened," he began. He didn't really know how to continue. This sounded so stupid! "I wondered if you knew what it was. Or if it's normal for someone like me..." he trailed off, not knowing how to put the strange sensations he felt into words.

"What happened?"

"I don't know, exactly. It was just a weird feeling. A strange sensation in my body. I've never felt it before. It felt like my bones were vibrating. Like my chest was shaking on the inside."

Jenson was quiet on the other end of the line, but Danny felt the weight behind his silence. This *was* something serious.

"What is it? Is there something wrong with me? Am I sick or something? It only lasted for a moment, and then it vanished. But for a moment, it really scared me."

"You felt afraid?" he asked.

"Well, yeah!" he said, unable to keep the defensive tone out of his voice. This is the reason he didn't like discussing things with Jenson. He was so fixated on how Danny 'felt' about everything, as if he wasn't supposed to have any feelings. He tried to swallow his annoyance.

"Danny, are you sure it was... uh, did it feel like *your* fear? Or..." he cleared his throat. "Never mind," he trailed off.

"What do you mean?" he asked, confused by the question. *Did it feel like MY fear?* It made no sense.

"I don't think it is anything to worry about," he said. "But Danny, if it happens again, I want you to move away from it. You mustn't go chasing these sensations."

Danny frowned as he tried to understand this weird cryptic message. *Chasing these sensations?* "What do you mean?" he asked. The question came out with more aggression than he would have liked. He hated not understanding things.

"Just, if it happens again, I want you to stay calm, turn around, and walk away until you can't feel it anymore."

"What is it? Is it dangerous? Like a meltdown? Will I hurt somebody?"

"No, no. Nothing like that. As I said, it's probably nothing. Just promise me you will get away if you feel anything like it again. Okay? And call me immediately. You should probably talk to your dad about this too, Danny. He likes to know what's going on with you."

The line went dead without another word, leaving Danny dumbfounded. He stared at the phone in utter disbelief. Jenson normally liked to dissect every little issue in great detail. Everything from his thoughts and feelings to his blood pressure. He couldn't decide if this really was nothing to be concerned about, or if Jenson had blown him off, but why would he do that, when he was always so interested in everything that Danny thought, felt and experienced?

He wondered if he should tell his dad about it after all, but if Jenson wasn't any help, his dad certainly wouldn't be. One thing he could take comfort in was that anything he discussed with Jenson remained confidential. Jenson would always encourage him to confide in his dad, but that decision was ultimately left up to Danny.

He went to bed, full of questions. When the morning came, he confided in Tony about the strange experience he'd had in the taxi. Tony listened intently, but didn't show any signs of concern, and by now, Danny was wondering if he had made a fuss over nothing. It only lasted for a minute, and it hadn't happened again, and Jenson didn't think it was anything worth worrying about. He shook his head. The news of the Poly-Gen breakout must be influencing his mental health. It was making him paranoid or something!

He shoved it to the back of his mind and tried not to worry himself about it. Jenson had said it wasn't something that made him dangerous to other people, so he decided he could safely sit on it, and wait to see if it happened again before he worried about it anymore.

CHAPTER 14

Saturday 10th June 2102

Helstain Club Scene

It had been almost four months since Edel had fallen into Jay's life, and Jay was finally feeling comfortable enough to go out and socialise again. Maarku was about to order another round of drinks when he turned to Jay and nodded toward the pretty blonde by the window.

"She's checking you out!" he said with a grin.

Jay followed his friend's gaze, and his eyes settled on the pretty, young blonde. He lifted his glass, flashed her a smile and gave her a cheeky nod.

"She's gorgeous! Do you think I should ask her out?"

Maarku looked at him with a face that said, 'Not in your wildest dreams.' "Just drink your drink, lover boy," he said with a smirk. "She'd never date you! Especially since you are standing with a dirty foreigner like me."

"What do you mean?" he was smiling, but he knew what his friend was saying. Racism was part and parcel of everyday life. And Maarku was a casher.

"Don't you know who that is?" he asked, his jaw dropping in amusement. "That is Katie Stroud. As in STROUD. One of the wealthiest families in Helston. God only knows what she is doing in here. It's hardly upmarket, is it?"

Jay couldn't stop glancing over to her. He didn't think he would stand a chance with a girl like that, and she was only half his age, but there was no harm in looking at her...

Maybe it was his imagination, but he was sure she was checking him out too.

He and Maarku talked. Jay had divulged he had a new roommate, but he was trying his hardest to stay off the topic of Edel. Every time Maarku asked about her, he changed the subject. Eventually Maarku said, "If I didn't know any better, I'd say you were trying to keep me away from your new roommate. You never let me come over anymore! And you stopped coming out with me! What's going on?" He winked at his friend and made some rude gestures with his fingers. "Are you more than just house mates? Hmmm?"

Jay almost spat his drink across the bar. The idea he could be in a relationship with Edel was hilarious. "No. Definitely not," he said dryly. "She's just not good around new people, that's all."

When Maarku didn't look convinced, Jay embellished the truth a little. "She's a casher. She's been through a lot."

"Oh!" Maarku's voice was grave. Jay knew he would have drawn his own conclusions about what that meant. He would think exactly what Jay thought when he first met Edel – that she was a trafficked sex worker who had been abused in awful ways. "Sorry man, I didn't know."

Jay knew his friend had a lot of empathy for girls like that. He'd grown up knowing what happened to those poor girls.

They changed the subject after that and got onto work, and sports, and who was sleeping with who in the office. Maarku caught Jay's eye and nodded his head to indicate he should look behind him. Jay turned around to see the pretty blonde from the window standing next to him. He didn't put much thought into it; he just tapped her on the shoulder and said, "Hey! Have a drink with me."

He flashed her a smile which she returned, then she seemed

to look him up and down as if she were appraising him for sale before she said in husky tones, "White wine."

Jay stood talking with her for a while. Maarku was right, her name was Katie Stroud, and she lived in Helston. She didn't work; she didn't need to. She studied dance at the performing arts college and was hoping to be accepted into some upmarket ballet school soon.

"I should probably get back to my friends," she murmured, holding his gaze, and offering him an apologetic smile.

Jay didn't even think about it. "Let me take you out sometime," he blurted out.

She gave him a coy smile. "Do you have a phone?" she asked.

He handed her his phone, and she placed hers on top, automatically transferring the numbers. "I'm free Friday," she said, as she sashayed back to her table.

Maarku's mouth was hanging open. He was just about to erupt in cheers for the magnificent feat his stud of a friend had just pulled off, when Jay held his hand up in front of his face and hissed "Be cool man!" They both exploded with raucous laughter and clinked their beer bottles together.

Edel wasn't out of her room when Jay returned home. It was late, and he wasn't at all surprised she had gone to bed. She seemed to enjoy routine.

Their living arrangement was working well now they had become used to each other. She was nowhere near as terrifying now as when he first met her. The truth was, he felt sorry for her. The level of abuse she had lived through was incomprehensible and he felt a strong need to protect her.

He picked up his phone, feeling oddly nervous about texting Katie. Before Edel fell into his life, he had dated a lot. Never anything serious, not since Tanya, but he was no stranger to one-night stands, or casual flings, or even friends with benefits. She'd been living with him for three months now, and he hadn't even considered dating anyone.

It took him an age to get the message right. He wrote and rewrote it a dozen times before he finally had one he was happy with. His thumb hovered over the send button longer than necessary before he finally took the plunge and sent it. It came as quite a shock when his phone pinged with her response. He assumed that even if she got back to him, she would take a while to respond. Isn't that the done thing these days?

They texted back and forth, chatting a bit before they decided on a time and place. He offered to pick her up, but she said she would rather meet him there. She had chosen some fancy elite place in Helston, and Jay wondered if he would need a bank loan to pay for dinner there. His finances had taken a serious hit since Edel had come to stay. He'd had to feed her, and clothe her, and he had never known anyone spend as long as she did in the shower. Water was an expensive commodity.

Friday came, and Jay was dressed in his best navy shirt, fiddling with his hair, trying to get it to sit properly, when Edel came back from her run.

"Edel, I'm going out tonight," he said as she walked in.

She looked at him with a face that screamed *what are you telling me for?* But she didn't speak.

"Will you be alright?"

The look continued, and he shook his head in amusement. "I might not come home. Or, I might not come home *alone.*"

That got her attention. Her eyes narrowed, "You are planning to bring another person here?" she asked, clearly finding the idea of another person in her space upsetting.

"Well, not planning exactly, but it might happen. Would that be a problem for you?"

"Who? Why would you bring someone here?" He could hear the distress in her voice.

"I'm going out on a date, Edel. With a woman. She might decide to come back home with me." He paused to see if she understood what he was saying. "You know?" he asked, hoping he wouldn't have to spell it out.

She nodded, but Jay wasn't sure if she understood why a woman would come home with him. He assumed she didn't know much about sex.

"You won't tell her about me?"

"No! You should know that by now!"

She nodded. "If she comes home with you, I will stay in there until she has gone." She pointed to her room.

It was a better response than Jay had hoped for. He expected her to tell him he could never bring another person into his house ever again. He nodded, and that was the end of that brief conversation. She disappeared into her room, and he didn't see her again before he left.

He arrived at the restaurant early and waited impatiently for Katie to arrive, tapping his foot nervously. The restaurant was posh, and Jay felt out of place, looking at all the high wage earners here.

She arrived, and he couldn't help but be floored by her beauty. She looked stunning. Her long, wavy hair was pulled over her shoulder, flowing down one side of her body and revealing her backless black dress.

"You look amazing!" he said. She smiled with confidence and thanked him for the compliment.

They were shown to their table by the waiter, and Jay was surprised that the atmosphere between them was so easy and comfortable. Katie talked a lot of herself, but Jay didn't mind. It was a refreshing change after the weeks and weeks of talking at Edel and getting no response. At least this was easy, if a little tedious.

Jay couldn't deny that he'd had a perfectly nice evening, but once the meal was over, he didn't offer to take her to a bar, or to anywhere else. He offered to walk her to her car instead. She hadn't driven herself but had the family chauffeur on hand to collect her at a moment's notice.

She leaned into him, and he gave her a half-hearted kiss. It's not that he didn't find her attractive. She was by far the prettiest girl in the room, turning heads wherever she went. And it was such an ego boost that she was interested in him, but she simply didn't interest him, and they didn't seem to have an awful lot in common. Her political views on cash payers and illegal immigrants were the polar opposite of his own, and he wasn't sure he wanted to spend time with someone with such snobbery, who had no compassion for those so much less fortunate.

He couldn't tell if Edel was up or not when he returned home. Her door was closed, and he could hear no movements from her room.

The following morning, Edel peered out of her room and looked over to Jay in the kitchen. He looked across at her and said, "It's safe. There's nobody new here."

"Yes," she said. Jay wasn't surprised that she knew it already. She heard *everything*. It made him uneasy at the idea of bringing a girl back.

Edel walked into the kitchen and made herself a drink, and Jay couldn't help noticing how her confidence had grown. She took a seat at the table, and he couldn't help but smile. She still didn't initiate conversation, and when he spoke to her, it was still very stilted and one sided, but he still somehow enjoyed her company.

"What are your plans for today, Edel?" He asked, knowing full well she would struggle to answer this innocuous question.

She hesitated, the same look of fear in her eyes, like a rabbit caught in the headlights. She wasn't sure how to answer. Jay took pity on her, and said, "It's fine, Edel. You don't have to decide right now." He laughed at her, and she stared back at him, unable to understand what was funny.

Jay ignored her and went back to his usual morning routine. He picked up his phone and was shocked to find three messages from Katie. It surprised him – last night had been okay, but he couldn't see this going anywhere. He opened the first message.

< Thank you for last night, Jay.
I had a lovely time.

> K x >

He smiled as he read it. Going out on a date and having real conversation with someone had made a refreshing change. He hadn't realised how lonely he was until Edel had fallen into his life. But she wasn't much company. He opened the second text.

> < I'd like to see you again. >
> When are you free?
> K x >

He read the message again. Had she really enjoyed it that much? He wasn't sure he'd had that much of a good time that he wanted to repeat it. On the other hand, it was refreshing to have someone so openly admit interest. At least she wasn't playing games.

He opened the third and final text.

> < I'm attending a charity ball
> next week. Would you like
> to attend as my date?
> K x >

Jay stared at the message. She was more than just interested. She seemed a little desperate. He put his phone away without responding. He wasn't interested in anything serious, and she was half his age. What was he thinking when he asked her out?

He looked up to Edel. "I'm going out to the city today. Would you like to come with me?"

Her eyes moved across to his face, but she didn't give him an answer.

"I'm just going to run a few errands. You should come, it will be good experience for you."

He felt sorry for her already. It was obvious she was struggling with the idea and unable to say so. "We can take it slow. I promise I will look after you. I won't leave you," he said, wondering if he had put his finger on what was bothering her.

She looked at him, and he could tell she was building up to asking a question. It seemed she needed to psych herself up first. She took a breath and then hesitantly asked, "Will there be many people?"

He frowned at her. "No. There are no people in the city," he said, his voice dripping with sarcasm. He quickly realised she didn't get his humour, and sighed, all joking gone. "You need to get used to people," he said.

***

The boundary patrol stopped them on their way. Jay offered his ID to the man and vouched for Edel. Edel eyed the man, and did not speak, except to confirm that she was accompanying a legitimate of her own free will.

Jay opted for the train, deciding it would be a new challenge for her, but now they were travelling, he was regretting his decision. It was a short journey to the city, but it seemed Edel was already floundering. She was acting the same as the previous times she'd been forced into unfamiliar situations: her eyes and head darted around to face every noise. Apart from these jerking movements, she sat perfectly still and rigid. She looked uncomfortable and almost crazy.

Jay leaned forward to speak to her, but before any words left his mouth, she jerked herself back, as though she thought he was going to harm her. He studied her face, trying to understand what was wrong, what she was thinking. She was staring at the floor; her arms laying by her sides.

"Edel?" His voice was gentle, but it still made her jump, and the fear in her eyes was plain to see. "It's okay." He reached forward as if to comfort her, but before his hand connected with her arm, she attacked. It was quick as lightening. He didn't know how it happened, but one minute he was sitting across from her, reaching forwards. The next, his face was pinned into the seat where she had been sitting moments before, her hand pushing down on the back of his neck with force. He let out a terrified yelp, and other passengers looked up from their phones and conversations to see what the commotion was. She was almost hyperventilating, and her body was shaking as she removed her hand from his neck and dropped into the chair she had just dragged him out of. She stared down at her knees again, unable to meet his eye.

"What the fuck, Edel?" he hissed through gritted teeth.

She was still staring at the floor.

He shook his head, unable to process what had just happened. His heart was racing, and his body trembled with fear. It seemed every time he relaxed around her and let his guard down, she would show just how dangerous she was.

The other passengers quickly became disinterested again, turning their attention back to their conversations and phones, and Jay and Edel spent the rest of the short journey in complete silence.

The train approached the station in the city centre, and Jay muttered, "We're here."

Her eyes finally found their way up off the floor and she followed him, still in silence. Once outside, he turned to her and said, "You wanna tell me what happened on the train?"

She looked so afraid.

"Edel. You attacked me," he said. "Why?"

"I thought you were going to touch me." Her voice was quivering as she spoke.

"I wasn't going to hurt you."

When she still had nothing to say, he added, "I won't try to touch you again, okay?"

"Yes."

Yes! Is that all I get? No apology? No reassurance that it won't happen again? He bit his tongue and didn't say what was on his mind. Instead, he asked, "Are you gonna be okay now? Are you gonna stay calm?"

"Yes."

He raised his eyebrows at her short, abrupt answer. There was no point holding a grudge, and she didn't hurt him so much as startle him. Okay... terrify him. But it wasn't like the time she smashed him into the refrigerator. He let it go and moved onto new things.

"I guess you've never seen the city before. What do you think of it?" he asked.

"I've been here once," she said.

Her answer took him by surprise. "When?" He never imagined that she would have been here by choice.

"The M brought me here. He needed to collect his new identification papers."

"The M? The one who broke you out?"

"Yes."

They wandered along and she was doing well. Not as jumpy as he had seen her before, but she didn't like the crowds of people. They made their way to the huge glass fronted skyscraper in the centre of the grid, and he stopped outside the door.

"Do you want to come in? Or do you want to wait here?"

He may as well have asked her to choose her own gruesome death for the look she gave him. When would she realise choices were okay now?

He left her outside, deciding that having someone as obviously strange as Edel in his boss's company would draw unwanted attention to him. When he looked back at her as he walked in through the door, she was standing rigid. The only part of her that moved were her eyes, as they darted back and forth, settling on anything that moved. He hoped she would be okay.

Jay made his way up to the JoBi Corp offices. He'd been here a few times before, but it was still nerve-racking. There were a lot of important people. He had hoped to be in and out, without seeing anybody who knew him, but as he approached the office he needed, Frank Johnson was just walking out of another room.

"Jay!" He greeted Jay with warmth, which was more than he expected. "Just the man I wanted to see! Are you here to collect the cash permits for your stock team?"

"Yes, sir."

"Excellent. Do you have a minute? I'd like to discuss a few things with you." He was already walking away, towards his office with the air of a man who expected to be followed. This wasn't a question, it was an instruction.

Jay's heart beat a little quicker. He couldn't refuse his boss, but Edel was waiting outside, and he had promised her he would only be a few minutes. A sense of dread crept up on him as he followed Frank in through the door. He couldn't help thinking he was in trouble again.

"Don't look so worried, Jay," he said as he sat down in his chair. "Did you ever give that therapist a call?" he asked, clearly trying to sound casual.

Jay cleared his throat. "No sir, I haven't yet. But I will if I feel the need."

"You *are* off the alcohol though?"

Shame and embarrassment forced its way out of Jay's pores. His face coloured in anger as he said, "Yes. But that's really none of your business."

"It is my business! I can't be having one of my warehouse managers under the influence at work."

"I'm not," he said shortly. "There have been no instances of *heavy* drinking since our chat." Jay felt that the fact he hadn't got drunk should be enough for Frank. He wasn't an alcoholic, so there was no need to quit completely! He did wonder to himself why, if he was so sure that he didn't need alcohol, was he unable to give it up completely? But he wasn't about to address that here and now. And he certainly would not see a therapist about it!

Frank nodded. "Good," he said, with a tone of finality. "Now, the other reason I needed to see you… Why have you still not filled that stock checker position in your downstairs stock room?"

"We keep filling it, sir, but the employees don't last. It's a mundane job, and lonely. They spend all day alone, counting stock. Even the cashers can't stick it out."

Frank nodded. "We need that vacancy filled, Jay. Productivity is low."

"If we created two positions, so the work wasn't so lonely, we wouldn't have so much of a problem," Jay countered.

Frank's forehead knitted into a crease. "I'm not looking to improve peoples' social lives, Jay. I'm looking to run an effective business model. That post only requires one employee."

"I'm not trying to be difficult, sir, but nobody wants that job. They stick it for a few weeks, then they leave. Even the pickers argue over who is going to be shut away downstairs all day. If you want it filling permanently, you need to increase the incentive to stay."

"Are you proposing a wage increase?"

"Well, yeah. Or perhaps a loyalty bonus – stick it for so many months and get a wage increase. Anything to make it seem more appealing."

"Work isn't meant to be appealing. It's meant to be work. It doesn't make much business sense to offer more money for such a low-level and unskilled job. Any idiot can count stock."

Jay hated that Frank only saw his staff as workers, not as people. Especially cashers. It was as if he felt that because they are poor, they have no right to want anything out of life beyond working to earn enough to feed themselves.

"Yes, and it isn't difficult work. But training up new people every few weeks takes time. I have to waste time interviewing, then I have to remove someone from picking to train a new stock checker. The computer system is difficult to learn, especially for a casher with no IT skills. But no legitimate citizen would choose to do the work. If you want someone to stick at it, it needs to be better paid work."

Frank nodded, then he waved his hand as though he was disinterested in this conversation.

"Fine. Just sort it. Let me know what you think is a reasonable wage to offer and I will make it work." He handed Jay a card with an email and business number on it.

"Yes sir." He stood to leave, not sure how he, a lowly stock manager, had convinced one of the company heads that his ideas were worth listening to. He left the office and collected the cash permits. Cash permits were small cards with a chip on the back and a photograph of the person it belonged to on the front. They allowed non-legitimate employees the right to work in the area and had to be updated every six months. If a casher had an outdated card and were stopped by border patrol in a legitimate only area, they would be detained and possibly beaten. The law had little sympathy for rule breakers.

As he made his way back into the street, he spotted Edel. She stuck out like a beacon, standing in the same spot, rigid and still like a statue. Her eyes had settled down now, they were moving at a more 'human' pace. As he walked closer, she turned to look at him, almost as if she knew he was there. He smiled and said, "How are you doing?"

He should have known better than to expect an answer. Shaking his head, he ignored her lack of response. "Come on. Let's get some lunch."

He set off through the crowds, leading her to a quiet restaurant. He led her to a table and studied her as she took in her new surroundings. She appeared to be struggling. She closed her eyes, just as she had so many times before, and he found himself wondering how hard all this really was for her. He didn't interrupt her this time; he sat patiently and waited for her to relax.

She eventually came around, but she seemed jumpy.

"I thought you would be okay in here... It's quiet. There aren't many people." He was looking at her with interest, trying to work her out. Sometimes this girl was terrifying.

"There aren't many people. But it isn't quiet."

Jay didn't know what to say to that. "What do you mean?" he asked.   She surprised him with an actual answer. He had been expecting her to stay silent.

"There is a lot of noise, and many new scents here. Things I have never known before."

Jay nodded. If he thought about it, he could see her point.

The kitchen was open plan, and you could see right into it. He took a moment to listen to what he could hear. There were sizzling noises, and banging noises coming from the back, and shouting and laughing. Then there were the servers who were chatting and there was gentle music playing on the speakers. *Shit.* He hadn't noticed the music. She said music was hard for her ears.

"Does the music bother you?" he asked, concerned. She didn't need this to be any harder.

She frowned. "It's not painful today."

Jay assumed that was because it was a gentle melody. The other times she had heard music, it had been some sort of heavy beat, techno, dance crap. He couldn't blame her. That stuff made his ears want to bleed too.

"Do you like it?" He watched her tense up and look down to the table. Every time! Every time he asked her if she liked something, she closed down. "It's okay if you don't, Edel," he said, hoping she would see she wasn't doing anything wrong.

He knew she wouldn't answer, so he changed the subject. "What do you want to eat?" he asked, pulling out a menu. It was not the right way to go. *Shit! Choices are just as hard for her as opinions!*

He helped her out, seeing as she looked so terrified. "They do a tasty mac 'n' cheese. That's what I'm having. Should I get you the same?" He offered her a patient and sympathetic smile, but it seemed lost on her.

"Yes."

Jay smiled. Her one-word answer seemed much less irritating these days. He ordered and scanned his ID over the reader. Legitimate only restaurants usually had people pay upfront. "Um sir, your card has been declined. Would you please try again?" the waitress said.

"Declined?"

"It says insufficient funds," she whispered discreetly.

Jay pulled out a credit card and passed it over, acting casual, but he felt anything but calm. Once the waitress had left, he pulled out his phone and checked his bank accounts.

"What is wrong, Jay?" she asked out of nowhere. "You are showing signs of stress."

"I've got no money," he said. "I'm fucking broke!" The panic was rising in his voice. "My wages – they've deducted more than half of my wage for those missed days at work. And the authorities have fined me for being drunk and fighting. And I hadn't noticed. I've been so busy with..." he couldn't say it was her fault. "um, other things... I hadn't noticed that my money has been disappearing left and right."

He studied his statement a moment. "Oh, God!" he said, putting his hand to his face. "My rent hasn't even left yet." He tried to see where he had gone so wrong. He did a mental calculation of all the things he'd spent money on over the last few weeks. He had bought Edel a whole wardrobe of clothing and shoes, right down to underwear and socks. None of it was expensive, it was all second hand, but when he added it up, it came to more than he thought. Then there were his bills, especially his water bill. That had almost tripled in price, and the amount of food he spent on groceries had doubled too. He was feeding, clothing, and looking after Edel rent free, and he simply could not afford it. Then another thought hit him. His fancy dinner with Katie... that was expensive. His eyes ran through his statement again, hoping to see it, but it wasn't there, which meant that it was still pending. He would incur further fines if that left his account while he was overdrawn.

"Shit. Edel. We're in trouble here!"

"What will happen?"

He could tell she had zero concept of how serious this was. "If we don't pay rent, we will be evicted. I'm already on my final warning from missed payments last year. We won't be able to rent another place without at least a three-month deposit. They won't trust that we are good for it if we've been evicted from property for being unable to pay. Even if we get an extension, or payment plan in place, the arrears I've racked up here will leave us without money for months. We won't be able to afford to eat!"

"How do we get more money?" she asked.

"We can't. I already work full time." Then he looked at her and stated the obvious. "You need to find work. You need to pay your way, Edel. I can't afford to keep supporting you."

He took in her expression. She looked like she was unable to understand what he was saying.

"What skills do you have that we could use?" he asked.

She stared back blankly. "What skills?" she repeated, frowning.

"I'm sure there are loads of jobs you could do. Um, cleaning? Or..." he looked around the room, trying to draw inspiration from it. His eyes settled on the waitress bringing their food. "Waitressing?"

He took in her terrified expression.

"You'd get used to it," he offered.

She shook her head. "Too much stimulation. It would be dangerous."

The waitress set down their food and gave them a quizzical look but made no comment.

Jay watched the waitress walk away, then hissed at Edel, "What does that mean? What would be so dangerous?"

She looked away from him, unable to look him in the eye. "It's a design flaw. We are dangerous when overstimulated."

"What does that mean, though? Dangerous how?"

"We lose control of ourselves. The scientists call it 'meltdown'. Once meltdown occurs, there is nothing to be done, except wait for it to pass. Even activating the compliance chip doesn't stop a meltdown, it just incapacitates us long enough for us to be restrained, so we won't hurt anyone else."

"What do you mean, hurt anyone else?"

"I don't want to frighten you Jay, but I am dangerous. If I entered into meltdown, everyone in this room would die. I would not be able stop until it was over."

"You'd kill people?"

"Yes."

"You wouldn't kill me though?" he said, disbelievingly.

"It wouldn't be by choice."

"Oh, well, that's super reassuring!" he said with obvious sarcasm. "How would I know if you were 'over stimulated' or whatever?"

She stared down at the table, and he knew he was losing her.

"Edel! This is serious information," he hissed. "Are you saying you could attack me at any time and not stop until you have killed me? And there is no way you can control it?" He dreaded her answer.

She still wasn't answering him, and he was getting concerned for his safety. "Edel! I need to know what would cause that to happen. Or what to look out for."

She took a deep breath, but still didn't meet his eye. "I usually get some warning. I know when they are going to happen. If I tell you to run, you need to run."

"Peachy!" He couldn't believe she didn't think this was worth mentioning before. "So, what is too stimulating?"

"Noise and unfamiliar scents are the worst. Close contact with multiple humans. Physical contact. Too much movement."

"Too much movement?"

"When there are things moving across my field of vision or flashing lights," she clarified.

"So, you will work, but it needs to be in a quiet place, away from people. And then you will be okay?"

She nodded.

A slow smile spread across his face, and he slapped his hand down on the table in front of him in excitement. "Oh my God! I've got the perfect solution!"

He launched into telling her about the position at the warehouse. "It's quiet, I'll be there to help you, I will do the training with you, and the best part is, you will work alone! You will barely have to see or speak to another person." Then he added, "And, they have left me in charge of deciding how much this job role is worth. I can pay you whatever I like! We won't need to worry about money. And if you stick it out and don't quit, I'll be a fucking hero at work! It's a win-win for everyone!"

He ate his meal feeling like everything in his world had clicked into place, and all his worries were over. Edel remained silent. He knew she would be concerned about the idea of her comfortable and predictable life changing. He also knew that she would find it difficult to disagree with him or refuse to do what he said.

His phone buzzed as he received another message from Katie. Wow, she was coming across as *very* desperate.

< Need confirmation for the Charity Ball, Jay. It's invite only. Should I add your name to the list?
K x >

Oh, what the hell. Why not? His mood had just been seriously improved. He texted back,

< Sure. Sounds great. :) >

CHAPTER 15

Monday 26th June 2102

Jay's Apartment, Helstain, Harpton Main

Two weeks later, Edel was dressed in the plain black uniform Jay had supplied for her. It was short-sleeved, so he had given her a bandage to wrap around her wrist, to cover her identity stamp. She allowed the bandage to wrap further up her arm, to cover the worst of her scars, where they had poured acid on her to see how long her skin would last. Her other scars had faded to silvery white lines. They looked no worse than old stretch marks, and were not that noticeable, but the chemical burns on her body had never healed. It made her shudder to think of the pain now. It was strange to think how nobody had hurt her since she escaped.

"Edel, are you nearly ready?" Jay's words pierced her thoughts. She stood awkwardly in the doorway, not sure what to expect from this day. Nerves at this level were a new sensation. Jay had promised to help her as much as he could, but he wouldn't be with her all day, and she would have to interact with other people. She didn't know how to do that.

Jay was staring at her, an odd look on his face. "Hmm," he flicked a rubber band at her. She didn't know it was coming, but her hand reached up and plucked it from the air with ease, regardless. Her reflexes were astonishing.

"For your hair," he said, when she gave him a questioning look. "Your hair is getting long, Edel. You need to tie it back."

Her hand felt the back of her head and she touched her hair, allowing her fingers to run through the length of it. It was soft, not at all like she expected it would feel when it was short and stubbly on her head. And the colour was a dirty blonde, dark, almost ashy.

She looked at the band between her fingers, and then at Jay. She had no idea how to tie hair, having never had hair to tie. Fear sparked in her gut. What if she was meant to know?

Jay strolled toward her, displaying no nerves at all. "I can show you, if you like?"

She hesitated in front of him.

"I will have to touch your hair, Edel. Would that be okay?" he asked with a soft voice and encouraging smile.

Her head bobbed up and down in a miniscule nod.

"Okay. Turn around." He gestured with his finger, spinning it in the air in front of her.

Edel's heart jumped into her throat. Standing stationary with her back to him put her in a very vulnerable position. She fiercely reminded herself that Jay would not hurt her and did as he instructed. His hands came towards her, and she held her breath as he grabbed her hair and scooped it into a bunch, then started pulling the rubber band over it. She stood rigid, hating the feel of someone being this close to her. The sensation of her hair being touched felt repulsive. His hand bumped the back of her head as he wrapped the band around, and she flinched. Her skin felt hot and itchy, as though something was crawling over it. She wanted to shrug it off her body, shed it and leave it behind. Touching was not something she thought she would ever become used to.

"You okay?" he asked as he finished and backed away from her. "Well, I can see how much you enjoyed that," he said with a smirk.

Enjoyed? That was not something I wish to repeat. Her thoughts echoed in her head. Jay's sarcasm was lost on Edel. She found him so confusing.

"You look great," he said, smiling. She felt the back of her head and found the shortest little ponytail there. It pleased her to find her hair no longer fell into her face as she moved her head. Having hair had taken some getting used to.

They drove mostly in silence to the warehouse. He tried to make conversation, but she was too nervous to speak, and he eventually gave up trying to force words out of her. It wasn't until they pulled into his parking space that he turned to her and said, "It would be best if we don't tell anyone we live together, Edel. You're going to have to pretend you don't know me. When you speak to me, you need to call me Mr Powell, not Jay. Do you understand?"

"Yes."

"Are you feeling um, calm?"

She realised he was asking if she was in control of herself. He may as well have just asked, 'would she lose her mind and kill half his workforce?' She looked him in the eye. "I'm in control."

He nodded. She noticed how his nerves had spiked now, too, revealing his concern. This no longer seemed like a good idea, but it was too late to back out now.

She followed him out of the car, and he directed her to the front door. "Go on ahead and wait outside. If there are people waiting to get in, just nod, smile and say hello. Talk to them a little, okay?"

Dread filled her. How many people should she expect? What should she say to them? What if she did it wrong? What if they knew?

"Edel! You're going to be fine. I'm not asking you to do anything you can't handle," he said with an encouraging smile. She nodded and tried to believe what he was telling her.

There were approximately thirty-five other people stood outside the front door, each wearing similar uniforms to her. They were talking and laughing but stopped as she approached.

"New picker?" one of them shouted across to her. She couldn't help it – she froze, panicking with not knowing how to interact with these people. Her eyes stayed fixed to the ground in front of her. She could sense their curiosity, each one of them were staring at her. She stared harder at the floor, wishing it would open and swallow her, until she heard beeping from inside the building. Jay had entered through the back and was disabling the alarms. She felt relieved as she heard his feet shuffling towards the front door, and the locks and bolts being undone.

The others greeted him and then one of the young men said, "Think we've got a noob today, Mr P."

Jay looked across at her and pretended not to know who she was. "Oh. You must be Edel? You're here for the stock checker position, right?"

She heard someone's excited whispers of "Yessssssss". Jay looked across to the girl with a grin.

"Does that mean I can do picking today?" Then her face fell a little, and she added, "Or am I stuck with training?"

"No, Evie, I will do the training. You're needed on main deck today." They all wandered in, and everyone seemed so relaxed around Jay.

"Edel, follow me, please. There are a few things we need to sort out in the office."

She silently followed him, and he closed the door behind them, gesturing for her to sit down on the chair across from his desk.

"Did you talk to them?" he asked. A smile had appeared on his lips, but she didn't understand he was making fun of her. As far as she was concerned, she had failed her objective. She hadn't spoken to the other humans. She sat in silent dread, awaiting her punishment.

Jay seemed to realise what was going through her mind. "You're not in trouble, Edel. I'm not angry with you!" He had his usual look of concern on his face as he spoke to her. "I understand how hard this must be for you. It's something we can work on, okay?"

She didn't have an answer for his encouraging words. Instead, she looked around his small office space. It was a mess, with papers and empty coffee cups strewn haphazardly on every available surface. She smiled internally, thinking how this was just like Jay. She had never met anyone as disorganised or chaotic as this human.

Jay cleared his throat and then switched from her friend into a much more serious person. It was unusual for him to be so business-like. He had her sign a few documents, "Sign it Powell. It's fine if you use my name, nobody will know," he said, after it became obvious she didn't have a surname to offer. Next, he went through the emergency procedures and took her photograph. "For your work permit, so you have permission to be in the area unaccompanied," he said, seeing the obvious look of distrust on her face. Last, he handed her a small book with a map on it. These warehouses were huge.

"The stock you will check is done downstairs in the basement." He pointed to the correct page on the map, then he gave her a slip of paper detailing all the door codes. She studied it for a moment and committed them all to memory, then held it back out towards him, not understanding he had intended for her to keep it.

"It's so you can open the doors, Edel." he said, looking at her with mild amusement. "You need that. All the codes are different."

She took it back and didn't argue, even though it was highly unlikely she would need to look at it for reference. The information was there now, in her head. She would remember.

Jay led her to the downstairs stockroom, explaining why nobody else wanted this job. "It's dark, it's lonely, and the stock you are checking all looks the same. It's all batteries and light bulbs, and nondescript electrical cables and adaptors and stuff. Nobody can tell it apart just by looking, so they have to be scanned individually, and things get mixed up when they are shelved incorrectly. It's a pain in the ass."

She looked around. It wasn't well organised.

He spent the rest of the morning talking her through the computer system and showing her how to operate the scanners.

"Edel?" he spoke her name with hesitation, and she knew without a doubt he was going to ask her a question. She was getting the hang of conversations and social cues now. Her eyes rested on his face as she waited for more.

"How is it you know so much about computers? I mean, I never thought you would have had access to them before. I thought I would need to go right through the basics with you, but you already know how to do it all."

She looked down. She didn't know how to tell him she had learned none of this stuff in the traditional sense. Much of the knowledge in her head was implanted there before her awakening. She didn't want to tell him things about Poly-Gen. Every question he asked pulled memories forward she was trying hard to keep buried. She didn't want to think about her life before she met Jay.

She hadn't noticed how rigid she had become. "You don't like to talk about your past, do you?" he asked, concern etched on his face.

Another question about likes and dislikes! It was getting easier to handle these things under normal circumstances, but she was feeling the stress of too much new today already. She couldn't answer again, and stood solid, like a statue, eyes fixed on the floor.

"Hey, it's okay Edel. Look at me!"

She raised her eyes at his command.

"How about this? I will ask questions, and you can try to answer them. But if you can't answer them, you can just say no."

She stared at him. *No? As if I've ever told a human no!*

He seemed to realise the problem. "Or we can come up with a phrase that you can say, and I will back off, and not ask anymore? Like uh- 'off limits'? If I ask you something, and you can't tell me, or don't WANT to tell me, you can just say 'off limits', and I will back off, okay?"

She nodded feebly.

"So, how do you know how to work a computer?"

She hesitated a minute before finding her voice. "Off limits."

He smirked to himself but kept his promise and didn't ask her anymore. He spent another hour going over the procedures and quality control checks, then they broke for lunch.

"There is a cafeteria on the top floor." He held out some paper money. "They accept cash, and it's not expensive."

"Will you be up there?" she asked, but she already knew the answer. Management did not eat with the staff.

"You can do this, Edel. Just follow the others. Stand in line, choose what you want. Pay. Sit. Eat. Easy," he shrugged. "You may as well get it over with." He stared at her expectantly until she eventually plucked up the courage to leave the stockroom unaccompanied.

It felt odd to walk the hallway, surrounded by humans. She was dressed the same as them, and they all thought she was one of them. She'd had a sort of uniform at Poly-Gen. Grey shorts and grey vest. It was how they made sure the XJ's were easily identifiable. That, and the fact they shaved their heads. But this uniform didn't mark her as something different, or dangerous, or less than. It marked her as one of them.

She took the stairs to the top floor, the feeling of physical exertion helping to ease her anxiety about entering a room full of people. It was noisy; she could hear the racket from two floors below. The chatter was a loud hum from here. There were a lot more people who worked here than she first realised. At least two hundred in the cafeteria alone.

She walked on until she came to the top floor. The cafeteria took up almost the entire floor. Large windows spanned the whole corridor. She could see into it, see the people, laughing and joking, and chatting and eating. Her head jerked across to the table nearest to the door. They were speaking, but it wasn't the language she was used to. There was a strange sensation of information buried deep inside her head being pulled forward, and she stood for a moment, unable to react until she could make sense of it. It was a language she understood. They had implanted it in her head long before she was awoken. Her mind worked overtime as she translated the words involuntarily. Without warning, her internal voice shifted to that language, and her thoughts were coming out all wrong. The sentence structure was different. She heard one speak to the other in his language, a language she understood, but could not name.

"What's she staring for? You'd think she'd never heard cashers talk their native tongues before!"

"Maybe she's legitimate?" the other man said, looking her up and down. "Maybe she hasn't heard other languages being spoken before."

The loud shout from across the large room took her attention, and her mind switched back to English. It was a jarring sensation, and it took a second for her to understand the words. It looked like a confrontation of some sort, but the people were laughing. Edel didn't understand, but she knew she did not want to enter this room. It was too much. She hung back, and stared a minute longer, stuck between fear and failure.

Another small group of people walked past her and pulled open the door. Her feet stayed fixed to the floor as she observed them. They were so relaxed as they entered the room, laughing and talking. Choosing their meals was easy for them. She tried to follow them, but she couldn't seem to make her body work. Fear was not a new sensation, but somehow this was harder to contain. Maybe because she hadn't experienced it for some time. Or maybe because there were no other XJ's in her head, filtering a forced calm through their shared consciousness.

She knew she couldn't stand there for her entire lunch break and eventually went back and hid in her stockroom, away from the people, and hoped Jay wouldn't be angry with her. She considered the implications – he was her boss now, but she was unsure about what that meant. How much power did he hold over his workers? Did he punish them for disobeying? Would he punish her for not following his orders?

She got to work and began organising the existing stock. Jay had said it was hard because all the items looked similar and were easy to confuse, but Edel didn't find it difficult at all. She couldn't understand what was difficult about it when the numbers on each code were different.

She was busy, lost in the work's monotony. It was almost therapeutic, relaxing even. Reaching up, she grabbed a box of light bulbs she recognised had been shelved incorrectly and walked across the room to their correct space when it happened. It was instant. The feeling took her by surprise, just as it had a few weeks ago. She had hoped she had somehow imagined those sensations, but there was no mistaking the feel of another XJ. There was one then, and there was one here, now.

Panic erupted in every cell of her body. Had they found her? She took a minute to assess her responses and concentrated. *ONE. Only one.*

Her heart rate increased at speed as the fear took hold. This didn't feel right – she did feel scared, but her initial panic had subsided now. The fear she was experiencing was not hers. It belonged to the other. It was immense, almost uncontainable. Her hands shook with the adrenaline and her breathing drew in short shallow rasps as she tried to gain control of herself.

She closed her eyes, trying to find this intruder. There was only one, she was certain of it. She mentally located them; they were outside the building. She held her breath and waited, not knowing what else to do. It must be one of the eight who escaped, and she wondered how they had made it to Harpton Main. The M had spaced them out by hundreds of miles when he dropped them off, but then, she had no clue what had happened to the four in the other car. Whoever was out there was afraid. It almost felt as though they didn't understand what was happening. She remembered the strange sensation of being in the company of only one or two other XJ's before, when they first escaped. It felt as though the emotional connection they shared was concentrated. It was uncomfortable and unpleasant, but it was nothing to fear to this degree.

She stood stationary, waiting. The XJ was on the move. She sensed them enter the building. The pulsating in her chest vibrated harder as the intruder drew nearer, and the immense sense of fear increased to an almost unmanageable level.

Her thoughts raced. *They would find her. They would kill her. They would take her back.* She liked her new life. She wasn't ready for it to be over.

But the fear... it made no sense! The fear she was soaking up from this other was excessive. She closed her eyes and tried to uncouple herself from their consciousness and close herself down to shield herself from their emotion. She would still be aware of it, but the feelings would be lessened. But why did this other not do the same? Feelings were banned for a reason. They were uncomfortable for every connected mind.

The feelings assaulting her turned to ones of confusion. She felt a complete lack of understanding and uncertainty mixed with the fear now. It made no sense. Surely this other had not forgotten how to close down? XJ's do not forget easily.

Relief flooded her system, and she felt the pulling sensation retreat. Whoever it was was leaving. A long, slow, calming breath left her lungs as she began to relax again.

She tried to add up what had happened, but none of it made any sense. She had felt another, but it was as if the other didn't understand what was happening. If they were looking for her, she was not safe, they would know where she was now. But if they were looking for her, why would they send only one? And, if they were searching for her, she should be restrained and on her way back to Poly-Gen by now, or maybe killed on sight.

It took another half an hour before Edel was calm enough to continue with her work. The XJ, nor anybody else, had returned. It made her wonder if it had even happened at all. It had been a stressful day, learning new skills and being amongst so many humans... But then thoughts echoed in her mind from the night she had had the same experience, and she knew she wasn't imagining it.

Jay wandered into the stockroom and apologised for his absence, pulling her from her reverie.

"Wow, Edel! How have you got through all this already?" he seemed astounded at the volume of work she had accomplished.

She didn't answer him. Questions about Jay's loyalty forced their way into her mind. Had he betrayed her? Was he was working with the HGMR? Maybe they were waiting for the perfect opportunity to take her.

She studied him. He was calm and relaxed, and he didn't seem like he was lying to her. She tried to shake the idea from her head. Jay had been good to her. He was her friend.

"You okay?" he asked. "How was lunch?"

She swallowed hard. Time to confess. "I didn't eat," she said, not able to look at him as she spoke. She didn't know if he would be angry with her.

He smiled and shook his head. "I thought it might be a bit much for you."

Confusion hit her again. Why wasn't he angry? She had disobeyed a direct order! She looked up at him, wondering what punishment to expect, but when her eyes found his, there was nothing there but kindness and patience.

"It's okay, Edel," he was still smiling. "You must be hungry though?"

She shook her head. "I can manage for weeks without food." She bit her tongue, halting her words. She wasn't supposed to divulge information about herself to humans.

She looked at him to gauge his reaction, but he seemed unphased by this information. He only shrugged and said, "People will notice if you never eat, so you should bring some lunch with you, even if you don't eat in the cafeteria."

She had little experience of humans, but Jay's reactions to situations seemed so abnormal to what she would expect. It was as if he didn't care about anything.

She considered telling him about her experience before, but

she decided it would be best not to. She intended to wait and see if it happened again. Next time, she would be sure to confront them, if she was certain they were alone.

Jay took a stroll around the stockroom, "Edel, I can't believe how organised you are. How did you do this so quickly?"

She didn't know how to answer that question. She didn't think she had done anything exceptional, and she'd lost at least an hour when the other was nearby.

"Well, I came to help you, but it looks like you are picking things up fine without me! I was worried. I got waylaid in a meeting with one of the directors. That was a weird meeting..." he made a face. "He brought his son with him, he's supposed to be taking over some responsibilities from his dad or whatever, but he doesn't seem like he's fully switched on if you know what I mean..."

Edel did not know what he meant.

"You know? Like maybe a little slow, or he has some sort of learning difficulties or something. He hardly spoke, he just kept staring around the room and breathing like he was on the verge of a panic attack or something." He shrugged. "Or maybe he just isn't interested in hard work. You see it all the time with rich legitimates. They don't need to work, so they don't see why they should! Either way, he didn't stay long, he couldn't get away fast enough!"

Jay spent the rest of the day in the stockroom with Edel. It's not that she didn't like Jay's company, but he just never seemed to shut up talking. And about nothing. Their day came to a close, and he instructed her to wait for him in the loading bay at the back. He didn't want people to see her walking with him to his car.

Jay talked incessantly all the way home, congratulating her on a good job and telling her how well she had done. It didn't feel like she had done well. She was still stuck on her failures in the cafeteria and filled with worry about what she had experienced in the afternoon. She kept her thoughts to herself and allowed him to chatter away. He didn't seem at all bothered about her lack of response.

When they got home, Jay suggested going out to eat. "Come on! You must be hungry if you skipped lunch!"

She held her breath and answered with a silent shake of her head. Saying no was not something she was used to.

"You aren't hungry?" he asked, incredulously.

"Yes. But..." she forced herself to continue with an explanation. "I need a rest from people, Jay."

"Oh." He looked at her with a new understanding. "When you spend all day alone in your room, is that more of a need than a want?"

She didn't understand what he was asking her. She preferred to be away from people. It helped her to stay calm. When she didn't answer him, he asked, "Do you need a rest from me too?"

When she failed to answer him again, he threw his hands up in the air and shouted, "I'm going out." It wasn't an angry shout, but Edel still didn't know how to take it. He grabbed his phone and keys and called, "See you later!"

Edel was in her room when he returned. The solitude had done her good; she was calmer now. He shouted out to her as he entered, "Am I allowed in yet?"

She opened her door and peered out of it, unable to understand his humour. He was holding a delicious smelling bag with a hot rotisserie chicken inside. "I didn't know if you would have eaten," he said, holding it out towards her.

She came out and took the bag, suddenly aware of how hungry she was. "Thank you," she said as she took it.

"Holy cow! Did you just thank me for something?" He laughed at her, and she froze. *Wasn't that what people were supposed to say?* She had observed this countless times whenever somebody was given something in their hands. Her eyes fell to the floor, and her shoulders rounded, palms laying limply by her sides.

"I'm sorry, Edel. I didn't mean to upset you. That was just a joke."

"A joke," she repeated. The words meant nothing to her.

"What I should have said was, well done, you are learning how to communicate better every day, and it is always nice to be thanked when you have given something to somebody."

As she ate her food, she thought back to the strange experience in the stockroom earlier and felt sorry for doubting Jay's loyalty. He was good to her. He wouldn't betray her.

CHAPTER 16

Tuesday 27th June 2102

Unit 7 Warehouse, Harpton Main City Centre

The next morning was just like the previous one. Jay drove them both to work, and Edel walked around to the front door to wait with the others with a sense of trepidation. Nobody spoke to her, and she held back, out of the way until the doors were opened. It wasn't Jay who opened up today, but Maarku. She scurried past him with her head down, avoiding eye contact and ran into her workspace, away from everyone else.

She continued with her work from yesterday and got on with organising the existing stock. Occasionally Evie would come down and check the computer systems to see how much of an item they had on hand. At first, she tried to communicate with Edel, but quickly gave up. Edel wasn't being intentionally difficult, but her one-word answers and lack of eye contact made it tough for people to warm to her. Not that Edel cared. She wasn't looking for any more friendships with humans.

It was Edel's first delivery, and Jay came down to talk her through the process and give her a hand. He was impressed with the speed at which she learned and complimented her on the steady pace she worked, and how she didn't tire, even after lugging the huge pallets around. He said she was a perfect fit for the job.

At lunch, she remained in the stockroom and ate the sandwiches Jay had packed for her. Truth be told, she didn't need to eat three times a day. At Poly-Gen, she was only fed once in the morning and once in the evening. But Jay had said she should eat, so she ate.

The rest of the week passed easily. It hadn't taken long for her to become accustomed to the work, and she found she enjoyed the routine.

She quickly gained a reputation amongst the other members of staff for being unfriendly and a little peculiar. They didn't bother her; they didn't speak to her unless needed, and that was the way she liked it. She spent her days down in the stockroom, alone with her work, and found a sort of peace and serenity she had never known before.

"Okay, will you let me take you out to celebrate today?" Jay said when they got back one evening. "You have done a whole two weeks down in that stockroom, and you've managed incredibly well!"

"Nowhere too busy," was her only response.

He handed her a piece of paper. "That's your regular shift pattern. It's similar to mine, but we will work different days sometimes, and you know, sometimes I have to work nights." He looked at her for a moment. "Will you be okay there when I'm not around?"

"Yes," she said. She didn't add that she had hardly seen him since her second day.

Jay walked her into the quiet restaurant. She had never seen anywhere like it before. It was cosy inside, all the furniture was made from dark, shiny wood and the lights in the ceiling were subdued and dim, but whole panels of coloured light illuminated the walls. It was a strange place.

Jay ordered for both of them, not bothering to ask her what she wanted to eat, which she was thankful for.

They sat and talked, and for the first time, Edel felt unguarded. Jay still did most of the talking, and he spent a lot of his time with his attention split between Edel and texting Katie on his phone. They had been seeing each other for a few weeks now, and they talked all the time. He went out with her most nights, sometimes not returning until morning.

"Edel, there's something I need to ask you," he said.

Her eyes searched his face. She could tell he was nervous.

"I want to have Katie over, for dinner."

She looked at him, waiting for more. She didn't understand what he was saying at all.

"I mean like a sort of date, Edel. As in, just me and Katie."

"You want me to leave the house?"

"Well, don't say it like that! That sounds like I don't enjoy having you around! But, well, yeah. I'd like to have the place to myself for a few hours. Would that be okay?"

She blinked at him. Was he actually asking her permission? She wasn't used to this at all. "Yes."

"What will you do, though? Where will you go?"

She thought for a minute. "Running."

"For three or four hours?"

"Yes." She wondered why he was acting like that was a big deal. She could run for two solid days and not quit.

"Um, Edel? What would happen if she was still here when you got back?"

"What do you mean?"

"Well, if she spent the night. Would that bother you?"

The realisation of what he was asking her smacked her in the face. "Oh!" It took her by surprise, even though she knew about the human reproductive process, and about sexual desire. "I can stay in my room until you are done," she said, staring back at him with a plain expression.

A pink tinge flushed upon Jay's cheeks. She recognised it as embarrassment, but she wasn't sure how or why he was experiencing it. He sighed and tried to speak again, but it was clear he was struggling to get the words out. "Edel, how well do you hear? I mean, if you are in the room next door, and I'm with Katie... um..." He trailed off.

"I don't have to listen. I can tune most noises out," she assured him.

He nodded once and changed the subject back to work as their meal arrived. He chatted about lots of things, and she listened intently. She hadn't realised meals could be social events, but decided it was nice to eat meals with company, even though she still rarely had anything to add to Jay's often one-sided conversations.

His phone rang, and he made an apology. "I'm just going to take this, will you be okay?" he asked, as he was already standing up to leave.

Uncertainty crept up on her as she watched him leave. She was alone in a public place, and there were people all around her. Her heart raced as she swallowed down her unease. She hadn't considered how reliant she had become on Jay. Like he was her personal protection or comfort blanket. She felt exposed and alone and out of her depth if he wasn't here to guide her. She closed her eyes and tried to find her calm, but instead of the tranquil feelings of nothingness, a surge of sheer panic overtook her as she sensed another close by.

Her head snapped up in a jerking motion, like she was possessed, and her eyes scanned the room. Whoever it was, was close, but they were not inside this room. The vibrations grew stronger as they drew nearer and she concentrated hard, trying to locate them.

Her own panic was swelling in her chest, but there was also an unfamiliar and strange sensation of curiosity. She couldn't fathom it.

Her eyes stared out of the window and locked on Jay. The ugly sensation of doubt reared its head as she tried to listen to his words. Had he betrayed her? She zeroed in on his conversation and could just make out the woman's voice on the other end of the phone. They were discussing dinner plans. Shame weighed her down as she realised he was speaking to Katie. She shook her head and berated herself for doubting Jay.

The pulsating was getting stronger, along with the feelings of fear and apprehension, and curiosity and wonder. She'd never felt such a mixture of emotion before, and it sent her head spinning.

Her eyes caught sight of the small group of men and women as they entered through the door. She stared hard at them, taking in every ounce of information she could. Someone here was like her; she was certain of it. She looked at each one in turn, but she recognised no one.

She eavesdropped on their conversations. There was a lot to sort through, but one man had her attention, as he grabbed another man by the shoulder and spoke to him.

"Hey man! You okay?" he sounded concerned.

She watched and listened to his friend's response. He shook his head and said, "I'm just feeling a little... I don't know. Weird?"

"Weird how?"

"Like the other night." He grabbed his chest and supported his weight on the table in front of him.

"You need to sit?"

"No, no. I'll be fine. I'm just going to the men's room, okay?"

Edel watched him leave and sensed his movements as he walked through the room. It was him! He was an XJ. How was it she didn't recognise him?

She focussed her attention on the people he had entered with for a moment. Each one of them appeared to be normal, average humans, there was nothing unusual or special about any of them.

In her chest, she could still feel the familiar hum and pulsating of another XJ, but there was also an unusual sensation of wild and unbridled panic: the other was trying and failing to stay calm.

She concentrated hard and turned herself 'off' and sensed his confusion as her own feelings became shrouded from him. It did nothing to lessen his fear, it seemed to send him further into a mixed-up mess, but she couldn't understand why. It made no sense.

She looked back to Jay; he was still speaking to Katie on the phone. She turned her attention back to the small crowd of people who had entered with the XJ and listened.

"Where's Danny?" one of them asked.

"Oh, he's not feeling well. I think he might have gone home."

Her hand spontaneously gripped the table in alarm, as the question was asked – *his* fear and apprehension had peaked, and their shared conscious mind had caused *her* body to respond. She breathed through it as he relaxed back down, after hearing the other man's answer.

She pulled herself together, knowing she needed to act. This was a dangerous situation, and she needed answers.

Trying to act casual and go unnoticed, she picked her way through the crowd and entered the men's bathroom. He turned in shock as she pushed open the door, but she knew exactly where he was before she'd even laid eyes on him. There was no time to process his confusion or fear. She lunged at him, grabbing him by the throat and slamming him up against the wall with force. The pure sense of shock he was emitting was hard to contain. He was fearful for his life and the sticky feeling of repulsion seeped down her throat. XJ's do not show fear or weakness!

Shifting her weight, she grabbed his shoulder and slammed his head into the side of the sink in front of him. He fell to his knees, and she leaned her weight into his body, her hands grabbing the back of his head as she rammed it forward again, cracking the porcelain of the basin with his face with a sickening clang.

Fear *Uncertainty* *Panic*

The depth of his feelings was overwhelming. She tried her hardest to hold them at bay and not lose herself to his emotional weakness.

"IDENTIFY," she growled at him. It was an order. One she

had answered many times before.

He didn't respond, and at first, she thought perhaps he was too stunned from her assault. But she couldn't escape his complete lack of understanding. How did he not understand this basic command?

She shoved her knee hard into his back to keep him in place, as she reached forward and pulled down on the back of his shirt collar. She yanked it so hard he coughed and spluttered as the front of his shirt cut into the soft tissue of his neck, choking him, but it did not matter how far back she pulled it, there was no stamp.

Confusion

This time it was Edel's lack of understanding. *How is he not stamped? What is he?* She leant forward and grabbed his left arm, ripping the sleeve of his white shirt as she pulled it with force. She turned his hand over and studied the wrist, but there were no markings on him. His skin was perfect. Smooth and brown, like polished wood.

"Who are you?" The words left her mouth short, sharp, and aggressive. "You're not stamped. You're not chipped. But you're not human."

Another man entered the bathroom, and she backed up without hesitation, setting some distance between them. The man looked at them with unsure eyes, uncomfortable to see a woman in the men's bathroom.

"Stay away from me," she spat. It was a command. She wasn't asking him.

The new man didn't speak, he simply stared at the scene before him with his mouth hanging open and stepped aside to allow Edel to leave. He glanced at Danny, clearly wondering why he was bleeding and so dishevelled, and why the sink was cracked.

***

Danny pulled himself to his feet and bolted after her. He needed to know what the hell just happened – who was she? By the time he caught sight of her, she was speaking to a man seated at a table near the door. He listened to her words.

"I've had enough. I'll see you at home, Jay."

Danny watched her hurry out of the door. Part of him was desperate to follow her, but that was the most terrifying five minutes of his entire life. She was like him. She had to be! She seemed dangerous though, like they said on the news. And strong, too. As strong as him, for sure. He'd never met anyone who could match his strength.

He turned his attention to the man she had just spoken with and took a sharp intake of breath as recognition hit him. That was Jaydon Powell. He'd met with him only a couple of weeks ago at the JoBi Corp Warehouse. He remembered feeling similar sensations in that meeting, and the fear, and the anxiety. It had been so intense he could barely concentrate on anything at that meeting. Had she been there then, too?

Danny watched Jay pick up his belongings and leave. He decided he was going to set up another meeting at the warehouse.

He looked across to his friends. Nobody had noticed him standing on the other side of the room. And he'd heard Tony cover for him and tell everyone he'd already left. He retreated out the door before anyone noticed him, knowing he wouldn't be able to explain his current state to anyone without people asking questions he could not answer.

CHAPTER 17

Tuesday 11th July 2102

Jay's Apartment, Helstain, Harpton Main

Jay was impressed with how Edel was settling in at work. No one had ever worked so well in that stockroom without complaint. Her capacity for memory was astounding. She never needed to check the computer systems, she always knew how many of an item they had, and she knew where everything was. That stockroom was organised and immaculate.

He didn't feel one bit guilty for suggesting they pay her more than the others. He had discussed it with Glasby and mentioned he had Frank's authority to pay the new stock checker an increased wage as an incentive to stick it out. It angered Glasby. He didn't like that Jay had been discussing things with one of the company directors, but after seeing how efficient Edel was, he changed his mind, and signed off on the more than generous figure Jay had suggested.

Life had largely settled down now, and Jay felt like he was back on an even footing. His financial problems would soon be over now that there was an extra wage coming into his household. Edel was settling in and becoming more 'human' every day. She was relaxing around him and beginning to trust. Occasionally, she would even ask unprompted questions, and she was finding it easier to express likes and dislikes. Although that might seem like something minor, watching her grow as a person and seeing her personality develop was a beautiful thing. It was like watching a child grow, but on an accelerated level.

She still struggled socially, though. She froze up in any situation she wasn't comfortable with, no matter how small or insignificant it was. If someone spoke to her, she would freeze, her whole body going rigid.

Jay still hadn't introduced her to Katie yet. He wasn't sure he wanted to. He wasn't really sure what he had with Katie. If he was honest, she didn't interest him at all. She was dull and self-absorbed, and her snobbery was on a new level. But she had chased him around the town, showing up in bars he frequented and being chased by someone so much younger had been flattering. Plus, she was exceptionally pretty. And rich. And she was dynamite in bed. He'd never been with someone with so much energy before. He knew he only continued this relationship because he was lonely. He cared for Edel, but her friendship took a lot out of him. Her company wasn't enough, he needed something more.

It made him question what Katie saw in him. He wasn't rich; he had no power or influence, and he was almost twice her age. This wasn't love, but he must fulfil some use to her. He just didn't know what. The cynic in him suspected she was simply trying to piss her father off.

Jay had been with Katie a little over two months now. She had been to his apartment a few times, but Edel was always either out or stayed so quiet in her room, Katie never knew she was there. But there was one thing Jay couldn't get past. He hadn't allowed Katie to stay the night. He couldn't stand the thought of Edel being able to hear every noise, every moan, every thrust. The more time he spent with her, the more it became apparent her hearing was acute enough to rival a dog, and no matter what she said about not listening, he knew he wouldn't be able to concentrate.

He had stayed with Katie plenty of nights, though. She shared a house with two other girls. They were all dancers, and they all seemed to accept Jay just as he was; they didn't treat him any differently because he was older. He thought it made sense, considering his young and laid-back outlook on life. He didn't *feel* any older than them.

Jay was getting ready to leave when Edel wandered out of her room. "Are you working?" she asked, frowning.

He smiled. She knew his shift pattern better than he did. "I've got a meeting. Hopefully, it won't take too long." He handed her some cash. "Could you pick up some milk?"

She stared at him with a blank expression. He had been pushing her to do small tasks independently, but he was usually with her when he made her pay for things.

He grinned at her. "It's not rocket science, Edel. You go to the store, pick up the milk, hand it to the guy behind the counter, pay, then leave. Easy. You can do this!"

"You could do it," she said.

He laughed out loud. "Holy crap! Are you giving me sass?"

He instantly regretted saying anything. He saw her change in front of him, and revert to the unsure, nervous, childlike creature she was when they first met. Her face was serious, and she could not meet his eye as she stood, motionless.

"Edel, it's okay. I was just messing with you."

Her forehead knitted together into a series of worried lines as she raised her face from the floor. "So, you don't want milk?" she asked, confused.

"What? Yes, I want you to get milk. From the store. Today. That is literally the only thing I want from you," he said in mock exasperation. Sometimes he couldn't help himself. She was so easy to mess with.

She looked at the paper money in her hand, and he could see she was struggling with the idea of shopping by herself. He left before he took pity on her, telling himself this would be good for her. She needed to learn to do things for herself.

"I'll catch you later, I've got to go. Don't want to be late!" he yelled, as he skipped through the door.

"Keys," she yelled after him. He double backed a second later.

"I don't know how I ever coped without you, Edel!" he said, laughing.

"Neither do I."

Jay's head shot up to look at her. Had she intended to say that? The look on her face was one of pure fear. Her eyes were wide, and her trembling hand was covering her mouth as if she hoped to put the words back and stop them from escaping.

He couldn't help but laugh as he shook his head. She had some snark in her today and it was such a refreshing change.

Her expression didn't change. The worry about the outcome of saying something like that was displayed on her face. He didn't say anything more, he only turned and walked down the corridor, still snickering to himself. She was full of surprises.

The meeting was being held at one of the boardrooms in The Grid offices. Jay sauntered into the fancy foyer and informed the snooty receptionist he was here to see Frank Johnson.

The meeting was nothing of particular importance, and it felt like a giant waste of time to Jay. An hour and a half later, Frank was thanking everyone for attending and people began gathering their belongings together while one of the juniors collected the empty coffee cups. Jay was on his way out when Frank called out, "Jay. I'd like to see you. There is something I need to discuss with you."

One of the guys from another site shot him the raised eyebrow look. It never looked good when your boss needed to speak to you in private after a meeting. Jay held back as everybody left, and he noticed Frank's weird son hanging around at the back.

"Don't look so worried Jay, you're not in trouble," Frank smiled at him. "You remember my son, Danny?" he said, gesturing to the young man in the back. Jay looked in his direction and stepped forward to shake his hand. He seemed a lot more together today, not at all like he was the day they met.

"Danny had decided Unit 7 is the place he would like to learn the ropes. I'm sending him to your site, and I'd like him to shadow you and learn how you and your management team run things."

"Oh," was all Jay could say. This guy couldn't have been less interested last time they had met. He had to wonder whose choice it was for him to work at unit 7.

Frank, Jay and Danny had a brief chat about when Danny would start, and what he was going to be doing, before Frank made his apologies and left. "I'm afraid I'll have to leave him in your capable hands, Jay. I've got another meeting to get to, unfortunately." He checked his watch as he spoke, then he walked out of the room without even considering if Jay may have had plans or if this extended meeting time may be inconvenient.

Jay had a very different impression of Danny now to what he had when they first met. He was more switched on than he'd first given him credit for. He was confident and self-assured, but also polite and friendly. And he seemed to already know a lot about the business. Perhaps he was having an off day when he showed up at the warehouse with Frank.

"I don't want to keep you Jay, I'm sure you've got better things to do today," Danny said, after they had chatted a while.

"I don't mind. I've got no plans until later," he said, thinking how he couldn't blow off the director's son, even if he did have plans.

Jay found Danny to be pleasant and chatty. He asked him a lot of questions about where he lived and his home life.

"So, you live alone?" he pushed on.

Jay smiled. "I have a roommate."

"What's he like?" he asked.

"Who said it was a guy?" said Jay jokingly. "*She* is great."

"What is she called?"

"Edel," Jay said, an uneasy frown taking over his face. This conversation was turning into a bit of an interrogation.

"Where is she from?" he continued asking about her.

Suspicion clouded Jay's mind, and his forehead creased with worry. "Why the sudden interest in my roommate?"

Danny stalked to the door with long, confident strides, and closed it. Turning to face Jay and blocking their only exit, he squared his shoulders, and asked, "How much do you really know about her?"

The colour drained from Jay's face, and his heart beat faster. *What did this guy know?* "I don't know what you mean," he said evasively. "So, if that's everything about work, I guess I'll see you Monday?" he made a start towards the door, but Danny was blocking his path, his face set into a hard, almost angry expression.

"I know who she is."

The words hit Jay like a punch in the gut. All the air rushed out of his lungs, and he couldn't answer.

He finally found his voice after faltering a few times. "She's a casher, from Gromdon," he said, already sure that was what Danny was getting at. What else could he possibly know? "Look, I know it's not technically legal to rent, or sublet to cashers, but I'm not doing anything that will affect the business," he said.

Danny was still standing in front of the door, his arms folded across his chest. "You're lying." There was a quiet, simmering anger to his voice when he spoke.

Jay panicked again. How did this guy know? WHAT did this guy know? He swallowed and forced a placid smile onto his face, and he said, "I have to go. I've just remembered... there's somewhere I need to be." He tried to walk past Danny and reach for the door, but Danny grabbed him and shoved him hard into the wall.

"TELL ME WHAT YOU KNOW!" he snarled in his face. He was breathing hard, and his weight was pressing into Jay's chest, crushing him.

"Danny! What — the — fuck?" he gasped for breath between each word, unable to breathe for the crushing weight on his ribcage.

"Tell me what you know." His hand gripped Jay's throat, his fingers wrapping around and squeezing his windpipe. Jay coughed and spluttered, trying to breathe. He saw stars and felt the sharp pain explode in the back of his head. Danny slammed him into the wall, and then the grip around his throat abruptly relaxed.

"TELL ME," he growled, his hand slamming him up against the wall once more, and resting threateningly over Jay's throat.

"I don't know what you mean." The words were no louder than a whimper. Jay was unable to hide his terror.

"DON'T LIE TO ME."

The next thing Jay knew he was sailing through the air and landed headfirst onto the boardroom table, skidding across the polished wood on his face, his stunned mind unable to work out what had just happened. Danny advanced on him and grabbed him once more, yanking him up by the arm, and shoving his face down again. Jay let out a scream of agony as his shoulder popped out of the joint.

"I know you are lying. I can tell. Tell me who she is."

Jay was dumbstruck and terrified. Danny was completely deranged, and he looked like he wasn't done.

He couldn't betray his friend. He wouldn't. She hadn't divulged much about what they did to her at that place, but what little he knew was enough. Her whole life had been hell until she found her freedom.

"Please... please. I don't know anything. I don't know," he begged.

"LIAR," Danny shouted and grabbed him again.

This time Jay heard a woman's shrill scream as his head went into the table.

***

When Jay came around, he was being lifted onto a stretcher by the paramedics. His head was screaming in pain, as was his shoulder, and he was having trouble making sense of what had happened. All around him, concerned faces stared at him, but

Danny was nowhere to be seen.

He was taken to the local hospital and checked for concussion, and they fixed his shoulder up. All he could think about was getting hold of Edel. He made a mental note to get an additional phone on his account, so he could give it to her.

The nurse came to speak to him. "How are you feeling, Mr Powell?" she asked.

"I'm fine, I think. How long do I need to stay here? Am I allowed to go home?"

"The doctor is on her way to check you over, but everything seems fine with your scans. Your shoulder will be sore for days, though." She handed him a sheet of paper. "These are the recommended exercises to help, but we've injected it with a stabiliser which will keep the connective tissue strong but supple. You should have full use of it again in a few hours, but it may feel stiff for a week or two."

Jay thanked her and waited for the doctor to arrive. She was friendly enough, and she gave him the all clear. "Your medical bills have already been covered, Mr Powell. You don't need to do anything else. You are free to leave," she said briskly.

He got himself together and collected his belongings, still in a complete daze, trying to work out what had happened in the boardroom, and what the Johnson kid knew about Edel. As he walked along the corridor, he ran into a well-dressed, middle-aged man, who greeted him by name. "Jaydon Powell? Come with me, please."

Jay didn't argue. The man seemed so official; he assumed it had something to do with discharge papers or signing something. He followed the man into a private room. Jay's eyes rested on the man at the back of the room. Hovering awkwardly, and looking very uncomfortable, was Frank Johnson.

"Jay." He held out his hands in what seemed to be a calming gesture. "I can't apologise enough for what happened."

Jay stood there dumbly, looking at Frank, wondering how many times he had done this before. Danny seemed unhinged.

"Obviously, I've covered your medical expenses, and I don't

expect you to return to work straight away. Take as much time as you need, I'll see that you won't lose any pay."

Jay scowled at him. "Your son just tried to kill me. But don't worry, it's okay because you're going to pay me for any absence I need to take!" he said, glaring at him with contempt.

"Okay, how much?"

"How much what?"

"How much for you to keep quiet about this and not press charges?"

"You're trying to buy my silence?" he asked. The realisation hit that this wasn't the first time daddy had had to pay people to stay quiet.

"I'm looking at restructuring at the warehouse, Jay. I could move Glasby, opening a new GM position. It will come with a *very* generous wage, and more flexible working hours, and an attractive annual leave package. Of course, you can expect to receive generous compensation for what happened today on top. All I'm asking is that you don't press charges, and you don't talk about what happened with anybody."

"You're promoting me?" he asked, dumbly.

Frank smiled. "I think General Manager has a nice ring to it. I'm giving you the opportunity to negotiate your own salary here, Jay, and your own perks. In addition to that, I'm offering you a $25,000 lump sum, to keep quiet about what happened. And needless to say, I will ensure Danny stays away from you and your workplace."

Jay's mouth hung open as he tried to take in what was happening here. Was his boss bribing him to keep his mouth shut? "He's crazy! How many times have you had to pay people off? I bet I'm not the first. He could have killed me, Frank!"

"Danny isn't crazy. He has some issues we are working on. I can assure you; it won't happen again," he said with a forced calm.

"No, it won't if I press charges. He assaulted me. Do you even know why?"

Frank shook his head. "Jay, I hoped it wouldn't come to

this, but you know you won't get anywhere pressing charges against me, or Danny. Think *very* carefully about what you are saying. If you go down that route, I will have to terminate your employment, and believe me when I say I have A LOT of influence in all aspects of this city. I could make your life very difficult. Tyler tells me you live in Helstain," he said, pointing to the well-dressed man standing beside him. "Were you aware that my company owns the company who rent to you? Tyler has checked up on your accounts, and I know you have defaulted on rent payments recently... You'd find it difficult to get accommodation anywhere else in the area, if you were evicted for not paying rent on time."

Jay glared at Frank with a look of loathing. He had him between a rock and a hard place, and he knew it.

"I like you, Jay. I have a great deal of respect for you. I'd much prefer to keep you on my side than for us to be enemies."

Jay didn't know what to say. Any respect he held for this man had vanished.

Tyler handed him a document. "Sign here." It was an NDA. He was signing to keep his silence.

"I'll be in touch," Frank nodded to him as he strode out of the room.

***

"You are injured," Edel stated as soon as he walked through the door. Jay didn't even want to know how she knew that before she'd even looked at him.

"Jay! What happened to you?" she asked, looking at his bruised body and arm supported in the sling.

He swallowed hard. "Has anybody been here? Has anybody been to look for you?"

"Me?" Her face changed to one of distrust. "Why would anybody be looking for me? Nobody knows I'm here."

He could hear the accusatory tone in her voice, and he saw her stance change; she was readying herself to attack. "Edel, I swear I didn't tell anybody about you. I didn't! But he knew. I don't know what he knew, but he knew something."

"Who?" Her voice was short and abrupt.

"His name is Danny. He's my boss's son. He started asking questions about you, and when I wouldn't answer them, he attacked me."

"What does he look like?" The words were monotonous. She sounded neither angry nor upset, it was more analytical. Methodical, like she was trying to remain impartial until she had all the facts.

"Black, average height, short hair. Do you know him or something?"

"We've met."

"Does he know about you?" How would anybody know about her? She didn't have any friends. She didn't speak to anybody except him. There was so much here that made no sense.

Edel was silent, staring at the floor.

"What aren't you telling me, Edel?"

"I know nothing for certain. But I think he is like me."

Jay frowned. "Like you? An escapee from the facility?"

She shook her head. "I've never seen him before."

Jay considered his strength. He wasn't well built, or muscular, but he had thrown Jay across the room like a rag doll. "Why do you think that?" he asked.

"I can sense him. I can feel him."

"What do you mean?" he asked, shocked at the sound of it. The idea that they could 'sense' each other was news to him. "When did you meet him?"

She recounted the times she had sensed another XJ, and the tale of when she attacked him in the men's room of the restaurant.

"Shit, Edel! You didn't think to tell me about him?"

She stayed silent.

"Oh, for fuck's sake! After everything I've done for you, you still don't trust me?"

She backed up a step, away from him and his anger. "It's not that." She seemed to be struggling to find her words. "I want you to be safe. The more you know, the less safe you will be."

"I think it's a little late for that," he spat at her, gesturing to his bruised body and dislocated shoulder.

"What did you tell him?" she asked.

"Nothing. I swear."

She narrowed her eyes. "Then, how did you survive?"

"What?" The idea that Danny could have easily killed him was alarming. He was only just realising the seriousness of the situation he had been in. "I don't know. I heard screaming, I guess someone walked in and interrupted him, I don't really remember. The next thing I know, the paramedics were on me."

"He is the son of your boss?"

Jay nodded.

"You need to find new work. He knows where you work. Where I work. He will come back."

"Um..." Jay launched into a grovelling explanation of how he somehow ended up with a promotion and a $25,000 lump sum, and how he promised not to say anything to anyone, and how he cannot under any circumstances leave his job. He then told her how Frank knows his address, which meant that Danny also either knew, or had the means to find out.

Edel seethed with anger. She marched into her bedroom and returned with her shoes. "Where are you going?"

"To end this," she said, and she marched out of the door before he could stop her.

***

Hours passed, and Edel did not return. Jay was going out of his mind with worry. He tried to wait up for her, but the painkillers the doctor had prescribed were strong, and it was proving difficult to keep his eyes open. He was asleep on the couch when she finally returned but jolted awake with the sound of the door. "What happened?" he asked, pulling himself upright and trying to shake himself to alertness. It was light in his living room; she had been out all night.

She stared at him. "I couldn't find him."

A wave of relief washed over Jay, and he let his breath out in a whispered "phew" sound. Her head jerked up, and she glared at him with a look of distrust. "That was a sound of relief," she stated. "Why are you pleased I couldn't locate him?"

"What would you have done? Fought him? Killed him? You might have ended up hurt, or worse. If they called the police or discovered who you are, they would have taken you back to that place for sure. I was worried about you! Besides, you said you wouldn't kill any more people."

"He's not people." She walked past him and into her room and returned a moment later, dressed in her work uniform.

"What are you doing? You can't be serious! You've been out all night! Take the day off and get some rest."

"I can function for days without sleep." She marched right back out of the door.

Jay was beginning to miss the days when she was afraid to make decisions for herself. Things were easier when she did as she was told.

He spent the rest of the day recuperating. Katie spent the day with him, and he made up a story about being mugged by a group of cashers. She believed every word. It wasn't unusual for cashers to target legitimate citizens, and because the crimes were carried out by people with no identification, it made it difficult for the police to investigate or make any actual arrests. Half the time, people didn't bother reporting these types of crimes.

Katie was still with Jay when Edel returned. He hoped she would be polite at least, but he had no such luck. She opened the door and stood awkwardly in the doorway, staring at Katie.

"Oh, hi Edel!" He greeted her with a forced smile and a silent hope she would answer. She didn't. She just stood, unresponsive.

"Um, this is my girlfriend, Katie. Katie, this is Edel, my roommate."

"Hi!" Katie greeted her pleasantly. "I was starting to think you didn't really exist, and Jay made you up!" she joked.

Edel looked to Jay, then back at Katie. Her face remained serious; it was obvious she didn't understand Katie's attempt at humour. She walked through the room and passed Katie and Jay without speaking to either of them, disappeared into her bedroom, and closed the door.

"Is she always like that?" Katie whispered.

He laughed a little. "Yeah, pretty much. She doesn't mean to be, she's just not a people person."

CHAPTER 18

Wednesday 12th July 2102

Clearwater Hotel, Hawley

Danny stared absent-mindedly through the window of his hotel room, lost in his dark thoughts, feeling so angry with himself he could cry. What the hell had possessed him to confront that man about whoever that girl was, anyway? What had he been thinking?

His dad had made him leave town for a couple of nights until Tyler could sort out some damage control. Tyler was his dad's own personal fixer, who never asked questions about the problems he was 'fixing'. It was just a shame that Danny seemed to be his main problem. How much money had he just cost his dad to keep things hushed up?

He couldn't shake the knowledge that if Tracy, one of the interns, hadn't come in when she did, Jay would likely be dead, and he would be a murderer.

He sat alone, sinking ever further into the pit of despondency and self-hate. With nobody to talk to, his thoughts ran rampant through his head, repeating the same why's and what if's.

He shouldn't have lost it. He should have stayed in control. Even though deep down, he knew he hadn't really lost control of himself. That wasn't a meltdown. It was the build-up of years of frustrations of not knowing anything about who or what he was, exploding out of him. That man, Jay, could answer all his questions, or at least point him to somebody who had the answers he was so desperately searching for. But he wouldn't tell, and it was too much. To be so close to everything he had needed his entire life, and then have someone shake their head and lie to his face, to tell him they don't know. It was too much.

There was so much he needed to know. What were those sensations he had when he was near her? And why did his own emotions seem to get so out of control whenever she was close?

It wasn't only answers he needed. It felt shameful to admit it, but he wasn't the same as everybody else, and he knew it. When he was a child, he would daydream and obsess about meeting somebody just like him, but never in a million years did he think this dream could become a reality. He *needed* to know her. He *needed* to feel like he belonged, and to see where he fit. Were they similar in any way? Did she view the world the same as him? Did she become overwhelmed with the noise of a busy room? Could she smell who was on the other side of her door before she answered it? Did she ever forget information, or could she recall every last insignificant detail the same way he could?

His phone rang, and his dad's name flashed across the screen. He didn't want to answer, but he needed to know if Jay was going to be okay. What if he was seriously injured?

"Hi Dad," he said in a sullen voice.

"Danny," His dad's curt tones screamed disappointment.

"Is he okay?"

"Yes. He had a slight head trauma, but no concussion, and a dislocated shoulder. They've treated that. He'll be fine. Tyler and I have sorted everything out. He will keep this whole matter confidential. You, of course, will find somewhere else to learn the business."

Danny didn't have a response to that. He already had a reputation for having an explosive temper. He would not be able to show his face again.

"What about Tracy?" he asked. She had walked in just as he had slammed Jay into the table again. She had screamed hysterically and ran, calling out to anyone who would listen to call the police, call security, call an ambulance.

"Tracy is no longer employed by JoBi Corp," he said in a clipped voice. It was clear his father was disappointed, but would it kill him to show a little compassion? It's not like he meant for this to happen... *And now I've cost her her job*. He didn't think his feelings could sink much lower.

"What exactly did Jay do to upset you?" he asked, his voice thick with accusation.

Danny did not think it a good idea to tell Frank about the girl. He remained silent, and Frank's annoyance grew. "Danny!" he snapped. "You can't go around hurting people every time they upset you. What set you off this time?"

Danny didn't know what to say. No matter what reason he came up with, there was no excuse for his behaviour today. "I'm sorry," he said, although even he could hear the insincerity in his own voice.

"Sorry! Sorry isn't good enough, Danny. You could have killed him! And for what? You won't tell me. Which leads me to believe you are getting worse, not better. That's the third episode in six months! What the hell is going on with you?"

"I'm sorry," he said again, only with a little more desperation.

"It can't happen again, Danny," he warned.

"I know. It won't."

He heard his dad sigh, a long and weary sound. "How are you feeling?" he asked begrudgingly.

"I'm okay." He didn't elaborate. As long as his dad thought he'd had a meltdown, he would not be any more angry, upset or disappointed than he already was.

"Get some rest, Danny. I know you need it after something

like this. Come home in a couple of days when things have blown over."

They said their goodbyes, and Danny felt worse for their chat. He hated not being honest with his dad, but he couldn't admit that he almost killed a man simply because he lost his temper. It was better to allow him to believe he had suffered a meltdown. At least Jenson would back him up and say it was beyond his control. He couldn't tell his dad about the girl either. He wasn't sure what his dad might do or say about her, but he didn't want to risk it. There was a good chance he would either send Danny away or turn her in to the authorities. Either way, he didn't think his dad would support him trying to get to know her – which he still had every intention of doing.

Danny called Gemma and simply hearing her voice made him feel better. She wasn't angry with him; she wasn't disappointed. Her encouraging words and sympathetic ear were more than he felt he deserved, especially since he wasn't being entirely honest with her either. He didn't tell her about the girl, and he skated over the reasons behind the 'meltdown', playing for sympathy and claiming he didn't know what had happened or why. He tried to tell himself he was protecting her. This girl was dangerous, and he had the bruises to prove it. But his real reasons had more to do with him wanting to understand and figure things out on his own. Not even Gemma could understand how he felt about his differences.

When he finished talking with Gemma, he called Tony to let him know he would not be home for a couple of nights. Tony at least sounded more concerned for him than his dad did. After their brief chat, he sat back and continued to think about what a terrible person he was, and how he was lying to his friends and family and girlfriend. He'd often wondered if he was bad by nature.

Nature was the wrong word. Design was more accurate. He was designed to be a killer. A soldier, or whatever else they were made for. His train of thought led him to why he was earmarked for termination. He wasn't meant to survive. His mother had been tasked with killing him, and all the others in his batch. He was faulty stock. There was something fundamentally wrong with him that made him not worth keeping.

He tried to shake the dark thoughts from his head. Nobody knew the reasons why. Not his mother. Not Jenson. Or if they did, they didn't say. He often wondered what was wrong with him. What made him not worth keeping? This was just another reason to add to the list of why he was so desperate to connect with this girl.

He stayed cooped up in his room for the next two days and wallowed in self-pity and self-disgust. By day three he was missing Gemma, and he felt homesick. He was done feeling sorry for himself, and ready to go home to try to make things right.

He called his dad, with a much more heartfelt apology and a promise that he would try harder, and then was on his way back within the hour. He went straight to Gromdon to pick up Gemma and spent the afternoon basking in her love and understanding. She always knew what to say. She always made him feel better. As the evening rolled around, he didn't want their time together to end.

"Stay!" he said, looking up at her with his big puppy dog eyes.

"I have to work tonight, Danny," she said, untangling her arms from his.

"Call in sick. I'll cover your wages."

She rolled her eyes at him. He knew she hated it when he said things like that.

"You don't buy my time, Danny!" she snapped.

"I know, I know that. I'm sorry, I didn't mean that at all. I missed you, that's all." She laughed as he grabbed her and pulled her in close and kissed her.

"Stay," he said again, like a child whining for sweets.

"Noooooo," she answered back at him, in the same whiny tone.

"Can I at least come with you?"

"Sure, nobody minds as long as you order something. But I can't talk to you all night. I'm working." She smiled at him thoughtfully. "Don't you get bored hanging out at the restaurant?"

He smiled. It was hard to explain why he liked to go to the restaurant. "I enjoy watching you work. You always look happy and confident. Even when its mega busy and you're rushing around, and you're getting tired. You always smile, you always laugh. I like to see you happy."

Danny drove Gemma to work and took his usual seat at the bar. He felt peaceful as he watched his girlfriend. She really did enjoy her job, and she'd fought so hard to get well paid work. She was independent. That was one of the many things he admired about her. She was poor; he didn't know exactly how poor, but he knew she was self-conscious about her home. Her house embarrassed her so much, yet she had never asked him for anything.

He remembered when he first met her, and he bought her a ridiculously expensive piece of jewellery. He'd met nobody quite like Gemma before, and he was trying to impress her. The way she saw things, the way she understood things, she has a beautiful mind. She handed the diamonds back to him and simply said, "I can't wear those."

He had insisted, of course, and she got mad. In the end she had screamed at him that her friends and family were starving, and that necklace would feed them for weeks. She ranted about how grotesque it was that he thought she could parade around wearing something worth so much money, when all around her, her peers were being worked to death, used as a slave labour workforce, and still couldn't afford to feed their families.

After that he opened his eyes a little more to the real struggles of the cashers. He returned the necklace and tried to give the cash value to Gemma instead. She went even more crazy and refused to see him for weeks. That was when he knew he wanted to be with her.

There was a group of men at a table, who were getting rowdy and impatient. One stuck his hand in the air and clicked his fingers at Gemma and whistled at her like she was a dog. Danny watched her, she never faltered. She approached the table with grace and greeted the men as though they weren't the rudest people she had ever encountered.

She returned to their table a short while later and Danny hated the way they spoke to her. He wanted to knock their heads off their shoulders. They were so rude and treating her like she was nothing.

She appeared behind him and placed her hand on his shoulder. He looked at her face and she smiled a weary smile, shaking her head gently. "Don't let them get to you, Danny. I'm used to it."

"That doesn't make it okay!" he said, glaring at the men.

"Danny, I don't want any trouble here. Promise me you will leave it and keep your mouth shut."

He nodded feebly, wondering why she would allow people to treat her this way when she was worth so much more. Gemma returned to work, and he smiled at how she always seemed to know what he was thinking.

The table of rude men eventually left. One of them casually placed his hand around Gemma and rested it on the small of her back as she took payment for their meal. Danny seethed with anger, and it took every ounce of his self-control not to get up and grab him. *Gemma was not their property!* He glared at them, livid at the thought of someone touching his girlfriend.

Gemma handled it well. She manoeuvred her body, standing out of his reach, and returned his card, placing it directly into the offending hand. He took it naturally without thinking about it, and she thanked him for his custom as she walked away.

The restaurant was drawing to a close, and Gemma had finished her shift. She was retrieving her coat when Terri came and stood beside him.

"You've been here all night!" she said, offering him a cheerful smile. "Don't you get fed up, just waiting for Gemma to finish work?" She stood close to him, closer than he would have liked. She was wearing perfume, it was a thick, cloying scent. Danny reminded himself it probably smelled nice to other people. Gemma rarely wore perfume, and when she did, it was a gentle fragrance they had chosen together.

She reached past him to hand something to the barman, and her free hand casually found his body. She didn't remove it; it remained in place, resting on his waist, as she looked up and gave him a coy smile. "And don't you get fed up with seeing her flirt with other men? Those guys were all over her," she said, pointing to the table where the group of men had been sitting.

Danny was about to argue that she had not been flirting with anyone, but Terri continued speaking. "So, Gemma's working almost every night this week. What are you going to do with yourself?"

He stood and moved back a fraction, so she was no longer touching him, but she didn't seem phased. She was still smiling with confidence. "I'm free, I only need to work a couple of nights. I'm not a desperate casher."

Danny was stunned. Not only was she brazenly hitting on him, she was insulting his girlfriend to boot. Danny caught sight of Gemma and walked over to her, placing his arm around her shoulders. "Ready?" he asked.

She smiled up at him and said her goodbyes to the remaining members of staff.

"That Terri is a nightmare," he said as soon as they were outside.

Gemma laughed. "She's mean to me at work. She's a legitimate though, and more senior than me, so I have to do what she says."

Danny stopped and looked at her. They were standing in the restaurant's window, Terri still watching. He could tell she was hoping they were arguing about Gemma's supposed flirting with men. He grabbed her and kissed her passionately, leaning her back as if they were in some sort of musical.

Gemma was laughing, "Danny, what the hell? I work here!"

He sniggered at the look of jealousy and loathing on Terri's face as he pulled Gemma back upright and continued walking, saying, "She's going to be even meaner to you now, but that was so worth it."

He walked with her to Gromdon, and she said her goodbyes on the street as always. Craig, her brother, was staring at them through the window.

"Gemma, when will you let me get to know your family?" he asked, his eyes fixed on the figure inside the house.

"You already know them!"

"You know what I mean. When can I hang out with them? Why can't I take you all out for food and get to know them properly?"

She shook her head. "You know why, Danny."

"Your brother hates me. He's only met me twice, and he doesn't know anything about me."

"He doesn't understand, that's all. He can't see why you want to be with me. Neither can anybody else."

"I love you," he said, stroking her hair. "I love you so much."

She smiled and reached up to touch his face. "I love you too," she whispered. She made her way inside, and Danny heard Craig start on her straight away, making snarky comments that she should be ashamed of herself. He called her a 'cash traitor' and said she had turned her back on her family. It hurt Danny to hear how she was treated at home, but pride swelled in him as he heard his usually patient and passive girlfriend hold her own and tell him where to shove his opinions. He heard how she stomped through the house and then the sound of a door slamming shut. He assumed that was the end of it, and he set off walking back towards the restaurant to retrieve his car, but he couldn't shake the idea that Gemma had such an unhappy home life.

***

The following day, Danny tried to visit his dad, to make a more sincere apology for his behaviour in the boardroom. He arrived at the house to find only Lyssi was home by herself. She turned to look at him as he walked in through the door, and her expression was one of pure dread. Her heart pounded in her chest, and she backed away from him. Shame filled every inch of Danny's heart. She would never get over what had happened.

"Do you know where my dad is?" he asked, trying to sound casual and carefree. He kept his distance from her, hovering by the front door, trying to make her feel less uncomfortable.

"He said something about a lunch with a potential client," she said. Her tone was guarded, as though she was afraid to confirm she was alone.

"Do you know when he will be back?"

She shook her head.

"Would it be okay if I wait around for him?"

There was no mistaking her fear at the idea of being alone with him. He hung his head and whispered, "Lyssi, I won't hurt you. I'm so sorry that happened."

She didn't answer, she just nodded her head. His words were meaningless. She would know all about the boardroom incident by now, so there was no point telling her he wouldn't hurt her, when he had just put someone in the hospital for no reason. He couldn't blame her for being afraid to be alone with him. He was more monster than man when he lost himself to the rage. Lyssi was lucky to be alive.

Sighing, he asked, "Will you tell him I came by?"

Danny came back later. He wanted to speak to his dad in person, not on the phone. He wanted to apologise properly, and he knew his dad would want to discuss Danny's working arrangements. There was no way he would allow him to work at unit 7 now.

"Danny!" his dad greeted him as he entered. "Lyssi mentioned you came by earlier. I was just about to call."

There was no tone of accusation in his statement, which Danny was thankful for. He worried he wasn't welcome to visit home anymore unless his dad was here too. "I wanted to see you. I want to apologise."

Frank cleared his throat a little and patted his son on the shoulder condescendingly. "I know you didn't mean to Danny. It's all been sorted out now."

"Is Jay alright?"

"Yes. He will be fine. It's astounding what doctors can do these days. You realise you popped his arm right out of his shoulder? They injected it with some sort of stabiliser after they shoved it back in, and he has full use of it already. He says it isn't even painful, just a little stiff!"

Danny was relieved to hear he had caused no lasting damage. He took a deep breath and in a careful and measured tone, said, "I'd like to apologise to him in person."

Frank frowned. "That's not the best idea, Danny. You attacked him, and I've had to bribe him to keep the police out of it. I told him he would never need to see you again."

Danny considered how best to play this. He needed to speak to this Jay guy and find out what he knew about that girl. He cleared his throat and squared his shoulders, and said, "I need to start taking ownership of my actions, Dad."

"I guess I could call him and ask if he would be open to a meeting. I'm free tomorrow afternoon, we could go down together, and I can make sure things stay civil."

"No. I meant alone. I need to speak to him and apologise, alone."

"Absolutely not!" The words were so final, Danny didn't dare argue. Arguing with his dad would never get him what he wanted. He needed to be less forthright than that.

He hung around a while, chatting and catching up, then casually worked Jay back into the conversation, asking when he would be fit enough to return to work. He was going to confront this guy, with or without his dad's permission.

CHAPTER 19

Friday 28th July 2102

Danny's House, Helston, Harpton Main

Two weeks passed and Danny had spent most of his days obsessing about Jay and that girl. He had finally plucked up the courage to visit unit 7 and meet with Jay. Nerves churned his stomach as he set off. He had told nobody about his plans today, not even Jay knew to expect him.

He took one last look in the mirror before leaving the house and tried to tell himself things would be okay. His thoughts repeated like a mantra in his head, on his journey to the warehouse. *Keep cool, Danny. Don't get angry. This will be okay. Keep cool. Don't get upset. This will be okay...* He approached Jay's office door and let out a silent prayer as he held his breath and found the courage to knock. No amount of bribery or money would keep things hushed up if he killed someone on site. There would be no coming back from this if he lost control.

The last time he visited this building, he felt those strange vibrating sensations in his bones. Did that mean the girl was here then? Did she work here, too? He could feel nothing unusual right now. No strange sensations at all.

Jay was speaking on the phone as he pulled open the door.

He hesitated mid-sentence to whoever he was speaking with, his mouth falling slack with shock as he took in Danny.

"Uh, I'm sorry. I'll have to call you back." He didn't wait for a reply. He clicked the call off with a sharp jerk of his thumb and stood, staring open-mouthed at Danny.

Danny held up both his hands in front of him. "I just want to talk," he said, hastily. "Please Jay, may I speak to you?"

The look on Jay's face was a mixture of fear and shock, but he stepped back from the door and allowed Danny to enter. Danny closed the door behind him, and he sensed Jays nerves kick up a notch.

"I'm not going to hurt you. I came to apologise."

Jay didn't speak, he only nodded, regarding Danny with a plain and unsmiling expression.

"I am really sorry about what happened, Jay. There's no excuse for what I did," he said. They stared at each other for a beat of silence. "You're probably wondering why I got so angry…"

Jay held his stare, his eyebrows raised, as though he was waiting for an explanation.

Shit! He thought for a moment and then decided maybe he ought to just say what he came here to say. "Look Jay, I know you know more about her than you're letting on," he blurted out.

Jay's reaction surprised Danny. It wasn't a denial, but it wasn't a confirmation, either. He simply said, "Tell me what you think you know."

Danny breathed out a shuddering breath and held his gaze. This was dangerous territory. Once he said these words, he was endangering himself. "I think she is one of the eight escaped XJ5's from the Poly-Gen facility."

Jay didn't miss a beat. He showed no shock at Danny's words, he only continued to hold his stare and asked, "And, why do you think that?"

Danny held his tongue, unable to answer that question. They stood glaring at one another in absolute silence, neither wanting to give too much away to the other.

"Who are you?" Jay eventually asked, after the silence drew on too long.

Danny looked away from Jay, taking in the untidy office space in front of him. His eyes rested anywhere but on Jay's questioning face. He dared not say it out loud.

Jay allowed the silence to fill the small room. He continued to stare at Danny, squinting at him as though he were trying to decipher a puzzle. Then he spoke in carefully chosen words, "she thinks you are like her."

Danny's head snapped up, and he searched Jay's face as his heart pounded with a thrilling mixture of excitement and fear.

"Is she right?" Jay asked.

Danny's voice came out in almost a breathy whisper. "I need to speak with her. Please!" he fished in his pocket and produced a business card. "Tell her to call me. I can meet her any time, any place!"

Jay laughed out loud. "I don't think that's the best idea. She went looking for you after you attacked me. I think she was planning on killing you."

Danny's face fell, and he swallowed hard as he remembered their brief meeting in the restaurant's bathroom a few weeks before. She was violent, and she was strong. And there was no doubt in his mind that she was a killer.

"Why?" He couldn't understand why she wanted him dead. They'd only met once, and she had attacked him then. He started to wonder if she would have killed him then if she hadn't been interrupted.

Jay did not answer his question, and Danny found himself feeling concerned for his safety. What if she did want to kill him? "Is she dangerous?"

Jay glared at him. "Are you?"

Danny slumped into the chair opposite to Jay's desk and put his head in his hands, trying to make sense of this situation. "She lives with you. Does she work here too?"

Jay remained silent, glaring at Danny.

"Please Jay. Just tell me. Was she here that day when I came to meet with you, with my dad?"

Jay slowly nodded his head. "How did you know that?"

"I don't know. It's hard to explain."

"Could you *feel* her?" he asked, staring at him.

The question knocked the air from Danny's lungs. "Did she tell you? Is it normal? Could she feel it too?" he asked, shocked and surprised and full of wonder.

"Okay. Enough now. You haven't told me anything. I'm not saying anymore until I know you aren't a threat to her. Who are you?"

Danny drew a deep, calming breath. This was a big deal; he was about to out himself to a stranger. He was sure Jay knew the truth already, even though they'd danced around it, and nobody had confirmed it, but that fact didn't make this any less daunting.

"My mother used to work for the HGMR at the Poly-Gen site. I was meant to be terminated in infancy, but she took me home instead, and raised me as her son." He stared at his knees, unable to meet Jay's eye. It felt somehow shameful to admit he wasn't quite human.

"That's why she doesn't recognise you!"

Danny looked up at Jay, unable to take in his words. He didn't seem at all perturbed by the news that Danny wasn't human.

"When she's near, I feel strange things. There's so much I don't understand. I just want to know who I am, what I am, where I fit." Danny's eyes filled with tears as the weight of these wants engulfed him. He was so close to getting all he had needed his entire life. "I'm so sorry I hurt you, Jay, but you don't know what it's like. Nobody can imagine how it feels to be so different. I never thought I would meet anybody like me. I've got nobody to ask, nobody to help me. And suddenly, now there is someone! She has all the answers and I'm desperate to meet her. Desperate to understand things. But you wouldn't help me, and the only time I saw her, she attacked me and told me to stay away." He roughly rubbed his eyes, embarrassed by his tears.

Jay sat back and allowed Danny to collect himself. Once he regained his composure, Jay shrugged nonchalantly and asked, "What exactly do you want to know?"

Danny thought for a moment. "If we're the same, I guess. I know nothing about myself at all. My mom was going to tell me when I was older, but she died when I was still a kid." He didn't want to tell Jay about her suicide. That was too personal. "I need to talk to her, ask her some stuff."

Jay smiled with sympathy. "She's not much of a talker, Danny." He let that hang in the air for a moment and Danny wondered what he meant. "She's not like us. She's never known a normal life, and she's really sort of damaged. I understand why you want to talk to her so badly, but I don't think she will be what you think you are looking for."

"Does that mean I can meet her?" he asked, a feeling of hope blooming in his heart. It didn't matter what she was like, or if she didn't meet his expectations. She was like him. He needed to meet her.

"That is up to her. I can ask her for you."

"Did she really come looking for me? Did she really want to kill me? Is she like they say on the news?"

Danny listened to Jay's explanation of what she was like and how she acted. She sounded nothing like they described on the news reports, but she didn't sound entirely harmless, either. It didn't matter, he still felt the crushing, desperate need to meet her.

They talked for a long time, and it was absurd how relaxed Jay seemed. He didn't appear to be in any way nervous after Danny had admitted he was in fact a genetic experiment and not entirely human, and to Danny's surprise, he wasn't holding a grudge about the boardroom incident either.

It felt good to finally have somebody to talk to, and even though he didn't know the guy, he already felt he could trust him. Besides, they had a mutual understanding about confidentiality. Danny couldn't tell anybody about Edel without endangering himself. And Jay couldn't tell anybody about Danny without endangering Edel.

He explained he hadn't yet told his dad about Edel, and Jay agreed it would be best to keep this only between them for now.

They parted company, and Danny felt optimistic, hopeful that he would find the answers he had spent a lifetime searching for.

CHAPTER 20

Saturday 29th July 2102

Jay's Apartment, Helstain, Harpton Main

Edel could hear that Jay was not alone as she approached the apartment. She considered turning around and running a little longer, but evening was closing in, and border patrol cracked down harder after dark. She didn't know what she would do if they stopped her. According to Jay, they were checking every person they detained for the XJ5 identity stamp, regardless of how unlikely it was they would accidentally stumble upon an XJ5. XJ5's did not have 'a look'. They were not easily distinguishable from regular humans and didn't fall into any single category of ethnicity. They were made in batches, and each different batch was made in every conceivable race, meaning it was technically possible for any person without ID to be one of the escapees. It would look suspicious if she ran, but it would be far worse if they caught her. She didn't dare to risk it.

Katie and Jay were sitting close together, chatting and giggling. The laughter was a complete mystery to her. She hurried in with her head down and tried not to be noticed, but Jay called to her from the couch. "Hey Edel!"

She stopped in her tracks and looked at him, wide eyed. She felt nervous and exposed, as though they had caught her doing something she shouldn't have been.

"You wanna join us?" he asked, shooting her an innocent-looking smile.

"No." There was nothing pleasant in her voice, and she carried on walking, head down, until she reached the sanctuary of her bedroom, closing the door behind her. It set her on edge when Katie was here. She didn't know how she should act.

"Your roommate is so rude! Would it kill her to speak?" She heard Katie's affronted sounding whispers.

Jay laughed out loud, "It might!" he joked.

"What's her problem, anyway?"

"She's had a hard life."

"Hard in what way?"

Edel felt her insides constrict. She held her breath as she listened, wholeheartedly believing Jay was about to betray her secret to his girlfriend.

"Well, she's a casher... They've all had hard lives, one way or another."

Edel let out her breath as she listened to his evasive answer, berating herself for doubting her friend. She should have known he wouldn't say anything.

"Casher? You live with a *casher*?" Katie sounded disgusted as she spat the last word. "As in, she pays in *cash* to live here? Isn't that illegal? They're not supposed to be encouraged. We're supposed to be clearing the riff-raff out, not encouraging them to stay!" she said indignantly.

Jay did not sound impressed with her views. His response was snappy as he said, "It's not illegal. She is a guest. It's not illegal to have a houseguest, Katie."

"What? So, you let her sponge off you for free?"

"As far as anybody knows, she lives here for free. Our financial arrangement has nothing to do with anybody else, okay?" he sounded angry, his voice rising in a way Edel wasn't used to hearing. He never spoke that way to her.

Edel stayed in her room. She had no intention of spending time with them in the first place, but now they were arguing over her, she was afraid to show her face. Confrontations were hard for her to navigate.

She didn't understand Katie's problem, but it seemed that people without proper identification were not worth the same as the ones who had identification. It made no difference to her. She was used to being thought of as less than and worthless.

Jay and Katie didn't seem to recover from their argument. They weren't talking a great deal, and she heard Jay ask, "Are you planning to sulk all night?" Katie left a while later and Edel listened to Jay's movements, waiting as always, for him to settle down and go to bed. Instead of his usual movements, she heard him moving towards her room, then came his tentative knock on her door.

"Edel. Can we talk?" He opened the door a fraction and shot her a smile.

She swallowed down her apprehension and braced herself for another encouraging chat about talking to humans when they were in the house.

He motioned for her to accompany him, and she pulled herself to her feet and followed him out of the door.

"I need to talk to you about something important." She detected his nerves and stared at him, trying to work out what he had to say that was making him so tense.

He took a deep breath and said, "It's about Danny Johnson."

The name hit her ears and her body tensed with worry, though her face stayed passive as she allowed him to continue.

"He came to see me at work yesterday."

Edel wanted to ask why. She wanted to ask if he was okay. She wanted to ask if he had been hurt. Instead, she remained silent and waited for more information, as always.

Jay was looking at her, waiting for her response. She continued her blank stare; he wasn't going to get one.

"He wants to meet you, Edel. He wants to talk to you."

A rush of panic welled up inside her. *Why? Why? I don't want to be near another XJ. Not now. Not ever.* She had worked too hard at trying to fit in and learning to be human to give it up now. Being near another XJ would be a constant, tangible reminder of the horrors of her past.

Her brain worked at speed, trying to work out who he was and what he could possibly want from her. It became obvious she would never discover these answers on her own. "Who is he?" The question was curt and abrupt.

Jay didn't seem at all put out by her tone. "He says he was born at the Poly-Gen site, but he grew up away from there. Like a normal human. He's never met another XJ." He shrugged his shoulders haphazardly, as if this information was nothing noteworthy.

Edel couldn't take in his words. She stared at him, willing her brain to make sense of this unexpected news. All the XJ's were reared in special incubators until they resembled human babies. They were then placed in the nurture pods for almost a decade, where all the information they were likely to ever need was fed directly into their brains until they were fully developed. She couldn't imagine growing up the 'normal' way and experiencing a childhood.

Jay looked at her for a long moment, and then asked, "So, can he meet with you? I think he has a lot of questions."

"No." It was the first time she had ever told a human no, but somehow it wasn't as terrifying as she expected.

"Aw come on Edel, he's desperate! I can't help but feel sorry for him. He pretty much begged me."

"NO." The answer came with more force this time and she glared at him as she stood her ground.

"Well, at least tell me why!" he said, exasperated.

"OFF LIMITS," she said. The words were cold and harsh.

Jay let out an exasperated noise from the back of his throat. "Edel! Come on!"

"Tell him to stay away from me. I don't want to see him. I don't want to speak to him. I don't want to *feel* him. And if he comes looking for me, I will kill him." She stomped off back to her room and shut the door, shaking with a mix of fear at her little outburst, and shock at what she had learned about that XJ. She could hear Jay's muttering and swearing outside, but he didn't follow her, and for that she was thankful.

The following morning, the thought of seeing Jay again had her shaking with fear. Yesterday, she had told a human no, and then she had allowed her emotions and her fear to control her actions. She didn't know if she had crossed some sort of line. If she was still at Poly-Gen, she would be in a great deal of pain right now.

She scuttled into the shower before he caught sight of her and dressed for work, then she nervously peeked out of her door. He was waiting for her in the kitchen. "You over your strop now?" he asked, laughing.

She only looked at him, unable to understand his humour. Shouldn't he be angry with her? She didn't understand this man at all.

"I'm sorry about yesterday, Edel. If you don't want to meet the guy, you don't have to. And if you don't want to tell me why, that's up to you as well." He handed her a coffee. "I spoke to him. He was disappointed, but I think I convinced him to stay away."

She nodded, not finding the words she needed. She had given into emotional weakness and refused a direct order. And HE was apologising to her? It was unfathomable.

Life continued as normal for the next few days. Edel found the predictability of work/run/sleep to be comfortable. Her days off were more of a challenge. If Jay was home, and didn't have plans with Katie, he would make her go outside with him. Being in public places was not getting any easier, but Jay said it was good for her. If Jay was working, or busy, she would spend all day inside, sitting at the end of her bed, not thinking, or feeling, almost ceasing to exist, until it was time for her run.

She was waiting for Jay in the loading bay at the back of the building at the end of her shift when she felt it. The familiar pulsating and vibrations in her chest. The pull of another.

Her eyes scanned the area, but she saw nothing unusual. The pulsing continued and grew stronger with every breath she took. She could tell which direction he was in now; she could pinpoint his exact location. She felt more than just his location – a mixture of fear and apprehension, thrilling excitement, and feelings of longing invaded her consciousness, except she couldn't name this foreign mix of feelings. She'd never experienced them before.

Spinning around in one fluid motion, she glared at him as he approached her. He stopped behind the huge metal containers that contained surplus stock for the warehouse, holding his hands out in front of him as if he was calming an angry mob. "Hi." His voice was breathless and unsure; she could sense his fear.

He tentatively took a step towards her, and she automatically stepped back. Not out of fear, but out of habit. XJ's were not supposed to get close to each other unless instructed.

"My name is Danny." He spoke to her with slow words, as though she might not understand.

She continued to stare at him. He was emitting all sorts of feelings and emotions she didn't understand, and she was having trouble processing them. He felt things she had never known or experienced, and it was strange and uncomfortable to have them forced onto her. It felt wrong. Feelings were not permitted.

"I just want to talk," he said, taking another step forward.

She didn't want to talk. Jay had told him that already. Without warning, she shot forward and slammed into him. Her fist connected with his jaw, and he flew backwards into one of the huge metal storage bins.

Pain *Fear* *Confusion*

She felt it all. She couldn't feel his actual physical pain, but she could sense he was in pain, and that was uncomfortable enough. He didn't seem able to control his emotional responses or his pain the same way she could.

He pulled himself to his feet, his hand rubbing his jaw where her fist had made contact. "I just want to talk," he said again. This time there was hurt in his voice and other strong emotions she was unable to decipher.

"Stay away from me," she said. "Come near me again, and I will kill you. Your family too."

Jay was pulling up at the main gate. She turned on her heels and marched to the car. She pulled open the door and climbed inside without speech and stared out of the window with a stony expression.

"Hey! What's up with you?" he asked, clearly able to see she wasn't in the best of moods.

She shook her head. The XJ was out of sight from the car, still behind the huge storage units, and she didn't see the sense in telling Jay about this. She had promised she wouldn't kill, but she would make an exception for him if he didn't leave her alone.

Edel had little to add to Jay's usual chatter on the way home, but that was nothing new and he didn't seem to notice there was anything wrong as she stewed on what had happened. She went running as normal; they ate as normal, and she went to bed as normal, switching off her feelings, and trying not to think as she sank into sleep.

***

XJ545-12 stood alone with baby. She didn't know if baby was human or genetic experiment. It did not matter.

They'd left her alone now for two weeks, just her and baby. They told her that her objective was to keep baby alive. Could it be true? Was this her purpose now?

Nobody had hurt her since they gave her this tiny creature to care for. No tests. No endurance. No pain. They monitored her and baby daily, but baby was never hurt. Baby was special.

XJ545-12 had always been alone before now, but she did not find the company of baby unpleasant. Sometimes in the night, when she was alone, and she thought they weren't listening in to her, she would hold baby and whisper things.

Baby had bright blue eyes. Baby had no name, but if she had been ordered to name it, she would have called her Blue.

***

Baby was four weeks old now. XJ545-12 had never been given directions on how to care for baby. Her only instruction was to keep baby alive and meet baby's needs as best she could. They continued to monitor baby. They provided everything baby needed. The formula, water for bathing, blankets for warmth.

XJ545-12 had kept baby alive. She knew they were watching and keeping notes on her actions and interactions with baby. There had been no intervention from the scientists, or the guards. She was left completely to her own devices.

She didn't know how to care for an infant, but nobody had beaten her, and this was the longest she had gone without her compliance chip being activated, so she must be doing it right.

XJ545-12 had been told she had been selected for this task specifically. They said she was an ideal candidate for such an important task, though they never divulged why, and she knew better than to ask.

XJ545-12 didn't dare hope for things often, but she was sure that if this was life from now on, then her life would be less painful and maybe even... enjoyable? She shook the thought from her head. XJ's weren't created to enjoy.

Baby was awake and making sweet, quiet noise. XJ545-12 couldn't help herself. She smiled. For the first time, a strange warmth had radiated from within her chest. She was alarmed by the unfamiliar sensation. Baby smiled back at her. There was a feeling inside her she couldn't describe. She didn't feel alone, isolated. Had she just had a connection with another living being? Fear erupted inside. She wasn't sure that was what she was meant to be doing. Baby was looking up at her with big blue eyes. She could feel herself melting.

***

Baby was seven weeks old now. It seemed that XJ545-12 was meeting baby's needs. Baby would stare at XJ545-12. Baby would calm when XJ545-12 would hold her. Her heart rate would slow, and she would fall asleep in XJ545-12's arms.

XJ545-12 had felt a sense of calm she had never experienced before. She didn't know why she had been chosen for this task. She tried not to think too deeply about why they asked her to do anything, she just blindly obeyed. That was her function.

***

They came. They took baby and ordered XJ545-12 to follow.

The one they called Jenson was there, and the one they called Hobson. They weren't alone, there were two guards and a lab technician and an XF there also. The guards led her into a room and passed her baby.

Jenson spoke, "Congratulations 12, we are very pleased with the progress you have made. The baby seems healthy and happy, and in perfect condition."

XJ545-12 was silent. What was next? She had a feeling they were going to take baby away from her. Was that it? Had they given her the baby to see if she would become attached to it? To see if she would develop some emotional attachment to it? She could never admit it, not even to herself, but that baby made her feel. She knew she had broken the rules. Feelings were not permitted. She didn't know exactly what she felt, but the last eight weeks had been the most pleasant and least distressing of her life. Perhaps this is what happiness felt like? She knew she was wrong for feeling it.

Jenson spoke again, "It seems you have been the perfect candidate for this experiment. You don't appear to have developed any emotional attachment to the child. Would you say you have?"

She stood straight, shoulders back, chin parallel to the floor. She looked past him and focussed on the wall behind. "No."

"That's good. There is only one test left. You shouldn't find it difficult."

Hobson stepped up and took baby from her. She ignored the urge to hold tighter and not allow this monster to take something so pure and precious. Baby was crying, wailing with distress and XJ545-12 wanted to reach out and comfort her. Calm her.

He placed baby on the cold, hard, tiled floor and baby cried harder. She couldn't move. She couldn't help and the crying caused a sensation in her chest that could be described as pain, though she didn't understand why it hurt.

Hobson turned to look at XJ545-12. "Kill it," he ordered.

For a moment, the whole world stopped turning. She hesitated and stood unmoving, the first time she had ever disobeyed a direct order.

Hobson looked over to the guard and gave a single curt nod, and all too soon she was in a heap on the floor, unable to move, unable to think. Every nerve in her body was on fire. She couldn't see, literally blinded by the pain. Her limbs were twitching and convulsing. Her heart beat in sporadic bursts, nothing like a normal rhythm, and the pain in her chest gripped her like a vice. She couldn't breathe, and the noise she heard in her head was enough to make her ears want to bleed.

They didn't allow it to go on too long. Just long enough to give her a taste of what to expect if she did not comply.

"12. I gave you an order. I want you to take your foot, and stamp on that baby. Stamp the life out of it."

She wanted to beg for the life of this child, but she knew it would be no use. This was a test, and she needed to pass. She wasn't supposed to care for life, even that of a helpless infant. If she failed to complete the task, she had failed the experiment. She would be tortured or maybe even terminated.

She stood slowly, raising herself off the floor on shaking legs. The pain had subsided, her eyesight had returned, and she found the resolve to carry out her order. Her feelings turned cold as she stood over baby, who was still crying and kicking her legs on the floor. Slowly, she raised her foot and felt nothing as she slammed it down with force. She heard the sickening crack of the baby's neck as she slammed her foot down and the crying stopped instantly, throwing them into jarring silence.

***

Edel woke with a start. Her breathing was heavy, and her heart was racing. She was soaked with sweat and disoriented. *Where am I? What is going on?* She looked around the room, recognising the familiar surroundings. She sat up and tried to make sense of what had just happened. It was so real.

It was like she was back there, in that place. The memories of that terrible place were fresh in her mind, and she couldn't understand why or how they got there. More than memories. It was as if she was reliving those moments, as if she was there.

A sadness settled around her. She hadn't thought of baby Blue since the day she killed her. She didn't know what to do with these feelings. She did what she always did; pushed them aside and snuffed them out, turning cold and emotionless.

Her hand moved to the back of her neck, and she felt for the compliance chip. It was still there, buried deep under her skin. It was almost as though she could still feel the pain, even though it was months since it had been activated.

She couldn't settle, she couldn't make sense of what had happened. What was going on? She was there – but she isn't there; she is here, safe.

She wondered if she was going crazy, losing her faculties. Normally when she slept, time passed, and she awoke feeling rested, with no memory of anything that happened in the times between being awake.

She couldn't make sense of this. *Something must be wrong with me.*

The thought worried her immensely. Edel did not go back to sleep that night. She sat in the quiet and turned herself 'off'. She was able to think of nothing and feel nothing. She didn't worry about what had happened anymore.

The following day, she continued as normal. And that night, she slept. Nothing happened. Whatever she had experienced the night before had not been repeated.

CHAPTER 21

Sunday 30th July 2102

Unit 7, Harpton Main City Centre

Danny picked himself up from the ground and roughly rubbed his jaw as he watched her drive away with Jay. He felt so confused and rejected. Why wouldn't she just talk to him? Why wouldn't she explain to him what was going on? He couldn't make sense of the sensations he experienced when he was close to her. There was so much he didn't understand.

He couldn't 'feel' her anymore. He scuffed the toe of his shoe along the rough concrete as he tried to understand why. His best guess was that they had driven out of range or whatever, however it worked.

Danny set off for home, filled with a sense of shame and rejection. The only person he had ever met who was like him didn't want him.

Tony was home when he arrived back at his house, and he shuffled in, trying to act normal. It didn't work. Tony took one look at him and yelled, "Oh my God! What happened to you?"

He caught sight of his reflection in the mirror and groaned. There was a deep purplish bruise visible across his jawline. The bruise wasn't obvious against his dark skin, but he looked dishevelled, his suit had a dirty mud stain along the back of the pants where she had thrown him to the ground, and there was an obvious swelling on the left side of his face, where his head had made contact with the metal storage containers.

"It's nothing important," he said, making a move to walk by Tony.

"Nothing important?" he repeated, dumbly. "Danny! I've never seen a bruise on you, ever. I didn't even think you could bruise."

Danny shook his head and tried to brush off Tony's concern. "I can bruise. It's no big deal."

"Well, how did it happen? It looks like someone hit you!"

Danny's face gave him away immediately.

"Oh my God!" Tony said, without even trying to hide his shock. "Someone hit you hard enough to bruise you? Who? Some sort of body builder?" The smile on his face vanished and his tone changed to one full of concern. "Oh... Is he okay? I mean, you didn't..."

Danny sighed and shook his head. "I didn't hit anyone."

"Then what happened?"

Danny looked at his friend carefully. "You can't tell anyone. Promise me you won't tell anyone."

Tony frowned. "No, of course I won't. What's going on, Danny? You're scaring me."

Danny instructed Tony to sit down. He had a feeling this explanation was going to come as a shock. "Remember when I told you about those feelings? The strange sensations I've been feeling?"

Tony nodded his head, his eyes fixed on Danny, waiting for more.

"Well, you know how a few months ago, there was an escape from the Poly-Gen facility?" He waited for his friend to put two and two together.

"Are you saying the feelings are to do with them? And one of them did that?" he asked, stunned, pointing to Danny's bruised face. Danny instantly picked up on his friend's fear.

Tony blew the air out of his cheeks. "What was he like?" There was a fascination to his voice, mingled with the shock.

Danny smiled. "She," he corrected.

"What? A girl smashed your face in?" He laughed at the absurdity of it. Once he got hold of himself, he looked at Danny with a much more serious expression, and asked, "Why did she attack you? Is she dangerous?"

Danny explained everything. How he had seen her before and she had attacked him in the men's room at the restaurant, and how he had confronted Jay about her, and the reasons he had lost his cool and ended up almost caving Jay's head in.

"She won't talk to me. She pretty much threatened to kill me and everyone I care about if I go near her again," he said in a sorrowful tone.

"Wow!" Tony breathed out. "But why?"

Danny shook his head and shrugged his shoulders roughly. He would like to know the answer to that question, too.

"Do you think she means it? Do you think she's dangerous?"

Danny thought for a minute. "Yes. I think everything they say on the news is true. I think she would kill me without a second thought," he shuddered as a cold tingle spread down his spine. He was desperate to know more about her, and himself, but he feared what he might find out.

"What does your dad think?"

"He doesn't know about this. He doesn't have any idea why I lost my shit with Jay at The Grid. And I want to keep it that way."

"Okay. What about Gemma? What does she think about this?"

Danny shook his head. "She can't know. This girl seems dangerous. And Gemma wouldn't stand a chance. I can't risk her getting hurt – or worse," he said, the worry in his heart matching the tone in his voice.

"Okay, so what about this Jay guy? What's his deal?"

"I'm not sure, he's just a normal guy, I think. I don't know how they met or how she ended up living with him, or working at the warehouse, but I guess they're friends."

"How do you know, though? What if he's being forced to help her? What if he's terrified of her and can't get help?" There was a deep look of concern etched on Tony's face.

Danny shook his head. "I don't know. He seemed to really care about her. When I talked to him, he was protective of her. Plus, he didn't seem at all upset or flustered when I told him about me. He wasn't afraid at all."

It felt good to finally have someone to talk to. He'd been carrying this alone for too long. Tony was one of the few people who knew how Danny felt about his differences, and he was always sympathetic and compassionate.

Eventually Tony leaned back in his chair and cleared his throat. "Danny, don't you think we should tell somebody? Don't you think we should call the authorities? She's a dangerous killer, and she's threatened you."

"We can't! What's stopping her telling them about me? If they knew I existed..." he shook his head as he thought of all the horrific things they might do to him. All the disturbing nightmares he'd been plagued with since he found out about the breakout swam to the forefront of his mind. The thought terrified him.

Tony looked horror-struck. "Oh! Of course. Sorry man, I wasn't thinking straight," he said. "What are you going to do?"

"Nothing, I guess. She said she'd kill me and everyone I care about if I don't leave her alone," he shrugged. "I don't think there is anything else I can do." The feeling of loss was crippling. He was so close to everything he had ever wanted, ever needed, but she was denying him. She wouldn't even give him a chance and he didn't understand why.

Danny spent the rest of the week wallowing in self-pity, feeling dejected and thoroughly miserable, but he knew he couldn't do anything to change her mind. Eventually, he had to give himself a talking to and shake himself out of this depression, and finally, he awoke one morning with a fresh perspective on life. He would never get the answers he wanted by badgering the girl, and she was obviously unhinged, and possibly dangerous. Who knows? Maybe once things settled down, he could try again.

It doesn't matter, he told himself. Why was he so hung up on learning about his differences? His friends, family and girlfriend all loved him for who he was, and that should be enough.

Today, he was taking Gemma out to a romantic, secluded spot in the country. His intention was to ask her to move to Helston to live with him. They had spoken of it before, but she'd told him she didn't want to leave her home. At the time, he'd accepted her answer at face value, but he couldn't shake the awful conversations he overheard every time he dropped her off at home. Her brother was unnecessarily mean to her, and he couldn't understand why she put up with that sort of abuse.

He had made a picnic basket of all Gemma's favourite foods and packed some wine with two plastic wine glasses. Danny loved the countryside, but Gemma had never seen much in the way of open fields and forests before. After the war, any land that wasn't contaminated was quickly used up for farming, so the green recreation areas had only made a return a few years ago, after the conservation trust had made green space a priority. It was paid for by tax, so only available to legitimate citizens. But cashers could accompany a legitimate for an additional fee.

It was beautiful, the open fields spanned for miles, and there was a small woodland that felt magical to walk through. There was water too. A huge lake with reeds growing out of it near the banks, although it wasn't safe for bathing. Danny led Gemma to a huge tree and laid a blanket out on the grass for her to sit on. She was so happy and relaxed, and he felt it too. He wasn't going to worry about Edel. Gemma was all that mattered.

Danny sat with his back against the tree trunk, legs outstretched with Gemma ensconced between his legs, her head resting on his chest. He had his arms around her, and he was gently stroking her arm while they sipped their wine. It was perfect. He had never felt so at peace, and he knew Gemma felt the same way when she was here with him.

He took a breath and leant back, aiming for nonchalance, and asked, "Have you given any more thought to moving to Helston with me?"

Warning sirens exploded in his head. *This was a mistake!*

She shifted her weight and turned her body to look at him, rolling her eyes. "Not this again, Danny!" She sounded exasperated and worn down, like she was fed up with discussing it already, before they had even started.

"Come on, Gemma! You can't say you enjoy living in Gromdon. It's awful! It's poor and dirty and it's not safe. Come and live with me. I can give you a better life."

He knew his mistake immediately. Gemma didn't want him to 'give' her a better life. She wanted to earn it on her own merit.

"There's nothing wrong with where I live. And I'm perfectly happy with my life, thank you." Her mouth had set into a sour pout, and she folded her arms across her chest.

"Gemma, come on! I can help you. I can get you a proper job. You could do something you really love!"

"The restaurant IS a proper job," she snapped. "You know how hard I had to fight to get paid work. I like it there. I like my job."

"But you could be so much more than a waitress, Gemma!" He didn't mean that how it sounded. She looked so crushed, and her face contorted in anger. "I AM so much more than a waitress! I thought you could see that. I'm sorry I *embarrass* you so much."

"You know I didn't mean it like that, Gemma," he tried to explain, but the damage was done. He carried on anyway, trying to make it right, but this was a touchy subject with her. He was only making things worse. Why couldn't she see that he only wanted what was best for her? He wanted to give her a chance to be who she wanted to be and do the things she wanted to do. She had dreams of being a designer, and she was so talented. Her ideas were fantastic, but nobody would want a dress designed by an uneducated casher refugee from Gromdon. That's just not how the world worked.

He reached forward and stroked her tears away with gentle fingers. He hated to upset her. She struggled with self-esteem issues, and that she wasn't good enough for him was one of those issues. His poor choice of words about being a waitress had added fuel that fire.

"I don't belong in Helston. I'm not like you. I love you, but I want to be more than just your girlfriend," she said.

Danny's eyes flickered with possibility. "What do you mean? Are you talking about marriage? Gemma, I would marry you in a heartbeat! I love you!" There was nothing he wanted more than for her to be his wife.

She slapped him on the arm. "No! I don't mean marriage!" she said as though he was crazy, and the jolt of rejection felt like a sharp slap in the face.

"I mean, if I move to Helston with you, I'm just the poor girl who got lucky with a rich guy. Everything I ever accomplish after that will be because of you, and your money or your status. I don't want that. I don't fit in there. The people all know I'm lower class, and they treat me like it. I wouldn't even be allowed outside without you accompanying me, I wouldn't be able to do anything at all by myself! And my brother and sister wouldn't be able to visit, not without you or somebody else there to act as a chaperone."

"Well, what am I meant to do? Leave you in the grotty industrial shithole? People rot there, Gemma. Let me give you the things you deserve," he said, gripping her hands in his and lifting them to his lips.

"I don't want you to GIVE me things," she snapped back at him.

"Well, you won't get them on your own!" Those words came out all wrong. This wonderful afternoon was spinning into a disaster. He didn't mean she couldn't achieve great things without him, only that the world simply didn't work that way. Nobody got anywhere without money or status, and she had the chance to have both.

She didn't answer him. Tears slowly streaked down her face as she made a grab for her bag and stood abruptly.

Danny grabbed her arm and pleaded with her to stay. "I'm sorry Gemma, I didn't mean that."

"I'm worth more than you think. If you think I'm so useless, go and get yourself a high-class girlfriend. Preferably one who doesn't care if what she's dating is human."

She stormed off and Danny was too stunned to follow. Those words wounded him to his core. How could she say something like that? Shame filled every inch of his heart. She knew he hated being different, but she had always said it didn't matter to her. That he was perfect the way he was, and she wouldn't change him even if she could.

He slowly gathered up his things, feeling utterly worthless. The pain of being rejected again, by someone he thought loved him, felt like a weight that would break him.

This was possibly the worst week of his life.

CHAPTER 22

Sunday 13th August 2102

Jay's Apartment, Helstain, Harpton Main

*T*he gripping fear enveloped her, the rising panic. This was surely going to be the end of her, she couldn't hold on much longer.
XJ545-12 opened her eyes and tried to see. Her vision was blurred by the water, and the chemicals stung her eyes. She persevered and tried to see how the others were faring. The one to her left was panicked, struggling, trying desperately to free her limbs and rise to the surface. Her arms jerked frantically in sporadic movements, trying to escape the restraints. It was too late; she opened her lungs and took a breath. She continued to fight for the next minute, arms and legs jerking in sporadic movements, until her head hung forwards and all went still.
XJ545-12 tried, but she couldn't tear her eyes away. The horror of seeing how she was about to die was gripping. She couldn't look away.
The pressure in her lungs was crippling, and the urge to breathe was about to overtake her. To her right, she could make out the perfectly still shape of the male, head held forward. He was dead too.
All-encompassing fear surrounded her. For a long time now, all she

had wanted was for her suffering to be over, but now it was time, she didn't want to die.

She couldn't hold on. She drew breath and her lungs burned as they filled with the water. Her body jerked and twitched as her lungs tried to expel the foreign substance, but it was no use.

Firm hands gripped her underarms as she struggled and squirmed, and the cold air hit her face as she broke the surface of the water.

Edel woke screaming and sweating. Her hands clawed at her throat, and she coughed violently, as though she was choking and couldn't breathe.

It took her a few seconds to get her bearings and realise where she was. She stared around the familiar dim room – her bedroom – and tried to cling to the feeling of safety.

She closed her eyes and tried to calm her frayed nerves, unsure what was happening to her. This had been the same as three nights ago, as though she was reliving her days at PolyGen. It was more than memories. She was experiencing the horrors and torture all over again. Feeling it as though she was still there and had never left.

Edel jumped as Jay came bursting in through the door. She'd been so caught up in her thoughts she hadn't heard him outside her room.

"Edel? Edel, is everything okay? I heard screaming!"

"I'm fine." She was short with him, an unfriendliness in her voice, warning him to stay back.

He stared at her quizzically, but she offered no more information. She pulled on her pants and hoody, then walked straight past Jay without speech, grabbing a jacket on her way out. She left the apartment without looking back, even as Jay shouted after her, "Where are you going? It's the middle of the night!"

She didn't return until after he had left for work in the morning. She didn't know how she could explain to him she was losing her mind. That when she slept, she was transported back to relive the torture and the experiments. She didn't know if she was safe to be around, this surely wasn't normal. If she had shown signs of psychosis before her escape, they would have terminated her.

She feared for her sanity, and Jay's safety. There was nobody to ask, nobody to confide in. Nobody qualified to delve into what had gone wrong with her mind. She was certain humans never experienced this, at least not ones with sound and healthy minds.

When she saw Jay later that day, she offered no explanation for her behaviour the previous night and continued with her usual routine, as though there was nothing wrong. It happened again that night. And again, the night after. Edel stared at the bed and felt a touch of trepidation the next night. She didn't want to experience those things again. She had worked so hard at keeping those thoughts, feelings, and memories out. As she climbed into bed, she took a moment to calm herself, telling herself she was being ridiculous. It took her some time to fall asleep, and that was worrying. She had never not been able to fall asleep before.

Bright white light assaulted her eyes. It caused her pain to look at them. She squinted up, trying to understand what was happening. The noise was rushing into her ears, but the sounds were undecipherable. Rough hands grabbed her and forced her onto a bed, the sensation of feeling touch for the first time frightened her. She screamed aloud, and hearing her own noise took her by surprise. Her breathing was fast and shallow, but it felt so wrong. The first time her lungs had been used, and it felt harsh and gritty as she drew each breath.

The people in the room were speaking. It took her a moment to recognise that she understood their language. She tried to communicate.

"What is happening? Help me, help me."

A hand slapped her hard across the face, leaving a stinging heat in its wake. The first pain she had ever experienced. It shocked her into silence.

"You will speak only when spoken to," a harsh voice said.

The shock and the fear kept her silent. She watched in horror as one man grabbed her arm and forced it into a machine. It burned. Pain was new, and she didn't understand it. It was excruciating as the searing laser cut into her skin. She screamed aloud and tried to pull her arm free, but there were men holding her down. The man hit her again, hard across the side of her face, and she screamed out again. They freed her arm from the machine and her eyes rested on the black lines and numbers etched into her skin.

Still the men did not speak. She was smaller than them, only a child – she somehow understood she was not done growing. They forced her over onto her front and pushed her face into the bed and restrained her again.

Fear. All consuming, pure, and unending. Her heart was racing, and her body shook uncontrollably. She dared not speak again. She dared not ask. They forced her head into the machine, and she screamed again as the same indescribable pain seared into her neck. It was somehow worse this time.

Edel woke, hyperventilating and unable to make sense of anything. How could it be that she was seeing and experiencing the horrors and the torture while she slept? She had re-lived her awakening, and it was so real, the trauma of being pulled from sleepy nothingness and forced into bright, harsh reality. She didn't want to experience that again. The pure fear of being awoken, the confusion and the pain when they branded her with the stamp and after when they implanted the compliance chip.

There was nobody to ask about this. She couldn't admit to Jay that there was something wrong with her. It only happened when she slept.

She made the decision to stay awake for a few nights. It wouldn't matter, she was able to function without sleep for weeks. She carried on as normal, not seeming to deviate from her routine of work/run/sleep. The only difference was, instead of sleeping, she would close down her emotions, and sit at the end of her bed, staring at nothing, until the sun came up again. Then she would shower as normal and get herself ready for work.

The first three days were fine, but by day four she was tired. It made no sense. She could function for weeks without sleep. She assumed whatever was in the food at Poly-Gen made a difference to her stamina. That, and the fact it was a perfectly controlled environment. She hadn't considered how much extra energy she needed to expend, just to accept the 'busyness' of her new life. Her cognitive processes were working harder all the time.

By day five, she realised she was afraid to sleep. She couldn't stay awake indefinitely, but it only happened when she slept.

Jay still had no idea, and the idea she could be a danger to him played on her mind. She wondered if she should tell him. Jay was the only person who had ever helped her, and she didn't want to hurt him, but she was getting on edge with the lack of sleep, and she was no longer sure she could guarantee his safety.

As the evening ended, she sat rigid, waiting for an appropriate time to pretend to go to bed.

"Edel? Hey! are you even listening to me?"

The sound of Jay's voice made her body jolt with surprise. How had she not heard him speaking?

He was laughing at her. "Is everything okay?" he asked with a chuckle.

She hated that question. It wasn't a real question. "Yes," she lied.

"What's wrong?" he made a move to get closer to her. He was looking at her face with interest. "Are you sick?" he asked, his voice full of concern.

"No."

"You look pale." He reached out his hand as if to touch her face, and she jumped to her feet and shoved his hand away before he could get close enough to reach her.

"Don't touch me!" It came out almost as a scream. She was losing control of herself.

Jay was massaging his arm, just above the elbow joint where she had jarred it. When he spoke again, she could hear the fear in his voice. "Edel, I'm sorry. I didn't mean to... I wasn't going to..."

"Stay away from me." The pitch of her voice was rising. She couldn't seem to control it. She stepped back, away from him.

Jay shrugged. "Okay, whatever. I'm sorry."

There was no irritation in his voice when he spoke; he was acting as though this was all perfectly normal. He simply sat back down and turned his attention back to the TV, unaware of how close he came to almost losing his arm.

She left the apartment without thinking about where she was going. Her legs carried her as though they had a mind of their own. Her thoughts turned to Jay. Had she hurt him? The sleep deprivation was leaving her too tired to control her actions. She was becoming unhinged and dangerous. Her thoughts were becoming jumbled up, running wild from one thing to the next, as though she couldn't hold on to one long enough to complete it. This had happened before, when they kept her without sleep for weeks at a time at Poly-Gen.

Out of nowhere, she was assaulted by the pulsing, vibrating sensations in her body. The other was near. She should have felt it before, but her senses were all underperforming.

She froze. The sensations sent her mind careering right back to Poly-gen, and the strange experiences she had been having during her sleep were fresh in her mind. Panic rippled under her skin. She was close to losing it.

She stared at him, unsmiling. Danny didn't speak to her at first. He was addressing the human he was with. "Tony. Stay where you are," he warned. "I'll catch you up, okay? Just go on without me. I'll see you at home."

"What's going on?" he looked over to Danny and then to Edel. "Is that–?" The look on Danny's face cut him off.

As soon as Tony spoke, it set Edel on edge. What did he know about her? A surge of irritation shot through her. This other had no business telling anyone who she was.

Anger

Danny felt an unnatural, unexplainable sense of anger towards his friend. For seemingly no reason at all, he wanted to rip his friend's face off. "Tony. Just go. I'll explain later," he said through gritted teeth.

Tony eyed his friend, then looked at Edel. He hesitated a moment, unmoving.

Edel rounded on Danny. The stress of the last few days and the lack of sleep and the fear that she was going insane all made it so much harder to think. She was abrupt and to the point when she said, "What did you tell him?"

Anger

Danny was trying to stay calm, but he didn't understand this irrational fury that had engulfed him so suddenly. He ignored her question and spoke with a calm authority to Tony again. "GO. NOW."

This time, Tony backed away. He turned and walked a few paces but kept stopping to look. He eventually left them, and Danny let out a sigh of relief.

Edel and Danny stood stationary, facing each other in the street. It surprised Danny how attuned to her he was suddenly. As though he could feel her feelings. He was desperate to know what it meant, but common sense told him right now would not be the best time to ask. He spoke to her in soft tones, as though he was coaxing a frightened animal. "There's something wrong?" It was both a question and a statement.

She didn't answer him; she just continued to stare at him.

"You are afraid?" he asked.

Panic

His question sent her fear and anxiety skyrocketing. How could he ask her that? It was not okay to show fear. Ever. Not to humans, not to XJs. Fear was punishable and not permitted.

Danny exhaled, feeling adrenaline rush through his own veins. Her fear somehow affected his body and his mind, and he shook with a sort of terror. He took another breath and tried to stay calm, but it was proving difficult now. Was it always like this? These new sensations left him both awestruck and terrified at the same time. There was so much about himself he didn't understand.

"Come with me," he murmured. "Let's go somewhere we can talk."

Edel knew she needed help. She was tired and scared, and she didn't know what else to do. She wasn't used to feeling so out of her depth and desperate. Silently, she nodded her head and followed him as he set off walking. To anybody looking at them, they just looked like two people heading in the same direction, but there was a lot of silent communication occurring between them as they walked.

The act of walking soothed Edel. It gave her something to focus on aside from her crippling fear. As they walked, the shared tension they were both experiencing lessened considerably, but it did not disappear.

Danny felt lost in his feelings. For the first time in his life, he felt as though he found where he belonged. There was someone here who understood him, or at least understood what it was like to be like him. It was the first time he'd ever felt like he wasn't alone, an outcast, different from everyone else. And finally, she was here. Trusting him. He couldn't let this opportunity pass him by.

Edel found Danny's feelings repulsive as they ate at the edges of her mind. They felt odd and intense; she couldn't understand or decipher the sensations. She hated the feel of it, but they were so unfamiliar, she was unable to tune them out.

They reached an abandoned construction site, closed for the weekend. It was eerily quiet away from the noise of the city. Neither of them had spoken during their walk, and Danny felt as though there was an invisible wall between them, as though she had erected a defence system so he couldn't feel her anymore. He wanted to ask what it all meant. How could his feelings echo hers? Was that normal between people like them? Did he have the same effect on her? But he wasn't entirely certain if he would sound insane. Did she even feel it?

They came to a natural stop, with nowhere else to go without turning around. It seemed as good a place as any to talk. He swallowed down his nerves as he turned to face her and calmly asked her what was wrong.

She didn't answer at first, and he waited, allowing her to collect her thoughts. The invisible wall was still there between them, and he couldn't help but try to push through it, trying to feel how she felt.

She held her hand up, palm facing Danny. "STOP." She didn't shout, but it was more than words. More like a command hitting him on the inside. It stunned him, as though he had been shocked from inside his body. He didn't know how she had done it, but the unusual assault pulled him up short.

"Why are you afraid?" he eventually asked.

It took her a long while to answer him; she needed to get control of herself first. Admitting fear was not something she was comfortable with and admitting it to another XJ was unheard of.

She collected her thoughts and put her words together with care. "I've not been sleeping."

Fear *Worry* *Shame*

Danny absorbed the feelings like a sponge. He, too, suddenly felt afraid and ashamed, but he had no idea why. It was so bizarre. As quickly as the feelings arrived, they vanished again, leaving Danny confused.

"I'm worried I might hurt Jay," she added, after her initial surge of panic subsided.

He narrowed his eyes, trying to understand. "Why would you want to hurt Jay?" he asked.

"I don't want to. I'm struggling to regulate myself without

sleep."

"Why aren't you sleeping?"

Fear *Fear*

He couldn't escape her fear. It pulled him under, and he couldn't understand why his body shook with fright and his heart raced.

Fear *Fear*

The way his body and mind responded to her fear was reflected to her, echoing her own and magnifying it. Closing her eyes, she exhaled forcefully, and said, "Control that," as though it was all perfectly normal.

"What is it? How does it work?" he asked after he caught his breath.

The questions took her by surprise. She had never given it a second thought that he had never met another XJ. He had no experience of how the hive mind, or their shared responses worked. For the first time, she understood why he made her feel confused and overwhelmed.

She didn't answer, and they both stood in silence, trying to remain calm while waiting for the fear to retreat. Eventually, she took a deep breath and spoke. "When I sleep, it's as if I am back there, at that place. Like I remember things without choosing to."

"You mean you're dreaming?"

Dreaming wasn't a term she understood. She'd never dreamed at Poly-Gen. Her sleep always came easily, and when she woke, she remembered nothing about being asleep.

"Dreaming?" she said the word aloud, feeling it in her mouth. Is that what she was doing? "Do you dream?"

"Everyone does," he said with a shrug.

She shook her head. "Not me. Not before."

There was a shift in the atmosphere between them then. It was subtle, but Danny felt it. She was less afraid, more curious.

"How do you make it stop?"

"I don't think people control dreaming. I don't think you can stop them," he said. He sensed her unease. Her fear had shot back up, causing him to feel afraid too. It was intense.

"Sometimes it can help to talk about them," he offered.

She didn't answer, or she couldn't. He wasn't sure which.

"What happens in your dreams?" he pressed.

The fearful feelings intensified. Danny felt anxious, as though he was about to have a panic attack. How could speaking to another person have this effect on him?

"It's okay. Whatever they're about, they're only dreams. They can't hurt you." He thought that sounded reassuring, but he was wrong. She felt as though he was dismissing her fears. She didn't argue with him, but he picked up on her uncertainty. He felt how she pulled back away from him, as if the tiny bit of trust they had built between them had shattered into pieces.

"I'm not saying they're not upsetting," he said, trying to fix his mistake. "I'm just saying, they can't physically hurt you."

"They did hurt me. They hurt me every day for ten years."

Danny hung his head. The things she dreamt about must be utterly horrifying. He tried to steer the conversation a little better. "How long since you last slept?"

"Five days," she answered, as though it was nothing.

Danny stared at her with wide eyes. "Five days?" he asked. "Five days?" he repeated. "Do you mean five days since you've had a full night's sleep, or five days since…?" he could not bring himself to finish the question. Surely, she didn't mean she had been awake for five solid days!

"Five days," she said.

"You've not slept in five whole days?" he asked her again. He caught the surge of irritation from her.

She remained silent, but her annoyance was eating at her. *Am I saying it wrong? Or is he just mentally inferior? How many ways are there to say I've not slept for five days? How is he not understanding this?*

He stepped back, away from her and her irritation. He felt annoyed too, almost angry, but he was no longer sure if it was his feeling or hers. His jaw was set as he pushed his tongue into his teeth, attempting to keep his angry words inside.

Her hands came up again in front of her body, palms facing Danny in a position of surrender. "Stop," she said. "I'm not functioning properly. I can't process your anger. I didn't come to hurt you."

Danny didn't understand what she meant about processing his anger, but it didn't matter now. It had already passed.

"You need to sleep," he said. He felt her fear spike again at the mention of sleep. She seemed terrified at the idea. "Why don't you come with me? Come to my house. Sleep there."

She stared at him, wondering if he was out of his mind.

"You don't trust me?" he asked, picking up on her scepticism. "I only want to help you."

She still hadn't answered him. She was wondering why he wanted to help her. People rarely treated her with kindness or compassion.

"Look, you can't keep awake forever. You need to sleep. You're worried about becoming a danger to Jay or hurting someone. There's less chance you will hurt me, right?"

No, she thought. If anything, this strange XJ didn't seem to have any control over his senses, or his emotions. If she woke from a dream disoriented and afraid, things could escalate to an unmanageable level very quickly. Still, she didn't have any other options.

"Are you ready now?" he asked, motioning with his hand for her to follow as he turned around and walked back the way they came.

They walked in uncomfortable silence and Danny's eyes flitted in her direction often, wondering if this was a bad idea. Her worry and apprehension piled on top of his own, making him feel worse. If the news was to be believed, she was a crazy psycho killer. She could kill indiscriminately, and without remorse.

The silence drew on, but he could no longer feel her fears. That odd, invisible wall had arrived again. He could sense her still, but it was like she was empty and cold. It made him uncomfortable, but he couldn't put his finger on why.

Edel never faulted, her resolve was strong, even with the lack of sleep. She shrouded herself from Danny and protected herself from his relentless feelings and emotional assault. She couldn't understand why he wasn't switching off. It was hard to keep closed down when feelings snuck up unexpectedly. It was easy to get carried away, but once you have a hold of yourself, you are expected to keep closed off. Emotional responses hurt the entire group. They are uncomfortable for all and not permitted. And being in such close proximity to only one XJ made the feelings so much stronger. She'd never had such a strange mix of feelings forced upon her, and never with this much energy. She was beginning to regret her decision to follow him.

They walked in complete silence for thirty minutes. As they drew closer to Danny's house, the tension she was feeling from him spiked. He looked at her nervously and said, "This is it. This is my house." He smiled at her.

She didn't return the smile. She had never seen an XJ smile before. In fact, the way he spoke was all wrong. Gentle and full of concern.

Once inside, they both stood awkwardly while she took in her new surroundings. "I thought we would be alone," she said, hearing the movements of feet upstairs.

Her abrupt and to the point speech set Danny on edge. His answer was nothing like the way he normally spoke, but came out in short, informative sentences instead. "That's Tony. He lives here. He's my best friend. I trust him."

Her ears caught the term 'best friend', but it was meaningless to her.

Danny offered her something to drink, but she only stood rigid and refused to answer. In the end, after he couldn't stand the tension anymore, he said, "My bedroom is upstairs. Come on, I'll show you."

She followed him up the stairs, and Danny prayed Tony

would stay in his room. Would he have heard them talking? He was never sure how much a regular human could hear.

He hovered in the doorway, feeling awkward at the idea of allowing a perfect stranger access to his bedroom. "I'll just be downstairs if you need anything," he murmured. He felt her irritation flare again.

What could I possibly need? Her annoyance was fleeting, and she closed herself down again. She could feel his curiosity, another uncomfortable feeling. Questions were not permitted.

Danny closed the door as he left and felt relief as he walked down the stairs, setting some distance between them. He had felt nothing like these frightening, unusual, and nerve-racking sensations, but it was somehow comforting to know he wasn't alone in the world. So many questions swirled in his head. How did it work? Did she feel him the same way he felt her? What was the point of it? There must be a reason they were made that way. He wondered how it would feel to him if she dreamed. Would he know what she was dreaming about? She said she only dreamed of memories of her life before. Would he have the chance to experience what it was like, if she dreamed tonight?

He thought about it a little longer and came to the realisation that he only sensed her feelings. He didn't know what she was thinking. If she was dreaming tonight, he would feel what she felt, but he wouldn't have any idea what she was experiencing.

Danny didn't know what to do to occupy his time while he stayed awake. He sensed her sleeping already, and a sort of calm washed over him. He allowed himself to explore the strange sensations. It was weirdly intimate. He felt creepy, like he was violating her in some way. Intruding on her feelings while she slept, but he didn't know how to not feel her. The wall she put up before must be something she could control, but perhaps not something she could keep up during sleep.

He thought about calling Gemma. They hadn't spoken since their fight a few days ago. He had never gone this long without seeing or speaking to her, and he ached with missing her, but he couldn't shake the things she had said to him. *She hasn't tried to call me either;* he thought sullenly.

He wondered a lot about his feelings for Gemma. His feelings for her were intense, more than how other people described how they felt for the people they loved. He'd tried to talk to his dad about love, but Frank wasn't a touchy-feely type of man. It made it difficult to discuss anything so personal with him at all, besides, what if it wasn't normal? His feelings for Gemma bordered on obsession. His need to be close to her and to protect her was overpowering. He craved her presence. He never tired of seeing her, watching her, listening to her talk. She was the single most interesting person he'd ever met. When she was near, he didn't see anyone else. It made him question if he was broken in some way. Jenson had always maintained that he wasn't meant to have feelings. He wondered if this was why they had side-lined him for termination. He was faulty stock.

It was late, and Gemma was probably sleeping now, but he picked up his phone and dialled anyway. After a few moments, her voicemail picked up, and he felt almost bereft as he listened to the recording of her voice. He needed her. He decided he would make things right with her in the morning. Then he remembered Edel upstairs in his bed and wondered what would happen in the morning. Would she be any more friendly? Would she be less terrifying?

She was still sleeping, and the only sensations he could feel were peaceful ones. He didn't know what else to do, so he switched on the TV and settled down for the night. The government was still spouting its propaganda. There were videos and news reports about possible XJ sightings, but they had made no arrests or captures. Then the new ridiculous 'Know Your Neighbour' campaign started rolling. It might sound like an initiative to improve community spirit, but it wasn't. They were encouraging people to check for escapees hiding within their neighbourhoods. If you didn't know your neighbours, you were supposed to get to know them, and quickly.

The theory was that the escaped XJ5's wouldn't be able to answer questions about their past. Simple questions like 'How old are you?' or 'When is your birthday?' would be enough to give them away. Other questions included 'Where did you grow up?', 'What is your mother called?' and 'What is your favourite colour?' There was a number to call, should you meet someone who couldn't answer these basic questions.

Danny realised he should warn Edel. She would need to have answers lined up in case anyone approached her with these questions.

The night passed slowly and was uneventful, but he was thankful for that. Perhaps if she had enjoyed a dreamless sleep, she would be more amicable this morning?

He heard movement upstairs, but it couldn't be Edel. He assumed he would know if she was awake. Tony appeared in the doorway wearing nothing but his underwear, and he shuffled through sleepily.

"You been up all night?" he asked, then seemed to remember the strange girl from last night. "What happened after I left?"

Danny explained what was wrong with Edel, and how he had brought her home last night, and how she was currently sleeping in his bed. Tony's eyes were wide with shock as he took this information in.

"What do you mean when you say you can feel her? Like, can you *feel* her now?" he asked, a look of pure fascination on his face.

Danny shrugged uncomfortably. It was hard to explain how it felt, and he didn't want to freak his friend out. "You should get dressed. You should probably keep out of the way until she's gone, too. She's not very friendly."

Tony swallowed and stared at his friend. "Is she dangerous?"

Danny made a face. "Maybe. I'm not sure," he admitted.

Tony didn't need telling twice. He turned on his heels and disappeared back up the stairs and into his room.

CHAPTER 23

Saturday 19th August 2102

Gemma's House, Gromdon, Harpton Main

Gemma woke and saw the missed call from Danny on her phone. She gave a heavy sigh and looked across to her sister's already empty bed on the other side of their small room. Ali was already at the market.

Gemma threw on some old sweatpants and a t-shirt and went to see if anybody else was home. Craig was at work, but Gianni was home, and he greeted her with his usual smile.

"Good morning, Gemma! You've slept here every night this week! Are things okay with you and your boyfriend?"

Gianni wasn't being nosy, that was just how he was. He was technically their landlord, but he was so much more than that. He was more of a parental figure for the three of them. Their whole family had lived in this house at one point, the three children and their mom and dad, but Aoife, their mother, had died when Gemma was twelve, and their father, Craig Sr, had vanished months later. Gianni was the one who had stepped up and taken care of them.

He was the only person who was happy for Gemma and her relationship with Danny. It didn't matter to him that he was a rich legitimate. He had never turned on her and called her a cash traitor. Instead, he would make her some tea, and tell her that Craig would come around eventually, and that he was probably a little jealous.

"We had an argument," she confessed.

"You want to tell me about it?" he asked, already filling a kettle to make tea. They were lucky. They had running water and electricity in their house. Although, no gas and no heating.

She shook her head. It wasn't the sort of thing she wanted to discuss, even if she could talk about the details of their fight.

"It might help. I've had my fair share of arguments in my time!" he said with a wink, his thick Italian accent showing through as he spoke so animatedly.

"I don't even know what we were arguing over. But I know I said something that really hurt him. I mean, REALLY hurt him. I was just so upset. I didn't even mean it."

"Well, how did you leave it?"

"I told him to get a high-class girlfriend. You know, someone who's more suited to his class status." Her eyes fell to the floor. "I think we might be done."

"Nonsense!" he said, waving his hand, dismissing her words. There was a cheerful sharpness in his voice. "I see how that boy looks at you. I might have never met the guy, because you refuse to bring him inside… but I know what love looks like, sweetheart. One argument isn't enough to call it quits, no matter what hurtful thing you may have said."

"I don't know. He said some hurtful things too. He thinks I'm not good enough for him."

Gianni coughed. "Gemma, sweetheart, did he actually say that? Because that sounds like what YOU think, not what HE thinks."

She cast her mind back. He had said that, hadn't he? Didn't he say she should be more than a waitress? Wasn't he embarrassed to be with someone with such a low-level service position for a job? And he wanted her to move to Helston. Gromdon was an 'industrial shit hole' according to him.

Gianni didn't let her think for too long before he said, "I doubt that's what he said, but if he did, he won't have meant it. You said things you didn't mean. He would have too. You should talk to him."

She nodded and thought back to the missed call on her phone. She could call him back, but she didn't want to make her apology over the phone. An apology in person would make him see she didn't mean what she said. It didn't matter if he was made in a laboratory instead of being born the traditional way. He could have three heads for all she cared, she would still love him.

She decided to take Gianni's advice and go to Helston to see Danny and surprise him. It took her some time to get ready. She had to boil the kettle to fill the sink in the bathroom to wash herself, and she washed her hair too. She didn't bother to dry it, instead she put it up in a French plait that snaked across the side of her head, and then took the hair at the back and made it into a neat bun. It looked good, and nobody would guess it was still wet. She dressed in a pair of green trousers she had made herself out of left-over material, and she wore a plain black top with three quarter length sleeves to complete her outfit. She would need to pass for legitimate if she was going to Helston unaccompanied. Last, she applied a small amount of perfume. She knew to use it sparingly; Danny always said he liked to smell her body, not her perfume. She wasn't sure what he could smell exactly, but not owning a shower or having easy access to hot water made her very self-conscious.

She took the train to Branley and walked past her workplace. It was another hour's walk to get to Helston, and if border patrol stopped her, she would be in big trouble. She knew she ought to call him, and tell him to meet her here, instead of breaking the law, but she was caught up in the idea of what a huge romantic gesture it would be if she showed up at his house. He couldn't fail to see how sorry she was because of the effort she had made to get there.

She arrived on his street and looked up at his house. Now she was here, the doubts were creeping in. What if he didn't want to see her? What if he was still angry with her? The things she said were unforgivable. She drew a couple of deep breaths to steady her nerves and forced herself to walk up the steps to his front door.

When the door opened, it was Tony, not Danny, who was standing before her. "Gemma! What are you doing here?"

She noted his tone. He wasn't happy to see her. She wondered what Danny had said to him and how much he had told him about their argument. "Um, I'm here to see Danny. Is he home? Can I come in?"

Danny appeared behind Tony. "It's okay, man," he said, placing a hand on Tony's shoulder.

Tony gave his friend a look but had nothing to add. He shrugged his shoulders and walked off into the house, leaving them to it.

"Danny! I'm so sorry," she wailed and pushed her way into him, flinging her body into his and hugging him hard as the tears ran from her eyes. "I'm so sorry. I didn't mean what I said."

His strong arms found their way around her body, and he hugged her back. They stood holding each other for some time until Gemma's tears had subsided. When he eventually let her out of his embrace, she grabbed his hand and started for the stairs.

She only got halfway when he grabbed her arm and held her steady. "Let's stay down here," he said.

She looked at him, a nagging feeling creeping in the back of her head. "We need to talk. I don't want to talk with Tony listening in," she said. "Come on," she yanked his hand as she walked up a few more steps.

"No. We can talk here. We don't need to go up there." He pulled her into him.

Gemma frowned. They stood on the staircase, almost at the top, and he didn't want her to go any further. There was only one reason she could think why he wouldn't want her in his bedroom. She backed away from him, taking two more steps up the stairs, and looked at his face. "Why not?" She could hear the accusation in her own voice.

He looked away from her for a moment and brought his hands up to his face. She took her opportunity and turned and ran up the last of the stairs, taking Danny by surprise. He bolted after her, reaching her just in time to stop her from pushing open his bedroom door.

"Gemma, I can explain!"

"Explain what?" Her face was set with fear and disbelief. *Surely, he hadn't? He wouldn't.*

"Please, just come back downstairs with me. Okay? Just let me talk to you."

She studied his face, searching for some undeniable proof he hadn't cheated on her, when he suddenly grabbed the wall as if to steady himself, and he closed his eyes.

"No. No, stay there. It's fine," he whispered under his breath.

"Danny?" This strange behaviour was alarming; she'd never seen him act this way before. "Danny?" she said again, frowning with concern.

He opened his eyes and looked at her face, but it was almost as if he was seeing her for the first time that day. He composed himself almost immediately and said, "Come downstairs with me."

Gemma nodded, a look of concern on her face. He turned to walk away, and she waited until he had taken two paces away from her before her hand jutted out and took hold of the handle of his bedroom door. She shoved it open as fast as she could.

Danny was there in a second. His reflexes were far quicker than any average humans' and his speed was astounding when he allowed himself to use it. He grabbed the door and pulled it closed as soon as Gemma had opened it, but not before they both had an eyeful of the near naked girl rising from his bed.

"Gemma!" he called her name desperately, reaching out to grab her. She stepped back, shaking her head. "No. No." Tears had sprung up in her eyes. "How could you?"

"No, Gemma, it's not what you think. I swear."

Grief momentarily floored her. How could he have done this? How could he have taken her words at face value and found someone new? The sorrow turned to anger, and she vehemently hissed at him through gritted teeth, "Let me in. I want to see her."

She tried to push past him, fighting him with all her strength, although she knew it was pointless. He didn't budge from the doorway and the tears rolled down her cheeks, leaving splotches of wet on her shirt. "How could you do this?" she sobbed, all the while pointlessly banging on his chest with balled up hands. She didn't know if it hurt him. She wished it did.

Danny stood and took her pained assault. He didn't stop her, and he didn't move himself away from the door. She eventually ran out of energy, and her rage filled punches were becoming weaker, as her tears cried harder, and the sobs racked her chest.

"Gemma."

"No!" she screamed at him. She turned and ran back down the stairs and bolted out of the front door without looking back. Every ugly doubt she had ever had had been confirmed. She wasn't good enough for him.

CHAPTER 24

Saturday 19th August 2102

Danny's House, Helston, Harpton Main

E del woke. The events of yesterday and where she was swam into her consciousness. She had experienced no dreaming in the night, and she felt rested and calmer, and better able to process the world around her again. She took a minute to adjust to her new surroundings and think what was expected of her now. The other was close by. She could feel his trepidation as he realised she had woken.

She didn't know what she should do next. Last night, she had shown weakness, and it felt shameful. She didn't want to see him.

Her thoughts were pierced by a knock at the door downstairs, followed by voices, then out of nowhere, an intense feeling hit her hard. The weight of it floored her as the ache spread in her chest. It was unexplainable and so intense it made her teeth feel itchy. She felt ill with it. It left her head spinning, and she felt sick. She did not recognise this feeling, but it was overpowering and uncomfortable. Feelings of fear, anxiety and panic replaced the odd sensation. At least these were things she understood.

She heard a woman's voice; they were arguing. She felt a stab of fear, and what could only be described as a type of pain, but not a pain she had ever experienced before. A deep sorrow, mixed with guilt, and she couldn't understand. She'd never experienced feelings like this before. This other, he was different. He was wrong.

They were outside the bedroom door now. He was afraid. Terrified. As the shared space of their minds connected, she felt afraid too. Her brain had interpreted the sensations, and she perceived danger – why else would he be afraid? Not knowing what else to do, she muttered, "Do you need assistance?" under her breath. She knew he would have heard her through the solid wood of the closed door.

His stress response elevated at speed as she heard his whispered response of "No, no. Stay there. It's fine."

It didn't sound fine. She did not intervene, but she left the bed. She was undressed and if she had to leave on foot, she would surely draw too much attention to herself, running around naked.

She sat up, pushed her hair out of her face and stood from the bed. Her body jerked in alarm as the door opened quickly and was pulled closed again. Edel stood, ready to attack. This other better have kept quiet about who she was.

The other was panicked, his state of stress was climbing higher and higher. Her hand came to her chest and her knees buckled. She lost the ability to support herself for a brief second, as a wave of pain engulfed her, that same pain she didn't recognise or understand.

It was disorienting. She'd never experienced guilt, sorrow, or remorse before. She didn't know what it was to feel pain for hurting someone she loved.

The female human left, and Edel felt the torn indecision of the other. She was catching her breath and trying to make sense of the swimming feeling in her head and her pounding heart when she felt the other retreat too. She could hear him chasing the girl down and feel a strange sense of desperation accompanying him. Eventually, he disappeared out of her 'feeling' range, the pulsating stopped, and she knew he was nowhere near her now. She was alone again.

She dressed and tried to piece together what she had just experienced. That was the strangest interaction between human and XJ she had ever witnessed. She was still reeling from the intensity of emotion. There was nothing she'd ever known that had come close to that. Feelings of nearly every description were foreign to her, and she found it distressing that being near this other caused such a strong emotional reaction. The feelings were unnameable and not something she could define, but she knew without a doubt that she didn't want to ever feel anything like that again. It was wrong.

She didn't know what she should do now. The other had left her alone, and she didn't know if he would be returning. She should leave. There was no reason to stay here now.

As she opened the door and walked down the stairs, she realised Tony was here. She could smell coffee and toast being made and hear bare feet slapping the hard floor in the kitchen.

She was momentarily frozen. This human knew of her. Danny had told him things and she didn't know if he posed a threat to her. She stood silently in the hallway, weighing her options. Danny said they could trust this man, and she'd promised Jay she wouldn't kill anybody, but trust wasn't something she was used to. She wasn't entirely sure if she trusted Danny, let alone his human friend.

She stood a few more minutes deliberating with herself. Perhaps she should speak to him? Tell him she was leaving? Did Danny expect her to stay here until he returned? She wasn't sure if she had permission to leave. She took a deep breath and reminded herself that Danny was not her superior; and neither was Tony. Nobody owned her anymore.

Her gentle reminder to herself did her no good. She heard Tony approaching, and she froze with fear.

He absent-mindedly wandered into the hallway where she was standing and let out a frightened yell, jumping back, spilling hot coffee all over himself. She realised, too late, that she may have been a little too quiet. He had no idea she was there.

Edel could sense the fear. Smell it even. His heart was racing, and she could almost taste the panic radiating from him. She wanted to tell him she didn't mean him any harm. He was safe, but her words wouldn't come out. She couldn't communicate with him at all. The best she could manage was to gawk at him awkwardly. She knew she must look completely deranged as she stared at him, feeling every bit as afraid as he was.

Tony found his voice. "Erm... are you feeling better?" he asked, staring at her as though she might be some sort of rabid dog. There was a scared sort of pleading in his eyes, begging for his life as if he thought she would attack at any moment.

"Yes." She knew her abrupt and aggressive one-word answer was doing little to ease the tension between them, but she couldn't communicate any more effectively. Humans frightened her, and she simply couldn't hold a normal conversation with a stranger.

She couldn't stand it any longer. She backed into the door, and her hand found the door handle behind her, and she pushed it open and left. She didn't say goodbye or thank him for her stay. She didn't even look at him, but she heard his sigh of relief as he closed the door behind him.

CHAPTER 25

Saturday 19th August 2102

Helston, Harpton Main

Gemma ran. She had no idea where she was going, but she needed to get away. Tears blurred her vision as she pelted down the street, and her chest constricted with the weight of grief and heartbreak.

"Gemma!" Danny was chasing her; she could hear him calling her name. He had initially allowed her to put some distance between them, but he was catching up now, closing the gap between them.

She was becoming breathless, tiring from the physical exertion. It seemed pointless to run now, knowing he would catch up with her eventually. She slowed to a walk and then leaned up against a garden wall and her tears fell once more as she waited for him to reach her. She couldn't breathe. As soon as her lungs caught her breath, her sobs seemed to rob it from them again.

"Gemma." Danny was almost beside her now. She turned her head away from him. She didn't want to look at him.

"Gemma," he said a little more forcefully. "Please let me explain. It's not what you think."

She was still crying and shaking her head. "How could you,

Danny? It was one argument. One little fight and you jump into bed with another woman!"

"No! Gemma, you've got it wrong. I swear! I slept downstairs and let her have my room. Gemma, it's not... she's not... ugh, Gemma..." he seemed to struggle to get his words out. She assumed it was because there was nothing that could excuse what he had done. And what planet was he on, if he thought she would buy a cock and bull story about sleeping on the couch?

"She's like me. She's one of... like me," he blurted out.

Gemma's stomach collapsed into the soles of her feet and her mouth fell slack with shock. "What? She's – she's one of the escapees?" she said breathlessly. "How? I mean, is she–? Is she dangerous?"

Danny shook his head, "No. Yes. Maybe, she's... different. I don't think she wants to hurt anybody. She just needed some help last night, that's all."

"How did you meet her? WHEN did you meet her?"

Gemma calmed enough to really listen as Danny explained who Edel was, and how he instantly knew she was like him. She really paid attention, as he told her about how crazy and on edge she was when he ran into her the previous night, how she was scared she was going to hurt her roommate and didn't know what was happening because dreaming was a new experience for her. He told her how unstable she seemed, and he knew he was the only person who could help her.

"I had to get her away from the public places, it was like she was on the edge of losing it. It's hard to explain, but it was like I was too. Like her feelings or her state of mind was affecting mine."

Gemma stared open-mouthed, trying to take it all in. The first thing that hit her was relief. He still wanted her, he still loved her. He hadn't slept with another woman. But these reassuring thoughts quickly turned sour when she realised that this girl, this strange woman, was everything he had been looking for his entire life. She was the same as him. Gemma could never compete with that.

Danny smiled at her, his eyes shining with excitement, like he was about to tell Gemma some thrilling news. "It's so strange Gemma, I've never felt anything like it. I can *feel* her. I can feel her feelings, or she can feel mine. It's like we can make each other feel things."

Gemma wondered what type of feelings he was feeling for her. It's exactly what every girl wants to hear – that some random woman makes your boyfriend feel in ways you never have.

Danny didn't appear to notice Gemma's despondency. He was too caught up in the excitement of telling her all about this other woman. "Her name is Edel. She seems the same age as me. I guess maybe we are all the same age? I don't really know." His excited babble was hard to stomach. Gemma noted how he was smiling from ear to ear, so pleased with himself. She knew she should be happy for him. She knew what this must mean to him, but she felt so resentful already. This girl was everything she wasn't.

"I'm going to get to know her, I'm going to learn about her. She'll be able to tell me everything about myself."

She could hear the emotion in his voice and see the hope as it lit up his face. He wanted this so badly. It made her heart ache that the things he had been searching for, the empty space within him, could be filled by someone that wasn't her.

Her smile was weak, and half-hearted as she said, "That's great, Danny. I'm thrilled for you."

"I'm so sorry I didn't tell you about her Gemma, I just wasn't sure if she was safe. I'm still not to be honest, but she didn't want to hurt me last night, and she doesn't want to hurt Jay."

The name sent bells of recognition clanging in her brain. "Jay?" she asked. Her eyes narrowed, and she said in an accusing tone, "The guy you attacked at work a few weeks ago, for no reason?" as she connected the dots.

Danny closed his eyes and exhaled. She could tell he hadn't meant to disclose that information. Secrets! He always promised he wouldn't keep secrets from her. She threw him a disgusted look and shook her head as she walked away.

"Gemma!" he said, hurrying alongside her angry strides. "I'm sorry, I know I should have told you."

She didn't answer. She marched onwards, doing her best to ignore him.

"Gemma," he grabbed her by the shoulders and turned her body to face him. "I'm sorry!"

"How long have you known her?" There was anguish in her words, and mistrust. He must want more from her than information if he couldn't even see fit to tell her about the girl.

Danny admitted the truth, that he sensed her months ago, but he didn't understand what the sensations were. He told her about their first meeting in the restaurant bathroom, and how he had briefly spoken to her once after then, but she had told him to stay away from her.

"You lied to me," she said. It wasn't an angry or accusing voice. She was quiet when she spoke, like she was accepting some sort of awful fate.

"I didn't, not really. But I didn't want to worry you, Gemma. I didn't know how safe she was. I couldn't risk her hurting you," he said desperately.

"You promised you wouldn't keep secrets from me, Danny. You promised you would always tell me things. Especially things about what makes you different."

He hung his head in shame. He had no answer to that, except for another weak apology.

"Can I meet her?" she asked. She already knew the answer would be no, but she wanted to ask, anyway.

"Not yet, Gemma. She's not friendly. She doesn't act like people at all. Let me get to know her first. Let me make sure she won't hurt you, then I will ask her, okay?"

Okay? Why would I ever be okay with that? Her body and face contradicted her thoughts as she silently nodded her head.

He pulled her into his body and held her close. "I love you, Gemma," he murmured. "I missed you so much."

She allowed his words and his love to wash over her. And for a moment, she believed him. But the nagging voice in the back of her head was telling her she wasn't enough. She would never be enough. Not now he had found someone who was just like him.

"Um, Gemma, I know you came all this way. And I appreciate it. I really, really do. But I should get back home, and make sure she is okay. Tony is home alone with her, and I don't know for sure if he is safe. She said she doesn't want to hurt anybody, but I don't want to take any chances."

She nodded and swallowed. "Of course." she said, a false brightness to her voice. "I'll be fine. I've got things to do today, anyway." She tried to shrug off the sorrow and crushing disappointment she felt that her big reunion and her huge romantic expression of love had gone unnoticed and unappreciated.

"You're amazing, Gemma," he said, hugging her again. He pulled out his phone and called a taxi. "You're not walking all the way home unaccompanied. It's a wonder you didn't get detained on your way in."

He didn't wait with her. He gave her another tender hug, and kissed her, then he set off back home. *Back to his other woman,* the bitter thought screamed in her mind, as she waited for the car to collect her.

Slow, silent tears fell from her eyes as she walked up the path to her house. Nobody was home, and she was grateful for that at least. She couldn't stand to hear Craig telling her how he was right about Danny all along and how she was an idiot to think he would want someone like her.

CHAPTER 26

Saturday 19th August 2102

Jay's Apartment, Helstain, Harpton Main

Edel returned home and Jay started on her immediately. "Where have you been?" Jay asked as soon as Edel walked in through the door. "I've been worried sick!" he chided her.

She stared at him, unable to comprehend what he meant. *Worried about what?* she wondered.

"Are you feeling okay? You were acting a little weird last night."

She nodded and hoped she hadn't frightened him.

"What did you take off for anyway?" he asked her. "You normally seem to prefer your routine."

She looked down to the floor; feelings of uncertainty about her behaviour snuck up on her. Was she in trouble with Jay? Was she supposed to keep to her routine?

"Edel!" Jay said her name and she could hear nothing but exasperation. "Look at me."

She raised her eyes from the floor. It was absurd, but she was gripped with a sort of fear. What if she had broken the rules? She didn't know if he would hurt her somehow.

Her eyes met his, but he only smiled his gentle smile. "You aren't in trouble, Edel. I was just concerned about you last night, that's all. It's okay for people to worry about their friends."

She still didn't understand the concept of someone worrying over her. And she still wasn't entirely sure what it meant to have a friend.

"Were you out all night?" he asked. "Where did you go?"

It was slow going, but she finally explained what had been happening to her over the last five nights. He watched with patience, as she stood in her usual submissive stance, unable to meet his eye, while she explained she had been dreaming, but she didn't understand what was happening and she was too afraid to tell him about it.

"Edel. You can talk to me. You can tell me when you're having a problem."

"I didn't know it was normal. I thought my mind was failing, and I was going insane," she said matter-of-factly.

"So, you must be worn out, if you haven't slept for days. Have you been wandering about all night?"

She swallowed and looked down again, not knowing if it was allowed that she had spent the night at another house.

"You can tell me, Edel," he said, gazing at her with a patient stare.

"I found the other one, like me. Danny."

She noticed his immediate fear response. He stared at her for a moment and then found his voice. "Is he...? You didn't–?"

"I didn't hurt him," she cut him off. "He helped me. He took me to his house and allowed me to sleep."

Jay was looking at her like he didn't believe what she was telling him. Only a few weeks ago, she had searched all night looking to kill him. "You stayed with Danny? All night?" he asked.

She wondered why humans did this. Why, when you tell them something, do they need to ask again? Why do they need facts more than once?

"Yes."

"So, you guys are friends now?"

She stared at him with a blank expression. *No*, she thought. She did not consider them to be friends.

"How did you leave it this morning?"

"What do you mean?" she asked, not understanding.

"I mean, what did you say when you left? What did he say to you? Does he know you are feeling better now?"

Edel stood looking at Jay, not able to comprehend what he was asking. "We didn't speak. He wasn't there when I left."

"What? Why would he leave you? I thought he was looking after you? I thought that was the point of you staying there!"

"He knew I was awake. He knew there was no immediate danger. Why would he need to stay?" she asked, confused by his reaction.

Jay shook his head in bewilderment. "How could he know you were okay if you didn't even speak? He should have made sure! Did you arrange to see him again?"

She looked at Jay like he was mental. "No," she said slowly. "Why would I do that?"

"Because he helped you!"

She wasn't sure what he was getting at. Was this an actual comprehensive explanation?

"Does he even know you left?"

"No," she answered.

Jay pulled out his phone and dialled Danny's number from the card he left him before.

"Danny speaking," he answered straight away.

"Um, Danny, it's Jay. Jay Powell."

"Oh man, tell me she is with you? Tell me she got back okay?"

"She's here. She's fine," he said tightly.

"Can I talk to her?" he asked, and Edel noted the hopeful tone in his voice as she heard him speak.

Edel stared at the phone as Jay held it out to her. She'd never spoken on a telephone before. She took it robotically and held it to her ear. The sound of the static on the line sounded loud and there was a gentle high-pitched hum that accompanied it, although she knew the frequency was out of an average humans' hearing range.

"Edel? How are you feeling?"

"Fine," her answer was short and abrupt.

"Look, I'm sorry about Gemma, she saw you and jumped to the wrong conclusion."

She didn't answer, and the silence drew on a long time. She didn't understand the situation with that other woman.

"So, I was hoping to ask you a few things..."

She still didn't answer.

"Are you busy today? I could come to your place, I have so many questions."

"No."

"Great! What time is best?" he asked. He clearly thought she was telling him she wasn't busy.

"I said no," she snapped.

He hesitated on the phone. "Uh..."

She ended the call before he could ask her anymore questions. The last thing she wanted was to have him near her. He seemed utterly unable to control his senses or his emotional responses, and he had no idea how to handle their shared consciousness. His emotional responses ran wild. Not dampened, not filtered. It was a mess being near him. It was uncomfortable and the unusual sensations left her confused. Her body was still reeling after being assaulted by his feelings. She felt violated.

"That was harsh, Edel!" Jay said as she handed him the phone back. "What did he want?"

"To meet here."

"And you said no? He only wants to get to know you. It's important to him, Edel. Surely you can understand why?"

She stared at him. She knew he had a desperate need to get to know her, but she had no understanding of why. A need or want that extreme wasn't something she understood at all.

"He helped you, Edel. He only wants to be your friend."

"You are my friend."

"People can have more than one friend!"

"XJ's aren't designed to be friends," she said in a measured tone.

Jay looked at her questioningly. "You aren't there now. You don't have to follow their rules. You can choose for yourself."

"I am," she said. She stalked by Jay and headed towards the bathroom, knowing he wouldn't try to follow her there. It was such an unusual feeling, arguing and saying no when a human asked something of her. It still frightened her and left an uncomfortable, heavy feeling in the pit of her stomach.

She switched on the water and stood under the shower, allowing the heat of the water to cleanse her mind and body as it rushed over her. Once she was finished, she felt calmer, and her thoughts were more ordered. She shoved Danny Johnson to the back of her mind and tried to forget about him. It wasn't her responsibility to give him explanations.

She was drying herself with a towel when she heard a knock at the door. She froze, her senses instantly on high alert. People knew about her. What if the human had turned her in? She held her breath as she listened to Jay talking to a man and relief flooded her system as she realised it was a voice she recognised. It was one of the delivery drivers from the warehouse. She could hear the clink of metal, and heard Jay thanking him for dropping off whatever it was.

When she emerged from the bathroom, there was a small pile of fixtures and fastenings leant up against the wall near the door.

Jay caught her looking with interest. "They're for work," he said with a casual shrug and a cheeky grin. "I had Nikolai steal them from one of the other units." He gave her a wink.

"Isn't stealing a punishable offence?" she asked, wondering what the punishment would be for humans who broke human rules.

Jay laughed out loud. "It's not as bad as it sounds, Edel. It's all

JoBi Corp property. I'm not going to get into any trouble, even if I get caught. But 'borrowing' from another unit will save me a fortune out of our budget. It's not really stealing. It's just being resourceful!"

Edel never knew with Jay. He was always saying things that weren't true. Not lies exactly, but he often said the opposite of what he meant, then he would laugh and tell her he was joking. She could never make sense of his sarcasm. It was something she had never known in her life before.

"What are your plans for today?" he asked.

She gave him her usual blank expression. She had no plans today.

"I've got another meeting at The Grid, but after that, I've got nothing on until this evening when I'm seeing Katie. How about when I get back, we have a proper talk, about everything?"

She nodded in agreement, although there was nothing she wanted to talk about. She had a feeling he wasn't done trying to push the subject of her and Danny.

"Do you need help moving these to your car?" she asked, pointing at the heavy-looking shelves and rails. There was a mixture of poles, shelves, and brackets amongst the pile of 'borrowed' goods.

"Are you mad?" he said, laughing. "I can't take those into work yet. They'll have to stay there for a couple of weeks at least. I don't want anyone to know I stole them!"

She stared back at the pile on the floor, frowning. She didn't like clutter, or things being out of place. Her whole life things had been ordered and controlled. She owned no personal belongings at Poly-Gen, so there was never anything in her cell, and even now she had her freedom, her bedroom was bare apart from essentials. Jay was disorganised, and things like this didn't bother him at all. She hoped he wouldn't keep them there too long.

A while later, Jay left for work. He had questioned her again about Danny before he left and hinted she should get to know him. She didn't want to talk about the other XJ. She didn't want to get to know him. His emotions invaded her body and made her feel dirty and impure. XJs weren't designed for feelings and the fact that he *felt* such strong emotions was bad enough, but to actively force his feelings onto her, and not dampen them, not close himself off or even try to protect the other connected minds was reprehensible. It felt like he was defiling her when he forced himself onto her in that way. She tried to forget about him, and the uncomfortable feelings he left her with, and turned into herself, switching off all awareness. All her senses and thoughts turned to nothing, and for the rest of the afternoon, she ceased to really exist. This was how she was meant to behave. This was familiar.

CHAPTER 27

Saturday 19th August 2102

Danny's House, Helston, Harpton Main

As Danny returned home, he could immediately tell Edel had already left. The strange sensations he felt when she was near were nowhere now, and a wild sort of panic enveloped him as he burst through the door and frantically called out for Tony.

He ran through the downstairs and into the kitchen, but it was empty. He ran back through the house and bolted up the stairs, still shouting his friend's name as he burst through his bedroom door, but there was nobody here.

Danny tried to get a hold of himself and look at things rationally. There were no signs of a struggle of any sort, and no blood. Nothing out of place. He picked up his phone and dialled Tony's number.

"Hello?" Tony answered

"Thank God you're okay," Danny said, sagging with relief. He would never have forgiven himself if anything had happened to his friend.

"You left me with her!" Tony wailed. "I can't believe you left me with her. She. Is. Terrifying!"

"Where did she go? What did she say when she left?"

"Nothing. She literally said nothing. She just stared at me for ages, as though *I* was the dangerous one, and then pretty much ran out of the front door. Man, it was weird. She is scary." Tony was laughing, but Danny didn't find this funny at all. He didn't know how dangerous she was. For all he knew, she could have killed him.

Danny ended the call and was searching for Jay's number when his phone rang. Jay's name flashed across the screen and the tension and worry he felt eased immediately, as Jay told him she had returned home, and she was fine. He swallowed down his pride and put his vulnerabilities on the line, as he asked her to meet with him. He held his breath as he waited for her answer, knowing he was so close to everything he'd ever dreamed of. His hopes shattered in front of him, and he felt crushed as the line went dead and he was left staring at the disconnected phone, listening to the dial tone after she told him to leave her alone, then abruptly ended the call.

He stared at the blank screen, utterly deflated. Why wouldn't she see him? Why wouldn't she communicate? It's all he had ever wanted. It wouldn't hurt her to explain some things to him, or for them to discover if they had any similarities. He felt heartbroken.

Sighing in defeat, he put his phone down, and his thoughts turned to Gemma. She deserved a proper apology, and a proper explanation. And she came all that way to see him. He felt terrible about sending her home.

A little while later he was on his way to Gromdon. He wanted to bring her some flowers or some sort of gift, but he knew how she felt about being showered with expensive things. He called her and they arranged to meet at the riverfront. It wasn't exactly a pretty view, but it was better than the slums, the broken old buildings, and the endless grey concrete of the industrial zone.

He found her sitting on the grassy bank, her knees drawn up to her chest, and she looked thoroughly miserable. He could tell she had been crying. Tears had a gentle, but lingering fragrance. It smelled like she had cried hard, but there were no traces of it to see on her beautiful face.

She offered him a weak smile as he placed his arm around her and pulled her into him. "Gemma, have you been crying?" he asked, full of concern.

She shook her head. "It's nothing, I'm just being silly," she said. "How did it go when you went back home?"

"Not great. She'd already left. I called her, but she doesn't want to talk to me. I don't understand why, but I don't think I should push it." He couldn't help the sorrow in his voice.

Gemma stayed quiet, offering only a simple nod of her head. Danny didn't know how to talk to her like this. They had always been so open with each other, right from when he first told her about himself. There was nothing he couldn't talk to Gemma about. Except this.

"I guess I'll just leave it for a couple of weeks and try again? Maybe she just needs some time," he said, paying close attention to her every response as he spoke.

Gemma nodded, but her face was serious.

"Gemma, what's wrong? You know nothing happened, right? You know I'm telling the truth about staying on the couch all night?"

"Yes, of course I do," she said. "I'm sorry that I thought anything else. I know you wouldn't do that."

"Do you?" he asked, staring at her with intense eyes. "You should, Gemma. I love you more than anything else in this world. I wouldn't even look at another woman, let alone sleep with one. I only want you." The passion in his voice lit up his eyes as he said the words.

"But she is like you." The words seemed to escape without her meaning them to. Her eyes had already filled with tears again. He hated he had caused this pain.

"Gemma, I know it's hard, but it's not like that. I would be every bit as desperate to meet her if she was a guy."

She shook her head. "You said she makes you feel in ways

that I can't. She is everything you've ever wanted."

"No! NO!" he denied it with his whole being. "YOU are everything I've ever wanted, Gemma. But I need to know her. I can't explain it, but I just, I NEED it."

"You need her," Gemma said, tears streaming down her face. "I need you too."

They went around in circles and Danny didn't know how to make her see that there was absolutely nothing sexual or romantic between him and this other girl. An hour passed, and he had eventually talked her round enough to see sense and she stopped arguing, but he couldn't help wondering if she still felt the same way. How was it possible she didn't know how crazy he was about her?

***

Thursday 21st September 2102
Danny's House, Helston, Harpton Main

As the weeks passed, things settled down between Gemma and Danny. He hadn't mentioned Edel to her since that day. He hadn't seen or spoken to Jay or Edel either, but it was eating at him every day. She could help him. She had the answers he so desperately sought.

Jenson had arranged another one of his visits. They usually met twice per year. Jenson would give Danny a sort of physical examination and ensure he was healthy, and they would discuss any problems Danny may be having. Normally Danny didn't mind having these meetings. Everyone agreed they were important. It wasn't like he could see a doctor if there was anything wrong or bothering him, and Jenson knew what sort of things were normal or not. But with the news of the escape being plastered all over the news at every end and turn, the idea of seeing Jenson made him feel more like an experiment than an actual person.

"Are you going to tell him about her? He might be able to explain the feelings you have," Gemma asked.

Danny shook his head. "I don't think that would be a good idea. I called him the first time I sensed her. He didn't tell me what the feelings were, but I'd put money on it that he knew what I was feeling, and he didn't see fit to tell me. He only told me if I ever felt it again, I should get away and then call him straight away. Besides, people are looking for her. Who knows what they'll do to her if they find her? If they catch her, what's stopping her telling them all about me? They'll kill my dad, and Jenson, and I bet they will want you too. They'll want to know all about us, and our relationship."

The idea terrified him. He liked Jenson, but he didn't trust that he wouldn't turn Edel into the authorities. He didn't view the Poly-Gen experiments as human. It made him wonder how 'human' Jenson thought he was, too. He never openly admitted he thought Danny was anything less than human, but with all the endless questions, and his fixation on Danny's feelings, that was certainly the impression he gave.

"So, what happens in these meetings, anyway?" she asked, sidestepping the subject of Edel.

Danny shrugged. "Mostly we just talk. He does a bit of an examination, makes sure I'm healthy, and then we just talk."

"What about?"

"Hmmm, about life, I guess. You come up a lot." He glanced at her to see how she felt about being the topic of scientific research. Her face remained passive. She wasn't giving anything away. "He wanted to meet you, but I wouldn't let him. It's too weird, the type of questions he asks, he doesn't seem to know where to draw the line."

"What do you mean?" Her brow knitted together into a frown. "I'd meet with him, if it would help you."

Danny shook his head. "I've told him things Gemma, really personal things about us. I had to talk to him about love and how I felt about you, and I had to ask him about sex, and if he thought I would be any different to other men, or dangerous to you in any way. Sex seems to be a hot topic. That and feelings, he is a bit fixated on how I feel about things."

"Because you're not supposed to feel things? That's what they say about the escapees, isn't it? But you aren't like them, Danny. You aren't cold or unfeeling. You are kind and loving, and nurturing."

He couldn't help but smile. No matter what, she always made things better. She always knew the right things to say to ease his worries.

***

Danny arrived at his dad's house to find Jenson was already there, sipping coffee with Frank and Michelle.

He walked in and tried to be his usual confident and self-assured self, but it was always awkward. Danny never felt more different than when he was in Jenson's company, and it made him feel very self-conscious, as though every action he made was being scrutinised. He knew these meetings were important, and Jenson had helped him no end when he was a teenager growing up, but he still hated being 'observed' and 'monitored'. It was obvious he was continually making comparisons, and everything they spoke about seemed to answer some unasked question.

Jenson greeted him, and the usual stilted conversation took place. The 'Are you well?' and 'How was your drive?' They eventually retired to Danny's old bedroom, and it made Danny feel like he'd regressed to being a child again as he sat on his old single bed, surrounded by his old things. Jenson questioned him on everything from his eyesight to his bowel movements. He performed a short physical, taking Danny's blood pressure, pulse rate, and taking blood to test in his own personal lab back home. Then he requested a urine sample to take too.

They moved on from the physical, and discussed Danny's feelings about his relationship with Gemma, and how he was finding the new life of living with a housemate instead of his family.

Then came the more serious subjects.

"When was your last meltdown?"

A sense of shame crept up on him. "A long time. Not since before last time I saw you,"

"Danny. There's no need to lie to me. I already spoke to your dad. He told me about the incident at work," he said, fixing Danny with a penetrating stare.

Danny could have killed his dad. He kept quiet about Lyssi, and about Tony. Why would he tell Jenson about Jay? "It was an accident," he said through gritted teeth.

"Did you use the breathing techniques I showed you?"

Danny shook his head. "They don't always work."

He thought back to the last few meltdowns. Maybe he should be more honest with Jenson. When they happened, they happened fast. The meltdowns seemed to take over all at once, and he couldn't control what he was doing or who he was hurting, let alone think about breathing techniques. Maybe if he was more honest, Jenson would have another idea about how to control them.

But he was afraid. He had suffered three episodes in quick succession, and it made him question if he was becoming more dangerous, not less. If he was becoming a danger to people, Jenson might turn him in. Sometimes he thought it would be no more than he deserved.

After they had discussed the most recent meltdown and gone through the reasons Danny thought it had happened (he lied of course), Jenson asked him about the strange phone call he received in the middle of the night.

"Have you felt any strange sensations since that night you called me?"

"No," Danny lied. "What do you think it was?"

Jenson pursed his lips together. "It was probably nothing to worry about, if you've never felt it since." There was a dismissive quality to his tone, and he offered Danny a haphazard shrug. Then his demeanour changed into somebody much more serious, as he said, "Look, I wouldn't worry about it, but if you do feel it again, Danny, you need to get away."

"Why?" He wanted to know how much Jenson knew about these feelings, and how much information Jenson would share with him.

Jenson considered Danny for a long moment. "I've never told you this, because I didn't think it necessary, but XJ5s have the ability to sense each other's presence." He let that hang in the air for a moment and looked to Danny, who was feigning shock and surprise. He needed Jenson to believe this was brand new information.

"I could be wrong, but based on your description of the sensations you felt, I believe you may have encountered another XJ5. One of the escapees from the testing facility." Jenson looked at him with warning in his eyes. "I don't want you to go looking for it, Danny. I know how badly you want to meet others like yourself, but I mean it – if you feel it again, run. They are dangerous. They are everything the news says they are. They are trained killers. Their upbringing makes them damn near unstoppable and they will kill everything in their path, without remorse."

Danny nodded his head obediently. His thoughts ran wild. Edel didn't seem like that at all. She was unfriendly, but Jay was still alive, and she worked at the warehouse with hundreds of other people. As far as he knew, she hadn't killed anyone.

The meeting ended, and Jenson told Danny he could call and ask him anything as usual. It was strange. He may hate these meetings, but once they were over, Danny always felt a little better, knowing Jenson was there for him. Still, he would prefer it if he could talk to someone who understood what it was like to be like him. The ever-growing ache of want filled his heart as his thoughts turned to Edel again. Jenson's warning was sitting at the front of his mind, but he couldn't fully believe the things he had said about the escapees. He had to be wrong. He made his mind up there and then; he was going to try again to talk to her.

Danny mentioned nothing to Gemma about Edel that night. She asked him all about his meeting with Jenson, and she spent a lot of time reassuring him that none of his differences mattered to her. They spent the evening entwined in each other's arms, happily talking and laughing. He didn't want to spoil this perfect evening by bringing Edel into it.

The following morning, they enjoyed a lazy morning in bed together and all the worry about Jenson's visit was forgotten. It was almost lunchtime before either of them got up and dressed.

"I should get back. I've got some things to do at home before I go to work later," Gemma said, reluctantly peeling her body away from his chest. "What have you got planned today?"

It took him a moment to put his sentence together. He tried to phrase it as though it wasn't a big deal at all. "I thought I'd visit Edel, and see if she was ready to talk to me yet."

He looked at her from the corner of his eye. The relaxed and happy atmosphere between them had completely vanished. Her face was set into a sour pout, and she looked away out of the window.

"Why?" was all she said.

"Gemma, you know why. You know why I want to get to know her."

The argument that followed was huge. She cried and screamed that he didn't love her, and she wasn't enough for him. No matter how many times he tried to explain that all he wanted was answers, she couldn't see it. She couldn't get past the idea that he would want to be with somebody like him.

At first, he felt sorry for her. He reminded himself how hard this was for her, how little she thought of herself, and how this was literally her worst nightmare coming to fruition. But, as the argument drew on, and she wouldn't see sense, he became increasingly angrier.

The buzzing started in the back of his head, and the colours deepened around him. Everything in his room became more vivid, and Gemma's relentless crying and shouting seemed to have almost an echoing quality to it.

He lurched to his feet and threw his hands over his ears and said in a voice that sounded far calmer than he felt, "Gemma. I need you to stop." He screwed his eyes up, trying to block out the light and the colours.

"Stop what?" she yelled angrily. "Stop feeling upset that you want another woman?" She continued her tirade and Danny felt as though he couldn't breathe right.

He felt his hands curl into fists, and he felt the urge to smash her face in. He needed her to shut up. The anger was taking hold of him, and her noise was relentless.

"Gemma. Please. Stop," he said, forcing the words out through his clenched jaw.

"Stop what?" she yelled again, and then drew a sharp intake of breath, as she quickly realised the danger. "Danny?" Her voice was much more hesitant this time, and she took a tentative step closer to him, her arm outstretched.

She didn't get close enough to touch him. He slammed past her, shoving her roughly onto the bed, and bolted out of the bedroom, running down the stairs and out of the front door. His whole body was shaking with unspent rage. He had been on the verge of meltdown, AGAIN! He continued running, and he reached the riverfront before he slowed to a walk and allowed his body to calm down. With the calm came worry. Was Gemma okay? Was she hurt? It was agony to think how easily he could have hurt her. Then came the blame. What the hell was she thinking? Didn't she know how close he just came to losing it? It left a sickening feeling in his stomach that he blamed her. A normal man, a *good man*, wouldn't victim blame like that. Not that Gemma had been a victim of anything today, but it was close. He hated he couldn't even have an argument without the fear of killing the woman he loved. He hadn't ever been so close to losing control in front of Gemma before. It made him shudder to think what might have happened if he hadn't run.

He had calmed enough to see sense again, and thought of going back, but every time he thought of her his anger would stir again in the pit of his stomach and he knew full well he wasn't over it. He couldn't go back. Not yet.

His thoughts turned to Edel. She seemed so controlled. And the way Jay described her, she didn't seem like she was always clinging onto her sanity, hoping she didn't rip other people's heads off their shoulders. This didn't happen to her. Or if she did have any experience of meltdowns, she must have a way to handle it better than he did. He needed to speak to her. She could show him how to control himself. Why wouldn't she help him?

He didn't give himself chance to talk himself out of this decision. He made his way to the warehouse on foot, determined to get answers one way or another. If she was there, she wouldn't have a choice but to see him. He was one of the junior directors of JoBi Corp. That technically made him her boss, and there was little she could do about it if he wanted a meeting with her.

CHAPTER 28

Friday 22nd September 2102

Unit 7 Warehouse, Harpton Main City Centre

Edel's head snapped up as she felt the presence of the other. What did he think he was doing, coming into her space? She tried her best to close herself off and ignore the sensations as she continued counting her stock in the warehouse.

He was getting closer. He was now in 'feeling' range. She allowed herself to feel him, testing to see if he was any better controlled. He wasn't. The instant she opened herself up and let down her defences, she was assaulted with a strange mix of nerves and excitement. Her heart raced and hands shook. He sensed her too, and the excited and nervous feelings increased immediately. She closed her eyes and tried to block him out again. It wasn't natural to feel things so deeply. It felt so wrong.

She heard Jay approaching her stockroom. She knew it was him, she could pick his scent out of a crowded room by now.

"Um, Edel?" He hung in the doorway, looking at her with a placid smile on his face.

She stopped her work for a moment and glared at him. "I don't want to see him," she said, before he spoke another word.

"Edel!" he gently coaxed her. "He only wants to talk to you. What is the harm in talking?"

"Off Limits."

"Edel!"

"NO!" she yelled, as her head suddenly jerked in the door's direction, and she stared past Jay, out into corridor. "I said no," she said again.

She wasn't speaking to Jay, Danny was standing out of sight, at the far end of the corridor. She felt his odd mix of rejection, sorrow, and sadness. It sent a lump to her throat that made her feel sick. It was disgusting to feel such things.

Her own feelings were ones of simmering anger. She said no, and Jay said that was her choice. This other was trying to take her choice away. The difference was, she knew better than to act on her feelings, or acknowledge them. She kept a handle on her anger, and held it close to her chest, trying not to allow it to spill out into their shared conscious space and contaminate it. He offered her no such courtesy.

She let out a sigh of relief as she felt his acceptance. He was walking away. He was leaving.

Jay shook his head in disbelief. "Why are you so against helping him? He helped you!"

"Being in close proximity to him is dangerous."

Jay scoffed at her, laughing out loud. "Dangerous how?"

"Off limits."

Jay let out an exasperated huff as he stomped back to his office, muttering under his breath how he wished he'd never invented the safety phrase. It impressed Edel that he stuck to his word and never pushed her when she said something was off limits. She didn't want to have to explain how uncomfortable being near the other XJ5 was. She didn't think he would understand. And she was telling the truth about it being dangerous. That one was unstable, he had almost no control over his feelings. Things could escalate quickly if they were together.

She got back to work and tried to push him from her mind,

hoping he would stay away from her from now on.

The drive back home was tense. Jay would not allow her to dodge the subject of Danny Johnson.

"He was devastated, Edel!" he whined at her. "Don't you feel a tiny bit sorry for him? He just wants to know about himself. Can't you put yourself in his shoes? Don't you have any empathy at all?"

She had no idea what he could mean, but there was no way she could adequately explain what it felt like to be near him. She only knew she didn't want to be forced into spending time with him. And she didn't want to *feel* him.

Once they arrived home, she got herself ready for her run. She noted the pile of fixtures and various bits and pieces that were still by the door and shook her head at Jay's complete disregard for organisation. He was so different to the humans she had known at Poly-Gen. She wondered if Jay was ever going to get around to taking them into work.

"I won't be home when you get back. I'm seeing Katie tonight," Jay said as she was about to leave.

Edel stared at him blankly, still unable to understand why he would be telling her his plans.

"I won't be back until morning, okay?"

"Yes." *Why wouldn't this be okay?* she wondered.

Edel followed her usual route, but somehow, it wasn't having the usual calming effect on her. She didn't know what was wrong. That other was still on her mind, and it was unusual for her to be stuck thinking about things. She couldn't shake the feel of his rejection. She had never known a feeling like it.

It made her question what was wrong with her. She had never cared about anybody's feelings before, but then, she'd never felt feelings, not properly. Maybe she was broken. She wasn't designed for this.

She tried to push thoughts of Danny Johnson and his ridiculous feelings aside and concentrate on running. She sped up, sprinting to the end of the park, really giving her lungs a chance to work hard. It had been a while since she had pushed herself, and although it felt good in one way, she was left with a feeling of failure when she actively chose to stop before her body gave out. She slowed to a walking pace and tried to understand how she felt. The sensations were a minefield of uncomfortable memories. She would have been punished for slowing or stopping before.

She made the choice to return home. She needed to shut herself away from the world, close herself down and not think or feel. It was the only way she could survive.

She rounded the corner and turned onto her street, and she felt it immediately. The other was here. Silent rage built in her chest. Why wouldn't he leave her alone?

She crossed the road and headed home, willing him to stay away. Her wishes were ignored, and she was suddenly hit with the full force of his begging and desperation.

"Edel." He spoke her name from where he stood, outside Jay's apartment building. "Edel, please. I only want to talk with you."

She turned cold and tried to ignore him. Seething anger pulsed through her veins, but she tried her best to shield it from him. Getting angry wouldn't make this better for either of them. The problem was, anger wasn't something she was too familiar with, and it was proving difficult to keep inside. As she approached, the strange hot angry sensations shifted slightly to take on his flurry of confusion and desperation.

"Edel, please," he begged again. His face screwed up, distorted with some sort of fury, his hands went up to his head. "What is this?" he almost screamed at her as he tried to make sense of the anger that didn't belong to him.

He was afraid. These sensations weren't normal, they weren't okay. He couldn't understand how or why his body reacted to her the way it did. It was as if he was enraged, a violent temper rising inside him. He wanted to hurt her. Or maybe it was her who wanted to hurt him. He could no longer tell where his feelings ended, and hers began.

Edel backed away, slowly. "Calm yourself down," she said, in a robotic voice with nothing in the way of feeling. She concentrated hard on holding herself together, in the hopes she could dampen his spiralling emotions. It wasn't doing much to help Danny.

She turned cold, and the empty feeling seeped into Danny's chest, rising from the pit of his stomach. Heavy, like a stone, it weighted in his body. He hated it. It was uncomfortable, and he didn't understand it, but he knew SHE was causing it.

His anger climbed another notch, and she felt it. Her body spontaneously responded the same way as his, her heartrate increased, and hormone levels changed. Her anger matched his, and she felt an urgent need to expel some of this energy, she wanted to hurt him. He wanted to hurt her.

She drew breath and said as calmly as she could manage, "Stay away." She barged past him and into the building, racing up the stairs two at a time, trying desperately to put some distance between them.

Danny followed. She was fast, but he was coming up behind her. He *needed* this. He needed to know what this was, what this meant. She had the answers. She could help him. It made him so angry he could barely see. What gave her the right to withhold this information from him? It's what he'd been searching for his entire life, and she was dangling it in front of him. Taunting him with it. Driving him close to madness.

Edel reached Jay's apartment, her key was just turning in the lock when Danny rounded up behind her.

"Talk to me. Tell me what this is." His speech was angry and aggressive.

She didn't turn around, and it made him angrier. She opened the door and tried to close it behind her, even though she knew they were well past the point of a door keeping them apart now. His hand jutted through the gap, preventing her from closing it, and he slammed his weight into it, pushing her back.

The overpowering emotion she felt right now was fear. It was hers, not his. He was on the edge; he was close to meltdown, and she was in danger of being taken with him.

She tried to pull away. She tried not to feel it, not to feel anything, but the out-of-control sensations were pulling her in every direction. She was falling, tumbling down into the black pit of rage and release.

Danny knew he was headed for meltdown. He knew but he couldn't stop. Her feelings seemed to pour fuel on the fire. As he inched further into the blackness, the rage, the hurt, and the need to destruct, her fear seemed to egg him on. It heightened the need for it all. He was hungry for it in a way he never had been before.

He lunged at her, but she was quick. She dodged out of his reach as his fist came at her.

"Danny don't do this," she pleaded with him.

He flew at her again, his fist connecting with her face, and she was launched backwards, her body flying through the air like a puppet, smashing onto the kitchen floor. She skidded on her back as she landed, and her head connected with the cupboards.

The burst of pain exploded behind her eyes, but pain was the least of her worries right now. She stood quickly as he advanced on her further. He was so close, but he wasn't lost to the madness yet.

"Danny. Please don't do this," she said again. Her voice was gentle, not much more than a whisper, but her gentle tones didn't speak to him the same way her fear did. She hadn't experienced another's meltdown since her days at Poly-Gen, and this experience had brought back too many unpleasant memories and feelings. She was desperately trying to keep control of herself, knowing that if she allowed herself to lose control, one or both of them would end up dead.

Danny was on the edge. He was so close to tipping over. Edel held her breath and braced herself for the mental assault that was another's meltdown: the temporary loss of understanding about who or what she was, the feeling of free falling at a million miles an hour, not knowing which way was up and having no clue where she would land. She closed her eyes and held on tight to any shred of sanity she could find. She heard the screams, and she felt his anguish. He didn't know who he was anymore. He didn't know what he was doing or why they were fighting. He only knew he needed to get it out. Whatever was inside him needed to come out.

He hit the heavy wooden dining table. The loud dull thud of his forearms connecting with the solid surface caused Edel to jump. He felt her startle reflex in his own body, and it sent him careering further into his downward spiral. The slightest amount of stimulation during a meltdown only made everything worse. He was reacting to her current frightened state. She knew she needed to handle this better.

He hit it again, but harder this time, and the wood split and splintered with a sickening crack. He flipped the table in one swift motion. It upturned, and he shoved it out of his path as though it weighed no more than a cardboard box. He was still screaming. The noises were not human, but they were well known to Edel. She backed away and got out of his way as he lunged forward again, trying to grab her. Hoping to break her.

She was breathing heavily, and her heart was racing. She knew these sounds would be magnified to Danny right now, and they weren't helping this situation, but there was little she could do to slow her heart. The motor of the refrigerator clicked on and temporarily took Danny's attention. It took a fraction of a second before he ripped it from its space in the kitchen and threw it across the room. The door flew open as it contacted the upturned table and it smashed into one of the table legs with such force, it snapped it clean off with a sickening crack. The contents of the fridge scattered across the floor. The humming from the motor had stopped, but Danny was already advancing on Edel. She was the only thing to be making noise in the apartment right now.

Edel didn't know what to do for the best. If she left, he would follow. He would hurt not only her, but everyone they encountered. There was a high probability she would lose herself too, if she was in a public place, amongst people.

If she stayed, it was likely she would still lose herself to the impending meltdown. She could feel it smothering her mind, trying to suffocate her and pull her in. If that happened, there was no doubt in her mind that he would die.

Her mind was frantic, searching for another way out. She promised Jay she wouldn't kill anyone, and even though she had tried to explain the concept of meltdown to him, she knew he didn't really understand.

She thought fast. A sense of shock and a sense of closure were often enough to end a meltdown. If the thing that was causing it could be stopped, it might be enough to pull him around.

She was the thing that was causing it. She knew she needed to allow him to have her.

He advanced on her again but paused and turned to the door. There were people out in the hallway, talking and laughing. He wasn't in control of his own body; the noise seemed to pull him forward. It wasn't a conscious thought, all he knew was he needed to make it stop.

Edel watched with horror and yelled his name as he reached the door. She needed to keep him in here with her. Her senses were fraught and on edge, every sound seemed to seer into her brain. She could not hold on much longer.

As he heard the noise of his name, he turned to look at her. He didn't recognise the words. He didn't recognise Edel, but the unexpected sound somehow fractured his intent to leave. He was caught in the confusion. He just needed it all to stop. He kicked out hard at the pile of items at the front door that Jay had yet to take to the warehouse, sending them scattering in all directions. The sound of metal hitting metal seemed to echo in his head. He saw the pole rolling across the floor. His arm darted forward, and he picked it up from the floor, stopping the strange tinkling sound it was leaving in its wake.

The pole was solid and heavy, and he slammed it down across his leg. The pain felt good. It was somehow helpful, like the release was easing the pressure on the inside of his body. He did it again, and let out more howling, inhuman screams.

Again, the noise, the pressure, the anxiety and the fear had caused Edel's body to respond in unhelpful ways. There wasn't a lot she could do. He turned to look at her, his eyes almost completely black as his pupils had dilated to cover almost all his iris. She knew he could see her, but he wouldn't recognise her now. He was lost.

The pole was still in his hand, and she knew. She just knew he was going to stab her with it.

The choice was instant. She could either fight, and they would both be in meltdown, or she could allow this to happen and take the chance that if he drove that pole into her, he would have that sense of completion and maybe the shock of it would be enough to end his madness.

He was quick, there was no consideration involved. He lunged forwards, pole in hand, and drove it into her body. Even though she had made this decision, her survival instinct kicked in, she grabbed his hands as the pole came towards her, trying desperately to save herself, but he was too strong, and she couldn't overpower him.

It slid in with ease, sinking into her soft flesh as if she was made of butter. She screamed out in agony as it pierced her body. He impaled her with so much force the pole went all the way through her body, between her shoulder and chest, and drove into the plaster of the wall behind her. She found herself stuck, pinned to the wall and unable to move.

It was as if someone had flicked off a switch. Danny fell to his knees, panting and sweating. He looked up at her as she tried to keep quiet, holding the agony inside and trying not to set him off again. His confusion was immeasurable. He wasn't aware of who he was, where he was, or who she was. He wasn't in a fit state to help, apologise, or even take in what he had done.

He stayed kneeling on the floor for a moment, his eyes opening and closing in extended blinks, as though he was hoping each time he opened them things would make sense.

Edel's breathing was laboured, but she tried to remain as silent as possible. She was stuck in pain and bleeding heavily, but she had control over her senses and over her body. She closed herself off and tried to block out the pain. She could still feel it, of course, but it was manageable. If she was going to die, she didn't need to die in pain.

Danny got to his feet. He looked at her, but he didn't seem to register what he was seeing. He stumbled out of the door without looking back.

CHAPTER 29

Friday 22nd September 2102

Jay's Apartment, Helstain, Harpton Main

Danny stumbled out onto the street. The brightness of the streetlights assaulted his eyes, and he squinted as he tried to shield himself from them. He was disoriented. The noise of the traffic in the streets and the motion of the shining headlights moving toward him in each direction made his head spin.

He didn't know where he was going. He wasn't even aware that his legs were walking. He drifted in and out of awareness. One minute he recognised his surroundings, and he had a vague recollection of who he was. The next he was lost again. Afraid and alone.

His next coherent moment was by the river. Hazy memories flooded back to him. He had had a meltdown. Another one. There was no mistaking these heavy and aching limbs and fuzzy rambling thoughts. This felt bad, like the loss of control had been severe. He took a moment to assess the damage. His body ached. His right leg in particular was singing with every step he took. He looked over his arms, there were bruises down the length of his forearms, and angry looking lumps. He knew he must have hit them against a solid surface. These injuries were the usual.

He tried to remember, but the brain fog was not clearing. The exhaustion was weighing him down. He knew he should care. He knew he should want to know the details, to make certain he hadn't hurt anyone, but the lethargy was too much. It ate at his ability to think. He sat on the grassy bank and allowed the exhaustion to take him.

***

It was dark when he awoke. He opened his eyes and tried to work out where he was. His eyes stung as they tried to focus on his dim surroundings. His face was pressed into the cool damp grass and an earthy scent filled his nose. It took a second for him to realise he was laying on the riverbank. *How did I get here?* He searched his pockets, looking for some sort of clue as to what had happened. He pulled his phone from his pocket. The time said a little after 3 a.m. He pulled himself up to sitting position and felt the earth lurch forward as he lost his balance. He only ever felt light-headed and dizzy after meltdown. Fuzzy memories of wandering around, unable to think, forced their way into his head. That's how he ended up here, but he couldn't see past it to the events before. He sat quietly for a moment and tried to remember. He was still confused; his brain wasn't cooperating at all.

The tiredness was weighing him down again. The simple act of sitting had somehow sapped his energy once more. He felt his eyes start to close, and he laid back down on the grassy bank and allowed sleep to take him again.

***

Danny jumped awake to the sound of his phone ringing. The noise and the brightness of the daylight startled him. His eyes hurt; his head hurt. His mouth was dry, and his body ached.

He fished in his pocket and stared at the phone. It was his dad calling. Danny sat staring at it but didn't answer. It eventually stopped, and he took a minute to understand what he was doing outside, and why he felt like he had been hit by a bus.

The time was 10 a.m. He remembered checking the time at 3 .a.m. He remembered the feeling of knowing he had gone into meltdown but not having the energy to care. He cared now.

He swallowed hard and tried to piece together the events of yesterday. He had been arguing with Gemma. She didn't want him to have a relationship with Edel; she was jealous and insecure, and it made no sense. He remembered getting angry. For a second, the cold tingle of dread gripped his chest. *Not Gemma, please not Gemma.* He silently begged and pleaded with any God that might listen. Memories of her hurt, tear-stained face flashed before his eyes and snippets of their conversation filled his head, "I need to do this Gemma. I need to know. I need to talk to her." He had left her crying. She didn't understand. She was convinced he would find everything he ever wanted in this new girl. Relief flooded his system and tears pushed their way up through his eyes. He could never live with himself if he hurt Gemma. He would never forgive himself.

The realisation that he went to Edel last night hit him hard. Her face, her angry, set face flashed before his eyes. She was not pleased to see him. She wouldn't talk to him, and he got angry. The angry feelings echoed in his body now. Had he hurt her?

The noise of his phone was jarring as it pulled him back to the present. He stared at it. It was his dad again. He couldn't bring himself to answer. He needed to work out what he'd done. He needed to remember.

"Danny, please don't do this," her voice seemed to echo in his head. He saw images of her frightened face, and he remembered the feel of her fear in his body. She was afraid. She begged him to stop. Her words and her feelings seemed to spur him on. He remembered hitting her. He saw how her small fragile looking body sailed across the room, how she had skidded across the floor and into the cupboards. Had he killed her? He concentrated hard and more memories came to the surface. She was up, she was still begging him to stop. Begging him to stay calm.

NO. NO. Please please please, no. He remembered. He remembered picking up the metal pole, and driving it into her body easily, like she was made of wet clay. He stabbed her, and he left her to die.

Panic quickly rose in his chest. He checked the time again. 10:33. He remembered it was only around 7 p.m. when he arrived at her house. He had no idea what time it was when he left, but it was getting dark. He vaguely remembered the cars with their shining headlights. If it was almost dark when he left, that would make it around 7:30 p.m. He stabbed her over 14 hours ago. He picked up his phone and checked it out. There were no missed calls from Jay, only his dad. His dad had tried to call twelve times but left no voice messages. Twelve missed calls set alarm bells ringing in his head. What could be so urgent? Did he know what he had done?

His hands shook and his breathing became short and shallow as he fully took in the weight of what he had done. He had murdered somebody. Not just anybody, the only person who could help him. The only person who had a chance of understanding him. The tears that he so desperately needed to fall seemed to freeze on their way out. The lump in his throat seemed to grow into a solid mass, and it weighed him down. His chest felt so heavy. It had finally happened. There was no going back from this.

There was no way to undo this. No way to make it better. His dad could pay or bribe whoever he liked, but it wouldn't change the fact that he was a killer.

His thoughts raced. Ugly awful thoughts, *maybe I could say she attacked me. Maybe I could say it was self-defence.* He hated himself for thinking it. He wished it was true, that he wasn't a murderer. Worse thoughts entered his head still, *at least she wasn't human.* How could he even think that? She was the same as him. They were the same! *Nobody will report her death.*

Nobody will look for her killer. He knew Jay wouldn't be able to tell anyone. Jay would know that if he reported it, he would be under arrest and investigated for harbouring an XJ5. Her death would have to stay a secret. A dirty, unforgivable secret.

His phone rang again. It was his dad, again. He connected the call, but he didn't speak. His dad was frantic on the other end, "Danny? Danny. What did you do? Come home. We need to sort this out. Danny? Danny? Answer me."

Danny cut off the call without speech. So, his dad knew, but how exactly were they meant to fix this? His dad might be able to keep Jay quiet, he might be able to pay people off to keep things hushed up, but nothing would change what he did. What he was. He was a killer. He shouldn't be near people.

He sat for what seemed like an eternity. He couldn't seem to make his body move. What would Gemma say? What would she think? There was no way he could even *pretend* to guarantee her safety now he had killed someone.

He sat, dazed and confused, in a state of shock, replaying Edel's final hour over and over. He was angry before he even set eyes on her. He should have known better than to try to see her. She made it perfectly clear only hours earlier that she wanted nothing to do with him. Now he understood why.

He couldn't seem to function properly. He couldn't seem to put it into one coherent thought. All he knew was, he despised himself. He was a monster.

He called Gemma. He just needed to hear her voice. She answered with her usual cheerful hello, yesterday's argument already forgiven, but Danny's words were stuck in his mouth.

He tried to speak, but each time, only a small croak left his lips. "Hello? Danny? Can you hear me?" her sweet sounding, loving voice filled his heart. He tried to commit it to memory. He never wanted to forget her beautiful voice.

"I'm sorry, Gemma. I love you," he whispered, then abruptly ended the call. He stared at the river water, idly wondering how long it would take him to drown. His phone rang immediately, with Gemma's name flashing across the screen, but he cancelled the call and blocked her number, then stared despondently at the blank screen. *She deserves better than you,* his thoughts screamed at him.

He didn't know how many hours had passed before he heard his friend's shouts.

"Frank! Frank, over here. I've found him!"

He stared blankly at Tony and then his eyes travelled to his father behind, running towards them. He didn't speak. There were no words that could have helped in that moment.

He knew he was on his final warning. His last chance. His dad had meant what he said. If it happened again, he would have to leave Harpton Main. There were only so many times you could cover something like this up and pay people off. Over the years, he had cost his dad a fortune in hush money, but he had never killed. This was a line that could not be uncrossed. He didn't want to be forgiven. He didn't want people to be silenced. He was everything the government said the escapees were. He should be contained, like them. He was dangerous.

His dad hugged him hard, which was more than he felt he deserved. He wanted him to say how much he hated him, how disappointed he was, how ashamed he felt and how disgusted he was that he had a murderer for a son.

Instead of the angry words he wanted to hear, his dad only whispered, "Come home, Danny. I can fix this."

The end.

ACKNOWLEDGEMENT

I've had a really good imagination for as long as I can remember. I can imagine entire worlds of totally made up people and things, and I grow attached to them, and the people in them, as though they were real.

Edel and Jay have lived in my head for twenty something years, and I never once thought about writing them down. Writing was not something I was ever planning to do. I thought writing was for other people - the clever ones, the ones with degrees in literature. It turns out that all you really need is a good story, a lot of practise, a willingness to learn, and a few good friends to tell you when it's good- and when you are writing utter shit!

So, on that note, I'd like to thank the following people.
SARA and SEANA. Without the two of you and your encouragement, this book would never have been written, let alone published. You have been with me from day one, and although we have never met face to face, I feel like you know me better than the people I see on a regular basis. Thank you for your continued support and your words of encouragement. And the chats. All the chats!
LOUISE. You were the first real life person I told about my plans to write a book. You were the first person to get your hands on it and the first person to read it. Without your enthusiasm, I would have probably never finished writing it. You will never understand how happy it made me to get emails and texts daily, asking for more.
FIONA. You were a perfect stranger, who offered advice on a

scene I was writing for a future book. And it's thanks to you and your eagerness to read my story, that I have a published novel today. I was on the fence about publishing it, and full of self-doubts, wondering who would want to read it. I had resigned myself to the fact that I was happy enough to have written it. I didn't need to publish it. Then you came along, full of excitement, and read it faster than I could have ever hoped. And the fact you loved it so much- a perfect stranger, who had no reason to lie- it gave me a new perspective. So thank you!

REBECCA my editor. You have done a fantastic job of pulling my story together tightly and making sure every end is woven in. You pointed things out to me that I absolutely would have missed and made it an all round better and more polished book.

And lastly, LEE, my loving husband, who has had to listen to me prattle on about Edel and Jay for years. Without your support, your love, your help and your encouragement, this book would not be published. I only have one more thing to say to you: Stop rolling your eyes at me when I talk about them. They're real to me!

ABOUT THE AUTHOR

Ashleigh Reverie

Ashleigh lives in South Yorkshire, England, with her husband, two children and one nutcase dog. When she isn't writing, she is usually working as a personal trainer. She loves walking and has recently discovered a love for camping. She also loves to train at her martial arts class, though everyone can agree that she is absolutely terrible at it.

BOOKS BY THIS AUTHOR

Almost Human: Discovery

The controlling and secretive New American Government has created a series of perfectly compliant, genetically modified human soliders. Emotion, independent thought, and all forms of communication are forbidden. Their only purpose is to obey.

Used as a pawn in somebody else's escape plan, Edel finds herself with unexpected freedom. She has been taught everything she needs to survive - except how to be human.

Danny is one of Harpton Main's rich elite, but beneath the shiny surface of his perfect world lies a dangerous secret, frequent bouts of uncontrollable rage, and endless questions about his origins.

A chance encounter with Edel leads to more questions than answers, and Danny will stop at nothing to discover the truth about himself.

Almost Human: Evolution

In hindsight, stabbing the only person in the world who could give him answers probably wasn't Danny's smartest move. When the haze clears and he can finally see sense again, his world has crumbled, and he is overcome with self-disgust at finally crossing that line and becoming a murderer. But his shame soon turns to fear when he learns he didn't stab her as well as he thought.

Danny can't believe his luck when Edel doesn't act out in revenge. She wants what she's always wanted: To be left ALONE. Just when it seems Danny's hopes of ever finding the answers to his questions are disintegrating, an unlikely ally helps him to forge the friendship he has spent a lifetime craving.

With Danny and Jay's help, Edel is learning to accept this new life of freedom and choices, and is slowly evolving from terrified and traumatised, to someone who resembles a normal, happy human. But her happiness is shadowed by a dark secret that threatens her life, and it seems, Edel isn't the only one hiding something.

Soon, Danny and Edel will both learn that mixing secrets with friendship can have devastating consequences.

I do sincerely hope you enjoyed this book. You can find and follow me on social media.

Facebook on my Ashleigh Reverie Author page at https://www.facebook.com/reverieashleigh

Instagram at ashleighreverie

Twitter @AshleighReverie

If you enjoyed this book, please consider leaving me a review. They really do help to get my work seen by other readers.

Book 2, Almost Human: Evolution is out now.

Please look out for book 3, Almost Human: Recovery, due to be published late 2022, along with two novellas which accompany the story.

Printed in Great Britain
by Amazon